When Cana[...] novels in high sch[...] [...]ed for such an awe[...] [...]ecades without pub[...] by the romance message that if you hang in there you'll find a happy ending. In May of 2012, Mills & Boon Modern bought her manuscript in a two-book deal. She's since published more than thirty books with them and is definitely living happily ever after.

Michelle Smart is a *Publishers Weekly* bestselling author with a slight-to-severe coffee addiction. A book worm since birth, Michelle can usually be found hiding behind a paperback or, if it's an author she really loves, a hardback. Michelle lives in rural Northamptonshire in England with her husband and two young Smarties. When not reading or pretending to do the housework she loves nothing more than creating worlds of her own. Preferably with lots of coffee on tap. www.michelle-smart.com

Tara Pammi can't remember a moment when she wasn't lost in a book, especially a romance which, as a teenager, was much more exciting than mathematics textbook. Years later Tara's wild imagination and love for the written word revealed what she really wanted to do: write! She lives in Colorado with the most co-operative man on the planet and two daughters. Tara loves to hear from readers and can be reached at tara.pammi@gmail.com or her website www.tarapammi.com

Ever After

COLLECTION

Passionately Ever After

DANI COLLINS

MICHELLE SMART

TARA PAMMI

MILLS & BOON

First Published in Great Britain 2021
by Mills & Boon, an imprint of HarperCollins*Publishers* Ltd,
1 London Bridge Street, London, SE1 9GF

www.harpercollins.co.uk

HarperCollins*Publishers*
1st Floor, Watermarque Building,
Ringsend Road, Dublin 4, Ireland

PASSIONATELY EVER AFTER © 2021 Harlequin Books S.A.

The Ultimate Seduction © 2014 Dani Collins
Taming the Notorious Sicilian © 2014 Michelle Smart
A Touch of Temptation © 2013 Tara Pammi

ISBN: 978-0-263-29914-4

MIX
Paper from
responsible sources
FSC® C007454

This book is produced from independently certified FSC™ paper to ensure responsible forest management.

For more information visit: www.harpercollins.co.uk/green

Printed and bound in Spain
by CPI, Barcelona

THE ULTIMATE SEDUCTION

DANI COLLINS

I've been lucky enough to work with a few different editors at Mills & Boon London. They're all made of awesome, but I must send a huge shout of appreciation to my current editor, Laurie Johnson. Not only has she made the transition into her care utterly painless, but this is our first book completely midwifed from start to finish by her. No spinal block required! Writer and book are happy and doing well. Thanks, Laurie!

CHAPTER ONE

TIFFANY DAVIS PRETENDED she wasn't affected by the hard stare her brother and father gave her when she entered her father's office. It wasn't easy to let people she loved pass judgment on whether she'd used sufficient concealer on her scars. Sometimes she wanted to throw the bottle of liquid beige into the trash and scream, *There. This is what I look like now. Live with it.*

But her brother had saved her life pulling her from the fiery car. He felt guilty enough for putting her in it. He still grieved for her groom, his best friend, and everything else Tiffany had lost. She didn't have to rub salt in his wounds.

Good girl, Tiff. Keep biting back what you really want to say. It's not like that got you into these skin grafts.

She came to a halt and sighed, thinking it was probably time for another visit to the head doctor if she was cooking up that sort of inner dialogue. But her harsh exhale caused both men to tense. Which made her want to rail all the louder.

Being angry all the time was a character shift for her. Even she had trouble dealing with it, so she shouldn't blame them for reacting like this. But it still fed her irritation.

"Yes?" She clicked her teeth into a tight smile, attempting to hold on to her slipping patience.

"You tell us. What's this?" Christian kept his arms folded as he nodded at the large box sitting open on their father's desk. The lid wore an international courier's logo, and the contents appeared to be a taxidermist's attempt to marry a raven to a peacock.

"The feather boa you asked for last Christmas?" Lame joke, sure, but neither man so much as blinked. They only stared at her as if they were prying her open.

"Be serious, Tiff," Christian said. "Why is the mask for you? Did you request to go in my place?"

A claustrophobic band tightened around her insides. A year in a mask had left her vowing to never feel such a thing on her face again. "I don't know what you're talking about."

The frost in her voice made both men's mouths purse. *Why did all of this have to be so hard?* The touchiness between her and her family was palpable every minute of every day. If she was short, they were defensive. If she was the least bit vulnerable, they became so overprotective she couldn't breathe.

They'd nearly lost her. She got that they loved her and were still worried about her. They wouldn't relax until she got back to normal, but she would never be normal again. It made the situation impossible.

"Where is it you think I want to go?" she asked in as steady a tone as she could manage.

"Q Virtus," her father said, as if that one word sufficed as explanation.

She shook her head and shrugged, still lost. Did they realize she was in the middle of an exchange worth five hundred million dollars? She didn't have much, but she did have a job now. Seeing as it involved running a multibillion-dollar company, she tried to do it well.

"Ryzard Vrbancic," Christian provided. "We put in a request to meet him."

Pieces fell together. *Q Virtus* was that men's club Paulie used to talk about. "You want to meet a puppet leader at one of those rave things? Why? The man's a despot."

"Bregnovia is asking for recognition at the UN. They're a democracy now."

She snorted in disbelief. "The whole world is ignoring the fact he stole the last dictator's money and bought himself a presidency? Okay."

"They're recovering from civil war. They need the sort of infrastructure Davis and Holbrook can provide."

"I'm sure they do. Why go the cloak-and-dagger route? Call him up and pitch our services."

"It's not that simple. Our country hasn't recognized his yet so we can't talk to him openly, but we want to be the first number on his list when recognition happens."

She rolled her eyes. Politics were so fun. "So you've set up this clandestine meeting—"

"It's not confirmed. That happens when you get there."

"That would be the broad 'you,' right? Like the universal 'they'?"

Christian's mouth tightened. He lifted out the feathery contents of the box. It was actually quite beautiful. A piece of art. The blend of blue-black and turquoise and gold feathers covered the upper eyes and forehead and—significantly—splayed down the left side in an eerily familiar pattern. Ribbons tailed off each side.

It was like looking in the mirror, seeing that reflection of her scar. A slithery feeling inside her torso made her heart speed up. She shook her head. She wasn't going anywhere, especially in public, with or without a crazy disguise.

"You understand how *Q Virtus* works?" her brother prodded. "This mask is your ticket in."

"Not *mine*."

"Yeah, Tiff, it is." He turned it around so she could see where her name was inscribed on the underside, along with *Isla de Margarita, Venezuela*. "See? Only you can attend."

His terse tone and shooting glance toward their father made it clear they'd spent some time pondering alternate solutions. Both men showed signs of deep frustration, a level of emotion usually reserved for when approval ratings were low. To see them so bent out of shape activated her don't-make-more-waves genes.

Your father is under a lot of pressure, dear. Do as he asks for now.

No, she reminded herself. She was living her life, not waiting for it to make everyone else's list of priorities. Still, she'd been raised to have civilized conversations, not be outright defiant. "I would think that taking off the mask to show your name defeats the purpose."

"There's a chip embedded. They know which mask belongs to which person, and as you can see, they only fit one face."

"They obviously know a lot about *me.* That's creepy. Doesn't it seem weird they would know how to cover my scars?"

"*Q Virtus* has an exceptional history of discretion and security," her father said, defending it with a kind of pompous grumpiness that surprised her. "Whatever they know about us, I'm sure it's kept very well protected."

A remarkably naive comment from a man who'd been in politics and business long enough to mistrust everyone and everything. Heck, he'd dragged her in here because he thought she'd undermined him with his brotherhood of secret handshakes, hadn't he?

"Dad, if you want to become a member—"

"I can't." He smoothed his tie, one of his tells when his ego was dented.

"Too old? Then Christian—?"

"No."

She was quite smart, had always had better marks than her brother, who fudged his way through just about everything, but she was missing something. "Well, Paulie was a member. What does it take?"

"Money. A lot of it. Paul Sr. was a member and once Paulie inherited, he had the means to pay the fee," her father said in a level tone.

Of course. Therein lay her father's envy and reverence. It must have eaten him alive that his best friend and rival for her mother's affections had possessed something he hadn't.

"When you were still in the hospital, I applied on your behalf, hoping to go as your proxy," Christian explained. "I didn't hear back until today." Glancing at their father, he added, "It is kind of creepy they know Tiff has finally recovered and taken over the reins of Davis and Holbrook."

"Everyone's talking about it. It's hardly a secret," her father dismissed with a fresh heaping of disapproval.

Tiffany bit back a sigh. She would not apologize for grappling her way into running the company now that she was well enough. What else would she do moving forward? Trophy wife and having a family was out of the question with this face.

Still, it was so *unladylike* to work, her mother reminded at every opportunity.

"I don't understand why they've accepted her. It's a men's club," her father muttered.

She eyed the mask, recalling the sorts of stories Paulie used to come home with after attending one of these *Q Virtus* things. "It's a booze-fueled sex orgy, isn't it?"

"It's a networking event," her father blustered.

Christian offered one of his offside grins. "It's a chance for the elite to let their hair down," he clarified. "But a lot of deals are closed over martinis and a handshake. It's the country club on a grander scale."

Right. She knew how that worked. Wives and daughters stood around in heels and pearls planning the Fourth of July picnic while husbands and fathers colluded to keep their money amongst themselves. Her engagement to Paulie, Jr. had been negotiated between the seventh and ninth holes of the top green, her wedding staged on the balcony by their mothers, her cake designed by the renowned chef, and all of it exploded into flames against the wrought-iron exit gate.

"This is all very interesting." It wasn't. Not at all. "But I'm in the middle of something. You'll have to sort this out yourselves."

"Tiffany."

Her father's stern tone was the one that made any good daughter spin, take a stance of dutifully planted feet, knees locked, hands knotted at her sides. She caught her tongue firmly between her teeth. "Yes?"

"Our friends in Congress are hoping for good relations with Bregnovia. I need those friends."

Because his hat was in the ring for the next election. Why was that always the only thing that mattered?

"I don't know what you expect me to do. Pitch our services while wearing a showgirl costume? Who would take that seriously? I can't go into a meeting without it, though. No one likes face-to-face interactions with this." She pointed at where her ear had been reconstructed and a cheekbone implant inserted.

Her father flinched and looked away, not denying that she was hard to look at. That hurt more than the months of screaming burn injuries.

"Maybe I could be your date," Christian said. "I don't know if members are allowed to bring an escort, but…"

"Bring my brother to the prom?" That certainly reinforced how far down the eligibility ladder she'd fallen. Her hands stayed curled at her sides, but mentally she cupped them around her tiny, shrunken heart, protecting it. *Love yourself, Tiff. No one else will.*

"Get me into the club and you won't have to leave your room until it's over," Chris said.

Hide the disfigured beast.

She had to close her eyes against her father's intense stare, the one that willed her to comply.

You weren't going to let yourself be a pawn anymore, she reminded herself.

"How long is this thing?" she heard herself ask, because what kind of family would she have, if not this one? Her friends had deserted her, and dating was completely off the table. Her life would be very dark and lonely if she alienated her parents and brother.

"We arrive at sunset on Friday night, and everyone is gone by Sunday evening. I'll make the travel arrangements," Christian said with quick relief.

"I wear this thing in *and* out. That's the deal, because I won't do this if I'm going to be stared at." Listen to her, talking so tough. She was actually scared to her toenails. What would people say if they saw her? She couldn't let it happen.

"As far as I know, everyone wears masks the whole time," Chris said, practically dancing, he was so elated.

"I'll be in my office," she muttered. *Searching for my spine.*

Ryzard Vrbancic abided by few rules beyond his own, but he left his newly purchased catamaran as the shadow of its mast stretched across the other boats in the Venezuelan marina. If he didn't climb the stairs before the red sky had inked purple, he would be locked out of the *Q Virtus* Quarterly.

Story of my life, he thought, but hoped that soon he'd be as welcome worldwide as the famous black credit card.

Security was its usual discreet step through a well-camouflaged metal detector that also read the chip in his mask. One of the red-gowned staff lifted her head from her tablet as he arrived and smiled. "We're pleased to see you again, Raptor. May I escort you to your room?"

She was a pretty thing, but the *petite q's* were off-limits, which was a pity. He hadn't had time to find himself a lover for weeks. The last had complained he spent more time working than with her, which was apparent from her spa and shopping bills. They were as high as his sexual frustration.

His situation should improve now, but he'd have to be patient a little longer. Like the music that set a vacation tone, the *petite q's* provided atmosphere. They could stroke an ego, dangle off an arm, flirt and indulge almost any reasonable request, but if they wanted to keep their job, they stayed out of the members' beds. Being smart and career minded along with attractive and engaging, the *petite q's* tended to side with keeping their jobs.

Such a pity.

His current escort set up his thumbprint for the door then stepped inside his suite for his briefing. "You have a meeting request from Steel Butterfly. Shall I confirm?"

"A woman?" he asked.

"I don't have the gender of our clients, sir."

And if she did know, she wouldn't say, either.

"No other requests?" He was hoping for a signal from international bodies that his petition to the UN was receiving a nod.

"Not at this time. Did you have any?"

Damn. He'd come here knowing he had a meeting request, hoping it would be a tip of the hand on his situation. Now he was under lockdown and liable to be taking a sales pitch of some kind.

"Not at present. I'll accept an introduction on that one, nothing longer." He nodded at her tablet.

"The time and location will be transmitted to your smartwatch. Please let us know if I can arrange anything else to ensure your satisfaction while you're with us."

He followed her out, confident that everything he'd preordered was in the suite. Zeus was exceptionally good at what he did. Ryzard had never had an issue of any kind while at *Q Virtus,* which made the exorbitant membership fee and elaborate travel and security arrangements worth the trouble.

Entering the pub-style reception lounge, he saw roughly thirty people, mostly men in tuxedos and masks. They stood with a handful of gorgeous *petite q's* wearing the customary red designer gowns.

He accepted the house drink for this session, rum over ice with a squeeze of lime and a sugared rim, then glanced at his watch. At his four o'clock, a collection of dots informed him the small conclave of men to his right included Steel Butterfly.

He had no idea where Zeus came up with these ridiculous nicknames, but he supposed Raptor was apt for him, coming from the Latin meaning to seize or take by force. The bones of several dinosaurs in that category had been uncovered in his homeland of Bregnovia, too.

Eyeing the group, he wondered which one was his contact. One accepted a drink from a *petit q* and handed her his watch. It didn't matter, he decided. He wasn't interested in beginning a conversation in public that he was scheduled to have in private tomorrow. He waited until he was out of range in the gambling hall to activate his identity on his own watch. This resulted in an immediate invitation to join the blackjack table.

He sat so he could read the screen mounted near the ceiling in the corner. It subtly manifested and dissolved with blurbs on presentations and entertainment to be held over the course of the *Q Virtus* Quarterly. Tastemakers, trendsetters and thought leaders were flown in to provide rich, powerful, political forces such as himself with the absolute cutting-edge information and samples of global economics and technology. Meanwhile, at tables such as this one, he would pick up the other side of the coin: gossip about a royal's addiction, a cover-up of a coup attempt on a head of state, a lie that would be accepted as truth to stem international panic.

He could only imagine what was said about him, but he didn't let himself dwell on what was likely disapproval and distrust. His people were free, his country independent. That was the important thing.

Still, thoughts of what it had cost him crept in, threatening to inject disappointment and guilt into an otherwise pleasant if staid evening. He folded his hand, left the table and lifted a rum off a passing waiter's tray as he moved outside in search of entertainment.

CHAPTER TWO

TIFFANY WAS STUCK and it was a sickeningly familiar situation, the kind she'd sworn she'd never wind up in again.

She'd love to blame Christian. He had urged her to step through the door when he'd been refused entry. *Go in and ask,* he'd hissed, annoyed.

Since her worst nightmare these days was being stared at, she'd forgone arguing on the stoop and stepped through the entranceway. Inside, pixies in designer nightgowns had fawned over the arriving men in masks. She'd looked around for a bell desk, and a stud named Julio had come forward to introduce himself as a *petite q.*

She, a seasoned socialite, had become tongue-tied over the strapping young man in a red footman's uniform. It was more than two years since she'd been widowed on her wedding day. Even without the scars, that would be bad mojo. Men didn't call, didn't ask her out. If she was in a room with a live one, they rarely looked her in the eye, always averting their gaze. She didn't exist for them as a potential mate.

Julio didn't attract her so much as astonish her. He didn't know what lurked beneath the mask and was all solicitous manners as he offered his services. "I see this is your first visit with us," he said after a brief glance at his tablet. "Please allow me to orient you."

She was completely out of practice with his type—the valet who never overstepped his station, but still managed to convey that he appreciated being in the presence of beauty. She'd haltingly fielded his questions about whether her travel had been pleasant as he smoothly escorted her into an elevator.

When he asked if she had any specific needs he could attend to while she was here, she'd come back to reality. "My brother needs a hall pass, or a mask. Whatever. Can you make that happen?"

"I'll send the request to Zeus, but the doors will be closing in a few minutes. Once we're in lockdown, no one comes or goes. Unless it's an emergency, of course." He'd lifted his head from tapping his tablet.

Lockdown? Alarmed, she'd tried to text Christian only to be informed that external service was cut off while inside the club.

"Cell phones and other cameras are discouraged, as is the sending of photos outside the club. Security will locate him and communicate his options," Julio assured her, then explained that if her requested meeting was accepted, the time and location would be sent to her Inspector Gadget watch.

"Where *are* we? A hollowed-out volcano?" she asked as he set up her thumbprint entry to her room.

"No, but we're working on obtaining one," he said, deadpan. "Now, you'll want to wear your watch throughout your stay. It tells a lot more than time. May I show you?"

Hearing that her scheduled meeting with the Bregnovian dictator wasn't a sure thing was a relief. Her father would be furious if she didn't go in Christian's place, but if the request was rejected, she would be off the hook. Still, she hoped her brother would be granted entry and save her worrying about any of it. She pressed Julio out of her suite with instructions to inform her about Christian as soon as possible.

Her suite was enough of an oasis to calm her nerves. Her

privileged upbringing had exposed her to some seriously nice digs, but she had to admit this was above and beyond. No expense had been spared on the gold fixtures, original art or silk bedding. The new clothes in the wardrobe were a pleasant distraction. Christian had said something about samples of prototypes being handed out to members. *If you don't want them, I do.*

She supposed he was referring to the spy watch Julio had shown her, but she was more interested in the designer gowns. Discreet labels informed her they were from the best of the best throughout South America, all in stunning colors and fabrics. Several were off-the-shoulder, figure-enhancing styles that would cover her scars.

Interesting.

Not that she had anywhere to wear them. She didn't intend to leave her room, but she would make the most of the in-suite amenities, she decided. Call it a vacation from her family. She'd work in peace for a few days.

Work, however, was next to impossible without Wi-Fi service to the external world, and besides, a calypso band was calling to her from below her open French doors. She *loved* dancing.

Full darkness had fallen, so she sidled into the shadows behind a potted fern on her balcony and gazed longingly at the party below, feeling rather like Audrey Hepburn in that old black-and-white. It was such a world beyond her. The pool's glow lit up ice sculptures on the buffet tables. Bartenders juggled open bottles, putting on a cocktail show as they poured fast and free while women in red gowns cha-cha'd with men in tuxedos and masks.

This whole mask thing was weird. As they'd flown south in the company jet, Christian had explained it allowed the world's elite to rub shoulders in a discreet way. Sometimes it was best for the biggest players to take their meetings in secret, so as not to cause speculative dips in the stock exchange. Certain celebrities stole these few days to relax without interruption by fans. *Q Virtus* catered to whatever the obscenely rich needed.

I need a new face, she thought sourly, but even the cavernous pockets her husband had left her weren't deep enough to buy a miracle.

She looked to where she'd left her mask dangling off a chair back's spire.

Despite her anxiety with the abrupt change of plans when she arrived, she had felt blessedly anonymous behind her mask as she had walked through the lobby and halls to her room. It had been an extraordinary experience to feel normal again. No one had stared. She had looked exactly like everyone else.

Hmm. That meant she didn't have to stay here like Rapunzel, trapped in the tower with the real world three stories below and out of her reach.

With her heart tripping somewhere between excitement and trepidation, she fingered through the gowns hanging in the wardrobe. The silk crepe in Caribbean blue would expose her good right leg, but not so high as to reveal where her grafts had been taken. After months of physiotherapy, she'd moved back into her old workout routine of yoga, weights and treadmill. She possessed all of her mother's vanity along with the genetic jackpot in the figure department. Only family saw her these days, and she hardly dressed to impress, but she was actually very fit.

Alone in the suite, she held the gown up to her body, then, without her mother there to discourage her, dared to try it on.

Whoever this Zeus guy was, he sure knew how to dress a woman. Especially one with defects to hide. The single sleeve went past her wrist in a point that ended in a loop of thread that hooked over her middle finger. The bodice clung to her waist and torso, plumping breasts that remained two of her best original features. She had to give her back-side the credit it deserved, too. When she buckled on new shoes that were little more than sky-high heels and a pair of saucy blue-green straps, it was like being hugged by old friends. She almost wept.

Filtering her image through her lashes as she looked in the mirror, she saw her old self. *Hi, Tiff. It's nice to see you again. 'Bout time, too.*

Makeup didn't completely cover her scars, nothing could, but she enjoyed going through her old ritual after using the concealer, taking her time to layer on shadow and liner, girling herself up to the max. By the time she was rolling spirals into her strawberry blond hair, she was so lost in the good ol' days, she caught herself thinking, *I wonder what Paulie will say.*

The curling iron tagged her cheek where she would never feel it, and she nearly broke down. *You're not Cinderella, anymore, remember? You're the ugly stepsister.*

No. Not tonight. Not when she felt confident and beauti-ful for the first time since her wedding day. Had she been happy then? She couldn't remember.

Don't go there.

Gathering the top half of her hair over her crown, she tied the mask into place, then let her loose curls fall to hide the strap that circled her skull. Oddly, the mask wasn't as traumatic to wear as she'd feared. It didn't suction onto her face and make her feel trapped in a body that writhed in agony. It stood cocked like a fascinator to cover the left side of her face, while the feathers arranged around her eyes gave an impression of overly long lashes that layered backward to cover her forehead and hairline. She had ex-pected it to be heavy, but it was as light as, well, feathers. They tickled the edges of her scars, where her skin was extra sensitive, making her feel feminine and pretty.

Staring at herself in the full-length mirror, she allowed

that she *was* pretty. After painting on a coat of coral lipstick, she did a slow twirl and caught herself grinning. Smiling felt odd, as if she was using muscles that had atrophied.

She lifted the weighty watch on her wrist, the one that identified her as Steel Butterfly. More like a broken one. Her sides didn't even match.

It didn't have to make sense, she assured herself as she tossed her lipstick into her pocketbook then realized she didn't need either room key or credit card. Such freedom! For a few hours, she would be completely without baggage.

Taking nothing but lighthearted steps, she left to join the party.

Ryzard could drink with the best of them. He'd spent the older half of his childhood in Munich, had managed vineyards in France and Italy, and had lived in parts of Russia where not finishing a bottle of vodka was a gross insult to the host. He was restless enough to get legless tonight, but so far he'd consumed only enough to become mellow and hungry. The cashmere breeze and the scents of beach and pineapple and roasting pig aroused his appetite—all his appetites. He'd mentally stripped the nearest *petite q's* and was considering a pass at one of the female members currently being scouted by every other bachelor here—along with some of the married members.

Not Narciso, aka the Warlock of Wall Street, though. He chatted with his friend long enough to see the man wasn't just here with his wife, but besotted by her. Lucky bastard. Ryzard countered his envy by reminding himself that love was a double-edged sword. He wouldn't ruin his friend's happiness by saying so, but he had once looked forward to marital bliss. Luiza had died before they found it, and the anguish was indescribable. No matter how pleased he was for his friend, he would never risk that toll again.

He'd stick to the less permanent associations one found, enjoyed and left at parties such as this one.

Glass panels had been fitted over the lap pool, turning it into a dance floor that glimmered beams of colored light beneath the bouncing feet. People were having a lively time, keeping the band's quick salsa beat rapping. The drummer stared off to the left, however, his grin male and captivated.

Ryzard followed the man's gaze and his entire being crackled to attention.

Well beyond the pool's light, in a corner mostly blocked by a buffet table and ice sculpture, a woman undulated like a cobra, utterly fascinating in her hypnotic movements timed perfectly with the music. Her splayed hands slid down her body with sexy knowledge, her hips popped in time to the beat, and her feet kick-stepped into motion.

She twirled. The motion lifted her brassy curls like a skirt before she planted her feet wide and swayed her weight between them. The flex of her spine gave way to a roll of her hips, and she was back into motion again.

Setting down his drink, Ryzard beelined toward her. He couldn't tell if the woman had a partner, but it didn't matter. He was cutting in.

She was alone, lifting her arms to gather her hair, eyes closed as she felt the music as much as heard it. She arched and stretched—

He caught her around the waist and used the shocked press of her hands at his shoulders to push her into accepting his lead, stepping into her space, then retreating, bringing her with him. As he moved her into a side step, she recovered, matching his move while her gaze pinned to his.

He couldn't tell what color her eyes were. The light was too low, her feathery mask shadowing her gaze into twin glinting lights, but he reacted to the fixation in them. She was deciding whether to accept him.

A rush of excitement for the challenge ran through him.

After a few more quick steps, he swung her into half pivots, catching each of her wrists in turn, one bare, one clad in silk, enjoying the flash of her bare knee through the slit of her skirt.

How had she been overlooked by every man here? She was exquisite.

Lifting her hand over her head, he spun her around then clasped her shoulder blades into his chest. Her buttocks—fine, firm, round globes as if heaven had sent him a valentine—pressed into his lap. Bending her before him, he buried his nose in her hair and inhaled, then followed her push to straighten and matched the sway of her hips with his own.

Tiffany's heart pounded so hard she thought it would escape her chest. One second she'd been slightly drunk, lost in the joy of letting the salsa rhythm control her muscles. Now a stranger was doing it. And doing it well. He pulled her around into a waltz stance that he quickly shifted so they grazed each other's sides, left, right, left.

She kicked each time, surprised how easily the movements came back to her. It had been years, but this man knew what he was doing, sliding her slowly behind his back, then catching her hand on the other side. He pushed her to back up a step, bringing one of her arms behind his head, the other behind her own. A few backward steps and they were connected by only one hand, arms outstretched, then he spun her back into him, catching her into his chest.

He stopped.

The conga beat pulsed through her as he ran his hands down her sides. Her own flew to cover his knuckles, but she didn't stop him. It felt too amazing. His fingertips grazed the sides of her breasts, flexed into the taut muscles of her waist and clasped her hips to push them in a hula circle that he followed with his own, his crotch pressed tight to her buttocks.

Sensual pleasure electrified her. No one touched her anymore. After being a genderless automaton for so long, she was a woman again, alive, capable of captivating and enticing a man. She nudged her hips into his, flashing a glance back at him.

He narrowed his eyes and held her in place for one deliberate thrust before he spun her into the dance, their energetic quick steps becoming an excuse to look at each other as he let her move to the farthest reach of his hand on hers.

She had been a bit of a tease in her day, secure in the knowledge everyone knew she was engaged. She'd been able to flirt without consequence, enjoying male attention without feeling threatened by it. This stranger's undisguised admiration was rain on her desert wasteland of feminine confidence. Climbing her free hand between her breasts to the back of her neck, she thrust out her chest then let the music snake up and down her spine as she flexed her figure for his visual pleasure.

His feral show of teeth encouraged her while his sheer male sexiness called to the woman in her, urging her to keep the notice of such a fine specimen. He might have started out his evening in a tux, but at some point he'd stripped down to the pants and the shirt, which was open at the collar and rolled back to his forearms at the sleeves. The mask he wore was vaguely piratical in its black with gold trim and wings at his temple, but the nose piece bent in a point off the end of his nose, suggesting a bird of prey.

A hunter.

And she was the hunted.

Her heart raced, excited by the prospect of being pursued. She wanted to be wanted.

Splaying her feet, she allowed her knees to loosen. The slit of her skirt parted to reveal her leg, and she made the most of it, watching him as she rolled her hips in a figure eight, showing off her body, enticing him with a come-hither groove.

He planted a foot between hers, surrounding her without touching her, hands raised as if he was absorbing energy from her aura. The sultry tropical air held an undertone of spicy cologne and musky man. Reaching out, she shaped the balls of his hard shoulders with her hands and climbed them to the sides of his damp neck, sidling close so they sidestepped back and forth, swaying together in time to the music, bodies brushing.

His wide hands flattened on her shoulder blades and slid with deliberation to the small of her back then took possession of her hips. As his unabashed gaze held hers, he pulled her in to feel the firm ridge of his erection behind his fly.

A flood of desire, not the trickles of interest she'd felt in the past, but a serious deluge of passion, transformed her limbs into heavy weights and flooded her belly with a pool of sexy heat. She became intensely aware of her erogenous zones. Her breasts ached and her nipples tingled into sharp, stinging points. Between her thighs, her loins pulsed with a swollen, oversensitive need.

As if he knew, he shifted and his hard thigh pressed into her vulnerable flesh. She gasped and her neck weakened as he bent over her. She dropped her head back and he followed, taking her body weight on his thigh. His nose grazed her chin, then her collarbone. His lips hovered between her breasts. Slowly he brought her up again and leaned his mouth close enough to tease her parted lips.

He was a stranger, she reminded herself, but her lips felt swollen and she desperately wanted the pressure of his mouth—

A clap of thunder exploded in the sky.

Jolted, she found herself smothered against his chest, his hard arms tight around her, one hand shielding the back of her head, fingers digging in with tension. Her mask skewed, cutting into her temple. Beneath her cheekbone, his heart slammed with power.

The claps and squeals and whistles continued and his arms relaxed enough she could fix her mask and look up. Fireworks painted the starscape in flowers and streaks of red and blue and green that dissolved into sparkles of silver and palms of gold.

As people moved into their space, he steered her away from the crowd, into a corner around a partition where they were hidden in an alcove. She set her hands on the concrete rampart and leaned back into the living wall he made behind her, eyes dazzled by the bursts of color reflected on the water as the fireworks continued to explode before and above them. The band switched to an orchestrated classic that matched the explosions, filling her with awe and visceral excitement.

Already fixed in the moment, they became one being, she and this stranger, their bodies pressed tight as they watched the pyrotechnics. His hands moved over her, absently at first, shaping her to his front. She responded, encouraging his touch by rubbing her buttocks into the proof that she could still arouse a man. When his hands cupped her breasts, bold and knowledgeable, she linked her own hands behind his neck, arching into his touch, reveling in the pressure of his palms and the thumbing of her nipples.

Dropping her head to the side, she turned her face and lifted her mouth, inviting his kiss with parted lips. He bent without hesitation, nothing tentative in the way he captured her mouth. Thorough and unhurried, he continued to caress her as he took sumptuous possession of her lips.

She ran her fingers into his hair, greeting his tongue with her own, inhibition melted by pure desire. Distantly she was aware this was out of character, but she wasn't Tiffany. Not the Tiffany of today and not the old one, either. Tonight she was the woman she wished she could have been. She was every woman. Pure woman.

Tonight she had no man to think about but this one. She didn't care that she didn't know him. She and Paulie hadn't known each other, either, not really, not the way a husband and wife should. Not in the biblical sense. She hadn't slept with him or any man.

But she wanted to. She had ached for years to experience sexual intimacy.

A strong male hand stroked down her abdomen and skimmed off to the top of her thigh, making her mewl in disappointment. Then he fingered beneath the slit of her skirt and she had to pull away from his kiss to draw in a gasp as he followed bare skin into the sensitive flesh at the top of her leg.

She stilled.

His arm across her torso tensed and the hand on her breast hesitated briefly before he continued caressing her, lightly and persuasively, both hands teasing her with the promise of continued pleasure.

A moan of craving left her and she shuddered in acceptance.

A streak of light shot skyward and his touch moved into her center, exploring satin and lace that were damp with anticipation. She couldn't help covering his hand with her own, pinning his touch where she ached for pressure.

He seemed to know what she needed more than she did. As he fondled her, her eyes drifted closed and her head fell back to rest against his shoulder. She bit her lip, ripples of delight dancing through her. Was she really doing this? Rubbing her behind into his erection, not caring they were in public, that she didn't know him, that this was all about her pleasure?

He started to draw his hand away and she turned her face to the side, a cry of disappointment escaping her, but he was only hooking her panties down her hip and returning to trace and part and seek and find.

She released a moan of pure joy.

He caught her chin in his other hand and tilted her face up for his kiss while his touch on her mound became deliberate and intimate and determined.

She let it happen. She held very still and kissed him back with naked passion, aware of the light breeze caressing where she was exposed to the shadows of the rampart and the velvety night air. She let him stroke her into delirious intensity, her awareness dimmed at the edges so she was focused on the pleasure he was delivering, plucking and teasing and bringing her closer.

Over the water, the biggest rockets exploded like thunder, sending shock waves through her that made her quiver in stunned reaction. The reverberations echoed inside her, sparking where he stroked, sending a wild release upward and out to the ends of her limbs. He pinched her nipple, and like a flashpoint, she was blind to everything but white light and astonishing pleasure. Glorious waves of joy crashed in, submerging her in tumultuous ripples that he seemed to control, pressing one after another through her with the rub of his fingertip.

As the fireworks dimmed to puffs of smoke surrounding a barge in the bay, her climax receded, leaving her a puddle of lassitude in his steely arms.

He adjusted her panties and started to turn her. She obeyed the command in his hands, wanting to kiss him, to thank him—

Without a word, he drew her across the balcony to a set of shallow stairs leading to the beach. She wobbled, partly because her legs were wet noodles, partly because her heels couldn't find solid purchase in the sand. He scooped her up, carrying her along with easy strength into a cabana encircled by heavy curtains.

Inside he set her on her feet and steadied her with one hand while he raked the cloth door closed behind them. Without a word, he scraped the mask off his face and yanked his shirt open, peeling it off his shoulders and throwing it aside.

She couldn't see his face, not really. It was barely a shade above pitch-black in here, but the glow of satin skin increased as he toed off his shoes and opened his fly, stripping without ceremony.

Sweet Lord, what a man. He stepped closer and she couldn't help reaching out to test the flat muscles of his abdomen, learning them by feel more than sight. Hot and damp, he reacted to her touch with a tense of muscles and a muffled curse, making her smile in the dark, pleased she had an effect on him.

Her hand bumped into his. He was applying a condom.

Curious, she lightly explored his latex-covered shape. As she did, the pressure of her mask shifted.

She knocked his touch away before she thought about what she was doing.

Stillness came over him.

She tried to penetrate the dark and read his face—which was what he was likely doing. He probably thought she was having second thoughts.

Hell, no. She might never have another chance to lose her virginity. Not like this, so caught up in desire she was shaking with it.

"Leave it on," she whispered.

His hands lowered to her shoulders, one skimming down the edge of her bodice under her arm. She knew what he was looking for.

"That, too." Catching his hand away from her zipper, she drew him toward the bed.

In the same way he'd taken her over on the dance floor, he took the lead. A tip of his weight, a knee in the bed and she was lifted and placed half under him in one smooth motion. Her startled exhale clouded between them as a hand sought beneath her skirt, catching at her panties then pausing.

She couldn't help chuckling, understanding the implicit question. Lifting her hips, she invited him to strip them off her. They caught on her shoe, and neither of them bothered to finish the job.

He hitched her skirt then tucked her neatly under him, his legs moving with practiced ease to part her knees wide.

More surprised than shocked, she stilled, bracing herself, wanting this, but not as lost in the moment as she'd been. That was okay. She'd had her fun and she wanted to remember everything about this encounter. Cataloguing the flex of his shoulders under the stroke of her hands, the weight of his hips, the roughened texture of his legs on her smooth inner thighs, she waited.

He teased her, rubbing the head of his erection against her and reawakening her senses. As she hummed a response, he kissed her, deeply, dragging her back into the well of desire she thought she'd left outside on the ramparts.

Sliding her knee up to his hip, she hooked her calf over his buttock and quite suddenly, it was happening. His flesh was pressing for entrance, stretching her. Oh, wow. It hurt, but not bad. She'd experienced pain way worse than this, but it was still very intimate. She bit her lip and concentrated on accepting him, breathing through the sting and countering her instinctive tension—

He swore and the hand in her hair tightened enough to pull, even though she suspected it wasn't intentional. His big body shook with tension.

"I'm hurting you," he said in a voice so gruff she couldn't discern what kind of accent he had.

"It's okay. It feels good. I like it." This was so primeval. Drinking in his scent, she licked his neck, wanting this delicious, mysterious man imprinted on her for all time.

Arching, she discovered there was more of him to take. Squeezing her leg to encourage him, she met resistance. Rather than press into her, he kissed her again, using his tongue, and lifted enough to sidle a hand between them, caressing where they joined. In moments he had her twisting in excitement, and a second later, he slid deep into her.

Ah, *this* was what it was all about.

Eyes wide open to the dark cabana, she hugged his rugged body and learned the dip in his spine and the shape of his buttocks. His tense muscles flexed as he retreated from her depths, pulling strings of sensations through her: echoes of sting, loss, but delicious friction, too. He smoothly filled her again, his big body trembling with strain as he controlled his movements. The smart was still there, but the pleasure was incredible.

Purring, she lifted her hips to his, clasping him with her inner muscles, kissing him with extravagant joy, telling him she loved everything he was doing to her.

For a second, he let her feel his full weight, the full power of his muscles as he caged her beneath him and pressed a hard, hungry kiss on her. The fingers tangled in her hair pulled again, and he held himself in stark possession of her. She could swear she felt him pulsing deep inside her.

Then his fingers massaged her scalp in gentle apology and he lifted slightly, withdrew and slowly began to thrust again. The music dimly entered her consciousness from far away as they danced, him leading her through the erotic steps as he lowered her zip and exposed her breast to his hand and mouth.

She sang breathy notes of acute pleasure and sensual agony, wanting this twisting, exciting play to go on for the rest of her life. But everything he did made the sweet pleasure intensify. Their lovemaking grew better and better, driving her up the scale of passion to exquisite heights. When he ran his hand up the bare thigh that bracketed his hip, and branded her buttock with his palm, lifting her into his quickening thrusts, she moaned in approval, needing that faster pace, that wild stimulation.

Climax arrived suddenly and more powerfully than the first. She clawed at him, stunned by the release, fixated by the intense sensation of his fullness inside her while she orgasmed. He cried out raggedly and shuddered over her and within her, pushing to take deep possession of her, holding them both on that place of ecstatic perfection.

Suffused with bliss, she didn't move afterward, just waited for her heart to slow and listened as his breath settled. In the distance, the music continued and voices rose in conversation and laughter.

At the first shift of his body to relax and leave hers, the first easing of his implacable lock of his hips against hers, she dropped her hands and removed her leg from his waist. Her long history with bandage changes gave her the knowledge that quick and ruthless was best, even though it hurt like hell.

He surprised her by merely shifting his weight off her a little before he pressed a kiss to the corner of her mouth then nuzzled his lips down her bare cheek to her ear. "That was incredible. Thank you."

She couldn't help the smile that grew unseen in the dark, or the way she warmed with pride and eye-stinging gratitude. "Thank *you*. I didn't expect anything like this to happen tonight," she confessed, even though she could hear the delight in her voice. He thought she was *incredible*.

"I'm pleased I could make your first time memorable."

Her heart stopped. "You could tell it's my first time?" She felt like the most gauche girl alive.

"I come to all of these. I know the regulars, and I've

never seen you before. I would have remembered," he added with another buss of warm lips against her cheekbone.

Oh, God, *that's* what he meant. She swallowed her relieved laughter, then stiffened as voices approached their cabana.

"We should go somewhere more private." He gently lifted off her, chivalrously flicking her skirt to cover her as he rolled away.

Everything in her protested, but she sat up on the other side of the narrow bed. As she tucked her breast back into her dress and closed the zipper, his hand curled around her upper arm, hot and commanding, drawing her into tipping back against him.

"I'm on the top floor. Are you closer?"

"I can't," she whispered with genuine regret, senses distracted by the musky scent surrounding him and the damp heat of his chest so close to her nose. She tilted her face to find his lips in a soft kiss of reluctant goodbye.

He didn't move his lips against hers except to say, "Why not?"

"It's complicated. I shouldn't have come out at all." Their breaths mingled. "I hope you *will* remember me," she admitted, feeling safe to reveal the bald longing here in the anonymous dark.

"I'll always wonder why, won't I?" he said with edgy dismay.

"And then you'll remember I wanted to keep this unspoiled by real life."

This time when she pressed her mouth to his, he kissed her back. Hard and thorough, so her heart rate picked up and her arms wanted to snake around his neck.

She wasn't about to hang around until the lights came on, though. She didn't want to see his face when he saw hers.

Pulling away, she stood and shook out her skirt, stepped her underwear off her heel and left them on the mat. Quite the cheeky Cinderella move. Her mother would never quit the slut-shaming if she knew.

Tiffany felt no guilt, however, no shame and no embarrassment as she slipped out of the cabana and up the stairs, past the pool and its raging party, toward the elevators and back to her room. Only sensual satisfaction and poignant *what-ifs* followed her steps.

CHAPTER THREE

RYZARD'S WATCH GAVE a muted beep, reminding him he had a meeting in ten minutes.

Annoyed, he rose from the small table where he'd sat for the last thirty minutes eating a meal he would have preferred to have taken in his room. He swept the breakfast room once more for a certain woman in a mask that made him think of a falcon's smoothly feathered head. A woman who was both gloriously uninhibited, yet had been so tight, he had feared as he entered her that she would call a halt.

A light sweat broke over him as he recalled possessing her, never having felt so—

He cut short the thought, stung by a dart of shame that he was on the verge of elevating a meaningless hookup past the only woman he would ever love. There was no comparison. Forget it all.

Good thing he hadn't allowed the *petite q* to send a message on his behalf. He'd been tempted, but the tight security here did him a favor, preventing him from a weak moment. All he'd had was a description of her mask, but when he had inquired to the nearest *petite q,* she had assured him she could deliver an invitation to the mysterious woman to join him at breakfast. She couldn't, however, divulge the member's name or moniker.

He'd declined, not wanting to look desperate. Not wanting to feel so desperate, but after the blood-chilling thought he'd just had, he *didn't* wish to see her again. Their somewhat literal bumping of two strangers in the night was nothing significant. A letting off of steam. If it had seemed particularly intense, that had been leftover adrenaline from the false alarm when the fireworks had exploded. For a second he'd been back in the heat of Bregnovia's civil war, his life in danger along with the woman in his arms.

Shaking off that terrifying second of *not again,* he assured himself this urgency to see her again was merely his libido looking for another easy pounce and feed.

That's why he'd had to force himself to take his time rising and dressing in the cabana last night, despite a nagging desire to hurry. It wasn't that he'd wanted to catch another glimpse, to actually catch *her* and convince her to strip down completely and stay with him all night. No, he was merely still horny.

Wondering why she hadn't stayed was pointless. He'd never know. Everyone at *Q Virtus* had places to go and people they preferred not to be seen with. Did she know who *he* was, he wondered?

She hadn't been wearing a watch that he'd felt. He'd checked his own as she'd left, trying to read her identifier before she had moved out of range, but no luck. Perhaps she'd run off to rejoin her husband or lover.

That thought infuriated him. Waiting to marry Luiza until it was too late was one of his few regrets. When you did make a lifelong commitment, you didn't break it. If she had…

He refused to dwell on any of it. She was a wet dream and he was awake now. Time to move on. He had an introduction to suffer through—would in fact drag his feet getting there so as to use up most of their time.

Then he would put out feelers for the meeting he really wanted. Someone here would know what was being said in the UN about his country's chances for recognition. Whatever he had to do to bestow legitimacy on his people, he would. They were his priority. It was Luiza's dream. He owed it to all of them to stay focused on that.

Not on some easy piece he'd picked up for a few hours of distraction.

Until the accident, Tiffany had always been fashionably—some would say chronically or even rudely—late. Once she began working, she'd discovered how irritating it was to be on the other side of that. Nowadays she strove to be early, and to that end she followed the directions on her watch, only to come up against yet another set of sliding doors. Rolling her eyes, she watched the timepiece count down how long she'd have to wait until they opened.

"Come on, come on," she muttered, wanting this meeting over with.

She'd almost forgotten it completely and wished she had. Unfortunately, her watch had been returned to her with her breakfast. "It was left in the reception lounge last night," Julio had said. "You have a message. That's what the blue light means."

"It was heavy and men kept coming up to me, saying my watch indicated I was open to being approached," she complained.

"Excellent feedback on the weight. A woman's perspective is so valuable for the manufacturers. But please let me show you how to set your Do Not Disturb."

He'd also shown her how to follow the directions to her meeting.

"Can I wear my mask?" she'd asked, peering at him from behind her feathers while trying to keep them out of her orange juice.

"Of course. Members typically wear their masks the entire time they're here."

With her main argument for blowing off the meeting disintegrated, she'd managed only a quiet, "Thanks."

Biting her thumbnail after Julio left, she'd debated whether to risk leaving her room. What if she saw *him?*

Heated tingles awakened, hinting at how exciting it could be to bump into him, but she tamped down on the wild feelings. Her behavior last night had been a crazy combination of being away from the stifling proximity of her family and, well, she had been a little drunk on rum, having almost finished her second drink by the time she'd begun dancing.

With a stranger.

Her lover.

A burble of near-hysterical laughter almost escaped her as she walked, thinking of their incredible encounter. Part of her reaction was delight that she had it in her to be that bold and daring. Before the accident she might have fantasized about something like that, but it would never be something she could imagine actually doing. There was no such thing as impulse in her family. The consequences to Daddy's career always had to be considered.

The rest of her giddiness had a sharply disappointed edge. This was the sort of secret she might share with a close girlfriend, but she didn't have any. Her friends, some closer than others, had all continued on with their lives during her recovery, living the life she was supposed to have. Hers had stalled and taken a sharp left turn. She would never have much in common with them now except the good old days. That topic just invited pitying stares.

Work was what she had now. A career. She had Paulie's corporation and men in her life who loved her as a daughter and a sister. Last night had been exciting and fun, but she couldn't repeat it. What was she going to do? Come to these events every quarter and sleep with a different stranger each time? The alternative, to expose her scars and hope a lover could overlook them, made her shudder in appalled dread.

No, she had to stay serious and focused and do what she'd been sent here to do. Last night was her personal secret, something to keep her glowing on the inside through the cold years to come. Today she represented Davis and Holbrook, one of the largest construction firms in the world, thanks to her marriage merging her father's architecture firm with Davis Engineering. As the one person with claim to both those names, she supposed she could take ten minutes out of her life to hand over the letter of introduction her brother had prepared.

Even if she didn't entirely approve of this man they wanted to court.

At least she could hide behind her mask. Kinky was her new normal, apparently, since she was becoming really fond of it, but it rejuvenated her confidence.

These gopher burrows under the building she was less sure of.

"Am I in an abattoir?" she asked a *petite q* when she found one.

"Absolutely not," the perky young woman replied, obviously not paid to have a sense of humor. "To ensure complete privacy for our guests, the doors only open if the next hallway is empty. Several people are moving around at this time, causing minor delays. Your meeting room is at the end of this hall and will open to your thumbprint."

As she stepped into the empty meeting room, however, she had to admit that this particular man's world was astounding. Given the industrial decor she'd traversed to get here, she had expected more of the same with the conference rooms. Instead she was in an aquarium—a humanarium—in the bottom of the sea. Stingrays flew like sparrows across the blue water over the glass ceiling and a garden of tropical fish bobbled like flower heads in a breeze, poking from the living reef that fringed the glass walls.

Amazed, she set down her black leather folder on a table between two chairs in the center of the room and walked the curved wall, keeping one hand on it to maintain her equilibrium as the distorted image of swaying kelp made her dizzy. She reminded herself to breathe and oriented herself by turning back to the room to take in the pair of chairs on the white area rug. They faced the windows and were separated by the table that held a crystal decanter of ice water and two cut-crystal glasses.

As she leaned her back against the window, the door panel whispered open and *he* stepped in. Her stranger.

Shock ran through her in an electric current that held her fixed, stunned.

Yes, that was the mask from last night, and she recognized his powerful build even though he was dressed differently. His gray shirt was short-sleeved, tailored close to his muscled shoulders and accentuated his firm, tanned biceps. The narrow collar of his shirt was turned down in a sharply contrasting russet, drawing her eye to the base of his throat.

She watched him swallow and lifted her gaze to his green-gold eyes.

How had he found her?

Behind him, the door whispered closed. The noise seemed to prompt him into motion. He took a few laconic steps into the room, hands going into his pockets. He wasn't taken aback by their incredible surroundings. His eyes never left their lock on hers as he paused next to the chairs, lifted a hand and removed his mask. He dropped it into one of the chairs, still staring at her.

Barefaced, he was beautiful. Not pretty, not vulnerable, but undeniably handsome with his narrow, hawkish face and sharply defined cheekbones. His blade of a nose accentuated the long planes of his cheeks to the rugged thrust of his jaw, making his mouth appear sensual by comparison, even though his lips weren't particularly full.

They weren't narrow, either, and neither were his eyes, but the keen way he watched her spoke of focus and intelligence.

Don't think about last night, she ordered herself, fighting the inner trembling of reaction.

"You could have given me your name last night and saved us taking up a room when they're so highly in demand."

Her throat closed as she processed his thick accent first. It was more pronounced when he spoke above a whisper and charged his deep, stern voice with husked layers. Then his words sifted through her mind, allowing her first to absorb that he recognized her, but didn't know her name. How—? The criticism in his tone penetrated, distracting her. She was rather sensitive to being called thoughtless, willing to admit she'd been quite the spoiled brat before she'd learned that even charmed lives could be hexed.

Finally she grasped the whole of what he'd said, and it sounded as if he thought she had known whom she was messing around with last night. Which meant he hadn't come here because he was looking for her, but because…

Oh. My. God.

"Ryzard Vrbancic?" she managed faintly. Please no.

His gorgeous mouth twisted with ironic dismay. "As you can see. Who are you?"

Of course she could see. Now that her brain was beginning to function, it was obvious this was the self-appointed president of Bregnovia. The leader of a resistance movement turned opportunist who had claimed the national treasury—from a fellow criminal, sure, but claimed it for himself all the same—then used it to buy his seat in his newly minted parliament.

How did a name such as Ryzard go from being something vaguely lethal and unsavory to noble and dynamic simply by encountering the man in person? How had she not sensed or realized—

"There's been a mistake. I've made a mistake." Oh, gawd, she could never tell her family. Her *virginity?* Really? To this man?

And yet her body responded to being in his presence. Even though she wasn't drunk and no music seduced her, her feet didn't want to move and her eyes kept being dragged back to his wide chest, where a sprinkle of hair had abraded her palms. His arms flexed as she watched, forcing memories of being caught protectively against him when the fireworks had started then carried like a wilting Southern belle when sex had been the only thing on their minds.

His wide-spaced feet in Italian leather drew her gaze, making her recall the way he'd shed his shoes and the rest of his clothes so deftly last night. His burnished bronze skin had been anything but cold and hard. He'd been taut and alive.

And generous. He'd touched her with incredible facility completely devoted to her pleasure. She tried not to look for his hands, but she was fervently aware of the way he'd tantalized her so intimately toward orgasm. In public.

Mortified heat burned her to the core, especially because she yearned to know it all again. Everything about him called to her, feathering over her nerves like last night's velvety breeze, not just awakening her sensuality, but exciting her senses into full alert. Why? How? The rapid plunge back into sexual arousal was incredibly confusing. Disconcerting. She needed to get out of here.

Pushing off the glass wall, she took two steps and he took one, blocking her.

Her heart plummeted through the floor. This undersea

garden had suddenly become a shark cage, and she was trapped inside it with the shark.

Warily she eyed him. "I didn't know who you were last night."

"No?" His brow kicked up, dismissing her claim as a lie.

"No!"

"You sleep with strangers often?"

"Apparently you do, so don't judge me."

His head went back a fraction, reassessing her. "Who are you?"

She folded her arms, debating. If she left now, without telling him, Christian might salvage something. She, of course, could never show her face in public again, but she didn't intend to. Except—

Her gaze involuntarily went to the black dossier on the table, the one that held their letter of introduction and a background on the company. She jerked her gaze back to his, panicked that he might have followed her look, but trying not to show it.

His vaguely bored gaze traveled to the table and came back to hers. Intrigue lit his irises, turning their green-gold depths to emerald. A cruel smile toyed with his mouth.

"That's not for you," she said firmly. "I have to go." She took one step toward the table and he reached without hurry to pick the dossier up.

"I said—"

He only flashed her a dangerous look that held her off and opened it with an elegant turn of his long finger. *Don't think about those fingers.*

Leave, she told herself, but there was no point. She couldn't outrun this sizzling mortification, no matter where she went. Her stomach turned over as she waited for a sign of his reaction to what he read.

A muted bell pinged. "Your reserved time has reached

its limit," a modulated female voice said through hidden speakers.

Thank God. Tiffany let out her breath.

"Extend it," Ryzard commanded.

"Will another thirty minutes be sufficient?"

"I can't stay," Tiffany insisted.

Grim male focus came up to hold her in place, locking her vocal chords.

"Send a full report to my tablet on Davis and Holbrook, specifically their director, *Mrs.* Paul Davis. Thirty minutes is plenty."

"Very good, sir." The bell pinged again and Tiffany thought, *run.* The threat he emanated seemed very real, even though he didn't move, only stared at her with utter contempt.

Bunching her fists at her sides, she lifted her chin, refusing to be anything less than indignant if he was going to jump to nasty conclusions about her. *He* could be married for all she knew—which was a disgusting thought. Her brain frantically tried to retrieve knowledge one way or another. She was no poli-sci major, but she'd always kept up on headlines, usually knowing way more than she wanted to about world politics because of her father's ambitions. There were gaps because of the accident, of course, months of news she'd missed completely that coincided with the coup in Bregnovia.

She had no memory about his marital status, but something told her he wouldn't be nearly so scornful of her if he had his own spouse in the wings.

Ryzard tossed the folder into the empty chair and hooked his hands in his pockets to keep from strangling the woman who wanted to play him for a fool. Her being married was bad enough. She might shrug off little things like extramarital affairs, but he did not.

The fact she thought she could buy his business was even more aggravating, partly because he was so affected by last night. As much as he wished he wasn't, his body was reacting to her even though she was dressed very conservatively. Her loose, sand-colored pants grazed the floor over heeled sandals he'd glimpsed when she had moved. They were clunky-looking things, but their height elongated her legs into lissome stems he wanted to feel through the thin fabric of her pants. Her yellow top was equally lightweight and cut across her collarbone, hiding skin that had seemed powder white last night.

What he'd seen of it, anyway. He couldn't see much today and found that equally frustrating. He might have detected her nipples poking against the fine silk of her top, but while her flat green jacket nipped in to emphasize her waist, it also shielded her breasts from his view.

Nothing about her appearance hinted at the exciting, sensual woman he'd met last night. Even her wild curls had been scraped back, which might have been an elegant display of her bone structure if he could see her face.

"Take off your mask," he ordered, irritated that his voice wasn't as clear as he'd like.

"No."

The quietly spoken word blasted into his eardrums. It was not something he heard often.

"It's not a request," he stated.

"It's not open for discussion," she responded, body language so hostile he could practically taste her antagonism.

Curious.

No. He wouldn't allow himself to be intrigued by her. Pulling himself together, he did his best to reject and eject her from every aspect of his life in one blow.

Glancing away as if his senses weren't concentrated upon her every breath and pulse, he said dismissively, "Tell your husband you failed. My business can't be bought. He

might enjoy your second-rate efforts that offer no real pleasure, but I'm more discerning."

Her sharp inhale, as if she'd been stabbed in the lung,
drew his gaze back to her. Her lips were white and trembled
just enough to kick him in the conscience.

He forced himself to hold her hurt gaze, surprised how
effective his insult had been. Her startling blue eyes deepened to pools of navy that churned with angry hatred. He
didn't flinch from it, but instead held her gaze as if he was
holding a knife in a wound, ensuring he would fully sever
himself from a repeat performance of his weakness.

"How do you propose I tell him?" she asked with a bitterness that bludgeoned him, implacable and final. "Hire
a psychic? He's dead." She pivoted to the door.

A blinding flash, like white light, shot through him.
Not an external thing, but an inner slice of laser-sharp pain
that he felt as an echo of hers. He knew that sort of grief—

Before he realized what he was doing, he'd moved to
catch her arm and spin her around to him.

She used her momentum to bring her free hand up, sending it flying toward his face.

He caught her wrist and jerked back his head, his re-
flexes honed by war and a natural dominance that always
kept him on guard. Still, a heavy blanket of regret suffo-
cated him as he held her while she wordlessly struggled.
He'd insulted her because he was angry, but he would never
wound someone by dangling such a loss over them. An
apology was needed, but holding on to her was like trying
to wrestle a feral cat into a sack.

"Stop fighting me," he ground out, surprised by her wiry
strength and unflagging determination.

"Go to hell!"

He got her wrists in one hand behind her back, her knee
scissored between his own tightly enough to prevent it ris-

ing into his crotch. Squeezing her enough to threaten her breathing, he loosened off as she quieted.

"Big man, overwhelming a helpless woman," she taunted in a pant.

"You're not that helpless," he noted, admiring her fighting spirit despite his inherent knowledge that he shouldn't like anything about her.

She was widowed. That was tremendously important, even though he refused to examine too closely why he was so relieved. Or why he was now determined to learn more about her. He'd been serious about not being corruptible, no matter how his body longed to be persuaded.

Her shaken breaths caused her breasts to graze his chest, increasing the arousal their struggle had already stimulated. She recognized his hardness and squirmed again, forcing him to pin her even closer to hang on to her.

"Let me go," she said in a furious voice that provoked more than intimidated.

"In a minute." He reached to remove her mask—

She tried to bite him. He narrowly snatched his fingers from the snap of her teeth.

"You little wildcat." He couldn't help but be amused by her streak of ferocity. Her bared teeth were perfect, her pinched nostrils as refined as a spoiled princess's.

"I'm reporting this assault," she told him.

"I have a right to see whose body I was in last night," he told her, unconsciously revealing with the low timbre of his voice how disturbed he was by the memory.

"No, you don't. I'm discerning about who sees any part of me. And maybe I didn't bring my best game last night because I was bored and wanted it over with. Did you think of that?"

"I suppose I deserved that," he murmured, but her insult still landed like a knee in the gut, making his abdominal muscles clench in offense.

Digging his fingers around the knot of her hair, he tugged lightly, deliberately overwhelming her with his strength, exposing her throat and making her aware she was at his mercy. Not because he got off on hurting women. Never. But she needed to understand that even though she was utterly vulnerable to him, he wouldn't harm her.

"Now we've both said something cruel, and neither of us will do it again."

Her outraged "Ha" warmed his lips, making him deeply conscious of the shape of her Kewpie-doll mouth with its peaks in her top lip over a fat strawberry of a bottom one. Her scent, like Saponaria, somewhere between dewy grass and sun-warmed roses, threatened to erase all thought but making love to her again.

"I only said what I did because I thought you were married. And you tricked me. I don't like your trying to take advantage of me. To even the playing field…" He reached for the tailing ribbon that held her mask.

"Noooo." The sharp anguish in her voice startled him. She was genuinely terrified, straining into a twist to escape his loosening of the mask.

He let go of the ribbon and her, horrified that he'd scared her so deeply, but he couldn't help reaching to steady her when she staggered as she tried to catch the falling mask. Her shaking hands fumbled it before her, turning it around and around, trying to right it so she could put it on again. A desperate sob escaped her.

It was too late. He'd seen what she was trying to hide, and the bottom dropped out of his heart. He touched her chin, wanting a better look.

She knocked his hand away and flashed a look of fury at him. With her jaw set in livid mutiny, she stopped trying to replace her mask and stared him down with the kind of aggression that would make him fear for his life if she'd been armed.

"Happy?" she charged.

Not one little bit.

As he took in the mottled shades of pink and red, all he saw was pain. He'd been in battle. He knew what bullets and flames and chemicals could do to the human body. That's why his world had stopped last night when he'd thought a bomb was landing on the ramparts of the club.

But these were healed injuries, as well as they'd ever get anyway. The ragged edge of the facial scar followed a crooked line like a country's border on a map, sharply defining rescued flesh from the unharmed with a raised pink scar. It hedged a patch from over her left eye into the corner of her lid—she might have lost her sight, he acknowledged, cold dread touching his internal organs. Under her eye, it cut diagonally toward her nose before tracing down to the corner of her mouth and under her jawline, and then wound back to her hair.

The side of her neck was only a little discolored, but the way the color fanned at the base of it made him suspect the scarring went down her arm and torso, too, maybe farther.

As he brought his gaze back up to her face, he met eyes so bruised and wounded, he was struck with shame at causing her to reveal herself. He hadn't been trying to humiliate her. This wasn't meant as a punishment.

The hatred in her eyes took it as such anyway, stabbing him with compunction.

"I wouldn't work for you if your country was knocked back into the Stone Age and we were overinventoried in animal fur and flint. I'm leaving. Now."

He didn't try to stop her, sensing he'd misjudged her on a grand scale.

She tied her mask into place without looking at him. When she pressed the button to open the doors, they didn't cooperate, remaining closed while she swore at her watch.

"Tiffany," he cajoled, pulling her name from what he'd read, but not sure what he would say if he could persuade her to stay.

"Die," she ordered flatly.

The doors opened and she walked out.

CHAPTER FOUR

FOR THE FIRST time in months, Tiffany cried. Really cried as she hugged her knees in the shower and released sobs that echoed against the tiles. They racked her so hard she thought she'd throw up. She hated her life, hated herself, hated him.

She'd still been processing his remark about her efforts being second-rate when he'd yanked back her curtain and looked at her as if she was an object of horror. As though he was repulsed.

Sex was not worth this. Men weren't. She was old enough, and educated enough, to know that having a husband and kids were not necessary ingredients to a woman's happiness. Why then was she so gutted every time she was forced to face that no man would ever want her? That a family life would never be hers?

It was self-pitying tripe, and she had to get over it.

Forcing her weak legs to support her, she turned off the shower and leaned against the wall, cold and dripping until she worked up the energy to pull on a robe. As she moved into her room, she felt empty. Not better, not depressed, just numb.

That was okay. She could live with numb.

Perching on the foot of the bed, she stared at her wrinkled fingers and wondered what she should do. Hide in her room until this ridiculous clubhouse opened its doors again? Fake appendicitis for a helicopter ride to the mainland? She felt sick. She was damp and feverish, aching all over, weak and filled with malaise.

A yawn took her by surprise and she thought, *Siesta.* One small thing in her favor. Crawling up to her pillows, she escaped into unconsciousness.

The sun crept around the edge of his balcony, likely to begin blistering his bare toes soon, but Ryzard was ready to stretch away the stiffness in his body anyway. He'd been motionless for over an hour as he read through the report he'd been provided by the *Q Virtus* staff.

Davis and Holbrook was an exceptional organization, very well regarded in the international construction industry. He could definitely do worse as he looked at rebuilding the broken roads and collapsed buildings in his city centers. They had wanted to land on his radar as he moved toward those sorts of goals, and now they were.

The rest of the report, about Mrs. Paul Davis, was even more interesting. She had started out as a wealthy society darling. Her marriage to a family friend had all the markings of a traditional fairy tale, right up to the wedding gown with a train and the multitiered cake.

Except a wedding gift from the bride's brother of a prestigious sports car had been more temptation than the drunken groom could resist. He'd taken it up to ninety between the courtyard and the gates of the golf and country club, detonating it against a low brick wall before the guests had stopped waving.

After a flurry of death and memorial announcements accompanied by touch-and-go mentions of the bride, the reports had dried up. Fast-forward two years and his widow was taking the reins of her dead husband's corporation. Her brother had held her power of attorney during her recovery, but his talents were better suited to hands-on architectural engineering. The plethora of awards he'd earned spoke to that very loudly.

All of this would have been flat information if it didn't reinforce to Ryzard that he'd made a mistake in assuming she'd been trying to influence him with sex. What reason would she have? Her company was flourishing—somewhat surprisingly, given that her credentials amounted to an arts degree and attitude, but her grades were exceptional. She was certainly intelligent.

And he could personally attest that she was a ballbuster, he allowed with irony. He had no doubt she was more than a figurehead. If she had a vision, quite likely one formed in her husband's name, she would achieve it.

Turning from that disturbing thought, he allowed that if Bregnovia had already attained recognition, she might have tried for an advantage while he had a wider playing field to draw from, but it would be a risky move until his government was recognized.

Did their interest in his business mean an acknowledgment for Bregnovia was in the works? Or was their rendezvous exactly what it seemed to be: two healthy people enjoying the pleasures of the mating ritual.

Heat pooled in his lap as he dwelt on the possibility she'd welcomed him because she'd been as caught up as he had in their physical compatibility.

A twinge of conscience followed, but he had long ago rationalized that his heart and his body were separate when it came to sex. He had the same basic needs as any living thing, requiring nutrition, a sheltered environment and a regular release of his seed. If a peculiar mix of chemistry intensified his reaction when that last happened, well, he couldn't be held responsible. It was hormones, not emotion.

It was not infidelity against Luiza.

And Tiffany would have no reason to pursue him for sex

to gain his business. It would only complicate what might otherwise be a wise and lucrative association.

Something he should take under consideration, he supposed, scraping the side of his thumb against the stubble coming in on his jaw. It didn't matter how he cast their tryst. It shouldn't happen again.

Except there was one other fact from this report that kept teasing him.

Mr. Holbrook, Tiffany's father. An architect by education, he'd quickly become a career politician who'd worked his way up the ranks of local councils into a senator's mansion. He was now running for the presidency.

Suppose last night had been pure coincidence. Why then had the Holbrooks requested he meet them here, under the discreet curtain of *Q Virtus*? If they feared making a play for his business would hurt the senator's chances, they wouldn't have met him at all. No, it must mean they knew the United States was leaning toward recognition.

A flush of excitement threatened to overtake him, but Ryzard reminded himself to be patient. Backing from the United States would influence many other countries to vote in his favor, but nothing was confirmed.

Still, one thing was clear: he needed another meeting with Tiffany Davis.

Tiffany woke foggy-headed to a noise in the main room like dishes rattling on a cart. Leaping from the bed, she staggered to the door into the lounge and found Ryzard Vrbancic directing one of the *petite q's* to set a table on the balcony.

"What are you doing?" She turned the lapel of her robe up against her cheek.

"I thought you were showering, but apparently you went back to sleep."

"What?" Tiffany scowled at him. "How do you know

what I've been doing? I thought these rooms were completely secure," she charged the woman in the red gown.

"I used my override to bring in the meal you ordered… didn't you?" The young woman looked suspiciously at Ryzard, but he was quick.

"We did, thank you. I'll manage from here. You can go." To Tiffany, he said, "Don't confuse the staff just because we've had a tiff." A mild snort and, "You're aptly named, aren't you?"

"Get out of here," she cried.

The *petite q,* already hurrying, ran to the door and out.

Goggling at Ryzard, whose mouth twitched, Tiffany said, "Seriously?"

"You're overreacting."

"I want you to leave."

"I'm about to make you an offer you can't refuse. Quit hiding and accept."

She narrowed her eyes on his back as he moved onto the balcony, not interested in anything from him except assurances her family would never find out what had happened between them. Not that she was willing to say so.

It took everything in her to stand tall and say, "What kind of offer?" She was writhing inside at everything that had happened, yet had wound up dreaming about him. It had been erotic until it had turned humiliating.

"I can't hear you," he called from the balcony.

Clenching her teeth, she wavered in the doorway, hanging back while telling herself not to let him get away with this manipulation. At the very least, she ought to cover up. She didn't so much as go for milk in the middle of the night without concealer for fear of frightening the staff at home. The only reason she'd forgone it this morning was because she'd expected to keep her mask on.

Ryzard Vrbancic had seen her, however, and she was

still flopping like a fish out of water, gasping for air, waiting for the boot that would send her careening off the boat.

Everything in her cringed with a need to hide, but maybe seeing her again like this would repel him into moving along.

Yanking tight the tie on her robe, she marched to the open French doors and said, "I'm not interested in any offers from you. Please leave."

"I thought you were dressing," he remarked, squeezing fresh lemon across raw oysters in their half shell. They were arranged on a silver tray of ice. Next to them sat a tapas platter of fritters, flatbread, shredded meat, guacamole, salsa and something that looked like burritos but they were wrapped in a type of leaf.

Her stomach growled. She tried to cover the sound with her hand, but he'd heard.

"You're hungry. Eat," he urged magnanimously. As if he wasn't trespassing in her room.

"I prefer to eat alone." She indicated the door, not subtle at all.

He picked up an oyster and eyed her as he slurped it into his mouth, chewed briefly, then swallowed. Raw oysters were supposed to be an aphrodisiac. She'd always thought they were disgusting, but what he'd just done had been the sexiest thing she'd ever seen. She followed the lick of his tongue across his lips, and a wobbly sensation accosted her insides.

Reacting to him made staring him down even more difficult than it already was, but she held his gaze, inner confidence trembling as she waited for another flinch to overtake him like the one this morning. His expression never wavered, though. He let his gaze slide to her scarred cheek, but then it went south into her cleavage, where the swells of her breasts peeped from between her lapels. His perusal continued over her hips, lingered on the dangling ends of her belt and ended at her shins, one white, one mottled.

Involuntarily, her toes curled as she reacted to his masculine assessment. She couldn't tell if she was passing muster or being found wanting. She told herself it didn't matter, that she didn't want his approval or any man's, but in her heart she yearned for a hint of admiration.

He pulled out a chair. "Sit down."

Swallowing, telling herself to keep a straight head, she deliberately provoked a reaction to her flaws by saying, "I'm not supposed to go in the sun."

He shrugged off the protest. "It will set in twenty minutes."

"Look, I'm running out of ways to tell you to get lost without pulling out the big one. I don't want anything to do with you. I was against giving you that letter in the first place, and I'm sorry I came here at all. We won't work for you."

He finished another oyster, but she had his full attention. She could feel it. When his tongue cleaned his lips, she imagined he was licking her all over.

Ignore it, she chided herself.

"Why?" he asked.

Why what? Her brain had lost the plot, but she quickly picked it up, reminding herself of *his* flaws.

"Because I don't like your methods. You're no better than the criminal you replaced."

"I'm a lot better than the criminal I replaced. Check my human-rights record," he growled while a flush of insult rose to his cheeks.

It was enough antagonism to give her pause and make her reconsider deliberately riling him, but despite how much she hated herself for having sex with him, she was still aware of a pull. She desperately needed to cut him down and out.

"You're living pretty large while your countrymen starve. How many people died so you could eat raw oysters and watch the sun set?"

"You know nothing about what I've lost so my people can eat," he said in a lethal tone.

As he spoke, he turned aside to toss his empty shell on the cart, but she glimpsed such incredible pain she caught her breath against an answering stab of anguish. She quickly muffled it, but something in her wavered. Was she misjudging him?

She shook off the thought, scoffing, "Did I strike a nerve? Do you not like having your repulsive side exposed?"

He shot her a fierce look and she thought, *Shut up, Tiffany.*

"You're acting out of bitterness, and it's not with me. We promised not to be cruel."

That gave her a niggle of guilt, which she didn't like at all. She looked at her perfectly manicured nails.

"You might have promised," she said haughtily. "I didn't."

"You like to deliberately hurt people? You do have an ugly side."

That lifted her gaze, and his expression made her heart tremor where it clogged the base of her throat. He had very patrician features. Very proud and strong. Right now they were filled with contempt.

Shame lunged in her. She might have been spoiled and self-involved, but she never used to be mean. But she was angry. So angry. And there was no one to take it out on. She had to look away from the expression that demanded she apologize.

She wavered, uncertain of her footing, but she had enough unscrambled brain cells to remember he was a dictator, not some do-good pastor.

"What do you expect, a welcome mat?" she hazarded, tucking her fists behind her upper arms, affecting a bravado she didn't feel. "You've invaded my territory—"

"You're not angry I'm here. You're angry you had to face the man you made love to last night. That I saw your secret. You're not repulsive, Tiffany."

"As I said, you're stepping into places you haven't been invited."

"I was invited." He picked up an oyster, and his tongue curled to chase and catch the slippery flesh before he pulled the morsel into his mouth.

Inner muscles that were still vaguely tender from their lovemaking clenched involuntarily, sending a shimmer of pleasure upward to her navel and down the insides of her thighs.

When he took a step toward her, she took a hasty one back, bumping into the rail of the balcony.

He raised his brows as he pulled out her chair another inch, reading way too clearly what kind of nervousness she'd just revealed.

"I want you to leave," she insisted.

"We'll clear the air first."

She almost mumbled an adolescent, *I don't want to clear the air*. Because she didn't. She wanted to hit and bite and push away.

She wanted to be left alone to die of loneliness.

Oh, don't be such a baby, Tiffany.

It was true, though. She was like a wounded animal that snarled at anyone who tried to help it. It was the source of the horrible tension with her family. They didn't know what to do with this new Tiffany who hated her life and everything in it.

She glared at Ryzard, loathing him for being the man to show her how twisted she'd become. He'd caught her in a moment of terrible weakness last night, playing pretend that she was normal. He'd sliced past the emotional scar tissue she'd grown, and he seemed to still be doing it. That made him dangerous.

"The sun is about to set. It won't hurt you to be out here," he said.

She whipped around to see how close it was to the horizon. She hadn't been in the sun for more than a handful of steps between a house and car in two years. As she stepped into its rays, the heat on her face felt good. The fading red ball filled her with rapture as it lowered toward the sea.

Holding her breath, she strained her ears.

The band started below, making her slap a hand on the rail in disappointment. "I wanted to hear it!"

"Hear what?" he asked, standing next to her.

"When the sun touches the water."

He gave her a skeptical look that said, *Aren't you a bit old for that?*

She turned away, hiding that yes, she clung to certain childish fantasies that reminded her of easier, simpler times. Being lighthearted and silly didn't come naturally to her anymore, and she desperately longed to find that part of herself again. Tiny moments of happiness were like bread crumbs, hopefully leading her back to a place of acceptance. Maybe even contentment.

"You're really quite sensitive, aren't you?" he mused.

"No."

"And contrary." He waved at the chair he'd pulled out for her. "I have some questions for you. They're important. Sit."

"I'm not a dog."

"No, you're as aloof and touchy as a wet cat. The purring version is worth all the scratching and hissing, though."

"I don't want to talk about that," she rushed to state, unnerved by the suggestiveness in his remark.

"We won't. Not yet," he agreed, and his touch on her shoulder nudged her to sit.

She did, mainly to avoid the way the light contact of his hand made her stomach dip in excitement, and partly because her mother was lecturing her in her head. The members of their family, in all their greatness, were ambassadors, obligated to set an example of good manners and rising above the unpleasant. Such an annoying legacy.

She was also starving. Taking care of herself had become a habit through her recovery. Good food was one of her few real pleasures these days, and this stuff looked awesome.

He watched her build a flatbread into a soft taco, not being shy with the high-calorie avocado paste, either.

"What?" she asked defensively.

"I'm not used to seeing a woman eat like that."

She bit back a spiteful, *Too busy watching them starve?* She really didn't want to be that person, but she didn't know how else to handle him.

"Why are you here?" she asked instead.

He paused in preparing his own flatbread. "Why are *you* here, Tiffany? Why did your family send you to meet me?"

The weight of his gaze turned her shrug into a shiver. "Apparently I'm the only one who is a member."

His brows went up in surprise.

"I inherited my husband's fortune. My father isn't exactly struggling, but he doesn't qualify."

"I read about your accident. I'm sorry for your loss."

She prickled, waiting to see if he would make more of it, dig deeper, question how a married woman could have been a virgin.

"I'm also a member and was one long before our civil war. The money you accuse me of stealing is Bregnovia's. It's earmarked to fund our recovery."

She eyed him, seeing a contrary mix of Euro-sophistication and obdurate leader. When he caught her looking at him, her heart skipped. She looked away.

"I'll have to request a report on you from the powers that be. Find out how you made your fortune," she said.

"I'll tell you. It's a spigot system I developed for the oil industry, inspired by what I learned working in vineyards after finishing my engineering degree."

Despite her inner warnings to hold him off, she was intrigued. "That seems an odd choice. What was an engineer doing in a winery?"

"Rebelling," he said flatly, not inviting more questions as he reached to the wine bucket and drew out a dripping green bottle. "This is from my country. You'll enjoy it."

Of course she would. Who would dare not?

His arrogance was growing on her if she was finding it more amusing than annoying.

"What do you mean, you were rebelling?"

He drew a subtle breath, as though gathering himself for something difficult. "If you were to order a report on me, you would learn my parents sent me to live in Germany when I was six. For my safety and to give me a better life. Our country has been annexed by one neighbor or another since before the First World War. There were constant outbreaks of independence-seeking followed by terrible repression. My parents couldn't leave, but they smuggled me out to friends. I can't complain. My foster parents were good people. The husband was an automotive engineer who pressed me to follow in his footsteps. As a vocation I didn't mind it, but when I graduated I felt as most young people do. That this was my life and I could do as I liked." He shrugged, mouth twisting in self-deprecation. "I'm not proud of abandoning my potential to pick grapes, but it allowed me to bring a fresh perspective when I went to Russia, planning to make my fortune drilling for oil."

"Where you fashioned this doodad that is so popular it made you into a bazillionaire?"

"Da," he confirmed with a nod.

"Humph." She reached for her wine. "Does the rest of the world know this?"

He lifted a shoulder dismissively. "The press prefers to sensationalize what I did with my money."

"Which was to fund a war."

"I freed my country."

"And now you own it."

"I lead it. What do you think of the wine?"

She was no sommelier and didn't bother with sniffing and swirling, but she thought the light color was appealing and she enjoyed the way the initial tang, almost fruity, eased into something more earthy. Not oaky. Vanilla?

She tried again, wanting to determine what it was. But as much as she loved wine, alcohol had been off-limits as her body had needed every advantage to recover. That made her a lightweight. She had to be careful about losing her head around him.

As the memory of their dirty dancing and everything that followed bathed her in heat, the proximity of a bedroom and sitting here in her robe suddenly seemed incredibly dangerous and intimate.

Ryzard watched a glow of awareness brighten Tiffany's skin, filling her compelling blue eyes even as she looked into the crisp white wine she set aside. Her reaction might be in response to the alcohol, but his male instincts read her differently.

He shifted in his chair, widening his knees to make room for the growing reaction tugging insistently between his legs.

Tricking the waitstaff into granting him entry to her room had been the oldest one in the book, but as he'd suspected, she wouldn't have seen him otherwise and he wanted answers. At this precise second, however, he found himself with only one thing on his mind: her. She was more complex than he'd given her credit for, both when he'd lost himself in the mecca of her flesh and when he'd assumed she was attempting to manipulate him.

She was far more beautiful than he'd taken the time to notice this morning, too. Then his attention had been drawn to the scarring, his focus on the pain it indicated. Now he could see what had existed before discoloration and a raised jagged line had bisected her cheek. Blonde, blue eyed, with skin like a baby and the bone structure of an aristocrat, she was Helen of Troy.

Not that he was prepared to go to war ever again, but he could imagine men who would. Her young husband must have been intimidated, knowing how coveted she was.

"It's rude to stare," she said, growing redder in one cheek.

"I'm not staring. I'm admiring."

Her mouth shrank in rejection, and so did his brain. He forced himself to look away from thick lashes that swept down to hide her eyes. This meeting wasn't about kindling an affair that had barely started, no matter how much the thought appealed.

It appealed far too much. He could barely concentrate as memories of her pushing her ass into his groin as she writhed with pleasure under his slippery touch filled his head. The heady power of fondling her to orgasm had made him drunk and was overshadowed only by how good she had felt squeezing him in her hot, perfect depths.

But his country came first. He couldn't forget that. Couldn't forget anything.

He shook himself out of his fascination and spoke briskly.

"Your father seems exceptionally well connected in Washington. By sending you to speak to me, he is signaling that your country is likely to support my petition for recognition at the UN, is he not? Has he told you this is forthcoming?"

"He's under that impression, but who knows what the attitude will be tomorrow? Welcome to politics. You know how these things work."

He did, and the hardest lesson he had learned after being in a war was when to back off and use diplomacy instead of force to get what he wanted. It was also standard practice to weigh a person's impact on an agenda before developing a relationship.

Maybe he hadn't properly examined how their affair could affect his goal before he made love to her, but Tiffany's knowledge and connections suggested she could have a very positive influence.

A wild rush of excitement flew through him as he found a rationale to continue their affair, but he forced himself to hold on to a cool head and gather information first. "Does your father have any sway over your country's decision makers?"

"He has followers. Believers in his vision. Isn't that how you got elected, by cultivating the same?" The remark was somewhere between haughty and ironic.

"You don't seem to be one of them. His followers, I mean. It's quite obvious you're not one of mine. Yet."

"Ha," she choked, but she lowered her lashes as if to prevent him reading something different in her eyes. "Never yours and while I'll always cheer for Dad, I'm tired of living my life by his career," she said with dour humor and popped a cherry tomato into her mouth, pursing her lips in a pout as she chewed.

"When is the election?" he asked, trying not to watch her plump lips too closely.

"Not for a year, but the campaigning is well under way. He was leaving for Washington as we were coming here."

"We?" he asked sharply, territorial instincts riled.

"My brother and I."

"Ah. That's fine then." He frowned. Whatever relief he felt in knowing there wasn't another man in her life was buried under the discomfort of revealing he saw himself in the role. What was it about her that not only affected him but also lowered his ability to hide how much?

She lifted her brows. "Jealous?" Her smile was taunting, but her voice thinned across the word, suggesting a vulnerability that further undermined his resistance to her.

He shouldn't want her this badly, but he did. Last night had been exceptional, and she was a practical connection to cultivate. Where was the sense in fighting it?

"Possessive," he corrected. "You have a lover, *draga*."

Her shocked expression masked into something complex. Her lips tightened in dismay while her brow flinched in pain. A stark yearning drew her features taut while her swallow indicated a type of fear. Then it all smoothed away, leaving him unsettled, wondering if an affair with her could become more complicated than it needed to be.

"Had," she said in a husky voice. "Past tense."

"I'm not talking about your husband," he growled, stirred to jealousy after all.

The blank look she sent him disappeared in a raspy laugh. "Neither am I."

His sharp brain caught a hidden meaning, but she kept talking, distracting him.

"Last night was a departure from my real life, not something I'll ever do again. Why would you even want to—" Dawning comprehension waxed her features before her face gradually tightened in rejection and something more disturbing. Anguish. "Wow. Nice to know some things haven't changed," she said bitterly.

"What do you mean?" Clammy palms seemed an overreaction to being rejected as a one-nighter. He'd done it himself in the past, but he didn't like it. Not from her.

"I'm still capable of being used," she answered. "You think that if you keep me close, you'll keep my father's cronies closer."

A pinch of compunction gave him pause, but that's not all that was going on here. And now she'd piqued his curiosity.

"Who used you in the past? How?" It was a tender point for him. Only a blind fool would fail to see the advantage to him in associating with her, but there were lines, especially with women. When Luiza was taken, it was to use her as leverage against him. She'd ended her life to prevent it. He never took manipulation of the unwilling lightly.

"Who *hasn't* used me?" she demanded. "I thought if there was one silver lining to this—" she drew a circle around her face "—it was that I was no longer a pawn. Thanks for dinner." She stood up, tossing him a pithy look. "A girl in my position is lucky when a man shows her a bit of attention. You're a helluva guy, Ryzard."

Her contempt burned like acid as it dripped over him. It might not have seared so deeply if he hadn't grasped at the advantages of an affair to justify exactly how badly he wanted to continue theirs.

He didn't want to admit how fierce his hunger for her was, but the hurt beneath her words told him she didn't see any at all. Wounding her, especially when she was so sensitive about her desirability, had a disturbing effect on him. Guilt assailed him and provoked something deeper. A compulsion to draw her close and make up with her.

He didn't want to be so enthralled. It went against everything he'd promised himself and Luiza's memory. Nevertheless, he reacted to the way she rejected him with a pivot of her body. It incited him to strike fast to keep from being shut out. Fear that had nothing to do with the best interests of his country goaded him to act.

"Don't underestimate what's between us, Tiffany." He

inwardly cringed at revealing so much, but he was even more averse to her thinking he was capable of low motives. "The attraction between us is real and very strong."

"Oh, give it up! You don't want me. You—"

"Shall I prove it?" He rose and easily stalked her across the tiny space of the balcony, using her outstretched hand to tug her close and pulling her resistant body into to his own.

"What do you think you're doing?" she demanded, wriggling for freedom then stilling when she felt his arousal. "You—" Confusion stilled her and she searched his expression.

"As I said." He lowered his head, setting a determined kiss over her protesting mouth.

Tiffany continued to press for distance, but he wasn't being mean, just insistent. Still, she was awfully confused. The way he'd given her that moment of hope that she could be attractive to someone before she realized it was all a ruse had been devastating. Now he was coming on strong, making her want to melt into him. Really, seriously, turn to mush in his arms. It was so frightening to be this affected. She did the only thing she could think to do. She tried to bite him.

He jerked his head back. "Are we playing rough, *draga?*" He shot his hand beneath her robe, grasping her breast in a firm hand, dislodging the slippery tie of her robe so it started to fall open.

"Don't!" she cried, hunching and scrambling to keep as much cloth in place as possible. "Please, Ryzard, don't do this. Not out here where anyone could see."

He froze, then slowly withdrew his hand. The tips of his fingers grazed a distended nipple, sending a pulse of pleasure-pain through her. She was too humiliated to respond and too shaken by the fear of exposure to appreciate his obeying her plea.

"Tiffany," he scolded as he held her in loose arms. "I'm not trying to hurt you."

Pushing back until he reluctantly let his hold on her drop away, she ensured she was completely covered, but couldn't lift her head.

"I've seen battle scars, you know." The hand he used to smooth her hair back from her bad cheek was surprisingly compassionate.

Rather than turn into his caress, she averted from it.

"I'm your first lover since the accident? That's why you're so shy?" Ryzard was still trying to catch up to the way her shield of toughness had fallen away so quickly into such tremendous vulnerability. One second she'd been a worthy adversary, the next a broken fawn in need of swift protection.

"Yeah." Her snorted word held a hysterical note. She tried to step over the chair he'd upended, trying to move away from him. Tears sheened her eyes, her emotions so close to the surface he knew she was near a tipping point.

He bent to right the chair, allowing her to move away into privacy because pieces were falling into place in his mind in a way he couldn't quite believe. Her back seemed incredibly narrow and bowed under a weight as she entered the suite. He could hardly countenance what he was thinking, but her gasp of pain last night rang in his ears. He had thought she just wasn't quite ready, but...

Cautiously he followed, one hand going to the door frame to steady himself as he asked, "Tiffany. Am I your *only* lover?"

She didn't turn around, but her shoulders seemed to flinch before she lifted her head to say cockily, "So far, but with my looks and connections, I'm encouraged to believe there's more in my future."

He bit back a curse while his free hand clenched into a

fist at his side. He wanted to shake her out of sheer frustration with her cavalier attitude, but at the same time he had a deep compulsion to cradle her against him. The erotic memory of their coming together grew sweeter even as he struggled with the ramifications of being a woman's first. He'd done it once before. He knew the emotional ties it pulled from both parties.

A splintering sensation accosted him as he once again compared her with Luiza. His first instinct was to walk away. Confusing emotions tumbled through him like a rockslide, tainted with the intense grief he'd managed to avoid as the aftermath of war had consumed him. He once again hated himself as a traitor for having more than a passing interest in Tiffany, but learning he was her first changed things. He wasn't so archaic he thought virginity was a seal of quality, but losing it was an important marker in a woman's life. He couldn't be dismissive of her or what she'd offered him, even if she was trying to be.

"Can you explain to me how this is possible, *Mrs.* Davis?"

Tiffany looked to the ceiling, battling back stupid tears and a deeper sense of vulnerability than she'd ever felt. There had been a time when her confidence, her belief in her own superiority, had been unflagging. In an instant she had become weak and broken and dependent. Finding her way back from that seemed impossible, and she hated that Ryzard saw her at this low point. He was so strong and sure of himself. Where had he been when she'd had all her defenses in place and could have handled his forceful, dynamic personality?

A dozen sarcastic responses to his question came to her tongue, but the nearest she could get to flippant was to say, "I was afraid I'd fall in love with someone else if I didn't save myself for Paulie."

She tightened her belt and turned, surprised to catch him in an unguarded moment.

The faraway look in his eye suggested he had dark thoughts of his own. Seeing he might not be as completely put together as he seemed gave her the courage to continue with more outspokenness than she'd ever allowed herself.

"Our marriage was written in stone. Our fathers were friends, and his mother was my mom's maid of honor. Paulie and my brother, Christian, were inseparable through childhood. The architect and engineer designed the bridge between our families when Paulie and I were still in diapers. By the time I was in high school, no other boy had the guts to ask me out. They knew I was already taken."

"You didn't date? Didn't sleep with him?"

"*Paulie* dated. He sowed enough wild oats for the both of us. He took me to the Friday night dances, and on Monday I would hear what had happened at the parties he went to after he dropped me at home. He came *here* and had affairs."

"And you put up with that?"

She sighed, hugging herself. "I believed him when he told me he was getting it out of his system. He swore that once we were married, he would never stray. I still believe he meant it. He encouraged me to do the same," she offered with a shrug, "but like I say, no one offered and I told myself it would be romantic to wait."

"Did you love him?"

She sighed, chest aching as she admitted what she'd never told anyone. "I adored him like a best friend. That's a good foundation for a marriage, right?" She had needed to believe it, but hearing it now only made her hug herself tighter.

She tried to stem the emotions swelling in her, but the rest of her feelings, the churning doubts and anger and grief, gathered and poured out. "I miss him like crazy. He's the one person who would have been right beside me through all of this, keeping my spirits up, saying all the right things. But I don't know if I'd even be speaking to him because I'm so angry. I hate him for dying, really truly hate hi—"

A sob arrived like a commuter train with a whoosh and a suck of air. She held herself steady as grief rose and peaked. She blinked and trembled until she could assimilate it. After a long minute, she found control again and managed to continue.

"I hate him for getting behind the wheel that night. I hate Christian for giving him the car. I hate myself for thinking one spin up the drive when we were all so drunk would be okay."

Something tickled her jaw, and she realized a tear had bled down her numb cheek to burn her chin. She swiped it away and sniffed back the rest.

Through blurred eyes, she saw Ryzard looked gray, but she was coming back from a dark place. The whole world looked dull and bleak.

"I've never admitted that to anyone," she confessed. "I think it needed to come out. Thank you." She rubbed her arms, becoming aware she was frozen and achy.

Ryzard's long legs and wide chest appeared unexpectedly before her. He drew her into his arms even as she drew a surprised breath. His expression was stark and filled with deep anguish.

"Don't say anything," he said heavily, overcoming her automatic stiffening and pressing her into the solid strength of his body. "Just be quiet a minute."

He smoothed hands along her back to mold her into him, warming her. It wasn't a pass. It was comfort. After a hesitant moment, she let her head settle into the hollow of his shoulder and closed her eyes. He stroked her hair and she let her arms wrap around him, hugging him so the bruise that was her heart still ached, but felt covered and protected by the shield of his solid presence.

"Sometimes anger and hatred are the only things that get you through the injustice," he said so quietly she wasn't sure she really heard him, but the tickle across her hair told her his voice was real. "I envy people of strong faith. They never seem tortured by the why of it."

She swallowed, floored to realize they were sharing a moment, something so deep and personal it didn't need a name of a lost one for her to know he understood her utterly and completely. He suffered as she did.

Her hand moved on his back, soothing the tension in the muscles alongside his spine. She relaxed into him and they held each other for a long minute.

Gradually she realized he was becoming aroused. He wasn't overt about it, but she knew and an answering thread of response began subtly changing her own body. Her internal organs felt quivery and her breasts grew sensitive. Awareness of their stark physical differences expanded in her mind along with how intimately they'd fit themselves together last night.

As heat suffused in her, she tried to pull away and keep her head ducked so he wouldn't see how she was reacting.

He kept her close and tilted her face up. His mouth twitched ruefully, but his eyes remained somber. "You see?" he murmured. A sensation of pressure made her think he might have stroked his thumb over the scar tissue on her cheek. "We're a good fit. You should let me give you the after-party you deserved before your wedding."

"Tempting," she said, backing out of his hold because a resurgence of warmth that had its feet in embarrassed longing tingled through her. "But I'm not a charity case you need to offer a pity lay. Give me your email and I'll let you know if my father learns anything."

"My desire for you has nothing to do with my political

agenda," he dismissed with a heavy dollop of annoyance. "I want you."

She snorted. "Why?"

"Because, Tiffany, if you had any experience with men, you would know that last night was remarkable. There are people who have been together years and not been so attuned to each other." He flinched a little as he said that, but she was too busy reacting to his outrageous claim.

"That's not what you said this morning." She tried to sound unaffected, but she was still feeling unfairly spanked. It reflected in the raspy edge on her tone and filled her with debasement long after the insult had landed. She couldn't even look at him.

"I was under a wrong impression and behaved unpleasantly. I apologize."

She eyed him, skeptical.

"I don't apologize often. I suggest you accept it."

"No doubt," she allowed with a twitch of her lips. His arrogance ought to turn her off, but he seemed to have a right to it. His inner strength was as compelling as his obvious physical virility. When it wasn't turned against her, that combination was lethally attractive.

"Come here," he cajoled in a smoky invitation, even though he stood within touching distance and only had to reach out if he really wanted to.

"Why?" She stayed where she was, but everything in her gravitated to him.

"I want to kiss you. Show you how good we are together."

"Seduce me?"

He offered a masculine smile so tomcattish and predatory, it made her stomach dip in giddy excitement. "I would very much like to make love to you again," he said.

An image of her naked body, the one she avoided in the

mirror every day, flashed in her mind. She drew the lapels of her robe together and shook her head.

"Find someone else. I'm not playing hard to get. I just don't see the point."

Rather than argue, he pursed his mouth in regret. "I've damaged your trust in me."

"There wasn't much to begin with," she assured him with a tight smile.

"And the claws are revealed once again." He seemed more amused than irritated. "You trusted me enough to share your—what does your American singer call it? The wonderland that is your body."

"Yes, well, I was pretending to be someone else," she dismissed with false breeziness, inner foundations unsteady as she recalled how completely she'd deluded herself into believing what she'd done was okay.

"Do it again," he commanded.

"Ha!" She couldn't help it. The man was so lofty and single-minded.

"I'm serious," he insisted. "Put on your mask. We'll go downstairs and find that woman capable of such delightful spontaneity."

"It's—no. I can't."

But she couldn't think why. At least, not fast enough to have an answer ready when he demanded, "Why not?"

"Because…" She searched for a reason.

"We could dance again. We both enjoyed that. Of course, we could do that here." He glanced to where the balcony doors stood open. The music from the band below drifted in with the sea-scented air and the swish of waves on the shore.

The mood and music came across as a lazy, exotic throb.

"No," she said firmly, smart enough to be wary of his power once he got his hands on her. The way he'd felt her up on the dance floor last night had obviously been a spell of some kind.

"Downstairs it is. Shall we say one hour? I can shave and change in fifteen minutes, but you women need twenty just to find a pair of shoes."

"He said," she mocked, "demonstrating his vast experience with the opposite sex."

"I won't apologize. We're adults. We can enjoy each other if we want to." He moved forward to set a brief but profound kiss on her startled mouth. "Sure you don't want to stay in?" he asked in a private tone that made her blood flutter in her arteries.

Oh, she was tempted, but she shook her head. "I'm not sure I even want to see you again."

"Meet me downstairs, Tiffany, or I'll come looking for you. But I don't want to waste time searching. Set your watch."

She shook her head. "I don't like people thinking they can talk to me. I'd rather leave it on Do Not Disturb."

"Set it so *I* can find you." At her blank look, he gave her a head shake of exasperation. "Where is it? I'll show you."

A few minutes later she stood in her empty suite wondering how she'd gone from crying in the shower to having a date, one that made her feel more awake and alive than— this was dangerous—any other time in her life.

Oh, Tiffany, be careful. You could still fall for the wrong man.

No, she wasn't that pathetic and vulnerable, she assured herself. Nor was she strong enough to stay in her room and risk his coming for her. Besides, she had enjoyed feeling normal. There was no crime in that, was there?

She liked even more the idea of making him see her as beautiful. Turning, she went to see what treasures the designers might have left her.

CHAPTER FIVE

RYZARD MOVED THROUGH the three-dimensional images of a *carnivale* parade. He had to be careful. There were real people, *Q Virtus* members and *petite q's,* dressed as colorfully as the fake partiers, but for the most part he walked right through projections of extravagant floats and scantily clad women wearing beaded bikinis and feather headdresses. He stopped for a troupe of men in checkered pants and neon elephant masks when they began a tumbling routine in front of him, nearly convinced they were real.

His watch hummed, indicating Tiffany was close by, but *where?*

His need to see her again, to know she'd come down here for him, was out of proportion to any normal sort of anticipation. He brushed it aside, thinking if he could have her just once more, he'd be able to forget about her. It didn't matter that she'd revealed more about herself than he'd ever heard from all other *Q Virtus* members combined. Like most of the happenings here, their private conversation would stay locked in his own personal vault, not even to be revisited by him.

He especially refused to dwell on their comforting embrace when her mixture of grief and anger and self-blame had struck a chord in him. Even though, for the better part of a minute while he held her, he'd been at peace for the first time in a long time.

He stepped on a man's hands and looked through the feet that would have struck him in the nose if the vision was real. Music blared, voices cheered, and the holographic players were so dense he might as well have been in a crowd on the street.

There. All the hairs stood up on his body as he took her in.

She had her head bent to study her watch and pivoted as though trying to orient herself with a compass. The movement allowed him to take her in from all sides.

She really was strikingly beautiful. Tall and slender, but generously curved in the right places. He swallowed. She wore some kind of jumpsuit that clung from knees to elbows, then flared into ruffles down her forearms and over her shins. It had a subtle sparkle in its midnight blue color and clung to her ass so lovingly, his knees weakened.

He mentally recited the populations of Bregnovia's cities, trying to keep hold of his control as he approached her. Sidling up behind her, almost touching, he inhaled where she'd left the right side of her neck bare, gathering her hair to the left so it covered the scars.

"What the hell are you wearing?"

Her head came up. "You don't like it?" She jiggled the watch in her hand. "This thing was buzzing at me, but I couldn't figure out if you were over there or over there."

"I'm here," he growled, wanting so badly to palm the firm globe near his crotch his hand burned.

"So you are." She turned to study his mask from behind her own. "Hello again, Mystery Man. Buy me a drink? I've had a terrible day with the most arrogant, self-aggrandizing jerk you can imagine."

Few people could get away with insulting him so openly, but he found her brashness refreshing. Maybe even reassuring. She wasn't as vulnerable as she'd seemed in her suite. Good.

Testing the waters, he said, "I'm looking forward to one myself. I was stuck all evening with the most infuriating female, smart as a whip, but *blonde*. No offense." He tugged one of her ringlets.

For a moment her mouth stayed flat and humorless, just long enough for doubt to creep over his conscience. Then her lips twitched and a pretty, feminine chuckle erupted, sounding a shade rusty, as if she hadn't laughed unreservedly in a long time, but it engaged him in a way he hadn't expected. He instantly wanted to hear it again.

"None taken," she assured him breezily, turning to grasp his arm above his elbow, demonstrating how much self-assurance she possessed when she wasn't paralyzed by self-consciousness. "Can you believe this parade? I thought it was real."

Despite wanting to remark on the sudden change in her, he decided to go with it.

"The first time I saw this technology, it was a rain forest. It wasn't as robust as this, but the rain effect was quite something."

"You've been coming to these shindigs for a while?"

"This is my twenty-fifth. I earned a pin." He lifted his lapel to draw her eye to the small gold button.

"Nice. What does it do? Beam you up? Shoot lasers?"

"It tells people I belong."

Ryzard's mouth tightened after he spoke, as if he hadn't meant to reveal that, which piqued her curiosity all the more. "What do you mean?"

He shook his head, trying to dismiss her curiosity. "They have a live performance on the beach tonight. Shall we check it out?"

"Are you sensitive to not belonging because of the UN thing? You must know how slowly the wheels of political progress can turn. If the old boys' network is refusing to pick you for their team, tell them to stuff it."

His mask annoyed her. He was already pretty stoic, and now she had to try reading his emotions from the way the corner of his supersexy mouth flattened with disgust.

"I've learned to do exactly that, Tiffany. And it really doesn't matter to me if I'm rejected or found wanting, but I can't bear for my country to be discriminated against."

Discriminated. There was a big word. As a woman she'd been on the short end of that nastiness even in her own home in favor of her brother, but she couldn't imagine it happening to a man who showed so few weaknesses. He wasn't a typical representative of the people she understood to suffer the worst end of biases.

"When were you picked on? Why?" she asked, allowing him to steer her through the shower of candies that should have landed with a sting or crunched under her platform shoes.

He shrugged as if the details were inconsequential. "Different times. When I was a child and didn't yet speak German. I was late to sprout and quick to fight, angry that I couldn't see my parents. My temper was a problem. Getting a legitimate passport was a nightmare, so I was forever in a country illegally. That's one of the reasons I picked grapes. Things like visas can be overlooked when the fruit is ripe and a transient offers to help. But when I tried to go to America, they wanted nothing to do with me."

"So you went to Russia."

"There are parts as wild as your early frontier. Misfits are the rule."

"Which country's passport do you travel on now?"

"Bregnovian," he asserted, as if that should be obvious.

"But it's not recognized? That still keeps you from entering America?"

"I wouldn't be allowed into Venezuela."

"But you're welcome here." She pointed at the floor of the club.

He nodded once, still seeming bristly.

She considered how that might feel, always being separated and left out. Being who she was had always ensured her entrée into virtually any situation. For all her father's faults and detractors, he was still welcome everywhere. Even with her scars, she wasn't locked out. It was her choice to stay home.

She looked up at Ryzard, wanting to ask how he'd come to finally go home and fund a war, but they had arrived on the beach. Bending, she removed her shoes and allowed him to take them so she could walk barefoot in the cool, powdery sand.

"That's an excellent cover band," she said as they moved toward the music.

"It's the real band," he told her, making her chuckle.

He looked at her and the corners of his mouth curled again, but his mask and the strobing lights made it hard to tell if he was smiling because he was in a good mood, or if he was laughing at her.

"I can't get used to this," she excused. "It's a lot to pay just for an exclusive concert, isn't it? The membership fee, I mean."

"If you hadn't been sulking in your room, you could have attended some of the lectures. There was an excellent one on the situation in Africa. Last quarter, I brokered a free trade agreement that will ease a lot of strain on our wheat and dairy production."

She weighed that, seeing new value in these meetings and wondering if she would come to another. Maybe see him again.

Or see him with someone else.

The chasm that thought opened in her chest was so great,

she quickly distracted herself by declaring with false cross-ness, "I wasn't sulking."

"You're still pouting," he claimed and took her jaw in a firm hand, nipping her bottom lip with the firm but tender bite of his.

A zing of excitement shot straight down her breastbone into her abdomen, then washed tingles into her limbs. Her hands instinctively lifted to his waist, but she held him off by proclaiming, "I've heard that all my life. I can't help it if my bottom lip is fat."

He drew back enough to sweep a gaze of masculine appraisal across her masked features, then bent to take a slower, more detailed tour of her mouth, allowing them both the luxury of a small feast. Absently she shuffled toward him, knees and thighs shifting so he could fit their frames together. His erection pressed into her stomach and her breasts ached as she flattened them to his chest. The music seeped through her and he began to rock them in a slow dance.

More like making love to her in public again, but who cared? No one even knew who they were. God, he felt good under her roaming hands.

"Come to my room," he intoned against her good ear.

She had her hands fisted in his shirt beneath the jacket of his tuxedo. Everything in her wanted to hang on to him forever. It was such a dangerous precipice to stand on, so threatening of a bad fall. But she couldn't escape how good it felt to feel wanted and beautiful and capable of giving him pleasure.

Without even doing much soul-searching—just like last night—she offered a shaky nod and let him guide her back into the club then into an elevator where they kissed with barely schooled passion. A minute later, he thumbed the sensor that opened his door and pivoted her into the foyer of his suite. It was grander than her own, but he *was* a twenty-five-visit member. Still, she barely saw it. One second later, she was in his arms.

Knocking off his mask, he dipped his head and kissed her again, discipline abandoned as he let her know with the thrust of his tongue exactly what he wanted to do to her. His hands roamed over her restlessly and he finally jerked back to say, "What the hell is this thing? I can't find a zipper."

Which was why she'd chosen it, she recalled dimly. Even the neckline was a difficult entry point. She didn't have the courage to be naked with him, but she wanted to make love to him.

Smiling secretively, she fingered open the buttons of his shirt and gazed appreciatively at the sleek bronze chest plate she revealed. A narrow line of hair delineated the center of his chest and outlined his squared pecs, which were flat, firm statements of strength.

Above his left nipple, a scrolled phrase in blue ink gave her pause. Some of the letters were oddly accented, but she thought she read the word *Bregnovia*. Framing it with the finger and thumb of her splayed hand, she asked, "What does it say?"

Tension stole through him. He seemed to expend a lot of effort drawing in a pained breath. "Luiza, Martyr of Bregnovia."

"Like our Lady Liberty?"

She drew a circle around his nipple and he jerked, making her smile.

"Yes," he rasped. "She's revered—damn. By all."

Other questions crowded into her mind, but she was too distracted by his gorgeous physique. Her hands couldn't resist smoothing over the hot satin of his skin. "You're so perfect, Ryzard. It's intimidating."

"Take off your clothes," he urged, plumping her breasts through her spandex suit.

Cruising her hand from his waist to his belt and lower,

she explored the shape of him. He grunted with pleasure and was so hard against her palm, her internal muscles clenched in anticipation. She swallowed and used her other hand to fumble his pants open.

He tried to remove her mask, but she pulled away and shook her head. "Not yet." She was too intent on being the anonymous Tiffany, the one who followed impulse and seduced a man if she wanted to. Lowering his fly, she managed to expose him, and *oh*. She went to her knees because he made her so deliciously weak.

"Tiffany," he groaned raggedly.

She was barely touching him, too new at this to do more than brush light fingertips over him. His breaths were audible hisses of anticipation, his erection jumping in reaction to her caresses. When she smoothed her lips against silky skin over steel, the weight of his hand came to rest on her head. The other stroked her exposed cheek, fingers trembling.

An experimental lick imprinted her with the taste of him. This was new territory for her, something she'd always been curious about, but it was so much more enthralling than she'd expected. She could sense how much power she had as she learned his shape with her tongue and open-mouthed kisses

When she took the tip into her wet mouth, he growled a string of foreign words, guttural and tortured, but sexy and thick with pleasure. If she could have smiled, she would have. Instead, she focused on finding his sensitive points, wanting this to be something he would never forget.

She never would.

Ryzard managed to hitch his pants back into place, but wasn't capable of much else. His head was swimming, his muscles trembling, and he was too wrung out to properly close his fly. He needed the wall to keep himself upright.

Water ran in the powder room, but he was barely aware of anything else. What Tiffany had just done to him had blown his mind. Her inexperience had been obvious in her tentative touch and first nervous licks, but after that she'd been so generous and given over to what she was doing, he'd lost it completely.

The door latch clicked and he turned his head. She walked out of the powder room with her clothes and mask in place, but there was an adorable self-conscious flush on her exposed cheek and an even more exquisite glow of arousal coming off her like an aura. Her nipples were pencil tips beneath her second-skin jumpsuit, and the way she walked held the hip sway of the sexually aroused.

Unbelievably, he twitched back to life below his unbuckled belt. He instantly wanted to strip her and have her under him.

"I'm going to eat you alive," he warned her.

She shook her head. "I have to go."

"The hell you do." He'd tie her up if he had to.

"No, I do," she insisted.

"What happened?" He looked to the powder room, wondering what had changed between seconds ago and now.

"Nothing. I just… This was really nice, but I want to leave it like this. As a nice memory for both of us."

"We can keep the lights off," he blurted in a burst of panic.

"Ryzard, please." There were tears in her eyes. "Just this, okay?"

He swiped his hand down his face, unable to think where he'd gone wrong. *Why the hell was she shutting him out?*

"I won't force you to make love with me. You don't have to go." Hell, the last thing he was capable of right now was *talk,* but it would be better than her leaving.

"I know you wouldn't, but I want to. Thank you again."

She skittered a wide circle around him and slid through the cracked door.

She'd got him off and thanked him twice. *What the hell?*

Tiffany was still trembling when she slid between her sheets, both angry with herself and relieved. Maybe she should have stayed with him. Maybe this was her chance to get over her scars so she could pursue a relationship with another man in the future.

But she didn't want anyone else, and she didn't have the courage to expose herself to Ryzard.

With a moan of despair, she rolled onto her stomach and groaned into a pillow.

A muted bell sounded. She lifted her head and noticed a light flashing on the bedside phone. Picking it up, she said a wary, "Yes?"

"It's me. Where are you?"

His voice sent a race of erotic excitement through her veins and into her loins. "In my room, obviously," she said, unable to control the husky edge on her voice.

"In bed?"

"Sleeping, yes," she lied.

"Liar."

She rolled her eyes. *So* arrogant.

"What are you wearing?" he asked.

"Flannel jammies and a nightcap."

"Well, take them off, *draga*. I'm about to tell you what you missed by running out of here."

"You're going to force me to have phone sex?"

"Hang up any time."

"I might have enough without adding more," she murmured in a considering tone.

"Hmm? Oh. Clever," he said with dry amusement. "I never know what to expect from you, Tiffany. Although

I'm quite sure you're still aroused. Have you been thinking of how you nearly killed me tonight?"

"Did I?" She couldn't help smiling.

"So smug. Yes, you did. I didn't thank you, and I should
have. You're a delightful lover."

She curled on her side so the phone was tucked under
her ear. "Thank you for saying that."

"Are you naked yet? Because if my hands will not be
stroking your gorgeous body, then I will listen as you do
it."

"You wish." But she tingled at the thought. He was right
about sexual excitement hovering under the surface. Her
skin prickled to sharp life, making her feel sensual and
deeply aware of all her erogenous zones.

"Satisfy my curiosity," he said in a low voice. "Are your
nipples still hard?"

"It's dark, I can't see."

"Feel them."

She closed her eyes, tempted, but, "Ryzard, I meant it
when I said we should leave it at tonight."

Silence.

Had he hung up on her?

"Are you still there?" she asked, hearing a forlorn note
in her voice.

"At least tell me why you're cutting me off." Underlying the brisk frustration in his tone was an edge of something she'd heard this evening when he'd said, *It shows I
belong.* She'd hurt him.

Through an aching throat, she managed to blurt out the
worst cliché around. "It's not you, it's me. I'm the biggest
head case going."

"You're concerned that I will be repulsed by these scars
of yours."

"Yes," she admitted, breathing a little easier at his understanding.

"Why would that bother you if I was?"

"I— What?" Her whole body tensed. *Did* she disgust him?

"Why would you care about my opinion? Who am I to you? Just some stranger you slept with on a wild night, right?"

So many protests choked her, she couldn't speak. He wasn't just anyone, not after some of the conversations they'd had and the physical intimacies they'd shared, but she couldn't admit that to him. He was already way too close to sensing he meant more to her than their brief association should warrant. His opinion mattered a lot.

"You're expecting me to get naked, be as exposed as I possibly could be, and risk being rejected," she said in a strained voice. "Wouldn't that bother you?"

"It bothered the hell out of me when you walked out tonight. I was as naked as a man needs to be the first night." His anger blistered off the receiver, making her squinch her face in a cringe. "You've done it to me twice."

"I'm sorry." The words burned from all the way in the pit of her sick stomach. "I didn't look at it from your perspective. I wasn't rejecting you."

"You need to start looking beyond yourself, Tiffany."

"I just apologized. That doesn't happen often. I suggest you accept it."

He sighed with frustration, then said with austerity, "You have been dealt a cruel blow from life. I won't dismiss that. But it didn't kill you, so start learning to live with it."

Wow. He didn't pull any punches, did he?

"How?" she demanded in a burst of angry despair. "You're not telling me anything I don't know, but how do I just get over it?"

"You want to be with a man, Tiffany. You like it when I touch you. Be with me."

He did make her feel more confident, but it would take

about a hundred of these heart-to-hearts before she'd be able to face being naked in front of him.

"We could meet for breakfast," she offered. The inside of her cheek stung and she realized she was biting it, feeling very insecure at putting herself out even this much.

"Where?" he asked.

"I assume they have a buffet or a restaurant downstairs."

"I meant your place or mine, but I see. Yes, they have a breakfast room. Nine?"

He wasn't making any effort to hide his disappointment, but she only confirmed, "Downstairs at nine. It's a date."

Ending the call, she rolled onto her back and stared at the dark ceiling. What was she doing? There was even less point in seeing him at breakfast on their last morning. They'd never see each other again after that.

Still, just thinking about seeing him made her body feel ripe and wanton. Running her hands over the hard swells of her breasts with their taut tips poking sharply against her rippling fingertips, she tried to erase the sensations nagging at her. The hunger deepened, provoking memories of Ryzard leaning on the wall, disheveled pants barely containing flesh she had memorized with her mouth, his eyes heavy lidded and voracious.

Rolling a frustrated moan into her pillow, she wished she'd said yes to the phone sex.

When she arrived in the dining room, Ryzard was standing in the entrance talking to another woman.

It was a low blow and nearly made her turn in retreat, but he lifted his hawkish mask and held out a hand to her even before he locked his gaze on her.

Stupid watches. Hers was shivering at its nearness to his, just like her to him. As she walked across, she experienced a little thrill at how good he looked in simple black pants and a white shirt open at the throat. His hair, clipped so short you could barely tell it curled, was still damp.

A dip of insecurity accosted her at the same time. The woman gesturing so passionately in front of him wore a light cover-up over a bikini that barely contained her flawless figure. Her mask was equally spare, just a sleek line from temple to temple.

Tiffany felt overdressed in her pants suit and elaborate mask as well as intrusive as she arrived, causing the woman to break midsentence.

Ryzard grasped her hand in a firm, warm grip, drawing her a step closer while continuing to give his attention to the other woman. "Please continue."

"I—" She was obviously disconcerted by Tiffany's arrival. Her body language changed from enticing to standoffish. "I just wonder if the sudden rumors being spread about this weekend, talk of dirty deals and Greek Mafia connections, could be true. Zeus's reputation is important for all of us, and if he's no better than a crook we should talk about it. Figure out what to do."

Tiffany was a little lost, coming in late and distracted by the strength and heat of her *lover*. He smelled freshly showered, and his flimsy white shirt was hardly any barrier, allowing her to nearly taste the texture of his skin.

Still, being excluded niggled at her. She'd been The Family Behind Him too many times for her father, a required face in a photo, but heaven forbid she open her mouth. Being relegated to arm candy here, where she was supposed to be an equal, was the final straw.

"Who *is* Zeus?" Tiffany asked.

"No one knows," the woman said, dismissing her with a patronizing jerk of her shoulder, adding, "Which is part of the problem. He should identify himself so we can decide if we want to continue associating with him."

Tiffany followed the entreating glance the woman sent

to Ryzard. She was obviously trying to pull him over to her side for reasons other than any real concern about the club.

"That seems hypocritical, doesn't it?" Ryzard said calmly. "When we keep our own identities secret?"

"I have to agree. It's quite possible to have a wrong impression about someone until you know them better," Tiffany said with a significant look upward to Ryzard.

"Well, we don't keep any secrets from Zeus, do we?" the woman insisted. She wavered with indecision a moment as her gaze touched on his hand holding Tiffany's so possessively. Then she made a noise of impatience and muttered, "I'm just saying," before she walked away.

Tiffany raised her brows, not that Ryzard could see them and appreciate her pique at coming upon a woman hitting on him so blatantly.

"Good morning," he said before swooping to kiss her.

She stiffened, but he took his time, working swirls of reawakened passion down through her torso and into her belly until she softened into his loose embrace. When he lifted his head, he said, "I'm starving. You?"

Food was the last thing on her mind, but she followed him through the indoor/outdoor dining room to a table near the lagoon-shaped pool. They accepted coffee and placed their orders before she lost her ability to stay silent and asked, "Do you pick up women at all these things?"

Setting down his coffee, he regarded her with a hard look. "Your pretty blue eyes have gone quite emerald, *draga.*"

"Who is she?"

"That's a question I can't answer. Members do not out other members. That's why I didn't introduce you."

She narrowed her eyes. "If I had looked at my watch, would I have seen her nickname?"

He shrugged. "Possibly. Mine is turned off except for

you. She only spoke to me because we happened to meet at the door and have spoken before."

"About?" she prompted.

"It's confidential."

"Have you seen her away from these things?"

"Also confidential."

"So you won't tell me anything."

"This is how the club works. That's why it works. But I will tell you that I have never had a sexual relationship with her."

"And she would never admit to one if you had because members don't out other members. I'm just supposed to trust that you're telling me the truth."

"Yes," he said firmly. "I do expect you to trust me."

Her gaze dropped to the button he'd only half pushed through its hole in the middle of his chest.

"If you had let me make love to you last night, you would not be feeling so insecure this morning," he added.

Her heart skipped at that, but she only said, "I'm not insecure. I don't *know* you."

"Exactly."

Oh, he was infuriating. And sexy. Her eyes were eating up the way his shirt was perfectly tailored across the line of his shoulders and hugged the strength in his arms. Her fingers itched to unbutton the whole shirt and expose his very promising chest again.

It's just hormones, she tried to insist to herself, not wanting to succumb to feelings that were a lot more complex than mere lust.

"I'm jealous of her for being pretty," she admitted in an undertone, ashamed that she was this shallow, but, "I used to be and it gave me confidence. Don't deny that being physically attractive is powerful," she warned with a point of her finger. "My mother still turns heads and uses it every day. And she places so much importance on looks."

The weight of that knowledge slumped her into her chair.

"Sometimes I wonder if that's why she chose Dad and not Paul Sr. He wasn't ugly by any stretch, but Dad's got that Mr. President, all-American look. Mom wanted the best-looking kids in the state and she got them. Now, when she looks at me…"

Time to shut up. Her throat was closing and it was impossible to fix.

"Your mother sounds very superficial." His tone of quiet observation told her he'd heard and weighed every word she'd said. Being such a tight focus of his concentration made her feel oddly vulnerable and safe at the same time. It made her think he genuinely cared about what she was revealing.

"She's the wife of a politician. Her world revolves around how things look. You're judged on everything in that position. Looks matter."

"I suppose," he allowed with a negligent tilt of his head. "Did she push your father into politics?"

"No, it was something he wanted, but maybe that's the real reason she married him." Tiffany considered her parents' marriage a moment. "Dad is a good father, a super husband, a really good man, but he aspires to be a Great Man and Mom aspires to be the wife of one. She set me up to…" want? demand? "expect the same thing."

"Was your husband planning to go into politics?"

"If our parents had anything to do with it, yes." She curled her mouth in mild distaste.

"You didn't want him to."

Once again she was able to speak a truth to him that she couldn't say aloud to anyone else.

"I honestly didn't think I had a choice. But I've seen how that life has affected my mother over the years. Every word she says is guarded. Half the time she's Dad's mistress. His work is his wife. Our family day at the fair was always a photo op with Dad glad-handing everyone except us. He couldn't buy me the candy floss I wanted. A taffy apple was a better message." She sighed, still more bewildered than bitter. "My life was staged to look like the life I wanted, but we weren't allowed to actually live it that way."

"Another reason why I will never marry. Too much sacrifice on a family's part."

"Another' reason? You don't intend to marry? Don't you want children? That's the one thing I looked forward to when I agreed to marry. I wanted to give my kids the childhood I hadn't had."

As the words left her mouth, she realized how leading they sounded. As if this was a conflict they'd have to resolve before proceeding with their relationship. She never talked this openly, except maybe to her therapist, but who else did she talk to these days? She was out of practice with hiding her real thoughts and feelings.

"You can still have a family," he said with a calm blink of his eyes within the holes of his mask. "Why couldn't you?"

Behind her own mask, she burned with self-consciousness, her gaze fixed to his. Her finding that kind of happiness wasn't as easy as he made it sound, and he knew it. With her teeth bared in a nonsmile, she said, "Why don't you want to marry?"

"I'm married to my country," he stated. "As you said, my work is my wife. Everything I do, I do for my people."

She tried to ignore the dull pain that lodged in her chest. That was good, wasn't it? She admired patriotism, and that certainly kept things simple between them. No false expectations.

"How did you become, um, president?" she asked, faltering because it was an impulsive question that sounded a lot more loaded than she'd meant it to.

"I was elected," he said coolly.

She waited while their meals were delivered, then said, "I meant, how did people come to know who you are and want to vote for you? I'm sure it was covered in the news, but as you've said, that's usually slanted, and quite frankly I've had other things on my mind for the last few years. I missed how it all happened. I'm really asking what drew you back to your country and into representing it."

"My mother was killed in a random attack. I went back for the funeral and my father was determined to fight. I couldn't leave him to it. I was angry with myself for not returning sooner, for thinking someone else would sort out the trouble and I could return when there was peace."

"You're either part of the solution, or part of the problem," Tiffany murmured. "I'm sorry about your mom." Was that whom he'd been talking about yesterday, she wondered, when he'd held her in shared grief? "At least your father is safe."

"He died, as well. Fighting."

"Oh. I'm so sorry."

He waved that away with a lift of two fingers. "I believe he wanted it that way. To be with my mother."

"Still…" She swallowed, ready to cry for him because he seemed so withdrawn and contained. Tears would never dare to seep from his bleak eyes. "I'm sure he would be very proud of you for what you've achieved."

"Once you've paid the price of a loved one, you don't stop until the job is done. I managed to bring enough of our various factions together to throw over our corrupt government and campaigned on a promise of peace. There is still a very long road. The biggest challenge is keeping the country from falling back into fighting, but we had some corruption charges work through the courts recently that gave people confidence. Small things like that matter."

She nodded, tipping a little further into the primordial

world of deeper feelings for him. Genuine admiration. Awe. Empathy.

Careful, Tiffany.

"Shall we take the art walk?" he asked when they finished eating.

"I didn't know they had one." She looked around, expecting artists with pads and a jumble of still lifes and caricatures had arrived to line the stones near the pool.

"They set it up inside to avoid sun and humidity damage."

"Really? What are we talking about? Priceless artifacts? Da Vinci?"

"If something like that is on the market, absolutely. Most of it is contemporary, but they're all good investments."

Moments later, they entered a gallery of comic book art competing with old-world landscapes and elegantly carved wooden giraffes. She fell in love with a stained glass umbrella, mostly because it was so ridiculously useless.

"How much is it?" she demanded, searching for a tag.

"The auction is in a few hours."

"We'll come back?"

"If you like."

"I want to use it as a parasol against the sun." It had to weigh fifty pounds. It was the most impractical object ever created and she *had* to own it.

"You have a beautiful laugh," he remarked, tugging her into a space behind a giant sculpture of ladies' shoes. "I'd like to see you smiling under this umbrella of yours, your face painted by the colored glass. I'd like to see you sunbathe naked under it," he added in a deeper tone that seemed to stroke beneath her skin and leave a tingle.

At the same time his words put a pang in her heart. She wished...

He bent to kiss her, pulling her into his aroused body as if they were the only two people in the room. A second later, as his tongue invaded her mouth, she forgot everything except the feel of him, shoulders to thighs, branding her.

"I want you in my bed," he told her huskily, as he found her bare earlobe and drew it between his lips.

Her body felt as if it swelled to fill his arms, breasts aching, all her skin thin and sensitized. Willpower and self-protection fell away as she confided in a whisper, "I want that, too."

He lifted his head. His possessive hands stilled and firmed on her. "Yes?"

Her heart stalled. He wouldn't accept any more waffling. She swallowed, still terrified by the idea of being naked in front of him, but she would hate herself forever if she refused him out of sheer cowardice. With breath held, she gave an abbreviated nod.

His smile should have alarmed her. It bordered on grim, but a light of excitement behind his eyes made her tremble with anticipation. He really did want her.

Blood rushed in her ears so she barely heard him speak to a *petite q* as they made their way back to the main floor.

"Early checkout?" she repeated as he led her through the door the *petite q* released with a thumbprint and security override card.

"Gold membership has its privileges," he said drily. "But they'll only let me leave early. They won't allow us back in."

"Oh, but what about my things—?" She paused on the ramp down to the marina, where several eye-popping luxury yachts bobbed like toys in a bathtub.

"Our luggage would be packed for us regardless. That's the level of service we pay for, Tiffany." He waved and called something in Bregnovian to a young man as they approached a catamaran. It was called the *Luiza* and had an orange sail wrapped around its single mast. The body was such a brilliant white she had to squint.

"We'll remain docked a few hours yet," Ryzard said in

answer to a question from his crewman. "Unless we have to move to let someone out." He nodded at the boat they'd traversed to reach this one. "Tell the captain we're aboard and will order lunch when we're ready, but we don't wish to be disturbed."

Tiffany blushed behind her mask, thinking Ryzard was making it incredibly obvious what they were about to do. He didn't seem concerned, however, as he led her through the interior salon of sleek curved lines, the colors a soothing mix of bone and earth tones. Panoramic windows slanted over the lounge and bar, bringing splashes of turquoise water and cerulean sky into the room. Bypassing a short staircase that led to an elevated pilothouse of some kind, he brought her down a half flight of steps into the master stateroom.

"This is amazing," she couldn't help blurt. No stranger to the finer things in life, she was awestruck by the simple elegance and understated masculinity in the surprisingly spacious room. Drawers and cupboards in blond teak lined the space below the windows that provided a one-eighty view. A door led to an exterior deck on this side and into a well-organized head on the other. One curved radius corner of the room was a scrupulously efficient work space, the other a rounded sofa that looked to a flat-screen television set into the wall offset from the bed.

The bed itself was a king-size statement of power, tall and stalwart, its linens almond colored with a bold chocolate stripe across the foot. She dragged her eyes away from it as she heard a whispery sound and the light changed.

Ryzard moved with deliberation to draw woven shades down into a clip, allowing filtered sunlight to penetrate, but giving them privacy.

Her stomach swooped and she put out her hand, not sure where to find purchase when the floor was dipping at the same time.

"I thought we'd go to a room in the club," she said, linking her hands before her to hide that she was trembling with nerves. And excitement.

He turned from the last window and brushed away his mask, tossing it aside. "As I said, I don't want to be interrupted."

By staff wanting to pack their belongings, she imagined he meant, but couldn't speak because he came close enough to remove her mask.

She stopped him.

"I've seen your face, Tiffany."

"I don't want you to see how scared I am."

He frowned. "Of me?"

"Your reaction."

He shook his head, dismissing her fear as he trailed light fingertips over her clothing, grazing the sides of her breasts and settling warm hands on her waist. "I'm afraid I'll hurt you again. I wish you'd warned me the other night. I wasn't nearly as gentle as I could have been."

"I know pain, Ryzard. That was nothing."

"It was something," he told her, pulling her close enough to brush his mouth against hers, not properly kissing her. Teasing. "I'll never forget it."

An odd expression spasmed across his face before he controlled it, as if he hadn't meant to admit that to her, but she drew in his confession like air, deeply affected, wanting to hold on to this special feeling he provoked in her. Everything in her yearned so badly to please him, and she was so sure she wouldn't.

Get it over with, she told herself. She had to let him see and judge and reject before she climbed too high in optimism and desire. A long fall from excitement to disgust would be more than she could bear. If she did it now, before they'd gone too far, she'd still be able to dress and trudge into the nearest town to phone her brother—the one she kept forgetting about.

For now, she had to gather her courage.

Gently removing Ryzard's hands from her waist, she took a step back. The mask seemed like a tiny bit of necessary protection so she kept it, reaching first for the single button that held her linen jacket closed.

Removing it exposed her arm, marbled in streaks of red and pink, some parts geometric patterns from the grafts, other edges random and white. Not looking at him, she opened her pants and stepped out of them. Her left leg was as bad as her arm, and the top of her good right thigh was peppered with rectangles where they'd taken skin to patch the bad. Her stomach had the same types of scars. She threw off her sleeveless silk top and stood there in her cherry red bra and underpants and gold gladiator sandals.

For the life of her, she couldn't lift her chin. Her eyes were glued to the floor, her mind full of the rugged road map her body had become. No ivory virgin here.

"You do know pain, Tiffany," he said quietly.

That brought her eyes up. He studied her gravely, all the way to her toes, and gradually climbed his gaze back to her face. Stepping closer, he touched her chin to bring her face up and looked into her eyes. His were somber, but glowing with something fierce.

"You humble me. I don't know if I could have fought through such a thing."

She had to bite her lips to keep them from trembling.

Gently he removed her mask and let it fall. She felt incredibly vulnerable, standing before him nearly naked when he was clothed.

"Do not be ashamed of your courage to survive."

She had wanted to be told she was pretty despite her scars, but what he said was better, filling her with an emotion she couldn't describe. Tipping into him, she hugged him tight.

And realized he was aroused. His hand swept her bare back down to where her thong exposed her naked cheek. With a purposeful clench of his fingers into the firm flesh, he tilted her hips into pressing where he grew harder by the second.

"You're turned on," she breathed in wonder.

"I've got you naked next to a bed. How the hell else would I react?"

That made her laugh, then she squealed as he picked her up and lightly tossed her onto the mattress. Coming up on her elbows, she accused, "Caveman."

"Believe it," he confirmed, yanking off his shirt and dropping it away. His pants came off with similar haste. "Off with the rest," he ordered, jerking his chin at her lingerie. "This time we're both naked."

He was, in record time, and pulled off her shoes without ceremony.

"Don't wreck them. I like those," she protested, pausing in finding the clip between her breasts to reach for the strap of her shoe.

"What about these?" he asked, hooking two fingers in her panties at her hip. "Special favorite? Because I'm out of patience." He snapped them.

"Oh!" Why his primitive act turned her on, she couldn't imagine, but the way he loomed over her, practically overwhelming her with his strength, gave her a thrill. Probably because she felt totally safe despite his resolute expression and proprietary touch. He was impatient, but not without discipline. He threw away her bra, but then he simply held her, his weight on one elbow as he studied her breasts.

"Does this hurt?" he asked, tracing where her scar licked like a flame up the side of her breast.

"I can barely feel anything. Just a bit of pressure. Nerve

damage. You know how your face feels after the dentist and the freezing is just starting to come out?"

"Good to know. I'll focus where you can feel it." He cupped her breast and flicked her nipple with his thumb.

The sensation was sharper than she anticipated, and she flinched.

"No?" he prompted.

"I— No, it's good, just really..." She blushed. This was surreal, lying in full light with a gorgeous man naked against her. Twin desires to curl into him and to stop and give herself time to take it in accosted her.

He lowered his head to lick, and her inner muscles clenched like a fist, tearing a sound of reaction out of her.

Almost experimentally, he switched to her other breast, teasing and making her shift restlessly. It felt incredible, but wasn't quite as intense as the other.

He moved to her left one again and another shot of extreme sensation went through her, flooding her loins with a heated rush of pleasure. She didn't know if her nerve endings were compensating for others nearby that had ceased to work, but the way his tongue toyed so delicately made her pinch her thighs together.

"That one is really sensitive," she panted, smoothing her hand over his short, thick hair and clutching at his shoulders, not sure if she wanted him to stop or take her over the edge.

"I can tell," he said with smoldering approval. Opening his mouth on her, he sucked delicately, nearly levitating her off the bed.

"Ryzard," she cried, knee bending and thighs opening as she tried to grasp more of him. With a growl, he slid down and bit softly at her inner thigh. "Do you know how many things I want to do to you?"

Moaning, she threw her arm over her eyes and surrendered. "Do anything. I love everything you do to me."

For a second he did nothing. She wondered if she'd done something wrong and started to drop her arm away. Then she felt his touch delicately parting her. His mouth. Pressing the back of her wrist against her open mouth, she muffled her throaty groan of abject joy. To be wanted like this, so deliciously ravished, brought tears of happiness to the seams of her closed eyes.

And *oh* that was nice. Pleasure coiled and built on itself through her middle, winding her into the sweetest tension. She wanted release and she wanted this to go on and on. Then he slid a testing finger in her, and she knew exactly what she wanted.

And told him.

"I can't wait, either," he said in a raw voice, as if the truth stunned him. In a sliding lunge across her, he nearly yanked the bedside drawer from its table and seconds later smoothed latex down his length.

When he pressed into her, she welcomed him with a gasp, nails tightening into his skin as he possessed her with ruthless care, slow and inexorable. Through her lashes, she watched him watching her and bit her lip, feeling deeply exposed, but moved by the intimacy at the same time.

"I can't believe I'm the only man who knows how amazing you are," he said gutturally, hands holding her head as he rocked side to side, settling deep inside her, sealing their connection.

Her body didn't feel like her own. She trembled in arousal, limbs both weak and strong, clinging to him. Her mouth offered itself, parting and begging for his.

With a tortured growl, Ryzard kissed her, thrusting his tongue into her, wanting more and more of her. All of her. Indelibly.

But that intense, deep possession couldn't be sustained forever. Eventually, he drew back enough for ecstasy to strum through him as her sheath stroked and clenched around him. She smelled incredible, felt even better, tasted like forbidden substances. He became animalistic, purely in his physical state, senses captured and held by this creature who entranced him. Nothing entered his vision except the expression of exquisite torture against the unique pattern on her face.

In a rare moment of unguarded openness, he removed his internal shields so he could fully absorb the pure, sweet light of her. His only thought was to fill her with the same all-encompassing rapture that held him in its grip.

She sobbed his name and he increased his tempo, reacting to her need and compelled to fulfill it. She met him thrust for thrust, their bodies so attuned they scaled the cliff together and soared into the abyss with perfect affinity. Clutching her tight under him, buried deep in her shivering depths, he let out a ragged cry of triumph as he gave in to pulse-pounding release.

CHAPTER SIX

RYZARD ROLLED AWAY, then settled on his back, his body brushing hers, but only incidentally. He wasn't embracing or meaning to touch her that Tiffany could tell.

She turned her head to see his profile was unreadable. Not displeased, but not…

Oh, she didn't know what she was looking for. A spear of inadequacy impaled her. While she had been caught up in their lovemaking, she'd been fine, but now she was back to being scared and self-conscious of her scars. She sat up.

"Don't go anywhere," he said, hand loosely cuffing her wrist.

Ha. Where could she go? They weren't allowed back into the club. *Hello, big brother, can you pick me up at the docks?*

Glancing over her shoulder, she tried to read his mood behind his heavy eyelids, but his spiky lashes made it impossible.

"You seem…" She didn't want to reveal how sensitive she was to disapproval right now. They might have been intimate in other ways before, but this was different. It wasn't just the physicality or revealing of her scars. She'd been incredibly uninhibited, exposing the very heart of herself.

"It's probably best if I go," she managed in a husky voice.

"I don't know what I seem, but I'm only trying to assimilate something that—" He breathed a word in his own language. She suspected it was a curse, but his tone was kind of awed and self-deprecating at the same time.

Facing forward, she closed her lids against a sudden sting, biting back an urge to beg him to continue what he'd almost said. It sounded as if he was as moved by their love-making as she was, which was balm to her tattered soul.

He released her wrist to stroke her lower back, making her lift her head from where she'd let it droop to rest on her knees.

"Are you okay?" he asked.

"Just trying not to act like a first-timer."

"This is unique for both of us."

She tried not to drink too deeply of that heady assessment. She was already falling for him in little ways and couldn't afford to become too enamored. This was merely an extension of their one-night stand.

"You keep condoms in the drawer by the bed," she pointed out. "I'm not that unique."

A beat of dark silence, then, "*I* never claimed to be a virgin."

She wanted to glare at him, but couldn't risk him seeing how hard it was for her to acknowledge his experience. Why? What right did she have to possessive feelings? She was lucky to be included in his special club at all.

"And this won't be the only bed I'll ever be in, so—hey!"

He had her on her back and under him before she realized he could move that fast.

"Here's a tip for someone new to this," he growled. "We don't discuss past and future lovers, particularly when we're still making love to each other."

She blinked in shock, heart hammering.

His aggression fell away to a baffled, tender caress that he smoothed along her good cheek. "Don't make me feel guilty for my life before I met you. How could I have known that what I thought was pleasure…" His expression clouded with a look of such angst, it made her heart hurt.

"It's just chemistry," she assured him, teetering inwardly against her own words even as she attempted to comfort him with them. The remark went directly against her girlish desire to hear that she was actually very special to him.

She held her breath, hoping against logic that he'd offer such a pledge.

"Exceptional chemistry," he agreed. His hungry gaze followed his hand as he caressed from her lips to her collarbone, across the damp underside of her breast and down to her hip where his thumb aligned to the crease at the top of her leg. "But you do understand this is simply an affair? It can't lead to anything permanent. I'm not the sort of life partner you're looking for."

His blunt statement fell between them like a metal wall, softened only by the expression of regret on his face.

"Glad you said it first," she said with a poignant smile, hoping it hid the way she tensed internally. She was as wary of certain fantasies as he was, but not nearly as adept at cutting her emotions out of her heart. "I told you what I think of being the woman behind the man. You're merely a guilty indulgence, like cheating on a diet."

His brow winged, indignant but amused. "Let's fatten you up then."

Ryzard gave up trying to work. They'd been sailing three hours already, so he had another word with his captain, then remained at the helm while his instructions were carried out. As the wind whipped his shirt through the open windows of the pilothouse, he once again congratulated himself on having the wisdom to switch from a single-hulled sailboat to the double construction of a cat. The three-sixty views and flexibility with anchorage were worth the ribbing he received from traditionalists.

Hell, if he had allowed his concentration to wander like this on his old schooner, they'd all be dead, but here he could indulge himself with recollecting every delicious minute of his day. He'd devoted several hours to learning each and every one of Tiffany's pleasure triggers, stimulating both of them as he expanded both of their educations in physical delight. Sweetest of all had been her generous straddling of him, broken voice asking for direction as she tugged him along her path to bliss.

They'd been like drunkards at that point, sheened in perspiration. Her eyes had been glassy, her pouted lips reddened by a thousand kisses. Her breasts had swayed with their undulations, her hips an instrument of torture he wielded on himself as he guided her with hands clamped tight in ownership.

He'd been sure he would die, it had been that good.

Rubbing his face, he dragged himself back to reality, yanking open his collar in search of a cool breeze to take his libido down a notch. They were flying over the waves, skipping at a light angle, demanding he pay attention, but all he could think was, how could he be this aroused again? She'd drained him dry. They'd collapsed into unconsciousness, utterly exhausted from making love.

He'd woken soon after, sweaty and thick with recovery, wanting her again.

When he'd shifted, she'd grumbled without opening her eyes, "Don't move. My hip hurts. I need to keep my leg propped."

He didn't doubt it. His joints had protested his rising from the bed, and he'd never crashed and burned in a roadster. He'd substituted a pillow under her thigh and watched her settle back into sleep before taking his insatiable libido for a cold shower in a spare cabin.

Then he'd made a decision he was still second-guessing, but it was done. She was his.

I love everything you do to me. The power of that statement unexpectedly exploded in his mind again, but that first bit, *I love...*

He scratched his chest where a sensation gathered like sweat trickling. The tickle was behind his breastbone, uncomfortable and impossible to erase. *It's just chemistry,* she'd said as he'd been reeling from a depth of pleasure he'd never experienced before.

He'd agreed with her, clinging to that simple explanation, but it was harder to blame chemistry when he'd found himself unable to wake her and send her on her way.

Why not? Why was his response to her, on every level, so much more intense than it had been with the woman he'd loved, the one he'd pledged to marry? He hated himself for it, but he couldn't deny it.

He and Luiza hadn't had the luxury of time and privacy to soak themselves in sexual intimacy, though. Their bond had been forged by shared secrets and ideals. She had loved him when he'd had no one else. Her vision had become his.

She'd died before her dream could become reality, but he was still striving to make it come true. There was no reason to suffer pangs of infidelity just because he wanted to play out an affair with a particular woman for a little longer than a weekend.

He clenched his hands on the wheel, telling himself that the fact Tiffany had been a virgin weighed into his decision to extend their association. No man wanted to be a woman's first and her worst. He owed her more time and consideration than the average jaded socialite.

And she happened to have a sexual appetite to match his own. He kept mistresses when it suited him for that very reason. This was still a temporary arrangement, and Tiffany understood that's all he ever intended to have with any woman. His heart belonged to Luiza. If he couldn't marry her, he wouldn't marry anyone.

Having relegated Tiffany to her rightful place in his mind, he was ready to see her again. He nodded at the first mate, and the young man swung the sail to catch more gust.

Tiffany was falling out of bed.

She woke with a cry and a start, arms splayed to orient herself on the mattress. The room glowed a brassy yellow, the bed was a wreck and her body felt as if she'd been thrown down a flight of stairs. She held very still, trying to come to grips with the odd feeling the boat was not just bobbing in its slip, but moving.

It was. They were at sail!

She'd been on sailboats, but unlike the sharp angle that resulted in stumbling around to grip her way across a deck, this catamaran was only a hair off level, allowing her to rush the window and snap up the blind. Yep. Not another boat in sight. Just a speck of land on the horizon and glittering waves in every other direction.

"What the hell, Ryzard?" she said aloud.

Glancing around for her clothes, she caught sight of herself and cringed. Her hair was naturally straight, and all that sweaty sex had weighed it down into a droopy haystack. The side of her breast felt raw where it had been abraded by stubble and when she turned her nose to her shoulder, she could swear she smelled Ryzard's unique scent on her skin.

An odd, sexy feeling overcame her, making her want to loll in bed and call him to her, but she gave herself a firm shake. Where the hell was he taking her?

A very quick shower later, she dressed in her pants and sleeveless top to go in search of him. She forced herself not to be so cowardly as to wear the mask, but she still peered around corners, avoiding his staff.

She found him lounging in the shade of the aft deck,

taking up all the cushions of the built-in sofa as he read his tablet and sipped a drink made with tomato juice. A stalk of celery rested against its salted rim. He set it down when she appeared.

"I thought a few sharp turns might shake you out of bed," he said.

"Are you familiar with the term *kidnapping?*"

"I have business in Cuba."

"You're taking me to Cuba?" She gave a wild look around. Nope, not one hint of assistance in sight.

"Much as I'd love to anchor somewhere private and shirk my responsibilities, I can't. My weekend was booked for *Q Virtus,* but now we'll have to carve out our time around other commitments."

"Commitments like the one I made to get on a plane with my brother two hours ago? He'll be frantic." Dumbfounded, she braced a hand on her forehead trying to gather her scattered wits enough to formulate a plan.

"My staff spoke to him when they collected your things."

"Your staff collected my things. And brought them here?" She pointed to the deck, so astounded she could barely form words. "After they informed my brother that I was carrying on with you?"

"They're discreet enough to simply say you're my guest. Naturally he needed to be told why you weren't meeting him as arranged. Why are you upset? Relax. I realize you avoid the sun, but you can enjoy the view from the shade. I have a masseuse aboard, if you need."

"Ryzard," she said with a ring of near hysteria in her tone. "You said we'd stay in dock."

"For a few hours. We did. You overslept."

"You should have woken me! Not said things to my brother. He doesn't need to know about this. No one does. It's nobody's business but mine!" She splayed a hand on the place in her chest where he was taking up way more room than he should. Where he was lodged very close to places no one was allowed to go.

"When you called me your dirty little secret, I didn't realize you meant it," he replied stiffly.

Oh, she would *not* feel guilty. Maybe she was overreacting, but he didn't realize what kind of firestorm he would have set off with her family. This was bad.

"You should have asked me," she insisted. "And let *me* talk to my brother. Is there some way I can contact him?" Panic gripped her.

"If your mobile doesn't work, ask the captain for the ship to shore." He still sounded stung, but dealing with Ryzard came second to smoothing things over with Christian. What would he think of her?

She'd left her mobile in her room at the club and found it in her purse in the cabin where her things had been unpacked. Not Ryzard's cabin, she noted, but a separate one—and why did that bother her? She was upset with him, not supposed to be mooning about what it meant if he set her up to sleep apart from him.

Keying her code into her phone, she saw that her brother had left her a dozen messages.

"What the *hell,* Tiff," were his first words when she reached him.

"I know." She closed her eyes. She really should have thought this through before dialing. She was just so frantic to undo what had been done. But how?

"How does something like this even happen?" he demanded.

His askance reaction crystallized the confused self-consciousness inside her, so she felt very fragile and very brittle all of a sudden. Ryzard, despite his assumptions and autocratic ways, was not the villain. The problem with her family knowing about their affair, she realized, was the impossible vision she was supposed to live up to.

"You're the expert on picking up women. You know how it works," she retorted. "He came on to me with a great line. I fell for it."

The door clicked and Ryzard entered in time to hear most of what she said.

She averted her gaze from his darkening expression, prickling as her brother said, "You're too smart for that."

"Am I? Maybe I'm weak and desperate. Maybe I'm grateful for attention from *any* man."

In her periphery, Ryzard's arms folded and he said in an ominous undertone, "Is that true?"

"I knew it. He's taking advantage of you."

She sucked in a jagged breath, more hurt than words could express, but it was the ugly truth they'd all been dancing around since her accident. She wasn't worth a man's attention.

She flashed a look of resentment at Ryzard, angry that he was witnessing her humiliation. At the same time, she wished he didn't look so thunderous. She was desperately in need of backup. Instead, he'd probably leave her on a sandbar somewhere, but that was almost better than sending her back to the bosom of her kin.

"Thanks, Chris," she choked. "Thanks for letting me know there's no way he could possibly be attracted to me. I'm some broken, awful thing that ceased to be valuable when I ceased to be perfect. Shame rains upon us and it's my fault. Has Mom taken to her room?"

A weighted pause. She didn't dare look at Ryzard.

"I didn't say that," Christian said quietly.

"But it's true! Tell me something. How many times have you stolen a weekend with someone? Hundreds," she quickly provided. "How many times have you had to answer for it? *None.* And I never worked up the nerve to even kiss another man because I had a reputation to uphold. Not just mine, but the entire family's. Paulie's even."

He swore. "Okay, I get it. You're entitled to a private life, but this isn't exactly the time, is it?" he seethed. "Or the man."

"You haven't told Mom and Dad, have you?"

"I didn't know what to think, Tiff! This isn't like you."

"When have I ever had a chance to be who I am?" she cried. "I've been Dad's daughter, Paulie's intended. The bride who wore bandages. For God's sake, I'm an adult. A married, *widowed* woman. I shouldn't have to defend myself like I've committed a federal crime."

"No, you're right, I'm sorry. Truly."

"How bad is it?" she asked, hanging her head, weighted by guilt despite all she'd just said. "Do I have to talk to them or better to wait?"

"They don't know what to think, either. But they don't want to see you get hurt in any way, ever again. Is this thing serious with Vrbancic?"

She glanced at Ryzard. He didn't look quite so much as if he wanted to wring her neck, but he had an air of imperative surrounding him. As if he didn't intend to wait much longer for her to give her attention back to him.

"Not, um, really," she murmured.

Christian's sharp sigh grated in her ear.

"Oh, I'm sorry, did I miss where you married everyone you ever slept with?" she railed.

"So it's gone that far."

He didn't have to take a tone like the septic was backed up!

"Goodbye, Chris. Tell Mom and Dad whatever you want." She stabbed the end button and threw her phone onto the bed. Then dropped a pillow on top of it for good measure. And added a punch that left a deep indent.

"I'd like to say I'm above caring what people think of me, but when my family judges me, it hurts." Her baleful gaze met one that didn't so much judge as measure.

"You knew they would disapprove. That's why you were upset."

"Not because it's you. They would have been scandalized no matter who I slept with. Although, I'm sure there's some shock value that they sent me to talk to you and here I am. As God is my witness, I'll never, ever tell my mother I didn't even see your face the first time, let alone know your name." She buried her hot face in her clammy hands, reacting to all that had happened since she'd woken so abruptly. "This isn't the way I usually behave, Ryzard. I can't blame them for being shocked."

"Be careful how much you hate your parents, *draga*. They're the only ones you have."

"You're going to judge me now?" She lifted her face in challenge.

"I'm only offering the benefit of my experience."

"You hated your parents?" She didn't believe it.

"I was angry with them for sending me away. Keeping me away from my home. It felt like a rejection."

He hadn't explained that part before. A pang struck at how lonely and discarded he must have felt.

Beneath the pillow, her phone burbled. Tiffany made a noise and started from the room, then said, "Actually, I want to change. It's too hot for long pants."

Ryzard closed the door, but remained in the room. Apparently he intended to watch. Hell. The man gave her goose bumps without making any effort at all.

Skimming past the one-shoulder and long-sleeved shirts and dresses, she pulled out a skimpy sundress she would have worn only in the privacy of her suite yesterday. It was patterned busily in neon pink and green and yellow, hopefully bright enough to draw attention from her equally busy skin patterns.

The scared mouse in her wanted to hide under layers, but a spunky, more daring part of her wanted to test whether she still held his interest.

Stripping unceremoniously, even dropping her bra, she shrugged her arms under the spaghetti straps and tugged it into place, then picked up the flared skirt in a little curtsy, spinning under the direction of his twirled finger.

"Adorable. Now come here."

"And risk making love on that telephone? Possibly landing on buttons that could have serious consequences? No. You promised me a meal and we skipped lunch."

"Yet I recall being very satisfied with everything I tasted," he mused, one hand on the door latch. The other caressed her bottom as she exited in front of him.

Her blood skipped in her arteries, and she was blushing hard as she led him outside to where a table was set and chilled wine was ready to be uncorked. The sun sat low on the horizon, ducking beneath the shade to strike off the silver and crystal.

Ryzard held a chair in a corner for her and asked for a filtered shade to be drawn.

"I'm sorry I was such a pill," she said contritely. "You took me by surprise with this." She indicated the extravagance of the cat. "I thought we'd part ways this afternoon and maybe I'd see you with someone else at a future *Q Virtus* event. This is better," she allowed, but met his gaze with a level one. "But I do have to work."

"Apology accepted. And I've already instructed my crew to set up a work space in the cabin where your things were unpacked. It should be completed by morning."

"They're going to work while I'm sleeping in there?" she asked, already anticipating his reply.

"You won't be in there, *draga*. And you won't be sleeping."

* * *

Ryzard flipped through his emails on his tablet while he waited for Tiffany to finish her call. They'd had a surprisingly productive morning, despite lazing in bed first thing. An easy, affectionate companionship had fallen between them after her rather explosive reaction to waking at sea yesterday.

He still chafed a little, recalling it, even though he now understood it to be her own baggage with her family that had caused her to push him away like that. His reaction, however, continued to niggle at him no matter how much he wanted to ignore it. Her claim that she was with him out of desperation had slapped him with a surprisingly sharp hand.

She was volatile. A woman as sexually passionate as she was would have strong feelings in every aspect of her life, he supposed. He could only imagine what kind of mama bear she'd be about her children.

Sucking in a breath at having taken such a bizarre turn in his mind, he lifted his head to see her set aside her phone.

"Done. Really sorry," she said.

"Don't apologize. We both have to work. I made you wait this morning."

She gave him a look that said, *Seriously?* and slid her eyes to the crewman setting out their air tanks.

He grinned, amused by her blushing over his referring to the way they'd been driving each other into a frenzy, fresh out of the shower, when he'd had to take a call that couldn't be put off. Afterward, they'd nearly ripped each other apart, and breakfast had been a quietly stunned affair when her bare foot atop his had pleased him well beyond what was reasonable.

They'd parted ways after, each moving to their separate work spaces, but he'd been distracted by her proximity. With most women, that would signal the end for him. Not with Tiffany. His brain couldn't even contemplate an end to this. It had barely started. She was too extraordinary.

Her phone rang and she turned from removing her wrap, clad only in her bikini as she stepped toward the table where she'd left the phone. "I don't have to get that. We'll pretend we're already in the water and— Oh shoot, it's my brother. I should answer. Why are you staring?" She followed his gaze to her torso, then sent an anxious look to the crewman who had lifted her tank, ready to strap it onto her.

"I'm staring because you're hot as hell," Ryzard prevaricated. "Take your call or you'll be wondering what he wanted."

Somewhat flustered, she stabbed the phone, then held the screen before her for the video call. "Hey," she said as she picked up her wrap and shrugged her arm into it.

Ryzard sighed inwardly. He hadn't meant to make her feel sensitive. He'd been looking at her scars, yes, but only thinking that a woman with less zeal for life would have succumbed to such injuries. Tiffany's ferocious spirit was the reason she'd survived, and he was very glad she had.

"You're naked?" Her brother frowned. "It's the middle of the day. I thought it would be safe to call."

"Excuse me, darling," Tiffany said to Ryzard. "My brother has called to ask if the sun is over the yardarm. Could you lift the sheet and see?"

Christian sputtered, Ryzard looked to the sky for patience and his crewman buried a snort of laughter into his shirt collar. Although Ryzard had to admit it was nice to know she gave others a hard time, not just him.

"We're about to go swimming, you idiot," she said to her brother. "See? Bathing suit." She ran her phone down her body as if she was scanning for radioactivity, showing him the strapless band and itsy slash of blue. Then she turned the phone to show him the equipment on the deck. "There are the breathing tanks and scuba flippers. There's the mask that's going to give me an anxiety attack so Ryzard will have to buddy-breathe me to the surface. Is my virtue restored? Want to tell me now why you called?"

"Dad hasn't come across anything useful yet, but said he'd ask around."

"Motivated, is he?" The way Tiffany's blond lashes lifted to send a resolute look toward Ryzard made his blood kick into higher gear. "Tell him I appreciate anything he's able to pass along."

"As do I," Ryzard told her as she hung up. "If you're talking about what I think you are."

"I asked Christian to put a bug in his ear. Dad's not speaking to me directly right now, but I don't know if that's because he's in Washington and doesn't have time for the kind of conversation he thinks we need to have or if he's genuinely angry. I hope you don't mind, but I was worried Dad might—" She shrugged apologetically. "I'm his little princess. I didn't want any grumpiness he felt toward you to come out with anyone in a position to affect your situation. If he knows I have an interest in the outcome, he'll take care to support your petition. Or at least not damage it."

His ears rang with the impact of what she was saying. "He has that kind of influence?" It wasn't like him to underestimate people, but his sexual enthrallment had temporarily shortened his sight of the bigger picture.

"He's very well connected. And I'm being overcautious," she assured him, moving to put a hand on his arm. "Don't worry. He wouldn't do anything rash. Something like throwing support behind a leader who hasn't been recognized… It's too big a gamble going into an election. If anything he'll be even more circumspect, couching his reaction while trying to find out everything he can. He's not going to stir up a lynch mob or anything."

"No shotgun wedding?" he prompted, throat dry. How far would her father go for his daughter's groom?

"Absolutely not," she assured him.

He should be relieved. He couldn't betray Luiza's memory by contemplating marriage to another woman, but in the back of his mind a voice whispered, *If it was for your country...*

He brushed the thought aside, trying to remind himself this was a simple fling. Two people enjoying sexual compatibility and the luxury of Caribbean waters. If he took a moment to reassess Tiffany, not just because she was lissome and golden, not simply because she had a quick, intelligent mind and a clear understanding of politics, but because she could soon be first daughter of the United States of America, that didn't mean he was being disloyal to his one true love. Luiza had had a dream for their country, and he was obligated to consider any avenue to achieve it. That's all he was doing.

He watched her frown at her diving mask, lips white where she pinched them together. She'd told him about her aversion to wearing things tight against her face, but he watched her draw in courage with a deep breath and wrestle the mask onto her face.

"I'm really worried I'll freak out down there," she said in a tone made nasal by the mask covering the upper half of her face. Her eyes behind the glass were anxious.

"You're tough," he told her, pride and regard moving in him. "You'll handle it."

"You don't know that." She set a hand on her bare chest. "My heart's going a mile a minute."

"But you're trying anyway, despite your anxiety. That's why I know you'll be fine," he assured her.

He quickly slipped into his own gear, not wanting to make her wait for the distraction of reef and shipwreck to take her mind off her fears. Holiday fun, he insisted to himself. Nothing so complex as wanting to coax her past bad memories because he felt compelled to share the wonder below the surface with her.

Why it mattered to him that she go with him was a puzzle he didn't study too closely. He could just as easily dive with one of his crew and had in the past, but he was aware of a preference for staying aboard with her over diving without her.

That wasn't like him. He was not a dependent person. Tiffany had been surprised the other day when he'd told her he didn't want a wife or children. He understood the reaction. Everyone in the world wanted a lifetime companion and offspring, but after Luiza, he'd closed himself off to the idea.

He *didn't* want emotional addiction to another being. It made a person vulnerable, and he couldn't afford such weaknesses.

But the thought of marrying Tiffany kept detonating in his mind, trailing thoughts of sleeping with her every night for the rest of his life.

It was because of the advantages she offered him. It would be a practical move, not something he did out of a need to connect himself irrevocably to her. He didn't want or need *family*.

He needed to stabilize his country and make good on his promise of peace.

"You look like a frog," she said as they readied to jump.

"So kiss me, Daddy's Little Princess. See what I turn into."

She did, quick and flirty, then bit her smile onto her mouthpiece and fell back into the water.

He leaped after her.

CHAPTER SEVEN

"THAT WAS FANTASTIC!" Tiffany panted, still breathless from their ascent from a shipwreck covered in coral and barnacles, populated with colorful fish darting in and out of fronds. Ryzard had carried a spotlight so the wash of blue-green from the filtered sunlight had disappeared, revealing the true brilliance below.

He handed off his tank to his crewman, then heaved himself to sit on the platform at the stern of the boat, legs dangling beside her. "Up?" He offered a hand.

"Still recovering. Give me a sec," she said breathlessly.

He relayed their gear as they both stripped, lifting her tank off her back, muscles flexing under the glistening latte of his tan. His black bathing suit was ridiculously miniscule, making American men such as her brother seem like absolute prudes with their baggy trunks. She'd heard people refer to those teensy tight suits as banana hammocks and budgie smugglers, but on the right man, they were sexy as hell.

A crooked finger came under her chin, and he lifted her face to look him in the eye. Beneath the water, his foot snaked out to catch her at the waist and guide her into the space between his knees.

"What?" she challenged, hands splaying on the steely muscles of his flexing thighs.

"Are we staying in the water a little longer?" he asked suggestively. "You can't look at me like that and not provoke a response."

She flicked her gaze downward and saw he'd filled out the tight black fabric to near bursting.

"Don't ever let anyone tell you you're not beautiful, *draga*. When you smile, you light up the room, and when you're aroused, I can't take my eyes off you."

The water should have bubbled and fizzed around her, she grew so hot and flushed with joy.

"Will you come to Bregnovia with me?"

Oh. It was an out-of-the-blue question with huge implications, the most important being, *he wanted to keep her with him.*

Surging upward, she straightened her arms and let her chest plaster into his, meeting his hot kiss with open-mouthed, passionate joy.

"Yes," she agreed.

One big hand came up to cradle the back of her head and the other dug into her waist, holding her steady while his calves pinched her thighs, bracing her in the awkward position. Their kiss went on for a long time, sumptuous and thorough.

With a tight sound of frustration, he jerked back. "No condom," he muttered.

"What? There's plenty of room in that suit for one."

"Not much room at all, actually," he growled. "You'll take the lead into the cabin."

Laughing unreservedly, she let him pull her the rest of the way out of the water and onto his lap. "At least we know what you turned into down there."

He raised his brows in query.

She whispered, "Horny toad."

He pinched her bottom as he urged her inside.

* * *

The landscape from the airport was one of a country in recovery. When her brother had said Bregnovia could use their firm's expertise, he hadn't been kidding. They left the partially bombed-out tarmac, wound past a scorched vineyard and turned away from one end of a shattered bridge that spanned a canyon to zigzag into the riverbed, where they four-wheeled over a makeshift crossing before climbing the hairpin curves on the far side to enter a city that looked like a child had kicked over his blocks.

But what a city it had been. Bregnovia's capital, Gizela, was a medieval fairy tale on a river that, until dammed for electricity and irrigation, had been a trading arm in and out of the Black Sea. Low canals still lapped at the stone walls in its village square. Beyond that quaint center, stark communist housing stood next to even more modern shopping malls, but nothing escaped the wounds of recent war. Rubble punctuated in a small landslide off a facade here, crooked fencing kept children out of a teetering building there.

Fascinated by the contrast of beauty and battle, Tiffany barely spoke until they drove through gates that were twelve feet high and thirty-six feet wide. Their ornate wrought-iron grillwork with gold filigree appeared startlingly new and grand.

"This is your home? It looks like Buckingham Palace."

"It is a palace," Ryzard confirmed casually. "Built as the dacha for a Russian prince during tsarist times. The communists spared it—a KGB general appropriated it—but it was the last stand for my predecessor. We're still repairing it from the siege. It's only mine while I'm president, but I'm paying for the refurbishment, as my legacy."

Despite the bullet holes and the pile of broken stones that might have once been a carriage house, the palace made the White House look like a neglected summer cottage, especially with its expansive flower bed that formed a carpet beneath a bronze statue of a woman with an arm across her breast, the other outstretched in supplication—

Tiffany read the nameplate as the limo circled it. Inexplicably, her heart invaded her throat, pulsing there like a hammered thumb. *Luiza.*

Ryzard had said she was his country's martyr, revered like their Lady Liberty, but this statue wasn't staid. It didn't project a state of peace and optimism with a torch to light the way forward. It was anguished and emotional and raised all the hairs on her body. This statue wasn't a symbol or an ideal. She was a real person.

Whose name was tattooed on Ryzard's chest.

Not wanting to believe the suspicion flirting around the periphery of her consciousness, Tiffany left the car and walked inside to confront an oil portrait of the same woman in the spacious drawing room. Here, Luiza's serene smile was as exquisite as Mona Lisa's, only eclipsed by her flawless beauty.

Again it didn't seem like a commemorative pose that a country hung in the National Gallery. There was a wistful quality to the painting. It was the kind of thing someone lovingly commissioned to enshrine a memory.

Luiza's eyes seemed to follow Tiffany as she accepted introductions to Ryzard's staff. Thankfully they quickly left her behind as Ryzard and his porters took her up the stairs and along the colonnaded walk that circled the grand entrance below and brought her to a place he called the Garden Suite.

"It's the only one in the guest wing that's habitable," he said with a minor twist of apology across his lips. "But your work space is here." He left the bedroom and crossed the hall to push through a pair of double doors into a sitting room that had been tricked out with office equipment and a replica desk that Marie Antoinette would have used if she had run a modern international construction firm. "You won't have any problem working outside your country? With the different time zone?"

"We're global and I've been working from the family mansion. The advantage to living like a recluse is that no one will expect me to show up in pers— My umbrella!" The stained glass piece hung at a cocked angle in front of the window, just high enough for her to stand under it. "You said we slept through the auction," she accused.

"I placed a reserve bid before we left."

Moving in a slow twirl, she closed her eyes and imagined she could feel the colors as they caressed her face. "You're spoiling me."

"I want you to be happy. You will be?"

She opened her eyes to the window and the back of Luiza's bronzed head beyond the glass. Her floating spirits fell like a block of lead. She couldn't shake the feeling that Ryzard had a statue of his old girlfriend on the lawn.

"Tiffany?" he queried, voice coming closer.

"Where will you be?" she asked, leaving the window and leading him back across the hall to the bedroom. Here, at least, the windows faced the river.

"Too damned far away," he replied.

"Why? Security? No outsiders in the president's bedroom?" she guessed.

"Certain customs remain quaintly adhered to."

"Mmm." She pushed her mouth to the side, hiding that she was actually quite devastated. "I don't suppose our president could get away with bringing women home, either." The porter had gone so she jerked her chin at the door, saying, "See if that door locks."

"Subtle," he said drily, "but I can't."

"I don't know what you think I'm suggesting," she challenged, tossing her head to cover up that she rather desperately needed to reconnect physically. The emotional hit of what looked quite literally like a monumental devotion to Luiza shook her tenuous confidence. Badly. Now he was rejecting her, inciting a quiet panic. "I only meant that if I'll be sleeping alone, I need to feel safe."

"You won't be alone."

"I can have a guard with me?"

"That would be detrimental to the state of peace I'm trying to maintain," he stated with one of his untamed smiles. "No, I will sleep with you, but right now I have to go outside and salute my flag. It's a custom I observe when I return after being away. People gather to see it. It reassures them of my commitment. Would you do me the favor of putting on something suitable and joining me? They'll be curious."

Here we go again, she thought with an unexpected face-plant into dread.

I bet Luiza would do it, a taunting voice sang in follow-up.

"Problem?" he asked, obviously reading something of her reluctance.

"Just disappointed we can't test the bed," she prevaricated.

"They stand at the gate, if you're worried they'll see you close up."

"It's fine," she assured him.

It was. When she stood outside thirty minutes later, face shaded by a hat from the surprisingly hot sun, her entire being swelled with admiration as she watched Ryzard in his presidential garb stand tall and make a pledge to his flag. He wasn't a man going through the motions. His motives were pure, his heart one hundred percent dedicated.

With tears brimming her eyes, she watched him step away from the flag with a bow, taking his respectful leave. Then he turned and saluted the statue of Luiza, first pressing the flats of his fingertips to his mouth then offering the kiss to her in an earnest lift of his palm.

Tiffany stood very still, fighting not to gasp at the slice of pain that went through her. It wasn't the gesture that struck her so much as the anguish on Ryzard's face.

Her suspicions were confirmed. He loved Luiza, really loved her as a strong man loves his soul mate. His pain was so tangible, she could taste its metallic flavor on her tongue.

She reached out instinctively, longing to comfort him, but he stiffened under her touch, catching her hand and gently but firmly removing it from his sleeve.

"When I asked about your tattoo, you never said—"

"I know," he cut in, releasing her and taking one step away. "It's difficult to talk about."

"Of course," she managed, curling her fingers into a fist even though the blood was draining from her head, making her feel faint. Would she have come here if she'd known? The starkness of his rejection felt so final she could barely stand it. "I'm so sorry."

She meant she was sorry for overstepping, but he heard it as a lame platitude and dismissed it with an agitated jerk of his shoulder.

"I never want to go through anything like it again. To love like that and lose— Never again," he choked, flashing her a look that was both adamant and apprehensive.

He quickly looked away, but that glimpse of his resolve struck like a blow. She knew what it meant: he would never *allow* himself to love again. It would make him too vulnerable.

Making another quarter turn, he bowed his head toward the gates.

That's when Tiffany noticed the crowd of fifty or sixty people with faces pressed through the uprights of the gate, witnessing his rebuff and her humiliation. They didn't applaud, didn't wave, just stared at them for a few moments before slowly beginning to disperse.

Even they seemed to know she had no place here.

As she followed Ryzard back into the palace, she couldn't tell if Luiza's portrait met her with a smug smile, or a pitying eye. Thankfully, they both had work to catch up on. She needed space, even one situated with a prime view of Luiza's last haircut.

Oh, don't be bitter, Tiffany.

Ha, she laughed at herself. Bitterness had been her stock in trade after the pain of her recovery had receded from blinding to merely unrelenting. She really had believed her life was over, but Ryzard had shown her she could have a measure of happiness.

She considered the boundaries of her happiness later, as she soaked in a tub of bubbles. Ryzard had had to take a call, leaving her to dine alone, and she felt very much as her mother must have for much of her marriage. Not so much slighted as resigned. This was the reality of living with someone in his position. If he had loved her, the sacrifice might be worth it, but he didn't.

His heart belonged to Luiza. Indelibly.

A tiny draft flickered the candles in the corner of the tub and sudden awareness made her glance toward the door, then sit up in a startled rush of water and crackling bubbles.

Ryzard slouched his shoulder against the frame, arms folded, hip cocked. The most decadently wicked glint of admiration gave his shadowed expression a sexy cast.

She'd set a stage for him if he chose to come looking for her. A delicate lily-of-the-valley scent hovered in the humid air and a low-volume saxophone hummed sensuously from the music player. That hadn't prepared her for the impact of his tousled hair, wrinkled collar under a pullover sweater, or the way her heart leaped when he reached to tug his sweater over his head.

"I came to sneak you down to my room, but you've made me an offer I can't refuse. Before I forget, though..." He leaned over her, one broad hand cradling her chin while he crushed her mouth in a hard, thorough kiss that made her murmur in surprised delight.

"You were in danger of forgetting to do that, were you?" she asked breathlessly as he straightened to take off his shirt and kick away his pants.

"An undersecretary from your State Department called. It's not a promise to vote in favor, but it's a promising sign they're leaning that way."

"Oh!" The impulsive clap of her hands sent bubbles exploding like flakes off a snowball. "That's wonderful."

"That's thanks to you." He eased into place behind her, his muscular body buoying hers as he pressed her to relax back into him.

"I didn't do anything."

"I'm sure it was your father's influence at play."

"Mmm." She let her head loll against his shoulder, absently playing with his fingers where he roped his forearm across her collarbone. Her brow pleated. She wanted him to be happy, wanted peace for his country—who wouldn't wish peace for everyone in the world? But a pang sat in her chest. She wished something more personal had brought him to her this evening.

"It's a very big step," he said, drifting his hand down the slippery slope of her breast. "Do you know how many countries hesitate to make a move because they fear instigating something with yours? If America supports us, the other two-thirds of the votes I need would fall into place fairly quickly. I know I said I wouldn't force any dress-up on you, but there may be a few state dinners in our future."

She bit back a huffing laugh. *So* not surprised.

Just say no, Tiffany.

But refusing to play her part meant refusing this relationship. Despite it's misty future, she wasn't ready for it to end.

Especially when Ryzard lightly toyed with her nipple, making her murmur approval and slide against him. Was he manipulating her with her own responses, she wondered distantly? He was hardening against her, so he *did* want her.

Still, she hated herself a little for being so weak and easily managed. If she couldn't have the same effect on him, she at least wanted to break through his control. Rolling over, she grasped him in a firm hold, the way she'd learned he liked, and nipped his bottom lip.

He jerked his head back. The gold flecks in his green eyes glinted like sparks off a sword. "It's like that, is it?" he growled.

She grinned and sent a small tsunami across the ledge as she dragged herself onto her knees and straddled his thighs. As she kissed him with all the passion releasing inside her, she used her whole body to caress him, wiggling her hips to encourage the palms that shaped her backside.

Licking into his mouth, she reached to caress his thick erection again and started to take him into her.

"*Draga,* wait," he rasped against her open mouth. "Protection." He leaned away to reach for his pants.

Inhaling anguish along with a small dose of shame, she wondered what she had been thinking, offering unprotected sex. Was she that desperate for something permanent with him?

"Actually, let's go to the bed," he said, pulling away to leave the tub and let water sluice off him onto the floor. "It'll be more comfortable." He reached to draw her onto her feet, then lifted her out, carrying her wet and dripping into her bedroom, where he followed her onto the bed.

She bit him again as he tried to kiss her.

"What has got into you?" he asked, pulling her scratching nails off him and pinning them above her head in one hand.

"Not you," she taunted, inciting him with the arch of her body into his. "What's taking so long?"

With a bite of the packet and a stroke of a finger and

thumb, he was covered and pushing into her, not rough, but not gentle. Inexorable. She was ready, but not entirely. The friction caused her to draw in a breath of both surprise and anticipation.

"Better?" he asked, holding himself so deep inside her, she released a little sob. He eased back. "Tiffany, what's wrong?"

She shook her head. "Just make love to me."

Ryzard did, because he couldn't be with her like this and not thrust and withdraw and savor and bask. But he held out, making it last a long time for both of them, sensing a wall that needed prolonged lovemaking to erode. He blamed himself for the distance. He was struggling with having her here. It had been an impulse to ask her and he didn't regret it, but he was still having a hard time adjusting.

For the moment, however, he closed his mind to his inner conflicts and opened himself to Tiffany.

She writhed beneath him, so beautiful in her struggle to resist the little death of orgasm, clinging to him as she hung on to their connection. It couldn't last forever, though. Nothing could. His heart stopped. The whole world did. Ecstasy overtook them and nothing existed for him except her.

He stayed in that trance for hours, trying to sate their appetite for each other with repeated joinings. The wall between them receded and he didn't worry about it again until the next morning, when she woke in his bed.

She glanced around with the perplexed befuddlement of the bubbleheaded blonde he sometimes teasingly called her. "Where am I?"

"The Presidential Bedroom," he answered, shrugging into his suit jacket while he enjoyed the show.

The sheet slipped as she sat up. Her blue eyes blinked and she smoothed a hand over her tangled hair. "Why?"

"Your bed was wet," he reasoned, distantly aware that wasn't the whole truth. He had wanted her in here before he'd ever gone looking for her, but he was distracted by the shadow that passed behind her clear-sky irises as she looked around.

"Problem?"

She only lifted the sheet and glanced at her naked body. "Please tell me you put clothes on me when you carried me here."

"You were awfully heavy. I couldn't manage another ounce."

Her baleful gaze held a dire warning that made him grin. He picked up her robe from the chair and tossed it to the foot of the bed in answer.

She stood to pull it on, not returning his smile. The niggling sense of being held off returned full force.

"Are you all right, *draga?*" he asked, moving forward to cup her cheek and force her to look up at him.

She didn't quite meet his eyes, only saying with an ironic twist to her mouth, "Let's just say it's a good thing I had a warm bath to loosen my muscles before we played for gold in that triathlon last night."

"Shall I rub you down?" he offered, stroking a hand down her back in concern. He was ready to insist, wanting the physical connection to her even if it wasn't a sexual one. The way she stayed resistant to his touch bothered him.

"I thought it was verboten for me to be in here? I'll be fine. I'll have a hot shower and do my stretches." She kissed him, but it was a minimal brush of her lips against the corner of his mouth before she disappeared.

He frowned as he crossed to pick up his phone from the nightstand. Absently he straightened the snapshot of him and Luiza on horseback, wondering if he was imagining the wedge between him and Tiffany.

It was probably for the best if there was one, he reasoned. This was an affair. They couldn't afford to develop deeper feelings.

Still, he left his room with a pain cleaved into his chest.

CHAPTER EIGHT

TIFFANY TRIED TO ignore the fact that Ryzard was in love with a dead woman and soak up what he offered her: generous lovemaking and a boost to her confidence.

On his catamaran, she'd quit trying to hide herself from his crew. Three days in Bregnovia and she was even more comfortable in her own skin. He kept threatening to take her along on his public appearances and she always managed to talk him out of it, but part of her longed to go on a date the way they had at *Q Virtus*.

Pressing a strapless dress in sunset colors to her front, she decided to have a pretend date with him tonight. She imagined that like all men he had a thing for short skirts and low necklines. She'd knock his socks off.

An hour later, she'd run the straightening iron over her hair to give it a sheen and applied a final layer of glossy pink to her lips, making them look pouty and ripe. The dress offered her breasts in half cups, hugged her waist and clung so tightly across her hips she could barely walk. The gladiator sandals didn't help, but man did she look hot. The fact her scars were fully revealed by the itty-bitty dress didn't faze her.

She paused to consider that. A light coat of concealer downplayed the mottled scar on her face, but she wasn't about to smear her whole body with the stuff. Ryzard wouldn't notice or care either way. He thought she was gorgeous exactly as she was. It was such a painfully sweet knowledge, she had to stop and cradle it and blink hard or ruin her carefully applied makeup.

Digging her nails into her palms, she focused on the sting to clear her head, aware she was dangerously close to tumbling into love with him. It was because he was her first, she reasoned. He was gorgeous and smart and *so* patient with her moodiness and baggage. He commanded everything around him with calm ease, and that would make anyone feel safe and protected and cherished.

The real tell would be when they separated. She couldn't hide from her parents forever. The one stilted conversation with her mother had centered on exactly how long she intended to be away.

Tiffany hadn't wanted to admit she was afraid to leave. Would Ryzard miss her if she went home for a week? Or would it be the end of their associations?

She shook her head, having learned to be present in a moment, especially if it lacked pain. No one had a crystal ball telling what would come next. For now, she and Ryzard were together and happy.

With a calming breath, she searched him out in his office. He was watching his favorite newscaster and remained behind his desktop screen as she entered, head bent in concentration as he listened, expression grim and contained.

"What's happening in the world to make you look so severe?" she teased as she sidled up to him. "A beautiful woman just walked in. Whatever you're watching, forget it and notice *me*."

His arm came around her waist, grasping her close and tight, but his other hand caught hers before she could press his head down for the kiss she wanted. The look in his eyes was not easily interpreted, and the voice beside her startled her out of trying.

"Should we continue this later?" the newscaster asked.

"No," Ryzard answered.

Tiffany cried out in surprise and jerked against Ryzard's arm, but he held on to her without laughing.

"I thought you were watching a broadcast," she gasped, covering her heart.

The familiar face on the screen gave a tight smile of acknowledgment.

"I didn't realize I was walking into a video call. I apologize. Oh, gosh," she realized with a belated hand going to the bad side of her face. "I can't imagine what you think of me, making an entrance like that."

"I was already aware you two were close," the talking head said. He was a globally known face, one who'd elevated from foreign-correspondence stories to hard-hitting investigative stories and in-depth analyses of world politics.

At the moment she didn't have much choice with regard to how close she was to Ryzard. His arm was like a belt of iron, pinning her to his side, his tension starting to penetrate as she read zero amusement in his expression over her mistake.

"What's wrong?" she asked, instinctively bracing herself.

"We had company after our dive," he replied.

"Paparazzi?" She tried to step back, but he kept a tight grip on her.

"It doesn't matter, Tiffany."

"Of course it matters! Otherwise your friend here wouldn't be calling to warn you. Is it photos or video?"

"Photos." Ryzard fairly spat the word.

"The photographer knew I would never touch something purely to incite sensation," the newscaster said. "So they didn't offer them to me or I would have kept them off the market completely. Instead I heard about it secondhand and I've suggested a countermeasure to draw attention from their release."

"What kind of countermeasure? What are they saying?" She looked between the screen and Ryzard, panic creeping into her bloodstream.

"They don't sell clicks by being kind," Ryzard said brutally. "We'll meet in Rome," he told his friend on the screen. "You're right that a face-to-face broadcast interview will have more impact than something thrown together remotely."

"I'm not going on camera!" Tiffany cried.

"No," Ryzard agreed with the full impact of his dictatorial personality. "But you'll accompany me to the interview—"

She shook her head, growing manic. Part of her wanted to explode in rebellion, the other desperately needed to crawl away and hide.

"I need to go home." Had her father heard yet? She struggled against Ryzard's steely grip, then froze, thinking of her mother's reaction. "My family will be livid. They're already barely speaking to me—"

"Calm down." He thanked his friend and promised to be in touch with his travel arrangements, then turned off the screen. "The sun will still rise tomorrow, Tiffany. No one has died."

"It would be better if I had. That's what they'll be thinking."

"Don't talk like that. Ever." He gripped her arms and gave her a little shake.

She quit struggling, but kept a firm hand of resistance against his chest. "We're not one of these families who has a disgrace every minute, Ryzard. My accident was the worst thing Dad has ever had to field with the press. Given it was more tragedy than scandal, it didn't do him any harm in the polls, but it was still a monumental circus. He won't appreciate this."

The look of wild outrage Ryzard savaged over her made

her shrink in his hold. "Your father enjoyed some kind of political *benefit* from your near death?"

"He didn't mean to! I'm just saying that's how it works. Chris and I know that. We don't go off and sleep with people who are shaking up the maps of an atlas, putting the UN on notice, then get ourselves photographed for the gossip rags so Dad has to make explanations for our behavior. This, what you and I are doing, has to stop. I have to go home." She tried again to push away.

"So you can be shunned and cloistered? No," he gritted through his teeth, holding her in place. "The photographer is the villain here, not you. Not us."

"I'm still about to be vilified, aren't I? And I don't want…" Her voice wavered. Her muscles ached where she still held him off. "Home is my safe place, Ryzard. I'd rather be there when— How bad are they? The photographs, I mean."

"Don't think about them," he commanded. "You'll never see them if I have anything to do with it." His voice sent a wash of ice from her heart to her toes, it was so grim. "But I can't allow you to be away from me when they're released. They'll say I've rejected you, and that's not true. Besides, it doesn't sound as if your family will support you, so no, you stay with me."

She drooped her head. "They would support me," she insisted heavily. "The wagons get circled at times like this. And after it blows over, they would still be there for me. They do love me. It's just complicated."

"I will *ensure* it blows over," he said, forcing her chin up and looking down his nose from an arrogant angle, but his touch on her gentled even if his voice didn't. "You're coming to Rome with me, Tiffany."

She held back from pointing out she was perfectly capable of booking a charter flight and getting herself anywhere she darned well wanted to go. If he was only being authoritarian, she probably would have, but he sounded concerned. He sounded as if her feelings mattered, not just his image. That softened all the spikes of umbrage holding her stiff, making her shudder in surrender.

"Okay," she acquiesced.

"Good girl."

"Don't push it," she warned, but turned her face toward the caress of his fingertips as he smoothed her hair back behind her ear. Her eyes drifted closed.

"I'd like your father's contact number."

"Oh, no, I'll call Dad." She straightened, but found herself still in the prison of his hold.

"No, Tiffany. This is my fault. I should have taken more care to shield you. He's already uncomfortable with our relationship. I should have introduced myself before something like this made our first conversation an unpleasant one."

"I really think—"

"We're not negotiating, *draga*. We'll stand here until you've given me his number, but I'd like to get to Rome sooner than later, so make this easier on both of us."

"You're unbelievable," she choked.

"His people will have questions about the arrangements I've made. Quit being stubborn," he pressed.

Her? Stubborn? Kettle. *Black*.

With a sigh of defeat, because she really didn't want to face down her father *and his people,* she offered up his private mobile number.

How could he kiss something so hideous?

She didn't know why she looked it up. She should have known better, but she'd been compelled to know what they were saying. It was horrid. Beyond cruel.

Ryzard had been furious when he had emerged from

his shower and found her with his tablet in her lap, fingers white, throat dry, eyes unable to meet his.

"Why would you take a dose of poison? It's self-destructive, completely against everything you are," he'd growled, nipping the tablet away from her and tossing it across the room onto the bed.

Somewhere in his words she supposed a compliment lurked, but all she heard was disapproval. It made her cringe all the more.

The flight to Rome was exhausting and silent, his mood foul, but she hadn't wanted to speak, either. She didn't want him to notice her. She seemed like a burden, something he was carrying with him because he had to, not because he wanted her. How could he want anything to do with her when she was bringing shame on him like this?

Like sleeping with snakeskin. She shuddered at the headlines and comments from trolls that would stay in her mind forever. *Her husband was lucky he died and didn't have to stay married to that.*

Ryzard's interview was staged in a hotel room, the pristine white decor too bright for her gritty, bloodshot eyes. Neither of them had slept despite lying next to each other for a few hours. He'd stroked her for a time, but she hadn't been able to respond, too frozen inside. Feeling betrayed. Her parents hadn't called, not even replying to her text that she was available if they wanted to talk. The only friend she had right now was Ryzard, and he was so remote he might as well have stayed in Bregnovia and sent a wax double in his place.

She'd been too afraid to ask what he intended to say and wound up standing at the side of the room, staring dumbly from the shadows into the light as he took his seat. The interview began.

Her father had done a million of these things, so she wasn't surprised to hear them tiptoe through a variety of political tulips on the way to the meat of the interview. Ryzard's devotion to his country was on full display, and she imagined the whole world was reevaluating him as he spoke passionately about Bregnovia's desire for peace and plans for prosperity. She hoped so. He deserved to be taken seriously.

She grew more and more tense as the interview dragged on, however. Didn't they realize the audience was waiting for the mention of her name?

Twenty-five minutes in, the question finally came.

"Photos have circulated showing you with American heiress Tiffany Davis. Is it serious?"

"I take very seriously that your bottom-feeder colleagues are making their fortune on photos that for all we know have been manipulated for a higher profit."

Nice of him to defend her with such an implication, but the photos had not been airbrushed. She genuinely looked that bad.

The interviewer smiled tightly. "I meant is the relationship serious?"

"That's between us. We're private people," Ryzard stated implacably.

Tiffany caught back a harsh laugh. Did he really think he'd get away with as little as that?

"My sources tell me you met at the notoriously secret *Q Virtus*," the newscaster continued.

See? she wanted to cry. The press never rested until they drew as much blood as possible, even when they called themselves a friend.

"That's true," Ryzard allowed.

"*Q Virtus* is a rather exclusive club, isn't it? What can you tell me about it?" the journalist pressed.

"I'm sure contacting them would get you more information than you'd ever get out of me," Ryzard said smoothly.

Oh. Ha. That was smart. She relaxed under a ripple of

humor. The public's insatiable curiosity would now turn to the club. Papers could trot out as many before-and-after photos of Tiffany Davis as they wanted, but viewers and readers would be more interested in learning the names of other people in the secret club. They'd hungrily eat up the scant yet salacious details of what went on there. She and Ryzard would be old news before the credits rolled on this broadcast.

In fact, when she watched later that evening, she noted that while the names rolled, her own image came forward to Ryzard's reaching hand. She shook hands with the newscaster and thanked him, all of them standing in friendly banter. Her good side was angled to the camera. Her hair was done and her makeup was decent. Wearing a simple alabaster suit, she looked...normal. Pretty even.

Ryzard clicked it off as it went to commercial. She collapsed on the foot of the hotel bed, emotionally exhausted. Could it really be over as easily as that?

Ryzard watched Tiffany as he unknotted his tie and released first the cuffs, then the front buttons of his shirt. As tough as she was, he'd seen what a toll this attack had had on her. She'd been shutting him out as a result, and that infuriated him. Her talk of running away where he couldn't reach her had nearly put him out of his mind.

He was still beside himself that this incident had happened at all. His captain had warned him that an unidentified boat kept turning up in their radar, but he'd shrugged it off. None of his mistresses in the past had warranted much attention, but he supposed his own profile was elevated to the international stage these days. Tiffany's family was certainly of a level to feed the appetite of her country's gossip columns.

And she's not just a mistress, is she? The question beat in warning like a jungle drum in his chest, ominous and dark.

His plans for his relationship with Tiffany were changing, but he hadn't wanted to allude to anything more in his interview. The last time his link to a woman had been public and indelible, she'd been used as a pawn in his country's civil war and the outcome was fatal.

Seeing Tiffany beaten and wounded by words shook loose his nightmare of losing Luiza. He'd grasped at anger to counter his resurgence of helplessness, hating that he couldn't stem the damage being done to her, but agony and guilt were constant. He should have protected her better. If he could have stopped Tiffany from searching out what they were saying about her, he would have. Humanity's capacity for ugliness astounded him. His job, the one he'd taken on for his country, for his own sanity, was to push brutality and attacks to the furthest fringes of existence that he could.

And keep himself apart so the pain of life couldn't reach inside him and wring him into anguish.

It wasn't easy when Tiffany sat with her spine slouched and her golden hair trailing loose from its neat bun, seeming incredibly delicate, like a dragonfly that had its wings crushed. When she was like this, she stirred things in him that needed to stay in firmer places. The chin-up, spoiled and cheeky Tiffany he could easily compartmentalize as a friendly partner in a game of sexual sport. Like a tennis opponent who gave him a run for his money, athletic and quick.

The vulnerable Tiffany frightened him. She made him feel so ferociously protective he would do violence if he ever found the photographer who'd reduced her image to a commodity in filthy commerce.

Shaken by the depth of his feelings, he tried to pull them both out of the tailspin with a blunt, "Dinner out or in?"

She sighed and looked up at him. Her heartrending expression was both anguished and amused. His heart began to pound in visceral reaction, and he swayed as though struck with vertigo, not sure why.

"My first thought is, *Duh, Ryzard.* Of course I'd never dine in public, but how could I be such a coward when you've just defended me so fiercely? No one else has. I can't tell you how much that means to me."

A sensation of wind rushing around him lifted all the hairs on his naked chest, as if he was free-falling into space. Her gaze was so defenseless, he couldn't look away. She reached inside him with that look, catching at things he couldn't even acknowledge.

"You already know I would only wish away your scars because I hate that you were hurt at all. But I see them as a badge of your ability to overcome," he heard himself admit. "Your sort of willpower, your deep survival instinct, is rare, Tiffany. You probably don't realize it because it's such an integral part of your nature to fight, but not everyone accepts such a life blow and makes herself live through it."

Luiza hadn't, he acknowledged with a crash of his heart into his toes. Thinking about her when he was with Tiffany, contrasting them, was wrong. Setting aside Luiza in his mind was like ripping an essential part of him away and abandoning it, but he had to do it. They couldn't occupy the same place inside him, and right now Tiffany needed him.

"All my life I heard, 'You're so pretty.' Like that was the most important thing to be. You're the first person to compliment me on having substance. I really thought I'd lost everything by losing my looks."

Where Luiza had built him into the man he was with vision and belief in him, Tiffany slayed him with honesty and vulnerability. His heart felt as though it beat outside his chest. When she rose and came to him, and went on tiptoe to brush soft lips against his jaw, he closed his eyes in paralyzed ecstasy. Deep down, at a base level, it felt wrong to be this gripped by her, but he couldn't help it. In this moment, she was all he knew.

"Thank you for wanting me exactly as I am."

He did. God help him, he wanted her in ways he couldn't even describe.

They shouldn't come together like this, with hearts agape and defenses on the floor, but he couldn't *not* touch her. Pulling her in, he settled his mouth on hers, tender and sweet. The animal in him wanted to ravish, but the man in him needed to cherish.

She drew an emotive breath and kissed him back in a way that flooded him with aching tenderness. The sexual need was there, strong as ever, but it sprang from a deeper place inside him. Hell, he thought. Hell and hell. Lingering feelings of infidelity fell away. This woman was the one he had to be faithful to. *This one.*

The rending sensation inside him hurt so much he had to squeeze her into him to stop what broke open, fearing his lifeblood would leak away if he didn't have her pressed to the wound. Her arms went around his neck, light palms cradling the back of his skull as she fingered through his hair, soothing and treasuring and filling the cavernous spaces in him with something new and golden and as unique as she was.

When they stripped and eased onto the bed and came together, it was with a shaken breath from him and a gasp of awe from her. She gloried in his possession, and he bent his head to her breast in veneration, golden lamplight burning the vision of her into his memory with the eternity of a primordial being caught in amber.

Twin fingers traced on each side of her scar, the sensation dull on one side, sweet on the other. She stretched in supreme pleasure and reached for him without opening her eyes, finding only cool, empty sheets where he was supposed to be.

"I'm already showered and dressed, *draga*," he said on her other side. "You said to let you sleep and I did as long as I could, but we have to leave soon. We have a dinner engagement in Zurich."

"Are you serious?" She rolled onto her back so she could see him where he stood over her, his knife-sharp suit of charcoal over a dove gray shirt set off with a subdued navy tie. He looked way too buttoned-down, hair still damp, chin shiny and probably tasting spicy and lickable. She skimmed the sheet away and invited, "Come back to bed."

"Your parents are expecting us. I already agreed to see them, but if you'd like to send our regrets…"

"They're in Zurich?" She sat up, bringing the sheet to her collarbone as if her father had just walked in the room. "How? Why?"

"I left it to our collective staff to work out the how. I simply extended the invitation when I informed him about the photos. He wanted you to come back to America. I said you were accompanying me to Rome and that I had a commitment in Switzerland, but that we'd be pleased if they could meet us there."

"How delightfully neutral. I guess that explains why they haven't been in touch. They've been traveling." She threw off the sheet and walked naked to find her phone, pleased at the way he pivoted to watch her.

Sending him a saucy smile over her shoulder, she clicked her screen and tapped in her code, reading aloud the message she found. "'Staying with the deHavillands in Berne.' That's the American ambassador. Mom went to school with her. Longtime friends of the family. 'Where will you be staying?'" She looked to him.

"At the hotel where the banquet will be held. My people should have sent the details already. I'll ask them to extend the invitation to include your parents' friends." He reached inside his jacket pocket for his mobile.

Tiffany heard only one word and lowered her phone, barely hanging on to it with limp fingers as she repeated, "Banquet?"

He gave her a long, steady look. "Something I arranged months ago. I've been trying to ease you into the public eye, *draga*. Don't look so shocked. It's not something I can miss since it's a charity I personally fund. We remove land mines and petition to stop their use completely. They're an appalling weapon."

She felt as though she stood on one, but he didn't coddle her over what attending would mean. Given everything that had happened, she supposed it was time to set aside her fear of being in public. As long as she had him by her side, she'd be okay, wouldn't she?

CHAPTER NINE

A FEW HOURS LATER, she wasn't so sure. She'd taken an *in for a penny, in for a pound* approach and forgone the one-shouldered gowns that would have disguised a lot of her scarring, deciding instead to let her freak flag fly. Her halter-style gown set off her breasts and hips beautifully and was the most gorgeous shade of Persian blue that glistened and slithered over her skin as she walked.

...snakeskin...

Stop it. She pretended she was her old self, the somewhat infamous fashionista who had graced more than her share of best-dressed lists. With her trained yoga posture reaching her crown to the ceiling, shoulders pinned back with pride, she entered the lounge and took the druglike hit that was Ryzard in a tuxedo.

"I knew you wouldn't disappoint me," he said. His smile was sexy and smug, but held a warmth of underlying approval.

Winded, she dissembled by checking her pocketbook, trying to grasp hold of herself as she reacted to him and the effect he had on her. Did he know how defenseless she was around him? She suspected he did. He was coming to know her very well, maybe too well. There was an imbalance there because he could see right past her defenses, but he remained unpredictable to her.

As if to prove it, he came forward and threaded a bracelet up her marred arm until it wrapped in delicate scrolls against her biceps. It was a stunning piece of extravagant ivy tendrils fashioned from platinum. Diamonds were inset as random pops of sparkling dew, fixating the eye.

"It's beautiful."

"When people stare, you can say, 'Ryzard gave it to me. He thinks I'm a spoiled brat, but wouldn't change a thing about me.'"

She wanted to grin and be dismissive, but she was too moved. Her voice husked when she admitted, "You do spoil me. I have no idea why."

"You inspire me," he confided, then swooped to set a kiss against the corner of her mouth. "Lipstick, I know," he muttered before she could pull away in protest. "In the future, don't put it on until I've finished kissing you."

"Then we'd never leave the room, would we?"

"And how is this a problem?" He held the door as he spoke, the light in his eye making her laugh, reassuring her the evening would turn out fine.

They stopped by another suite on their way downstairs. He'd arranged it for her parents and the ambassador. Her father greeted her with a long hug before he set her back. Then he looked between her and Ryzard, not seeming to know where to start.

She quickly introduced them and included the ambassador's husband, Dr. deHavilland, using Ryzard's title as the president of Bregnovia, and heard the crack in her voice as she queried, "Mom didn't come?"

"The ladies are fussing down the hall," the doctor said after kissing her cheeks. Taking her chin, he turned her face to eye her scar. "The specialist did wonders, didn't he? It's good to see you out, Tiffany. Ryzard, what's your poison? We're having whiskey sours."

He accepted one and she squeezed his arm. "Do you mind if I...?"

"Of course, go say hello, but we need to be in the ballroom to greet the guests in fifteen minutes."

"Five," she promised with a splayed hand and hurried in search of her mother, nervous of the confrontation, but experiencing the homesick need to reconnect.

Following voices through a bedroom to the open door of a bathroom, she approached and set her hand on the inner door only to hear a makeup compact click over her mother's voice. "Are we supposed to believe he's in love with her? Any fool can see he's using her for our connections."

"Any fool except me?" Tiffany blurted, pushing the door farther in while outrage washed over her. It was followed by a stab of hurt so deep she could barely see.

Nevertheless, her vision filled with the flawless image of her mother turning from the mirror. Shock paled her mother's elegantly powdered cheeks. An automatic defense rose to part her painted lips, but first she had to draw a breath of shock as her gaze traveled her daughter's appearance and measured the amount of exposure. A trembling little head shake told Tiffany what her mother thought of this gown.

"You won't be comfortable in that."

"You mean *you* won't," Tiffany volleyed back and turned to leave. A type of daughterly need for her mother's bosom had driven her in here, and now she wished Barbara Holbrook had stayed home.

"Tiffany Ann." The strident voice didn't need volume to stop Tiffany in her tracks. "He told your father he wanted to marry you. You met him last *week.* What are we supposed to think?"

Tiffany spun back, thrown by the statement. "He did not."

Her mother held her lady-of-the-manor pose, the one that had too much dignity to descend into a did-so, did-not quibbling match. Instead, she gave Tiffany another once-over and asked primly, "How on earth did you come to be his guest? I mean, if he had brought a party aboard, I'd understand you being swept along, but obviously he wants us to believe he has a romantic interest in you. What sort of promises has he made you?"

Tiffany heard the strange lilt in her mother's voice. Concern, but something else. Something shaken and protective…

She felt her eyes go wider and sting with dryness as understanding penetrated. Her mother genuinely believed she was being used—and was too blind to see it.

If her high school diary had been passed around the football locker room, she couldn't have felt more as though her deepest feelings were being abused. If only she could have defended Ryzard. If only she believed he had deeper feelings for her beyond the physical and amusement with her "great personality."

God, maybe he didn't even feel that much for her. Maybe it *was* all about who her father was. Insecurity nearly drove her to her knees, but she made herself stand proud and state what she'd let herself believe.

"He hasn't made any promises. He wants me for my body. It's mutual."

Dumbly she turned and walked out, floored by what her mother had said about Ryzard wanting to marry her. Was it true? Because if it was, her mother was right. It wouldn't be love driving his interest in her. They *had* met only ten days ago.

She tried to swallow away the painful lump of confusion that lodged itself high behind her breastbone.

Ryzard set down his drink as she appeared and held out his crooked arm. "Ready? We'll see you downstairs," he said to the men.

"Tiffany," the ambassador scolded, following her with a

swish of skirts. "You can't speak to your mother like that. She's been telling me how worried she's been for you, not just because you dropped out of sight with a stranger—I apologize if that sounds rude," she added in an aside to Ryzard. "But since—"

"I *know*. The accident. I've been a great burden on them, but can you understand how sick I am of having that define me? I'm better now. It's time for both her and Dad to butt out of my life."

She yearned for everyone to leave her alone so she could lick her wounds in private. It pained her horribly that everyone could see how weakly she'd fallen for this incredibly handsome, indulgent charlatan who had soothed her broken ego and wormed his way toward her heart. All in the name of advancing his own agenda.

"Where is this rebellion coming from?" her father clipped in his sternest tone. "You were never like this before. Your mother and I can't fathom what's got into you. Letting you go to work has obviously put too much stress on you."

"*Letting* me." She jerked up her chastised head, filling with outrage.

Beside her, Ryzard took her good arm in a warm, calming grip. "If you'll pardon an outsider's observation? Every child has to leave the nest at some point, even one who was blown back in and needed you very badly for a time. Your daughter is an adult. She can make her own decisions."

Despite that statement of her independence, she found herself letting him make the decision for both of them to leave. A crazy part of her even rationalized that even if he *was* using her, he was also helping her find the state of autonomy she longed for.

As they waited for the elevator, a jagged sigh escaped her. "I can't do this, Ryzard."

She meant the banquet, the evening, but he misunderstood.

"Don't let this upset you. Listen, I visited Bregnovia after finishing university. I could have stayed. My mother wanted me to, but I chose to drift across Europe like pollen in the wind. I was making a statement. They had forced me to leave as a child, but they couldn't make me stay as an adult."

"And now you hate yourself for not spending time with them. You think I should go back and apologize?" She looked back down the hall, hating the discord with her family even as she dreaded facing them again.

The elevator car arrived and Ryzard guided her into it.

"I don't hate myself as much as I should. Everyone does need to leave the nest at some point, *draga*. But be assured that your parents are operating from a place of love. Your father had some very pointed questions for me. He is the quintessential father who feels a strong need to protect his baby girl."

With bloodless fingers clinging to her pocketbook, she lifted her gaze to meet his. "Did you tell him you want to marry me?" Her voice sounded flayed and dead, even more listless than the tone she had used to discuss her prospective marriage to Paulie.

Surprise flashed across his expression before he shuttered it into a neutral poker face. "He asked me about my intentions when I called. I said they were honorable. What else could I say?"

"You told me this relationship wouldn't lead to anything permanent. When did you decide it could?"

He turned his head away, profile hard with undisguised impatience, then looked back, fairly knocking her over with the impact. "What are you really asking, *draga?*"

The car stopped and she swayed, stomach dipping and clawing for a settled state. "You weren't ever going to marry, but then you realized exactly how useful my father could be. Is that right?"

"Yes." No apology, just hardened, chiseled features that were so remote and handsome she wanted to cry.

"We talked about how much I enjoy being used, Ryzard."

The doors of the elevator opened. His handlers were waiting, one reaching to hold the door for them.

"We need a moment," he clipped.

"No, we don't." Her voice was strangled, but she stepped from the elevator into the bubble that was its own bizarrely familiar shield against reality. Her skin burned under the stares of his people, but she allowed only Ryzard to see how much that tortured her as she turned to glare up at him. "If this is what I'm here for, then let's do it. I'm probably better on stage than you are. Smile. Nothing matters except how this looks."

"Tiffany," he growled.

Arranging the sort of warm, gracious smile her mother had patented, she sidled beyond his reach and asked a handler, "Where would you like me to stand in relation to the president?"

Talk about land mines. Ryzard felt as though he stood in a field of them as he welcomed his guests and waited for the misstep that would cause Tiffany to discharge. She was the epitome of class though, greeting people warmly as he introduced her, maintaining a level of poise that made his heart swell with pride even as his blood ran like acid in his veins.

We talked about how much I enjoy being used.

He struggled to hide how much his conscience twisted under that. Did she think he couldn't see what this evening was costing her? He was so deeply attuned to her that he felt her tension like a high-pitched noise humming inside his consciousness, keeping him on high alert. It was fear, he realized with a *thunk* of dread-filled self-assessment. She would run given an opportunity, and that kept him so fixated on her he could hardly breathe, braced as he was to catch her before her first step.

He ought to let her go if that's what she really wanted, but he couldn't bear it when she hadn't even given him a chance to explain. The way she'd thrown her accusation at him in the elevator had been a shock. He'd answered honestly out of instinct, because any sort of subterfuge between them was abhorrent to him.

But distance was equally repugnant to him, and she was keeping an emotional one that didn't bode well for sifting through things he'd barely made sense of himself.

As for her pithy suggestion that all he cared about was his image, she was dead wrong there. He cared about her. Thinking about how much he cared made him feel as though the elevator's cable had been cut and he was still plummeting into the unknown.

They didn't have a chance to speak freely again until they were dancing after dinner. He kept his gaze off her, dangerously close to becoming aroused from holding her. Every primordial instinct in him wanted to drag her into the nearest alcove and stamp her as his own. The way they moved perfectly together no matter what they did seduced him unfailingly.

"Another one bites the dust," she murmured.

"What does that mean?" he asked with a flash of his glance into furious eyes that scored him with disdain.

"You can't keep your eyes off my mother. I told you she was beautiful."

He realized he'd been staring at the distraction of white hair swept in a graceful frame around aristocratic bone structure. Mrs. Holbrook's blue eyes stood out like glittering sapphires on the sateen of flawless skin as she watched them. Where Tiffany had a seductively full bottom lip, her mother's was narrow and prim, but that hint of severity lent her countenance keen intelligence. She was the height of elegance when she smiled and scrupulously well-mannered. She had thanked him warmly for inviting them even as her gaze consigned him to hell.

"She's not the one giving me a hard-on, *draga*. She's keeping it from becoming obvious. I'm in danger of catching pneumonia from her glare. I take it she doesn't approve of our affair?"

"I thought we were engaged." Limpid eyes, as capable of beaming frost as her mother's, glared up at him.

He involuntarily tightened his hands on her. "Not here, Tiffany. Not now."

She snorted, lashes quivering in a flinch, but it was her only betrayal of how much his deferral stung. He silently cursed, realizing he was forcing the taffy apple upon her.

"We'll talk upstairs as soon as I can get away," he promised.

"Mom and Dad are going back to Berne with the deHavillands first thing in the morning. They want me to come, so it would probably be better if I stayed with them—"

"Like hell," he said through his teeth. She was so stiff in his arms, he thought she'd shatter if he held her too tightly, but the idea she'd leave him made everything in him clench with possessiveness.

She showed him her good cheek, the skin stretched taut across it. Her voice wavered. "You were so appalled at the idea that Dad would use my accident for his own gain, but the minute you saw an advantage to your own precious country, you—"

"Enough," he seared quietly through gritted teeth. "Marriage is not something I take lightly. Even thinking of marrying you is the breaking of a vow I made to myself and a dead woman. You have no idea what it costs me."

With a little gasp, she stopped moving, forcing him to

halt his own feet. He looked down at her, as appalled by what he'd revealed as she seemed to be.

"Luiza," she stated under her breath, lips white.

He flinched. Hearing her say his beloved's name was a shock.

"Da," he agreed, nudging her back into dancing, feeling cold.

The air of thick tension surrounding them threatened to suffocate Tiffany, but she was a trained pony. The dance continued and her company smile stayed in place while all she could think about was the snippets of information he'd revealed about his tattoo, his lady liberty, his marriage to his *country.*

The rest of their waltz passed in a blur of tuxedos and jewel-colored gowns, glittering chandeliers and tinkling laughter. When he returned her to their table, her parents rose with their friends, ready to take their leave.

"Goodbye, Ryz—" she began.

"Don't even think it," he overrode her tightly.

"I have a headache," she lied flatly. "I'd like to leave."

"Then we will," he said with equal shortness. "Let me inform my team while you say good-night to your parents."

Seconds later he cut her from the herd and whisked her up to their suite.

"You're not making friends behaving like this, you know," she whirled to state as he closed the door behind them. "My father won't have your back in any arena if you continue to kidnap his daughter."

"I know your father hates my guts, but you will not let him separate us. If you're angry with me, then you stand here and tell me so," he railed with surprising vehemence, yanking off his tuxedo jacket to throw it aside. "Do not put yourself out of my reach. That is the one thing I will not tolerate."

Deep emotion swirled from his words at hurricane force, buffeting her. She unconsciously braced her footing, absorbing his statement with a wobble of her heart in her chest that left all the hair standing up on her body. It wasn't fear exactly. More of a visceral response to his revelation of intense feeling. Her body was warning her not to take his outburst lightly. He was startlingly raw right now, and anything but taking great care with how she reacted would be stupid and possibly hurtful to both of them.

She could hurt him.

A reflexive shake of her head tried to deny the thought. His face was lined with grief, emotions he felt for someone else, but a glint of something else in the stark, defensive gaze stilled her. A strange calm settled in her mind despite the racking pain of being used still gripping her.

The suspicion he feared being wounded by her was so stunning, she could only stand there hugging herself, not knowing what to say.

She had to say or do something. His hurting destroyed her. It was particularly intolerable because it had its roots in his love for another woman, but as much as she wanted to sublimate that knowledge, a masochistic part of her had to know the details. It was like assessing an injury so she'd know how to treat it.

"Was…" She cleared her throat. "Will you tell me about her?"

He turned away to the wet bar. Glass clinked as he poured a drink, drained it, then refilled his glass and poured one for her. When he brought hers across to her, his face was schooled into something remote while his eyes blazed with suppressed, but explosive emotion.

"Were you married?" she asked in a strained whisper. *Did you love her?* She couldn't bring herself to ask it.

"Engaged. She wanted to focus on winning the war, not planning a wedding. She was a protestor, an idealist, but very passionate and smart. I met her when I came back for my mother's funeral. I was beside myself, ready to seek retribution, but Luiza helped me develop a vision that people would rally behind. She was the velvet glove to my iron fist."

"You said she was your country's icon. That everyone revered her. What happened?"

He brought his glass to his lips, took a generous swallow then hissed, "She was captured and would have been used against me. She took herself out of the equation."

Appalled horror had her sucking in a pained breath, one she held inside her with a slap of her hand across her mouth. *Once you have paid the price of a loved one, you do not stop until the job is done.*

She stared at Ryzard over her hand, brutally aware there were no words to compensate for what he'd just told her. She didn't need the details. The horrifying end was enough. The truly shocking part was that he wasn't twisted into bitterness and revenge by loss.

He was stricken with guilt and anguish, however. It showed in the lines that appeared on his face before he turned away again.

"I'm so sorry," she breathed, reaching toward him.

He shrugged off her touch. "There's nothing that can be done. We both know that death is final. Nothing in the past can be reversed."

"No," she agreed, staring at her mottled arm folded across her good one. "You can only learn to live with the consequences. And preserve their memory," she added, feeling as though her chest was scraped hollow like a jack-o'-lantern. "That's what you want to do, isn't it? Achieve what she sacrificed herself for? That's why you'll do anything to bring peace to Bregnovia. You're doing it for her."

"I'm not the only one who lost people, Tiffany. I want it for all of us."

She swallowed, understanding, empathizing, yet feeling very isolated. Her heart ached for him, but for herself, too, because she instinctively wanted to help him. Maybe he was using her, but as he kept demonstrating, his goal was noble. And she loved him too much to refuse him outright when his need and grief were very real.

She loved him.

Staring at the red flecks in the carpet between their feet, she absorbed the bittersweet ache that pulsed through her arteries and settled in her soul. Part of her stood back and mocked herself for having such strong feelings after a mere week and a half of knowing this man. Surely her mother was right and this was a type of Pygmalion infatuation. God knows it was a sexual one.

But when she compared it with what she'd felt for Paulie—exasperated affection and the security of friendship— she knew this was the deeper, more dangerous shade of love. The mature kind that was as threatening as it was fulfilling because it made her needs less important than his. It gave him the power to cripple her with nothing more than his eternal love for another woman.

"I told myself if I couldn't marry Luiza, I wouldn't marry at all." He drained his drink and set it aside, turning to push his hands in his pockets. "Then I met you."

And realized how useful she could be.

"I understand." She fought to keep her brow from pulling.

"Do you? Because I don't. It wasn't a vow of celibacy. I'm not dead. I gave myself permission to have affairs. That ought to be enough. With every other woman it has been."

A strand of something poignant thrummed near her heart. She tried to quell it for the sake of her sanity, trying not to read anything into what he was saying. In a lot of ways what he'd offered her was more than she'd imagined she'd ever find, so she shouldn't be yearning so badly for more.

"I realize you have to look out for your country's best interest, Ryzard. You've been very kind and supportive of me—"

"Oh, shut *up,* Tiffany. Looking out for my country's best interest is how I've been rationalizing your presence in the presidential bed, but even that doesn't work. Do you think I can use you in good conscience after Luiza *died* as a pawn? *Hell, no.* But allowing you to push her out of my heart would be an even greater betrayal."

She could see the tortured struggle in him. He might never love her, not when to do so would mean accepting the debilitating guilt that accompanied it. Who could accept such a deep schism to their soul?

As she absorbed that reality, her breath burned in her lungs like dry smoke.

"But each time you talk of leaving for America, I start thinking about a length of chain about this long." He showed her a space between his hands of two or three feet. "With a cuff here and here." He pointed from his smartwatch to her wrist.

She couldn't help a small smile.

"For such a sophisticated, educated man, you're incredibly uncivilized. You know that, right?" She rubbed the goose bumps off her arms, trying to hide how primitive she was at her core, responding to his caveman talk like some kind of kinky submissive.

"Your parents have every right to be suspicious of me," he allowed drily. "But it's important to me that you know my intentions toward you are not dishonorable."

That's exactly what she had feared after overhearing her mother. It had gutted her. Meeting his gaze was really hard with that specter still haunting her.

"I don't expect you to love me, Ryzard." The words fractured her soul. "But I have to insist on honesty. If you're really just with me because of my father, please say so and I'll—"

"I can't believe I'm going to say this," he cut in impatiently, "but sometimes I wish to hell you'd had other lovers so you would appreciate what we have. *I* do."

"Oh, well, let me just accommodate that right now."

He grabbed her before she'd taken two steps toward the door.

"Gorilla! Brute! You're hurting me," she accused as she found herself bouncing over his shoulder toward the bedroom.

"Honesty, Tiffany," he reminded in a scolding tone. "You just demanded it, and so do I. Lie to me and so help me, I'll spank you. That is not a bluff." He flopped her onto the bed and retreated to slam the bedroom door.

"You scare me," she cried, sitting up. "Not like scared you'll hurt me," she protested with an outstretched hand, trying to forestall the outrage climbing in his expression. "The way you make me feel. I'm terrified you'll stop wanting me. You saw what I was like before you came along. I don't want to be that person again. I don't know how to handle how important you are to me, or how horrible I'll feel when this ends."

The tense line of his shoulders eased. "I can't imagine that happening."

"But I don't know how honorable *my* intentions are. I told you how I feel about living in the public eye. If it's just an affair…"

She trailed off, distracted as he joined her, his big body crowding and overwhelming, sending her onto her back under him with the force of his personality, barely even touching her. She melted in supplication, slave to his authority and the tenderness in his eyes.

"This is more than an affair," he insisted.

That didn't allay any of her misgivings, but she wasn't sure what she wanted him to say. She rather wished she had more experience with relationships herself, but from everything she'd observed, she doubted anyone was truly confident with whatever sorts of relationships they had. It came down to trust, and as much as she wanted to believe in Ryzard, she didn't have much faith in herself.

She touched the pad of her fingertip to his lips, tracing the masculine shape that so entranced her.

"Where do we go from here?" she asked, meaning emotionally, but he took her literally.

"I have quite a few appearances. I would like you to accompany me. Will you?"

Her heart stalled, but refusing meant bringing The End forward to now, and she could already see it would be horribly painful. She wasn't ready for that, so she said the only thing she could.

"Of course."

CHAPTER TEN

DESPITE TIFFANY'S AGREEMENT, despite the unflagging passion between them, she grew less like the cheeky woman he'd come to know and more like the chilly mother he'd met in Zurich.

Of course he was pressing her inexorably into her mother's role. He couldn't help it. The opportunity was too ripe, the timing at hand, and she was damned good at it. She stepped forward with a gracious remark when needed and backed off the rest of the time. No matter what came up or when, she accepted the pull of his attention with equanimity. If she didn't like it, no one could tell, not even him. When he asked, she assured him everything was "Fine."

A sure sign that it wasn't.

But neither of their schedules had room for the type of downtime that had brought them together in the first place. She'd been up for several hours two nights in a row trying to resolve a problem with her firm. Now he'd dragged her to Budapest for an Eastern European conference. A black-tie reception opened the event, and her best makeup couldn't hide the exhaustion around her eyes.

Still she smiled, always ignoring startled reactions to her scars or simply moving past an awkward moment with a calm "Car crash." Then she would distract with a compliment or question, her warm manner disguising the fact she maintained a discreet bubble of distance.

So why was she currently clasping two hands over a stranger's? Her expression was uncharacteristically revealing, not the cool mask she usually wore at these events. The man was older than Ryzard, somewhere in his fifties, but not someone he recognized. Tiffany was sharing deep eye contact with him, and her profile was somber.

He excused himself and crossed over to them, possessive male hackles rising to attention, especially when they both stiffened at his approach and lowered their gazes.

"Ryzard, this is Stanley Griffin, minister of international trade in Canada and my late husband's cousin. Well, cousin to my mother-in-law, Maude."

Despite the legitimate reason for familiarity, he used the introduction to extricate Stanley's hand from Tiffany's grasp.

They briefly chatted about his country's mission to, "Do what we did with the EU here in Eastern Europe." Ryzard expressed his desire to participate, but first he needed recognition so if that message could be conveyed to Canada's prime minister…?

Stanley left with a promise to do so, but made a point to ask Tiffany, "Please stay in touch." Once again, Tiffany had proved her worth to him politically, but her coziness with the man rankled Ryzard for the rest of the evening.

"You seemed very familiar with that Canadian," he said later when they were undressing in the hotel suite. He was tired of being away and wished they were home.

Home. Did she regard his country the way he did? She wasn't happy here in Hungary, despite her expressed desire to see the country and her interest in this city's history. He couldn't be sure she'd been happy in any of the places they'd been recently.

"He was at my wedding. I didn't remember him, to be honest, but he certainly remembered me. He started to tell me how much he loved it when Paulie had spent summers with their family, when the boys were young, and I thought we were both going to—" She clamped her lips together, then pressed a knuckle to her mouth, turning away.

Stricken by her edging toward breakdown, he moved to grasp her shoulders in bracing hands. "Shh. Don't talk about him."

She reacted with a violent twist away from his grip and glared up at him with eyes full of tears and betrayal. "Oh, that's rich. Why can't I talk about my husband? Luiza is right *there* every time we're naked." She poked two fingers into his chest.

Her hostility took him aback, as did the underlying challenge. He bristled, but managed to keep himself from pointing out her scars were an equally indelible reminder that she had had a life before he entered it.

"I didn't say you couldn't talk about him, but it's obviously upsetting you so you should stop," he managed, barely hanging on to a civil tone.

Her jagged laugh abraded his nerves, plucking his aggression responses to even higher alert. "Yeah, well, if that's the criteria, there's a lot of things I should stop doing."

Don't ask, he told himself, but the elephant in the room had grown large enough to put pressure on both of them. A few weeks ago she hadn't had the courage to go to the grocery store in her hometown. Today she was being shoved into a supporting role on the world stage. If she didn't want to do it, she ought to have said so by now, but apparently that was up to him.

"You're not happy in the spotlight. I understand that." He removed his belt and flung it away, angry with himself for turning a blind eye to what was obviously damaging their relationship, but he couldn't undo who he was any more than he was willing to have Luiza's name erased from his chest.

"Stanley said Paulie's mother was always jealous of my

mom because she looked like she had it all, but at least Maude had privacy. All I could think is, *What am I doing? Why am I here?*" She lifted helpless hands.

"Tiffany, you're good at this," he began.

"I'm good at sex. Should I do that with every man who asks?" she snarled back.

He recoiled, shocked by her vehemence and scored by a remark that made it sound as if she only tolerated sleeping with him. "As I said—" The words ground from between his clenched teeth. "You shouldn't do anything that fails to give you some level of enjoyment."

Her fierce expression flickered toward remorse, before she collapsed in a chair, elbows on her knees, head in hands, shoulders heavy with defeat. "I'm sorry. I know better than to have this fight. It accomplishes nothing because at the end of the day, you still need me beside you."

"I *want* you beside me, Tiffany. I don't need you. If you're feeling used then you know my feelings on that. I'll achieve my two-thirds votes with or without you."

She lifted her head out of her hands to stare at him, face like a mask, half of it tortoiseshell reds, the other side white. Slowly her flat gaze moved to the floor while her hands twisted together. She forced herself to sit upright, but her shoulders remained bowed.

"That certainly tells me where I stand."

The ice maiden was back, causing cold fire to lick behind his heart, leaving streaks of dead, black tissue.

"I'm saying you don't have to participate if you don't want to. We still be together. It doesn't have to change anything," he said rather desperately, sensing things slipping away without any chance to control it.

"It changes everything, Ryzard! What am I going to do? Sit in your presidential castle waiting for you to come home? *There's* a departure from turning into my mother," she said with a caustic laugh. "What else could I do? Follow you around but never be seen? That would be living as a recluse again. If you—" She bent her head to stare at her pale knuckles, but he saw the pull in her brow of deep struggle. "If we loved each other, it would be different."

He couldn't help his stark inhale of aversion. Marriage he might rationalize. Pulling his heart from the grave where he'd buried it next to Luiza was impossible. There, at least, it was safe from another blow of great loss.

Silence coated the room in a thick fog for a long minute. Tiffany was the first to move, swiping at her cheek before speaking haltingly.

"I thought my life was over, that I'd never be able to have a husband and family. I even reconciled myself to it and figured out how to fill my life with other things. I could live unmarried and childless with you, Ryzard. But you're the one who made me believe I shouldn't sell myself short. If someone could love me, if I have a soul mate out there, I shouldn't settle for anything less than finding him."

He clenched his hands into fists, trying to withstand a pain so great it threatened to rend him apart. She *did* deserve to be loved. He couldn't keep her here to serve his passion while he withheld parts of himself. It would wear on her self-esteem. If he wasn't capable of giving her all of himself, he had to let her go.

But the agony was so great he wanted to scream.

The weariness and misery in her eyes when she lifted them to meet his gaze was more than he could bear though.

"It's time for me to go home," she said gently.

He nodded once, jerkily, incapable of any other response. His throat was blocked by a thick knot of anguish, the rest of him caved in on itself so his skin felt like a thin shell, ready to crack and turn to powder.

"I'll go make the arrangements," her voice thinned over the last word as she stood and rushed from the room.

She didn't return.

When he couldn't stand it any longer, he went looking for her and came up against a locked door. He could hear her sobbing inside the bedroom, but he didn't knock. He silently railed at her for shutting him out, but the truth was, he was close to tears himself. Drowning himself in a bottle of vodka looked like a really good idea.

Taking one to his room, he sat on the bed then left it untouched on the nightstand as he stayed awake through the long, dark night, willing Tiffany to come to him.

CHAPTER ELEVEN

BARBARA HOLBROOK WANTED to know exactly what had happened.

"Mom," Tiffany protested, feeling cornered in her room, jet-lagged and wondering how she still had a doll propped on the pillows of her made bed. It was an antique, granted, but seriously. "I'm about ten years too late for having my heart broken by my first crush. That's all it was."

That's what she kept telling herself anyway. She sure as heck didn't want to deconstruct everything that had happened with Ryzard. It was too painful.

But she missed him. Sleeping alone sucked and stalking him on the web only made her heart ache. Or laugh aloud.

Mrs. Davis and I remain on excellent terms. Print something negative about her at your own peril, she read over breakfast one Saturday morning and got herself goggled at by her entire family for her outburst.

"What," she hedged, amusement fading. "It's funny," she insisted after reading it to them. She wanted to kiss his austere image, feeling as though he was flirting with her from far, far away. He'd been so contained that last night, so willing to let her go without a fight. That had made her feel insignificant, but reading that they remained "on excellent terms" bolstered her.

"You'll be seeing him again, then?" her father asked, sipping his coffee.

"Why? Does sleeping with him help your approval rating?"

"Tiffany," her mother gasped.

Christian sent her a hard look. "Come on, Tiff."

Setting her cup into its saucer like a gavel announcing a judge's decision, Tiffany said, "That was out of line. I apologize. But I'm tired of being a bug under a microscope. It's time I went into the office."

"You've been in there every day since you came home," her mother said with confusion.

"Not my office here, Mom. The real office. In the city."

"What? When?" Chris asked swiftly. "I can't drive you for a week at least. I told you I'm working from here until I get that design done, so I'm not interrupted."

"And I have to be in Washington," her father said with apology.

"I have an appointment in New York at the end of the month, darling," her mother offered. "You can come in for the day with me, but are you sure you're ready?"

She wished she'd had her tablet set to record. Ryzard would shake his head at this display and probably claim this coddling was the reason she was such a spoiled brat. She suspected he'd also remind her how lucky she was to be so loved.

Misty emotion washed over her in a flood of gratitude for the family she had and an ache of longing for the man she didn't.

"You guys are awesome. I love you," she said, meeting each pair of eyes in turn to let her sincerity sink in. She silently thanked Ryzard as she did it, finally able to see herself as a whole, independent adult because he had treated her as one. "But it's time for me to be a grown-up. I'll drive myself to New York and stay in the company flat until I find my own place."

Her mother's gasp and near-Victorian collapse didn't

sway her. On Monday she walked through the glass doors of Davis and Holbrook, palms clammy and half her face hidden behind giant sunglasses. By Thursday the worst of the buzzing and staring was behind her. Friday morning she was interrupted by a delivery of flowers.

"Wow," she couldn't help saying, stunned by the bouquet arranged to look like a culmination of fireworks. Her heart began to gallop in her chest. "Who is that from?"

"I couldn't say, ma'am." The uniformed man tapped the subtle *Q Virtus* crest on his shirt pocket. "I work for their concierge service. All I get is a pickup and delivery address."

"Oh, um, would it be from *Q Virtus* itself, then?" That was disappointing. And made the significance of portraying fireworks a little creepy.

"There's usually a 'compliments of Zeus' card if it is. Without one, I'd guess it's from one of their members, but I really couldn't say. I'm not privy to much that goes on there. *You* could be a member for all I know," he added with a shrug.

"I imagine there are members who don't know they belong," she murmured ironically, thanking him with a generous tip, then burying her face in the perfume of the bouquet. She wanted to gather the fragrant leaves and butter-soft petals into herself, trying to feel closer to Ryzard.

How could he be this sweet, this pleased by her stepping out of her comfort zone and taking control of her life, and not love her a little?

Luiza, she thought with a pang. She could never compete with a woman who had shown such a level of bravery.

Taking a page from Ryzard's book, she had *Q Virtus* arrange a nice lunch when her mother came to visit at the end of the month. Being scrupulously efficient, they located it in a penthouse that fit exactly what Tiffany was looking for as a new home. The decor was a bit too colorless for her taste. It needed a stained glass umbrella to jazz it up, but the floor plan and views were astonishing.

Her mother pronounced it excellent for entertaining, which only made Tiffany think of holding court with Ryzard and miss him all over again.

She sat across from her mother in tall wingbacks at a circle of white marble facing a floor-to-ceiling view of Central Park, sipping from crystal water goblets with brushed gold trim, thinking she'd rather be staring at that heart-wrenching statue if it put her back in his proximity.

"This isn't at all how I imagined things turning out for you," her mother murmured.

She seemed surprised that the words had escaped her and glanced toward the kitchen, where the noise and staff were well contained beyond a small service pantry.

Tiffany set down her glass and linked her fingers together, subtly bracing for reaction as she admitted, "I think it might have come to this eventually. I didn't love Paulie. Not in a way that would have kept us together forever."

"I know," Barbara sighed.

"You did?"

Her mother's perfectly coiffed head tilted in acknowledgement. "Not until you started up with that Bregnovian fellow, but once I saw the lengths you were willing to go for him, I realized you and Paulie never stood a chance. I should have seen it from the outset, but it would have been so convenient, Tiffany."

She sputtered a laugh at that. "Yeah, well, the situation with Ryzard was more convenience on his part. You were right about that much." Deep angst threatened to rise up and squeeze her in its clawed grip.

"Is that true? He seemed so protective of you. Still does."

"I think that's his nature," Tiffany said shakily, finding it really hard to hold on to her control. "He was so supportive, made me feel so good about myself, but when it came down to it he said he didn't need me or my connections. He—" Her voice broke, but she had to say it aloud so she could get over it and move on. "He doesn't love me."

"But you love him."

Through blurred eyes, Tiffany saw her mother's hand cover her own. The gesture was bittersweet and made her think of all the times her mother had held her hand through her recovery. Through her whole life. She was the wrong person to be mad at.

"I shouldn't have pushed you away so much lately," she husked.

"Shush. Your brother did it when he was eleven. I've been lucky enough to keep you close this long. I'm just glad I can be here for you when you need me."

"Are you going to tell me there's plenty more fish in the sea?"

"I'd like to, but there are so few worth reeling in," her mother bemoaned, making Tiffany chortle past her tears. "It's so good to see you smiling again," her mother added with her own misty smile.

She didn't know how often Tiffany cried. How she combed for news and photos of Ryzard, how she quietly kept tally of the countries recognizing him. She was doing exactly that one afternoon before going into a meeting, getting her fix to get her through one more day without him, when she came across a horrifying update.

Coal Mine Explosion in Northern Bregnovia, Dozens Unaccounted For, one hour ago.

Leaping to her feet, she shouted for her assistant.

Even though sabotage was not suspected, it was war conditions all over again. Ryzard could hardly bear it, but quick response on the recovery effort was critical. There was no time to ask the fates why his country should suffer this way. No way to reassure his people that they could live without fear. There were only feet on the ground, hands digging into the rubble, people trying to save people into the night.

Dark was receding, exhaustion setting in and spirits low when a throaty drone began climbing on the air. The latest batch of survivors, many badly burned, had just left on what aircraft he'd been able to muster on short notice. They hadn't had time to drop and be back so soon. That didn't bode well.

Squinting into the silver horizon, he saw what looked like an invasion, and his heart stopped. Then the hospital crosses on the underbellies of three of the helicopters became visible and he relaxed. Someone asked if the Red Cross was finally here. He had no idea. His phone was charging in the one small shack that had a power generator for electricity.

Jerking his chin at someone to greet and direct them, he threw himself back into the work at hand.

Sixteen hours later, he was knee-deep in rubble, numb and almost asleep on his feet, losing the light, when his eye—and half-dead libido—was caught unexpectedly by a pair of skintight jeans tucked into knee-high black boots. A blond ponytail swung against the back of a black leather jacket as the woman nodded at whomever she was speaking to.

He was seeing things. He clambered across to her, swaying on his feet as he pulled her around by a rather despondent grip on her arm, distantly surprised to catch at a solid person and still not believing his eyes, even when he saw the familiar patch of color on the side of her face.

"You're real," he said dumbly.

She smiled tenderly and set a hand against his cheek. Her touch was surprisingly warm, making him aware how cold he was. How utterly empty and frozen he'd been for weeks.

"All I could think was that no country would be equipped for this many burn injuries. We have a triage set up. I hope you don't mind, but I'm sending the victims with their families to whoever can take them."

He couldn't speak, could only string clumsy arms around her and drag her into him. Closing his eyes, he drank in the sweet, familiar scent of her hair.

Tiffany ran soothing hands over him, feeling the chill on his skin beneath his shirt, trying to ease the shudders rippling through his muscles. He was heavy, leaning into her, beyond exhausted.

"Come with me," she urged, dragging him stumbling across the trampled yard to the tent where cots and coffee were on hand for the rescuers.

His arm was deadweight across her shoulders. When he sat, he pulled her into his lap.

"You need to sleep," she insisted as she tried to extricate herself.

He said something in Bregnovian, voice jagged and broken. He snugged her closer, his hold unbreakable.

Not that she really wanted to get away. It felt so good to be near him. He was grimy and sweaty, but he was Ryzard. She blinked damp eyes where he was keeping her face trapped against his chest, surrounded in his personal scent.

"You need to lie down, Ryzard. You're not even speaking English."

He brought her with him so the cot groaned beneath them. When she tried to rise, he threw a pinning leg across her and tangled his fingers in her hair. "Don't leave," he murmured and the lights went out. He became a lead blanket upon her.

Since she was jet-lagged and had been on her feet for hours, she relaxed and dozed until activity around them woke her. Then she managed to climb free of his tentacle-like hold and carry on with the rescue effort. The trapped miners had been reached and the final victims would need transport.

* * *

Ryzard woke thinking he'd dreamed her, but the jacket draped across his chest told him he wasn't crazy. She was here, somewhere.

Coffee in one hand, jacket in his other, he went in search and found her trying to comfort an anxious wife as an injured miner was packaged into a helicopter. The woman clutched a baby and had a redheaded boy by the hand, and Tiffany held a matching toddler on her hip.

"Oh, Ryzard," she said when he draped her jacket over her shoulders, "Please tell her I'm sure her husband will live. The burns are bad, but they didn't find internal injuries. I've lost my translator and she's so upset."

Together they reassured the woman and made arrangements for her to catch up with her husband at the burn unit in Paris.

Calm settled as everyone was accounted for. There was a longer journey ahead to bring the mine back into operation, but the immediate crisis was over. Tiffany stifled a yawn as she thanked people and gave them final directions for breaking down the field hospital they'd erected.

"I can't thank you enough for this," Ryzard said.

"When you're part of a club, you pitch in to help your fellow members when they need it, right?"

She was being her cheeky self, but he wasn't in a frame of mind to take this gesture so lightheartedly.

"I'm being sincere, Tiffany. I hope your motives were not that superficial."

She sobered. "I told you last night that this struck close to home for me. But I don't suppose you remember, being pretty much sleepwalking at the time."

Was it only empathy for fellow burn victims that had brought her here? He flinched, wondering where he got off imagining she could have deeper feelings for him when he'd pushed her from his life the way he had.

"Hey, Tiff," some flyboy called across. "You catching a lift in my bird or…?"

"Oh, um—"

Ryzard cut her off before she could answer. "You'll come to Gizela with me."

"Will I," she said in the tone she used when she thought he was being arrogant, but he only cared that she acquiesced. He did *not* care for the way she hugged the pilot and kissed his cheek, thanking him for his help.

Ryzard lifted his brows in query when she turned from her goodbye.

"He grew up with Paulie and my brother. I've known him forever," she defended. "We needed pilots so I called him."

It was petty and ungrateful to think, we didn't need them *that* badly, but he was still short on sleep and deeply deprived of her. His willingness to share her, especially when he was so uncertain how long he'd have her, was nil.

His own transport arrived. They fell asleep against each other in the back of the 4x4 for the jostling four-hour drive back to Gizela.

The palace looked better than ever, Tiffany noted when she woke in front of it. Its exterior was no longer pockmarked by bullet holes and the broken stones were gone, giving the grounds a sense of openness and welcome. Inside, she went straight up the stairs next to Ryzard, both anxious for a shower. They parted at the top and she went to her room, where, he had assured her, everything she'd left was still there.

She wasn't sure what it meant. A dozen times she'd thought about asking for the items to be shipped, but she'd been afraid that contacting him would be the first step toward falling back down the rabbit hole into his world. Or it would have been final closure, something she hadn't been ready for. Had he felt the same? Because he could have had the things shipped to her at any time.

The not knowing hung like a veil over the situation, making her wonder if she was being silly and desperate when she dressed for his flag salutation, or respectful and supportive. He wouldn't have brought her here if he didn't want her here, she told herself, but she faltered when they met at the top of the stairs.

He wore his white shirt, black suit and presidential sash. His jaw was freshly shaved and sharply defined by tension as he took in her houndstooth skirt and matching wool jacket. "You don't have to," he said for the second time.

She almost took him at his word, almost let herself believe that he only wanted her, didn't need her, but his eyes gave him away. They weren't flat green. They burned gold. As if he was taking in treasure. As if she said she wasn't ready, he would wait until she was.

"I want to," she assured him, wondering if she was being an imaginative fool. Why would she want to do this? Pride of place, she guessed. It made her feel good to be with him no matter what he was doing. She admired him as a man and took great joy in watching him rise to his position.

Outside, it was blustery and tasting of an early-fall storm with spits of rain in the gusting wind. Leaves chased across grass and their clothes rippled as they walked to the pole. The flag snapped its green and blue stripes as he made his pledge and saluted it.

A burst of applause made them both turn to the crowd gathered at the gate. It was a deeper gathering than Tiffany had seen any other time. Hundreds maybe. A fresh rush of pride welled in her.

"Your predecessor wouldn't have cut up his hands freeing trapped miners," she said, picking up his scabbed hand. It was so roughened and abused, she instinctively lifted it to her lips.

The cheering swelled, making her pull back from touching him. "Sorry. That was dumb."

"No, they liked it. They're here for you as much as me. They know what you did for us." He faced the crowd and indicated her with a sweep of his hand and a bow of his head.

His people reacted with incendiary passion, waving flags and holding up children.

"They're thanking you, Tiffany." He lifted her hand to his own lips, and another roar went up.

They stood there a long time, hands linked, waving at the crowd. No one walked away. They waited for her and Ryzard to go in first.

"Are you crying?" he asked as they entered the big drawing room. It was such a stunning room with its gorgeous nineteenth-century furniture and view overlooking the sea, but she still wasn't comfortable in it.

Averting her gaze from Luiza's portrait, she swiped at her cheeks. "That was very moving. I didn't expect it. I had the impression they thought of me as an interloper." Now she couldn't help straying a glance at Luiza, as if the woman might be eavesdropping.

For a long moment he didn't say anything, only looked at the portrait with the same tortured expression she'd seen on him before, when his feelings for Luiza were too close to the surface.

She looked away, respecting his need for time to pull himself together, but taking a hit of despair over it, too.

"It's my fault you felt that way," he said in a low, grave voice. "But please try to understand what she meant to me. Luiza made me see that Bregnovia is my home. That if I fought for it and made it ours, *mine*—" he set his fist over the place where her name was inked forever "—I would always belong here. That was deeply meaningful after so many years of being rootless and displaced."

She nodded, unable to speak because she did understand and felt for him.

"I needed her love after losing my parents. I would have shut down otherwise. Become an instrument of war."

Instead of a leader who had retained his humanity. It was one of the qualities she admired most in him, so she could hardly begrudge the woman who'd kept his heart intact through the horrors of battle and loss.

"When I lost her, I couldn't let myself become embittered and filled with hatred. It would have gone against everything she helped me become, but I couldn't face another loss like it. The vulnerability of loving again, knowing the emotional pain of grief if something were to happen... It terrifies me, Tiffany."

He said it so plainly, never faltering even when he was exposing his deepest fear.

She wanted to look to the ceiling to contain the tears gathering to sting her eyes. It killed her to hear that he couldn't give up his heart, but she couldn't look away from him.

"It's okay. I admire her, too," she managed. Her voice scraped her throat with emotion, but she was being sincere. "I wish I'd met her. She had amazing willpower. I wouldn't have had the guts to do what she did."

"Guts." The harsh sound he made was halfway between a laugh and a choke of deep anguish. "Luiza had ideals. Now she is our martyr and a symbol of our sacrifice and loss. I would do her a disservice to forget or dismiss that, but it doesn't make you an interloper for living where she died, Tiffany. She had a vision. When I look at you, I see reality. Our reality. Scarred by tragedy, but so beautiful. So strong and determined to carry on."

His tender look of regard had its usual effect of striking like an unexpected punch into her solar plexus, making her breath rush out. She had to cover her lips to still them from trembling.

"I don't like comparing you. It's disrespectful to both of you, but you're right. You and Luiza are very different. You wouldn't have killed yourself. Given the same situation, you would fight with everything in you to stay alive until I came for you, no matter what happened. That's who you are. Your courage astounds me."

He ran his hand down his face only to reveal an expression of profound regret.

"When I sent you away, all I could think was that I didn't want to risk the pain of loss again. And did you crawl back in your cave even though I'd hurt you? No. You went on with your life without me, and I was so hurt and so proud at the same time."

She lowered her head, touched beyond measure, and saw a teardrop land on the hardwood. She swiped at her numb cheek, finding it wet. "Thank you for the flowers."

"The flowers were an apology. You made me feel like a coward, refusing to embrace love when it's as precious as life. I wanted to come to you and to hell with your Customs and Immigration, but I had to finish my obligation to Luiza first. I've done that. Official announcements will be made later in the week. I have the votes I need."

"Oh, Ryzard, that's wonderful!" She was elated for him, but still reeling from his mention of embracing love. Did that mean…? She searched his inscrutable expression.

"After the last few days, this country needs good news." He sighed and rocked back on his heels, regarding her. "It also means the worst is over for a time when it comes to state functions. I won't run in the next election. Could you live with two more years of being in the public eye, knowing it would be temporary?"

"What?" Her nails cut into her palms as she tried to stay grounded, not leaping too high on what he was saying. Not reading too deep. Definitely not wanting to hold him back in any way. "Ryzard, you *are* Bregnovia. It's barely on its feet. You can't hand it over to someone else so soon. I couldn't live with myself if all this stability you've fought for crumbled."

"I don't want to wait that long to marry you, *draga*. I ache every night and barely get through my days. I need you."

"You do?" Her voice hitched and stayed awfully small, but the world around her seemed to expand in one pulse beat, stealing the oxygen and filling the air with sparks. "You really want to marry me? *Me?*"

"*You.* Not the daughter of the next American president, not Davis and Holbrook, not the woman who charms heads of state without even trying. You."

"Because you love me?" she hazarded, curling her toes and pulling her elbows in, bracing for the worst.

"Because we love each other."

His tender gaze held hers, gently demanding she give up her heart to him. She did, easily.

"If I hadn't been trained from birth to pretend everything was fine no matter how miserable I was, I couldn't have got through these last weeks. I love you so much, Ryzard, and I hated myself for not letting my love be enough to keep us together."

"I shouldn't have made you feel like it was all up to you," he said, coming across to draw her into him. With his lips pressed to her forehead, he added, "I will never hold back from you again. I thought I was being noble, letting you find the man who would love you like no other could, but that man is me. I love you with every breath in me, Tiffany. A different man loved Luiza. This one is yours."

She relaxed her forehead against his nuzzling lips, touched to her soul. Fulfilled. Hopeful. *Happy.*

He traced a soft kiss along the raised line of her scar,

following it down to the corner of her eye and across her cheek until he was almost at her mouth.

"We should take this upstairs," she said against his lips. "I have a feeling it won't stay PG rated for long."

He quirked a rueful grin and led her upstairs. In his bedroom, he took a moment to lift the snapshot from his bedside table and walk it into his sitting room.

When he returned he found her seated on the bed, hands tucked in her lap.

"We have to talk about one more thing before we go any further," she said.

"What's that?" he queried.

"Children."

"At least two. I want them to have each other if something happens to us," he affirmed.

"I was going to say six, but okay. Coward."

"Ambitious," he remarked in a drawl. "I can keep up if you can." His smile was a slow dawn of masculine heat that twitched with amusement. "I've missed you, Tiffany. You make me laugh."

She threw herself into his arms.

EPILOGUE

THE MILKY WAY stretched from one edge of the horizon to the other, diffusing into more stars against Zanzibar's indigo sky than Tiffany had ever seen in her life. If Ryzard hadn't kept her pressed firmly against his side as he steered them down the jetty toward the island bar, she likely would have stumbled into the lagoon.

"What the hell are you up to?"

"I know, I'm sorry, but I've never seen anything like—wait, what?" She realized Ryzard had been talking to a man in a mask who'd just passed them on the jetty. She glanced back the way they'd come to see the member break off his lip-lock with a *petite q* and hurry her toward the interior of the club.

"Who was that?"

"A friend. One who knows better than to play with Zeus's toys." He dragged his puzzled gaze to her expectant one. With a low sigh, he bent to whisper, "His name is Nic." Straightening, he added, "Don't ask me to say more than that. Even though you're my wife, I still have an obligation to respect other members' privacy."

She grinned, pleased more by her title of "wife" than anything else.

The DJ's electronica pulsed louder as they finished their walk into the open-air bar. *Q Virtus* members and *petite q's* danced and jumped to the beat, making the wooden floor bounce.

Tiffany refused a drink offered by a passing *petite q,* but Ryzard drew her to a side bar. "Iced coconut. Nonalcoholic," he said.

Her condition wasn't official, especially since they'd been married only a day, but they'd stopped using protection weeks ago. She was pretty sure, and they were both so quietly, ferociously happy it was criminal.

The server tilted his array of cones for her to peruse. They were stunning, not merely shaved and frozen coconut with a splash of color, but intricately decorated works of art in more shades, flavors and hues than the stars above them.

Tiffany almost picked the one that looked like a bouquet of sweet peas, but maybe the mandala was prettier. The paisley?

"It just hit me," Ryzard said in a tone of discovery. "It was never about the taffy apple being better optics. You couldn't decide what color candy floss you wanted."

Grinning, she admitted, "You caught me."

"I'm convinced it's the other way around, *draga,*" he retorted.

She laughed in delight, but contradicted, "I distinctly remember a kidnapping on the high seas."

"I remember fireworks," he said with a smoky look from behind his mask. "Choose something or we'll miss these ones."

Face warm with pleasure behind her own mask, she took two cones and gave him one, leaning her weight into him as he hooked his arm across her shoulders and steered her toward the rail overlooking the Indian Ocean.

"I see them every night, you know. Fireworks. 'Cause I'm spoiled."

"You are," he agreed, leaning down to bite at her cone before he offered his. "So am I."

"Mmm. We're in the right place for the privileged, aren't we?" she mused, licking clove-and-orange-flavored coconut from her lips.

He stopped and turned her so they held each other in a way that felt perfect and familiar and right. "As long as I'm with you, I'm exactly where I belong."

* * * * *

TAMING THE
NOTORIOUS
SICILIAN

MICHELLE SMART

This book is dedicated to all the staff and volunteers at the John Radcliffe Children's Hospital, with especial thanks to the team on Kamran's Ward. Without their care, compassion and sheer dedication, my beautiful nephew Luke would not be here.

This book is also dedicated to the memory of Henry, Lily and Callum. May you all be playing together with the angels.

CHAPTER ONE

Francesco Calvetti brought his MV Agusta F4 CC to a stop and placed his left foot on the road as he was foiled by yet another set of red lights. Barely 7:00 a.m. and the roads were already filling up.

What he wouldn't give to be riding with nothing but the open road before him and green fields surrounding him.

He thought of Sicily with longing. His island had none of the grey dreariness he was fast associating with London. This was supposed to be *spring*? He'd enjoyed better winters in his homeland.

He yawned widely, raising his hand to his visor out of pure habit. After all, no one could see his face with his helmet on.

He should have gotten Mario to bring him home after such a long night, but being driven by anyone irritated him, especially in a car. Francesco was a man for whom *drive* had multiple definitions.

The light changed to green. Before twisting on the throttle and accelerating smoothly, he swiped away the moisture clinging to his visor.

What a country. At the moment it was like driving through a saturated cloud.

As he approached yet another set of lights, a cyclist on a pushbike just ahead caught his attention—or, rather, the fluorescent yellow helmet she wore caught it. She reached the lights at the moment they turned amber. If that had been him, Francesco mused, he would have gone for it. She'd had plenty of time.

But no, this was clearly a law-abiding woman with a healthy dose of self-preservation. She stopped right at the line. The car in front of Francesco, a large four-wheel drive, drew level on her right side.

She had the thickest hair he'd ever seen—a shaggy mass of varying shades of blonde reaching halfway down her back.

The light turned green and off she set, sticking her left arm out and turning down the street in that direction. The car that had been beside her also turned left, forced to hang a little behind her, with Francesco joining the convoy.

The road ahead was clear. The cyclist picked up speed....

It happened so quickly that for a moment Francesco was convinced he had imagined it.

Without any indication, the four-wheel drive in front of him pulled out to overtake the cyclist, accelerating quickly, but with the spatial awareness of a cauliflower, because it clipped the cyclist's wheel, causing her to flip forward off the saddle and land head-first on the kerb.

Francesco brought his bike to an immediate stop and jumped off, clicking the stand down through muscle memory rather than conscious thought.

To his disgust, the driver of the offending car didn't stop, but carried on up the road, took a right and disappeared out of sight.

A passer-by made a tentative approach towards the victim.

'Do not move her,' Francesco barked as he pulled off

his helmet. 'She might have a broken neck. If you want to help, call for an ambulance.'

The passer-by took a step back and dug into his pocket, allowing Francesco to stand over the victim.

The woman lay on her back, half on the pavement and half on the road, her thick hair fanning in all directions. Her helmet, which had shifted forward and covered her forehead, had a crack running through it. Her bike was a crumpled heap of metal.

Dropping to his haunches, Francesco yanked off his leather gloves and placed two fingers on the fallen cyclist's neck.

Her pulse beat faint beneath his touch.

While the passer-by spoke to the emergency services, Francesco deftly removed his leather jacket and placed it over the unconscious woman. She wore smart grey trousers and an untucked black blouse covered with a waterproof khaki jacket. On one of her bare feet was a white ballet shoe. The other was missing.

His chest constricted at the thought of the missing shoe.

He wished he could tuck his jacket under her to create a barrier between her and the cold, damp concrete, but he knew it was imperative to keep her still until the paramedics arrived.

The important thing was she was breathing.

'Give me your coat,' he barked at another spectator, who was hovering like a spare part. A small crowd had gathered around them. Vultures, Francesco thought scornfully. Not one of them had stepped forward to help.

It never occurred to him that his presence was so forbidding, even first thing in the morning, that none of the crowd *dared* offer their assistance.

The spectator he'd addressed, a middle-aged man in

a long lambswool trench coat, shrugged off his coat and passed it to Francesco, who snatched it from his hands. Francesco wrapped it across the woman's legs, making sure to cover her feet.

'Five minutes,' the original passer-by said when he disconnected his call.

Francesco nodded. For the first time he felt the chill of the wind. He palmed the woman's cheek. It felt icy.

Still on his haunches, he studied her face carefully, ostensibly looking for a clue to any unseen injuries. No blood ran from her nose or mouth, which he assumed was a good thing. Her mass of blonde hair covered her ears, so he carefully lifted a section to look. No blood.

As he searched, he noticed what a pretty face she had. Not beautiful. Pretty. Her nose was straight but just a touch longer than the women of his acquaintance would put up with before resorting to surgery. She had quite rounded cheeks, too, something else that would be fixed in the endless quest for perfection. But yes, pretty.

He remembered she'd had something slung around her neck before he'd covered her chest with his jacket. Carefully, he tugged it free.

It was an identity card for one of the hospitals in the capital. Peering closer, he read her name. *Dr H Chapman. Specialist Registrar.*

This woman was a doctor? To his eyes she looked about eighteen. He'd guessed her as a student...

Her eyes opened and fixed on him.

His thoughts disappeared.

Shock rang out from her eyes—and what eyes they were, a moreish hazel ringed with black—before she closed them. When they reopened a few beats later, the shock faded to be replaced by a look of such contentment and serenity that Francesco's heart flipped over.

Her mouth opened. He leaned closer to hear what she had to say.

Her words came out as a whisper. 'So there really is a heaven.'

Hannah Chapman leaned her new bike against the stone building and gazed up at the sparkling silver awning that held one word: *Calvetti's*.

She admired the explicitness of it. This belonged to Francesco Calvetti and no one else.

Even though it was 6:00 p.m. and the club wasn't due to open for another four hours, two hefty-sized men dressed all in black stood beneath the awning, protecting the door. She took this as a good sign—the past three times she'd cycled over, the door hadn't been manned. The club had been empty.

'Excuse me,' she said, standing before them. 'Is Francesco Calvetti in?'

'He's not available.'

'But is he in?'

'He's in but he's not to be disturbed.'

Success! At last she'd managed to track him down. Francesco Calvetti travelled *a lot*. Still, tracking him down was one thing. Getting in to see him was a different matter entirely.

She tried her most winning smile.

Alas, her fake smile wasn't up to par. All it resulted in was the pair of them crossing their arms over their chests. One of them alone would have covered the door. The pair of them standing there was like having a two-man mountain as a barrier.

'I know you don't want to disturb him, but can you please tell him that Hannah Chapman is here to see him?

He'll know who I am. If he says no, then I'll leave, I promise.'

'We can't do that. We have our orders.'

She could be talking to a pair of highly trained SAS soldiers, such was the conviction with which the slightly less stocky of the duo spoke.

Hannah sighed. Oh, well, if it wasn't meant to be, then… so be it.

All the same, she was disappointed. She'd wanted to thank the man personally.

She thrust forward the enormous bunch of flowers and thank-you card. She'd cycled the best part of two miles through London traffic with them precariously balanced in her front basket. 'In that case, could you give these to him, please?'

Neither made a move to take them from her. If anything, their faces became even more suspicious.

'Please? This is the third bunch I've brought for him and I'd hate for them to go to waste. I was in an accident six weeks ago and he came to my rescue and…'

'Wait.' The one on the left cocked his head. 'What kind of accident?'

'I was knocked off my bike by a hit-and-run driver.'

They exchanged glances, then drew back to confer in a language that sounded, to her untrained ear, as if it was Italian. Or she could have imagined it, knowing Francesco Calvetti was Sicilian.

Since she'd discovered the identity of her benefactor, she knew a lot more than she should about Francesco Calvetti. Internet searches were wonderful creations. For instance, she knew he was thirty-six, unmarried but with a string of glamorous girlfriends to his name, and that he owned six nightclubs and four casinos across Europe. She also knew his family name was synonymous with the Mafia in Sicily and that his father, Salvatore, had gone by the nickname Sal il Santo—Sal the Saint—a moniker allegedly given due to his penchant for making the sign of the cross over his dead victims.

She wouldn't have cared if his father had been Lucifer himself. It made no difference to what Francesco was—a good man.

The man who'd brought her back to life.

The stockier one looked back to her. 'What did you say your name was?'

'Hannah Chapman.'

'One minute. I will tell him you are here.' He shrugged his hefty shoulders. 'I cannot say if he will speak to you.'

'That's fine. If he's too busy, I'll leave.' She wasn't going to make a scene. She was here to say thank you and nothing else.

He disappeared through the double doors, letting them swing shut behind him.

She hugged the flowers to her chest. She hoped Francesco wouldn't think them pathetic but she hadn't a clue what else she could give him to express her gratitude. Francesco Calvetti had gone above and beyond the call of duty, and he'd done it for a complete stranger.

In less than a minute, the door swung back open, but instead of the bouncer, she was greeted by a man who was—and Lord knew how this was even possible—taller than the guards he employed.

She'd no idea he was so tall.

But then, her only memory of the man was opening her eyes and seeing his beautiful face before her. How clearly she remembered the fleeting certainty that she was dead and her guardian angel had come to take her to heaven, where Beth was waiting for her. She hadn't even been sad about it—after all, who would be upset about being escorted to paradise with the most gorgeous man on either heaven or earth?

The next time she'd opened her eyes she had been in a hospital bed. This time, the fleeting feeling was disappointment she hadn't gone off to paradise with Adonis.

Fleeting feeling? No. It had been more than that. Adonis had come to take her to Beth. To learn she was still alive had been on the verge of devastating. But then, of course, sanity poked through.

As she'd come back to the here and now, and memories of her Adonis kept peppering her thoughts, so, too, came the revelation that she truly was alive.

Alive.

Something she hadn't felt in fifteen years.

Limbo. That was where she'd been. She, hardworking, practical Hannah Chapman, for whom bedtime reading consisted of catching up on medical journals, had been living in limbo.

In the weeks since her accident, she'd convinced herself that her memory of that brief moment was all wrong. No one, surely, could look like he did in her memory and be a mortal? She'd had severe concussion after all. Even the pictures she'd found on the internet didn't do justice to her memory of him.

Turned out her brain hadn't been playing tricks on her.

Francesco Calvetti truly was beautiful...

But in a wholly masculine way.

His tall, lean frame was clothed in tailored dark grey trousers and a white shirt unbuttoned to halfway down his chest, the sleeves rolled up to his elbows. In the exposed V—which she was eye height with—he wore a simple gold cross on a chain, which rested on a dark whorl of hair.

A rush of...*something* coursed through her blood, as if a cloud of heat had been blown through her veins.

Unsettled, Hannah blinked and looked back up at his unsmiling face. Not even the forbidding expression resonating from his deep-set eyes—and what a beautiful colour they were, making her think of hot chocolate-fudge cake—could dent the huge grin that broke out on her face. She extended the flowers and card to him, saying, 'I'm Hannah Chapman and these are for you.'

Francesco looked from the flowers back to her. He made no effort to take them.

'They're a thank you,' she explained, slightly breathless for some reason. 'I know they're a drop in the ocean compared to what you've done for me, but I wanted to get you something to show how grateful I am—I am truly in your debt.'

One of his thick black brows raised and curved. 'My debt?'

A shiver ran up her spine at his deep, accented voice. 'You have done so much for me,' she enthused. 'Even if I had all the money in the world I could never repay you for your kindness, so yes, I am in your debt.'

His eyes narrowed as he studied her a little longer before inclining his head at the door. 'Come in for a minute.'

'That would be great,' she said, not caring in the least that his directive was an order rather than a request.

The two-man mountain that had flanked Francesco up to this point, guarding him as well as they would if she were carrying an Uzi nine-millimetre, parted. She darted between them, following Francesco inside.

After walking through a large reception area, they stepped into the club proper.

Hannah's eyes widened. 'Amazing,' she whispered, turning her head in all directions.

Calvetti's oozed glamour. All deep reds and silver, it was like stepping into old Hollywood. The only club she'd been to was at the age of eighteen when her entire class had descended on The Dell, their sleepy seaside town's only nightclub, to celebrate finishing their A levels. It had been one of the most boring evenings of her life.

Compared to this place, The Dell had been grey and dingy beyond imagination.

And, in fact, compared to Francesco, with his olive skin, short black curly hair and strong jawline, all the men she had ever met in her life were grey and dingy beyond imagination, too.

'You like it?'

Her skin heating under the weight of his scrutiny, she nodded. 'It's beautiful.'

'You should come here one evening.'

'Me? Oh, no, I'm not into clubbing.' Then, fearing she had inadvertently insulted him, quickly added, 'But my sister Melanie would love it here—it's her hen night on Friday so I'll suggest she drops in.'

'You do that.'

It didn't surprise Francesco to learn Hannah Chapman wasn't into clubbing. The women who frequented his clubs were a definite type—partygoers and women looking to hook up with a rich or famous man, preferably both.

Hannah Chapman was a doctor, not a wannabe WAG. He allowed himself to take in her appearance more fully, and noticed that she was dressed professionally, in another variation of the trouser suit she'd been wearing on the day she was knocked off her bike. The lighting in the club had the effect of making her white blouse see-through, illuminating her bra, which, to his trained eye, looked practical rather than sexy. Her thick blonde hair looked as if it hadn't seen a hairbrush in weeks, and he could not detect the slightest trace of make-up on her face.

He'd assumed when he'd seen her at the door that she

had come with an agenda. In his experience, everyone had an agenda.

He slipped behind the bar, watching as she set the flowers and card to one side. He had never been presented with flowers before. The gesture intrigued him. 'What can I get you to drink?'

'I could murder a coffee.'

'Nothing stronger?'

'I don't drink alcohol, thank you. In any case, I've been working since seven and if I don't get an enormous shot of caffeine I might just pass out.' He liked the droll way she spoke, the air of amusement that laced her voice. It made a change from the usual petulant tones he was used to hearing from her sex.

'You're back at work already?'

'I was back within a fortnight, as soon as I'd recovered from the concussion.'

'Any other injuries?'

'A broken clavicle—collarbone—which is fusing back together nicely. Oh, and a broken middle finger, but that seems to be healed now.'

'You don't know if your own finger's healed?'

She shrugged and hopped onto a stool, facing him. 'It doesn't hurt anymore so I assume it's healed.'

'Is that a professional diagnosis?'

She grinned. 'Absolutely.'

'Remind me not to come and see you if I need medical attention,' he commented drily, stepping over to the coffee machine.

'You're about twenty years too old for me.'

He raised a brow.

Her grin widened. 'Sorry, I mean you're twenty years too old for me to treat in a medical capacity, unless you want to be treated on a ward full of babies, toddlers, and kids. I'm specialising in paediatrics.'

It was on the tip of his tongue to ask why she had chosen to specialise in children but he kept his question to himself. He wanted to know why she had sought him out.

He placed a cup in the machine and pressed a button. 'Do you take milk and sugar?'

'No milk but two sugars, please. I might as well overdose on that as well as caffeine.'

His thoughts exactly. He added two heaped spoons to both cups and passed one to her.

His initial assessment of her had been correct. She really was very pretty. Of average height and slender, her practical trousers showcased the most fabulous curvy bottom. It was a shame she was now sitting on it. The more he looked at her, the more he liked what he saw.

And he could tell that she liked what she saw, too.

Yes, this unexpected visit from Dr Chapman could take a nice twist.

A *very* nice twist.

He took a sip of his strong, sweet coffee before placing his cup next to hers, folding his arms across his chest and leaning on the bar before her.

'Why are you here?'

Her eyes never left his face. 'Because I needed to let you know how grateful I am. You kept me warm until the ambulance arrived, then travelled in the ambulance with me, stayed at the hospital for hours until I'd regained consciousness, *and* you tracked down the driver who hit me and forced him to hand himself in to the police. No one has *ever* done anything like that for me before, and you've done it for a complete stranger.'

Her face was so animated, her cheeks so heightened

with colour, that for a moment his fingers itched to reach out and touch her.

How did she know all this? He'd left the hospital as soon as he'd been given word that she'd regained consciousness. He hadn't seen her since.

'How about you let me buy you dinner one night, so I can thank you properly?' Colour tinged her cheeks.

'You want to buy me dinner?' He didn't even attempt to keep the surprise from his voice. Women didn't ask him out on dates. It just didn't happen. For certain, they thought nothing of cajoling him into taking *them* out to expensive restaurants and lavishing them with expensive clothes and jewellery—something he was happy to oblige them in, enjoying having beautiful women on his arm. But taking the initiative and offering *him* a night out…?

In Francesco's world, man was king. Women were very much pretty trinkets adorning the arm and keeping the bed warm. Men did the running, initially at least, following the traps set by the women so the outcome was assured.

She nodded, cradling her coffee. 'It's the least I can do.'

He studied her a touch longer, gazing into soft hazel eyes that didn't waver from his stare.

Was there an agenda to her surprising offer of dinner?

No. He did not believe so. But Francesco was an expert on female body language and there was no doubt in his mind that she was interested in him.

He was tempted. *Very* tempted.

He'd thought about her numerous times since her accident. There had even been occasions when he'd found his hand on the phone ready to call the hospital to see how she was. Each time he had dismissed the notion. The woman was a stranger. All the same, he'd been enraged to learn the police had failed to track down the man who'd so callously knocked her down. The driver had gone into hiding. Unfortunately for the driver, Francesco had a photographic memory.

It had taken Francesco's vast network precisely two hours to track the driver down. It had taken Francesco less than five minutes to convince the man to hand himself in. By the time he'd finished his 'little chat' with him, the man had been begging to be taken to the police station. Francesco had been happy to oblige.

And now she had come to him.

And he was tempted to take her up on her offer of a meal—not that he would let her pay. It went against everything he believed in. Men took care of their women. The end.

If it was any other woman he wouldn't think twice. But this one was different. For a start, she was a doctor. She was a force for good in a world that was cruel and ugly.

Despite her age and profession, Hannah had an air of innocence about her. Or it could just be that she was totally without artifice. Either way, she had no business getting involved with the likes of him.

If he was a lesser man he would take advantage of her obvious interest, just like his father would have done if he'd been alive.

But he would not be that man. This woman was too… *pure* was the word that came to mind. If she were the usual kind of woman who frequented his world, he would have no hesitation in spelling out how she could repay her so-called debt to him. Naked. And horizontal.

'You owe me nothing,' he stated flatly.

'I do…'

'No.' He cut her off. 'What you consider to be your debt is not redeemable. I did what I did without any thought of payback—consider the fact you are alive and healthy and able to do the job you love to be my payment.'

The animation on her face dimmed a little. 'So you won't let me buy you dinner?'

'Look around you. You don't belong in this seedy world, Dr Chapman. I thank you for taking the time to visit me, but now I have business to attend to.'

'That sounds like a dismissal.'

'I am a busy man.'

Those hazel eyes held his for the longest time before she cast him the most beautiful smile he'd ever been the recipient of, lighting her face into something dazzling.

Then, to his utter shock, Hannah levered herself so her torso was on the bar and pressed her lips to his.

They were the softest of lips, a gentle touch that sent tiny darts fizzing through his blood.

He caught a faint whiff of coffee before she pulled away.

'Thank you. For everything,' she said, slipping back down onto her stool then getting to her feet. Her cheeks glowing, she finished her coffee and reached for her bag, her eyes never leaving his. 'I will never forget what you've done for me, Francesco. You have my undying gratitude.'

As she turned to leave, he called out after her, 'Your sister—she has the same family name as you?'

She nodded.

'I'll leave word that Melanie Chapman's hen party is to be given priority at the door on Friday.'

A groove appeared in her forehead. 'Okay,' she said slowly, clearly not having the faintest idea what he was talking about.

'Your sister will know what it means.' A half smile stole over his face. 'Tell her she'll be on the list.'

'Ah—on the list!' The groove disappeared. Somehow the sparkle in her eyes glittered even stronger. 'I know what *that* means. That's incredibly lovely of you.'

'I wouldn't go that far,' he dismissed, already regretting

his impulsive offer, which had come from where he knew not, but which unsettled him almost as much as her kiss.

Francesco never acted on impulse.

That same serene smile that had curved her cheeks when she'd lain on the road spread on her face. 'I would.'

He watched her walk away, his finger absently tracing the mark on his lips where she'd kissed him.

For the first time in his life he'd done an unselfish act. He didn't know if it made him feel good or bad.

CHAPTER TWO

HANNAH STARED AT the queue snaking all the way round the corner from the door of Calvetti's and sighed. Maybe the queue was an omen to stay away.

No. It couldn't be. Even if it was, she would ignore it. Just being this close to his sanctum was enough to send her pulse careering.

Meeting Francesco in the flesh had done something to her…

'Come on, Han,' her sister said, tugging at her wrist and breaking Hannah's reverie. 'We're on the list.'

'But this is the queue,' Hannah pointed out.

'Yes, but we're *on the list*.' Melanie rolled her eyes. 'If you're on the list you don't have to queue.'

'Really? How fabulous.' She'd thought it meant getting in for free—she had no idea it also encompassed queue jumping.

Giggling, the party of twelve women dressed in black leotards over black leggings, bright pink tutus and matching bunny ears hurried past the queue.

Three men in long black trench coats guarded the door.

Melanie went up to them. 'We're on the list,' she said with as much pride as anyone with a pink veil and bunny ears on her head and the words *Mucky Mel* ironed onto the back of her leotard could muster.

Hannah had guessed Calvetti's was popular but, judging by Melanie's reaction, she could have said she'd got VIP backstage passes to Glastonbury. Her sister had squealed with excitement and promptly set about rearranging the entire evening. Apparently Calvetti's was 'the hottest club in the country', with twice as many people being turned away at the door than being admitted.

Luckily, Melanie had been so excited about it all that she'd totally failed to pump Hannah for information on the man himself. The last thing Hannah wanted was for her sister to think she had a crush on him. It was bad enough knowing her entire family thought she was a closet lesbian without giving them proof of her heterosexuality—one sniff and they'd start trying to marry her off to any man with a pulse.

The bouncer scanned his clipboard before taking a step to one side and unclipping the red cordon acting as a barrier.

'Enjoy your evening, ladies,' he said as they filed past, actually smiling at them.

Another doorman led them straight through to the club, which heaved with bodies and pulsated with loud music, leading them up a cordoned-off set of sparkling stairs.

Her heart lifted to see one of the man mountains who'd been guarding the club the other afternoon standing to attention by a door marked 'Private'.

Surely that meant Francesco was here?

A young hunk dressed in black approached them and led them to a large round corner table. Six iced buckets of champagne were already placed on it.

'Oh, wow,' said Melanie. 'Is this for us?'

'It is,' he confirmed, opening the first bottle. 'With the compliments of the management. If you need anything, holler—your night is on the house.'

'Can I have a glass of lemonade, please?' Hannah asked,

her request immediately drowned out by the hens all badgering her to have one glass of champagne.

About to refuse, she remembered the promise she'd made to herself that it was time to start living.

She, more than anyone, knew how precarious life could be, but it had taken an accident on her bike for her to realise that all she had been doing since the age of twelve was existing. Meeting Francesco in the flesh had only made those feelings stronger.

If heaven was real, what stories would she have to tell Beth other than medical anecdotes? She would have nothing of real *life* to share.

That was something she'd felt in Francesco, that sense of vitality and spontaneity, of a life being *lived*.

Settling down at the table, she took a glass of champagne, her eyes widening as the bubbles played on her tongue. All the same, she stopped after a few sips.

To her immense surprise, Hannah soon found she was enjoying herself. Although she didn't know any of them well, Melanie's friends were a nice bunch. Overjoyed to be given the VIP treatment, they made sure to include her in everything, including what they called Talent Spotting.

Alas, no matter how discreetly she craned her neck, Hannah couldn't see Francesco anywhere. She did, however, spot a couple of minor members of the royal family and was reliably informed that a number of Premier League football players and a world-championship boxer were on the table next to theirs, and that the glamorous women and men with shiny white teeth who sat around another table were all Hollywood stars and their beaus.

'Thank you so much for getting knocked off your bike,' Melanie said whilst on a quick champagne break from the dance floor, flinging her arms around Hannah. 'And thank you for coming out with us tonight and for coming here—I was convinced you were going to go home after the meal.'

Hannah hugged her in return, holding back her confession that she *had* originally planned on slipping away after their Chinese, but that the lure of seeing Francesco again had been too great. It had almost made up for the fact Beth wasn't there to share Melanie's hen night. She wouldn't be there to share the wedding, either.

The wedding. An event Hannah dreaded.

She felt a huge rush of affection for her little sister along with an accompanying pang of guilt. Poor Melanie. She deserved better than Hannah. Since Beth's death, Hannah had tried so hard to be the best big sister they both wished she could be, but she simply wasn't up to the job. It was impossible. How could she be anything to anyone when such a huge part of herself was missing? All she had been able to do was throw herself into her studies, something over which she had always had total control.

But now her drive and focus had been compromised.

Never had she experienced anything like this.

Hannah was a woman of practicality, not a woman to be taken in with flights of fancy. Medicine was her life. From the age of twelve she'd known exactly what she wanted to be and had been single-minded in her pursuit of it. She would dedicate her life to medicine and saving children, doing her utmost to keep them alive so she could spare as many families from the gaping hole that lived in her own heart as she could.

At least, she had been single-minded until a car knocked her off her bike and the most beautiful man in the universe had stepped in to save her.

Now the hole in her heart didn't feel so hollow.

Since that fateful cold morning, her mind had not just been full of medicine. It had been full of *him*, her knight in shining armour, and meeting him in the flesh had only compounded this. She wasn't stupid. She knew she would never fit into his world. His reputation preceded him. Francesco Calvetti was a dangerous man to know and an *exceptionally* dangerous man to get on the wrong side of. But knowing this had done nothing to eradicate him from her mind.

That moment when she'd been lying on the cold concrete and opened her eyes, she had looked at him and felt such warmth.... Someone who could evoke that in her couldn't be all bad. He just couldn't.

'Come on, Han,' said Melanie, tugging at her hand. 'Come and dance with me.'

'I can't dance.' What she really wanted to do was search every nook and cranny of Calvetti's until she found him. Because he was there. She just knew it.

Melanie pointed at the dance floor, where a group of twenty-something men with more money than taste were strutting their stuff. 'Nor can they.'

Francesco watched the images from the security cameras on a range of monitors on his office wall. Through them, he could see everything taking place in his club. The same feeds were piped into the office where his security guys sat holed up, watching the same live images—but the only eyes Francesco trusted were his own. Tomorrow he would head back to Palermo to spot-check his nightclub and casino there, and then he would fly on to Madrid for the same.

A couple of men he suspected of being drug dealers had been invited by a group of city money men into the VIP area. He watched them closely, debating whether to have them dealt with now or wait until he had actual proof of their nefarious dealings.

A sweep of thick blonde hair with pink bunny ears

caught his attention in one of the central feeds. He watched Hannah get dragged onto the dance floor by another pink-tutued blonde he assumed was the hen of said hen party, Melanie.

Not for the first time, he asked himself what the hell Hannah was doing there.

She looked more than a little awkward. His lips curved upwards as he watched her try valiantly to move her body in time to the beat of the music. He'd seen more rhythm from the stray cats that congregated round the vast veranda of his Sicilian villa.

The half smile faded and compressed into a tight line when he read the slogan on her back: Horny Hannah.

That all the hen party had similar personalised slogans did nothing to break the compression of his lips.

It bothered him. Hannah was too...*classy* to have something so cheap written about her, even if it was in jest.

He downed his coffee and absently wiped away the residue on the corner of his lips with his thumb.

What was she doing here? And why did she keep craning her neck as if she was on the lookout for someone?

Since he'd dismissed her three days ago, he'd been unnerved to find her taking residence in his mind. Now was not the time for distractions of any sort, not when the casino in Mayfair was on the agenda. This particular casino was reputed to be one of the oldest—if not *the* oldest—in the whole of Europe. It had everything Francesco desired in a casino. Old-school glamour. Wealth. And credibility. This was a casino built by gentlemen for gentlemen, and while the old 'no women' rule had been relaxed in modern times, it retained its old-fashioned gentility. More than anything else, though, it was the one business his father had wanted and failed to get. This failure had been a thorn in

Salvatore's side until his dying day, when a life of overindulgence had finally caught up with him.

After almost forty years under the sole ownership of Sir Godfrey Renfrew, a member of the British aristocracy, the casino had been put up for sale.

Francesco wanted it. He coveted it, had spent two months charming Godfrey Renfrew into agreeing the sale of it to him. Such was Godfrey's hatred of Francesco's dead father, it had taken a month to even persuade him to meet.

What was more, if Francesco's spies were correct, Luca Mastrangelo was sniffing around the casino, too.

This news meant he absolutely could not afford to lose focus on the deal, yet still he'd found himself, an hour before opening for the night, giving orders to his hospitality manager to reserve the best table in the club—for a hen party of all things. He'd only ever intended to have Melanie Chapman's party on the guest list.

Under ordinary circumstances, free tables were given to the most VIP of all VIPs and only then because of the publicity it generated.

He hadn't expected Hannah to be in attendance, but now she was here he couldn't seem to stop his eyes from flickering to whichever monitor happened to be fixed on her.

Hannah tried heroically to get her feet moving in time with the music, aware her dancing was easily the least rhythmic of the whole club. Not that this seemed to put any of the men off. To her chagrin, a few seemed to be suffering from what her sister termed Wandering Hand Syndrome. One in particular kept 'accidentally' rubbing against her. When his hand brushed over her bottom the first time she'd been prepared to give him the benefit of the doubt, and had stepped away from him. The second time, when he'd been bolder and tried to cup her buttocks, she'd flashed him a smile and said in her politest voice, 'Please don't do that,' he'd removed his hand. Which had worked for all of ten seconds. The third time he groped her, she'd 'accidentally' trod on his foot. And now the sleaze had 'accidentally' palmed her breast and was grinding into her back as if she were some kind of plaything.

Did people actually *like* this kind of behaviour? Did women really find it *attractive*?

Just as she was wishing she had worn a pair of stilettoes like all the other women there so she could bruise him properly, a figure emerged on the dance floor.

Such was Francesco's presence that the crowd parted like the Red Sea to admit him.

Her sister stopped dancing and gazed up at him with a dropped jaw. The other hens also stared, agog, their feet seeming to move in a manner completely detached from their bodies.

And no wonder. A head taller than anyone else on the dance floor, he would have commanded attention even if he'd looked like the back end of a bus. Wearing an immaculately pressed open-necked black shirt and charcoal trousers, his gorgeous face set in a grim mask, he oozed menace.

Even if Hannah had wanted to hide her delight, she would have been unable to, her face breaking into an enormous grin at the sight of him, an outward display of the fizzing that had erupted in her veins.

She'd hoped with a hope bordering on desperation that he would spot her and seek her out, had prepared herself for the worst, but hoped for the best. She'd also promised herself that if he failed to materialise that evening then she would do everything in her power to forget about him. But if he were to appear...

To her disquiet, other than nodding at her without making proper eye contact, his attention was very much focused on the man who'd been harassing her who, despite trying to retain a nonchalant stance, had beads of sweat popping out on his forehead.

Francesco leaned into his face, his nostrils flaring. 'If you touch this woman again, you will answer to me personally. *Capisce?*'

Not waiting for a response, he turned back into the crowd.

Hannah watched his retreating figure, her heart in her mouth.

Melanie shouted over the music to her, her face animated, yet Hannah didn't hear a single syllable.

It was now or never.

Unlike the regularity of her life, where the only minor change to her schedule came in the form of the monthly weekend-night shift, Francesco's life was full of movement and change, hopping from country to country, always seeing different sunsets. Her life was exactly where she had planned it to be and she didn't want to change the fundamentals of it, but there was something so intoxicating about both Francesco and the freedom of his life. The freedom to wake up in the morning and just *go*.

He could go anywhere *right now*.

Hurrying to catch him, she followed in his wake, weaving through the sweaty bodies and then past the VIP tables.

'Francesco,' she called, panic fluttering in her chest as he placed his hand on the handle of the door marked Private.

He stilled.

She hurried to close the gap.

He turned his head, his features unreadable.

The music was so loud she had to incline right into

him. He was close enough for her to see the individual hairs in the V of his shirt and smell his gorgeous scent, all oaky manliness, everything converging to send her pulse racing.

'Why did you just do that?' she asked.

His eyes narrowed, the pupils ringing with intent, before he turned the handle and held the door open for her.

Hannah stepped into a dimly lit passageway. Francesco closed the door, blocking off the thumping noise of the music.

She shook her head a little to try to clear her ringing ears.

He leaned back against the door, his eyes fixed on her.

'Why did you do that?' she repeated, filling the silence with a question she knew he'd heard perfectly well the first time she'd asked it.

'What? Warn that man off?'

'Threaten him,' she corrected softly.

'I don't deal in threats, Dr Chapman,' he said, his voice like ice. 'Only promises.'

'But why?'

'Because he wouldn't take no for an answer. I will not allow abuse of any form to take place on my premises.'

'So you make a point of personally dealing with all unwanted attention in your clubs, do you?'

His eyes bored into hers, his lips a tight line.

Far from his forbidding expression making her turn and run away, as it would be likely to make any other sane person do, it emboldened her. 'And did I really hear you say *capisce*?'

'It's a word that the man will understand.'

'Very Danny DeVito. And, judging by his reaction to it, very effective.'

Something that could almost pass for amusement curled on his lips. 'Danny DeVito? Do you mean Al Pacino?'

'Probably.' She tried to smile, tried hard to think of a witty remark that would hold his attention for just a little longer, but it was hard to think sensibly when you were caught in a gaze like hot chocolate-fudge cake, especially when it was attached to a man as divine as Francesco Calvetti. If she had to choose, she would say the man was a slightly higher rank on the yummy stakes than the cake. And she liked hot chocolate-fudge cake *a lot*, as her bottom would testify.

'Thank you for rescuing me. Again.'

'You're welcome.' He made to turn the door handle. 'Now, if you'll excuse me...'

'Dismissing me again?'

'I'm a very...'

'Busy man,' she finished for him. God, but her heart was thundering beneath her ribs, her hands all clammy. 'Please. I came along tonight because I wanted to see you again. Five minutes of your time. That's all I ask. If at the end of it you tell me to leave then I will and I promise never to seek you out again.'

She held her breath as she awaited his response.

He eyed her coolly, his features not giving anything away, until, just as she feared she was about to run out of oxygen, he inclined his head and turned the handle of another door, also marked Private.

Hannah followed him into a large room that was perhaps the most orderly office she had ever been in. Along one wall were two dozen monitors, which she gravitated towards. It didn't take long to spot her sister and fellow hens, all back at their table, talking animatedly.

It occurred to her that she had simply walked away without telling Melanie where she was going.

'So, Dr Chapman, you wanted five minutes of my time...'

She turned her head to find Francesco staring pointedly at his chunky, expensive-looking watch.

He might look all forbidding but she could sense his curiosity.

How she regretted allowing Melanie to talk her into wearing the 'hen uniform', but it would have been churlish to refuse. She had denied her sister too much through the years. Dressing in a ridiculous outfit was the least she could do. Still, it made her self-conscious, and right then she needed every ounce of courage to say what she needed to say.

She swallowed but held his gaze, a look that was cold yet made her feel all warm inside. Seriously, how could a man with chocolate-fudge-cake eyes be all bad?

'When I was knocked off my bike I thought I'd died,' she said, clasping her hands together. God, but this was so much harder than she had imagined it would be and she had known it would be hard. 'I honestly thought that was it for me. Since then, everything has changed—*I've* changed. My accident made me realise I've been letting life pass me by.'

'How does this relate to me?'

Her heart hammered so hard her chest hurt. 'Because I can't stop thinking about you.'

His eyes narrowed with suspicion and he folded his arms across his chest.

Hannah's nerves almost failed her. Her tongue rooted to the roof of her mouth.

'What is it you want from me?'

Out of the corner of her eye she spotted the thank-you card she'd given him. Seeing it there, displayed on his desk, settled the nerves in her stomach.

Francesco had kept her card.

He'd sought her out and rescued her *again*.

She wasn't imagining the connection between them.

She sucked her lips in and bit them before blurting out, 'I want you to take my virginity.'

CHAPTER THREE

FRANCESCO SHOOK HIS HEAD. For the first time in his thirty-six years he was at a loss for words.

'God, that came out all wrong.' Hannah covered her face, clearly cringing. When she dropped her hands her face had paled but, to give her credit, she met his gaze with barely a flinch. 'I didn't mean it to come out quite so crudely. Please, say something.'

He shook his head again, trying to clear it. 'Is this some kind of joke?'

'No.'

'You're a virgin?'

'Yes.'

For a moment he seriously considered that he was in some kind of dream.

Had he fallen asleep at his desk?

Since the discovery of his mother's diaries ten months ago, he'd been consumed with rage. This rage fuelled him. Indeed, for the past ten months, his drive had been working at full throttle. Only a month ago his doctor had told him to slow down, that he was at risk of burnout. Naturally, he'd ignored that advice. Francesco would not slow down until he had eradicated every last trace of Salvatore Calvetti's empire.

And to think he'd almost missed those diaries. Had he

not given the family home one last sweep before emptying it for sale, he would never have found them, hidden away in boxes in the cubbyhole of his mother's dressing room. He hadn't even intended to go into his mother's rooms but the compulsion to feel close to her one last time had made him enter them for the first time in two decades.

Reading the diaries had been as close to torture as a man could experience. The respect he'd felt for his father, the respect that had made him a dutiful son while his father was alive, had died a brutal death.

His only regret was that he hadn't learned the truth while his father was alive, would never have the pleasure of punishing him for every hour of misery he'd put his mother through. Duty would have gone to hell. He might just have helped his father into an early grave.

He hoped with every fibre of his being that his father *was* in hell. He deserved nothing less.

Because now he knew the truth. And he would not be satisfied until he'd destroyed everything Salvatore Calvetti had built, crushed his empire and his reputation. Left it for dust.

The truth consumed him. His hate fuelled him.

It was perfectly feasible he had fallen asleep.

Except he'd never had a dream that made his heart beat as if it would hammer through his ribcage.

He rubbed the back of his neck and stared at the woman who had made such a confounding offer.

She looked ridiculous in her hen outfit, with the pink tutu, black leotard and leggings, and black ballet slippers. At least the other hens had made an effort, adorning their outfits with the sky-high heels women usually wore in his clubs. It didn't even look as if Hannah had brushed her hair, never mind put any make-up on. What woman went clubbing without wearing make-up?

Indeed, he could not remember the last time he'd met a woman who *didn't* wear make-up, full stop.

And she still had those ridiculous bunny ears on her head.

Yet there was something incredibly alluring about Hannah's fresh-faced looks. Something different.

He'd thought *she* was different. He'd resisted her offer of a date a few short days ago because of it; because he'd thought she was *too* different, that she didn't belong in his world.

Could he really have judged her so wrong?

What kind of woman offered her so-called virginity to a stranger?

And what the hell had compelled him to warn her groper off and not send one of his men in to resolve the situation? If he'd followed his usual procedures he wouldn't be standing here now on the receiving end of one of the most bizarre offers he'd ever heard.

It had been watching that man paw her—and her dignity when rebuffing his advances—that had made something inside him snap.

The rules were the same in all his establishments, his staff trained to spot customers overstepping the mark in the familiarity stakes. The usual procedure was for one of his doormen to have a polite 'word' with the perpetrator. That polite word was usually enough to get them behaving.

Francesco might have little respect for the type of women who usually littered his clubs but that did not mean he would tolerate them being abused in any form.

In the shadows of his memory rested his mother, a woman who had tolerated far too much abuse. And he, her son, had been oblivious to it.

A rush of blood to his head had seen him off his seat,

out of his office and onto the dance floor before his brain had time to compute what his feet were doing.

'I have no idea what you're playing at,' he said slowly, 'but I will not be a party to such a ridiculous game. I have given you your five minutes. It's time for you to leave.'

This *had* to be a game. Hannah Chapman had discovered his wealth and, like so many others of her gender, decided she would like to access it.

It unnerved him how disappointed he felt.

'This isn't a game.' She took a visibly deep breath. 'Please. Francesco, I am a twenty-seven-year-old woman who has never had sex. I haven't even kissed a man. It's become a noose around my neck. I don't want to stay a virgin all my life. All I want is one night to know what it feels like to be a real woman and you're the only man I can ask.'

'But why me?' he asked, incredulous.

Her beautiful hazel eyes held his. 'Because I trust that you won't hurt me.'

'How can you trust such a thing? I am a stranger to you.'

'The only men I meet are fellow doctors and patients. The patients are a big no-no, and the few single doctors I know…we work too closely together. You might be a stranger but I *know* you'll treat me with respect. I know you would never laugh at me or make fun about me being a twenty-seven-year-old virgin behind my back.'

'That's an awful lot of supposition you're making about me.'

'Maybe.' She raised her shoulders in a helpless gesture. 'I thought I was dead. When I opened my eyes and saw your face I thought you'd come to take me to heaven. All I can think now is *what if…* What if I *had* died? I've done *nothing* with my life.'

'Hardly,' he said harshly. 'You're a doctor. That takes dedication.'

'For me, it's taken everything. I'm not naturally bright—
I had to work hard to get my grades, to learn and to keep
learning. In the process I've been so focused on my career
that I've allowed my personal life to go to ruin.' The same
groove he remembered from the other evening reappeared
on her forehead. 'I don't want to die a virgin.'

Francesco rubbed his neck.

It seemed she was serious.

Of course, she *could* be lying. Having discovered who
he was, this could be a clever, convoluted game to access
his life and wealth.

Yet her explanation made a mad kind of sense.

He remembered the expression of serenity that had
crossed her face at the moment she'd opened her eyes and
looked at him, remembered her words and the fuzzy feelings they had evoked in him.

Something had passed between them—something fleeting but tangible.

There was no way Hannah could have known who he
was at that moment.

One thing he did know was that she had gained a false
impression of him. If she knew who he really was, he would
be the last man she would make such a shameless propo-
sition to.

Regardless, he could hardly credit how tempted he was.

He was a red-blooded male. What man *wouldn't* be
tempted by such an offer?

But Hannah was a virgin, he reminded himself—despite
the fact that he'd thought virgins over the age of eighteen
were from the tales of mythology.

Surely this was every man's basest fantasy? A virgin
begging to be deflowered.

'You have no idea who I am,' he told her flatly.

'Are you talking about the gangster thing?'

'The gangster thing?' His voice took on a hint of menace. How could she be so blasé about it? Was she so naive she didn't understand his life wasn't something watched from the safety of a television set, played by men who likely had manicures between takes?

Scrutinising her properly, her innocence was obvious. She had an air about her—the same air he saw every time he looked through his parents' wedding album. His mother had had that air when she'd married his father, believing it to be a love match, blissfully oblivious to her husband's true nature, and the true nature of his business affairs.

Hannah raised her shoulders again. 'I've read all about you on the internet. I know what it says your family are.'

'And do you believe everything you read on the internet?'

'No.' She shook her head to emphasise her point.

Deliberately, he stepped towards her and into her space. He brought his face down so it was level with hers. 'You *should* believe it. Because it's true. Every word. I am not a good person for you to know. I am the last person a woman like you should get involved with.'

She didn't even flinch. 'A woman like me? What does that mean?'

'You're a doctor. You do not belong in my world.'

'I just want *one night* in your world, that's all. One night. I don't care what's been written about you. I know you would never hurt me.'

'You think?' Where had she got this ludicrous faith in him from? He had to eradicate it, make her see enough of the truth to scare her all the way back to the safety of her hospital.

He straightened to his full height, an act capable of intimidating even the hardest of men. He breached the inches between them to reach into her thick mane of hair and tug the rabbit ears free. They were connected by some kind of plastic horseshoe that he dropped onto the floor and placed a foot on. He pressed down until he heard the telltale crunch.

She stared at him with that same serene look in her hazel eyes.

'Tell me,' he said, gently twisting her around so her back was flush against him, 'how, exactly, do you want me to take your virginity?'

He heard an intake of breath.

Good. He'd unnerved her.

Gathering her hair together, he inhaled the sweet scent of her shampoo. Her hair felt surprisingly soft. 'Do you want me to take you here and now?'

He trailed a finger down her exposed slender neck, over the same collarbone that had been broken less than two months before, and down her toned arm before reaching round to cup a breast flattened by the leotard she wore.

'Or do you want me to take you on a bed?' He traced his thumb over a nipple that shot out beneath his touch.

'I…' Her voice came out like a whimper. 'I…'

'You must have some idea of how you would like me to perform the deed,' he murmured, breathing into her ear and nuzzling his nose into a cheek as soft as the finest silk. 'Is foreplay a requirement? Or do you just want to get it over with?'

'I…I know what you're doing.'

'All I'm doing is ascertaining how, exactly, you would like me to relieve you of your virginity. I can do it now if you would like.' He pressed his groin into the small of her back so as to leave her in no doubt how ready he was. 'Right here, over the desk? Up against the wall? On the floor?'

Much as he hated himself for it, his body was responding to her in the basest of fashions.

He would control it, just as he controlled everything else.

He would *not* give in to temptation.

He would make the good doctor see just how wrong she was about him.

Hannah Chapman was one of the few people in the world who made a difference.

He would not be the one to taint her, no matter how much he desired her or how much she wanted it.

He was better than that. He was better than the man who had created him, who would, no doubt, have already relieved Hannah of her virginity if he'd been in Francesco's shoes.

He would not be that man. And if he had to come on heavy to make her run away, then that was what he would do. Reasoning clearly didn't work with her.

'You're trying to scare me off.'

Francesco stilled at her astuteness.

Although her breaths were heavy, he could feel her defiance through the rigidity of her bones.

It was with far too much reluctance that he released his hold and turned her back round to face him.

Hannah's hair tumbled back around her shoulders. Her cheeks were flushed, her eyes wide. Yet there was no fear. Apprehension, yes, but no fear.

'You are playing with fire, Dr Chapman.'

She gave a wry smile. 'I'm trained to treat burns.'

'Not the kind you will get from me. You'll have to find another man to do the job. I'm not for hire.'

His mind flashed to the man who'd been groping Hannah earlier—who, he imagined, would be more than happy to accede to her request. He banished the image. Who she chose was none of his concern.

All the same, the thought of that man pawing at her

again sent a sharp, hot flush racing through him. She was too...*pure*.

A shrewdness came into her eyes, although how such a look could also be gentle totally beat him.

She tilted her head to the side. 'Do I scare you?'

'On the contrary. It is you who should be afraid of me.'

'But I'm not scared of you. I don't care about your reputation. I'm not after a relationship or anything like that—the only thing being with you makes me feel is good. After everything you've done for me, how can I not trust that?'

He shook his head.

This was madness.

He should call his guards and have her escorted out of his club. But he wouldn't.

Francesco had heard stories about people who saved lives being bound to the person they'd saved, and vice versa. And while he hadn't saved her in a technical sense, it was the only explanation he could think of for the strange chemistry that brewed between them. Total strangers yet inexplicably linked.

Something had passed between them, connecting them.

It was his duty to sever that link. *His* duty. Not his guards'.

He would make her see.

'You think I'm worthy of your trust?' Unthinkingly, he reached out a hand and captured a lock of her hair.

'I *know* you are.' Reclosing the gap between them, she tilted her head back a little and placed a hand on his cheek. 'Don't you see? A lesser man wouldn't try to scare me off—he would have taken what I offered without a second thought.'

His skin tingled beneath the warmth of her fingers. He wanted to clasp those fingers, interlace his own through them....

'I'm not cut out for any form of relationship—my career matters too much for me to compromise it—but I want to *feel*.' She brought her face closer so her nose skimmed against his throat, her breath a whisper against his sensitised skin. 'I want one night where I can throw caution to the wind. I want to know what it's like to be made love to and I want it to be you because you're the only man I've met who makes me feel alive without even touching me.'

Francesco could hardly breathe. His fingers still held the lock of her hair. The desire that had been swirling in his blood since he'd nuzzled into her neck thickened.

When had he ever felt as if he could explode from arousal?

This was madness.

'If I believed you felt nothing physically for me, I would walk away now,' she continued, her voice a murmur. 'I certainly wouldn't debase myself any further.'

'How can you be so sure I feel anything for you physically?'

'Just because I'm a virgin doesn't mean I'm totally naive.'

In his effort to scare her away, he'd pressed his groin into her back, letting her feel his excitement through the layers of their clothing.

That particular effort had backfired.

Hannah had turned it round on him.

Well, no more.

Clasping the hand still resting against his cheek, he tugged it away and dropped it. He stepped back, glowering down at her. 'You think you can spend one night with me and walk away unscathed? Because that isn't going to happen. Sex isn't a game, and I'm not a toy that can be played with.'

For the first time a hint of doubt stole over her face. 'I

never meant it like that,' she said, her voice low. 'It's not just that I'm wildly attracted to you, it's more than that. I can't explain it, but when I look at you I see a life full of excitement, of travel, of so much more than I could ever hope to experience. All I want is to reach out and touch it, to experience some of it with you.'

'You think you know me but you don't. I'm not the man you think. My life is seedy and violent. You should want nothing to do with it.'

For long, long moments he eyeballed her, waiting for her to drop her eyes. But it didn't happen—her gaze held his, steady and immovable.

'Prove it.' She gave a feeble shrug. 'If you really think you're so bad for me, then *prove* it.'

He almost groaned aloud. 'It's not a case of proving it. You need to understand—once your virginity's gone you will never get it back. It's lost for ever, and who knows what else you might lose with it.'

She swallowed but remained steady. 'There's nothing else for me to lose. I'm not after a love affair. Francesco, all I want is one night.'

It was hearing his name—and the meaning she put into it—on her lips that threw him.

It made him want to find a dragon to slay just to protect her. Yet he knew that the only thing Hannah needed protecting from was herself.

He reminded himself that he did not need this aggravation. His mind should be focused on the Mayfair deal— the deal that would be the crowning glory in his empire. Hannah had compromised his concentration enough these past few days.

Maybe if he gave her some of what she wanted his mind could regain its focus without her there, knocking on his thoughts.

'You want proof of who I really am?' he said roughly. 'Then that's what you shall have. I will give you a sample of my life for one weekend.'

Her eyes sparkled.

'*This* weekend,' he continued. 'You can share a taste of my life and see for yourself why you should keep the hell away from me. By the end of our time together I guarantee you will never want to see my face again, much less waste your virginity on a man like me.'

CHAPTER FOUR

HANNAH HAD BEEN twitching her curtains for a good half hour before Francesco pulled up outside her house on an enormous motorbike, the engine making enough racket to wake the whole street.

It didn't surprise her in the least that he waited for her to come out to him. Once Francesco had agreed to a weekend together, he had wasted no time in dismissing her by saying, 'I will collect you at 7:00 a.m. Have your passport ready.'

He was taking her to Sicily. To his home.

She couldn't remember the last time she'd been this excited about something. Or as nervous.

Her very essence tingling with anticipation, she stepped out into the early-morning sun, noticing that at least he had taken his helmet off to greet her.

'Good morning,' she said, beaming both at him and, with admiration, at the bike. There was something so…*manly* about the way he straddled it, which, coupled with the cut of his tight leather trousers, sent a shock of warmth right through her. 'Are we traveling to Sicily on this?'

He eyed her coldly. 'Only to the airbase. That's if you still want to come?' From the tone of his voice, there was no doubting that he hoped she'd changed her mind.

If she was honest, since leaving his office six short hours

ago, she'd repeatedly asked herself if she was doing the right thing.

But she hadn't allowed herself to even consider backing down. Because all she knew for certain was that if she didn't grab this opportunity with both hands she would regret it for the rest of her life, regardless of the outcome.

'I still want to come,' she said, almost laughing to see his lips tighten in disapproval. Couldn't he see, the more he tried to scare her off, the more she knew she was on the right path, that it proved his integrity?

Francesco desired her.

The feel of his hardness pressed against her had been the most incredible, intoxicating feeling imaginable. She had never dreamed her body capable of such a reaction, had imagined the thickening of the blood and the low pulsations deep inside were from the realms of fiction. It had only served to increase her desire, to confirm she was following the right path.

She'd been his for the taking in his office but he had stepped back, unwilling to take advantage. Again.

Francesco was doing everything in his power to put her off, but she doubted there was anything to be revealed about him that would do that. What, she wondered, had made him so certain he was all bad? Was it because of his blood lineage? Whatever it was, she knew there was good in him—even though he clearly didn't believe it himself.

Face thunderous, he reached into the side case and pulled out some leathers and a black helmet. 'Put these on.'

She took them from him. 'Do you want to come in while I change? Your bike will be perfectly safe—all the local hoodlums are tucked up in bed.'

'I will wait here.'

'I have coffee.'

'I will wait.'

'Suit yourself.'

'You have five minutes.'

In her bedroom, Hannah wrestled herself into the tight leather trousers, and then donned the matching jacket, staggering slightly under the weight of it.

When she caught sight of her reflection in the full-length mirror she paused. Whoever said leathers were sexy was sorely mistaken—although she'd admit to feeling very Sandra Dee in the trousers.

Sandra Dee had been a virgin, too.

Hannah was a virgin in all senses of the word.

But, she reminded herself, with Francesco's help she was going to change that. Just for this one weekend. That was all she wanted. Some memories to share with Beth.

She took a deep breath and studied her reflection one last time. Her stomach felt knotted, but she couldn't tell if excitement or trepidation prevailed.

She checked the back door was locked one last time before grabbing her small case and heading back out to him.

'That will not fit,' Francesco said when he saw her case.

'You're the one whisking me away for a romantic overnight stay on a motorbike,' she pointed out. 'What do you suggest I do?'

'Let me make this clear, I am not whisking you away anywhere.'

'Semantics.'

'And I never said anything about us going away for one night only. We will return to the UK when *I* am ready.'

'As long as you get me back in time for work at nine o'clock Monday morning, that's fine by me.'

His face was impassive. 'We will return when my schedule allows it, not yours.'

'Is this the part when I'm supposed to wave my hands and say, "oh, in that case I can't possibly come with you?"'

'Yes.'

'Bad luck. I'm coming. And you'll get me back in time for work.'

'You sound remarkably sure of yourself.'

'Not at all. I just know you're not the sort of person to allow a ward full of sick children to suffer from a lack of doctors.'

His features contorted, the chocolate fudge of his eyes hardening. 'That is a risk you are willing to take?'

'No.' She shook her head, a rueful smile playing on her lips. 'I know there's no risk.' At least no risk in the respect of getting her to work on time. And as to Francesco's other concerns, Hannah knew there was no risk in the respect of her heart, either; her heart hadn't functioned properly in fifteen years.

More practically, she supposed there were some dangers. She could very well be getting into something way out of her depth, but what was the worst that could happen? Hannah had lived through her own personal hell. The worst thing that could happen had occurred at the age of twelve, and she had survived it. God alone knew how, but she had.

It was only one weekend. One weekend of *life* before she went back to her patients, the children she hoped with all her semi-functioning heart would grow up to lead full lives of their own.

'On your head be it,' said Francesco. 'Now either find a smaller case for your stuff, put it in a rucksack you can strap to you, or leave it behind.'

Her gaze dropped to her case. She didn't have either a smaller case or a rucksack....

'Give me one minute,' she said, speaking over her shoulder as she hurried back into the house. In record time she'd grabbed an oversized handbag and shoved her passport, phone, purse, clean underwear, toothbrush, and a thin sundress into it. The rest of her stuff, including some research papers she'd been reading through for the past week, she left in the case.

This was an adventure after all. Her first adventure in fifteen years.

'Is that all you're taking?' Francesco asked when she rejoined him, taking the bag from her.

'You're the one who said to bring something smaller.'

He made a noise that sounded like a cross between a grunt and a snort.

She grinned. 'You'll have to try harder than that to put me off.'

Nostrils flaring, he shoved her bag into the side case then thrust the helmet back into her hands. 'Put this on.'

'Put this on…?' She waited for a *please*.

'Now.'

How could *anyone* be so cheerful first thing in the morning? Francesco wondered. It wasn't natural.

What would it take to put a chink in that smiley armour?

With great reluctance, he reached over to help her with the helmet straps. Even through the darkened visor he could see her still grinning.

If he had his way, that pretty smile would be dropped from her face before they boarded his plane.

'Have you ridden on one of these before?' he asked, tightening the straps enough so they were secure without cutting off her circulation.

She shook her head.

'Put your arms around me and mimic my actions—lean into the turns.'

Only when he was certain that she was securely seated did Francesco twist the throttle and set off.

Francesco brought the bike to a halt in the airport's private car park.

'That was amazing!' Hannah said, whipping off her helmet to reveal a head of hair even more tangled than a whole forest of birds' nests.

If his body wasn't buzzing from the exhilaration of the ride coupled with the unwanted thrum of desire borne from having her pressed against him for half an hour, he would think she looked endearing.

His original intention had been to take advantage of the clear early-Saturday-morning roads and hit the throttle. What he hadn't accounted for was the distraction of having Hannah pressed so tightly against him.

And no wonder. Those trousers…

Caro Dio…

Behind that sensible, slightly messy exterior lay a pair of the most fantastic legs he had ever seen. He'd noticed how great they looked the night before, but the ridiculous pink tutu had hidden the best part: the thighs.

Not for a second had he been able to forget she was there, attached to him, trusting him to keep her safe.

Where the hell did she get this misplaced trust *from*?

In the end, he'd kept his speed strictly controlled, rarely breaching the legal limits. Not at all the white-knuckle ride he'd had in mind.

His guards were already there waiting for him, forbidden from following him when he was riding in the UK. It was different on the Med, especially in Sicily. The only good thing he could say about England was he never felt the need to have an entourage watching his back at all times.

In as ungracious a manner as he could muster, he pulled

Hannah's bag from the side case, handed it to her, then threw the keys of his bike to one of his men.

'What are you doing?' he asked, spotting Hannah on her phone. It was one of the latest models. For some reason this surprised him. Maybe it was because she was a virgin who dressed in a basic, functional manner that he'd assumed she'd have a basic, functional phone.

'Answering my emails,' she said, peering closely at the screen as she tapped away.

'From who?'

'Work.'

'It is Saturday.'

She peered up at him. She really did look ridiculous, with the heavy jacket clearly weighing her down. Still, those legs... And that bottom...

'Hospitals don't close for weekends.' She flashed him a quick grin. 'I'll be done in a sec.'

Francesco had no idea why it irked him to witness Hannah pay attention to her phone. He didn't want to encourage her into getting any ideas about them but, all the same, he did *not* appreciate being made to feel second best.

'All done,' she said a moment later, dropping the phone back into her bag.

Once the necessary checks were made, they boarded Francesco's plane.

'You own this?' she asked with the same wide-eyed look she'd had when she'd first walked into his club carrying a bunch of flowers for him.

He jerked a nod and took his seat, indicating she should sit opposite him. 'Before I give the order for us to depart, I need to check your bag.'

'Why? It's already been through a scanner.'

'My plane. My rules.' He met her gaze, willing her to

fight back, to leave, to get off the aircraft and walk away before the dangers of his life tainted her.

He thought he saw a spark of anger. A tiny spark, but a spark all the same.

She shrugged and handed it over to him.

He opened the bag. His hand clenched around her underwear. He should pull it out, let her see him handle her most intimate items. The plane hadn't taken off. There was still time to change her mind.

But then he met her gaze again. She studied him with unabashed curiosity.

No. He would not humiliate her.

His fingers relaxed their grip, the cotton folding back into place. He pulled out a threadbare black purse.

Resolve filled him. He opened it to find a few notes, a heap of receipts, credit and debit cards, and a photo, which he tugged out.

Hannah fidgeted before him but he paid her no heed.

She wanted him to prove in actions how bad he was for her? This was only the beginning.

He peered closely at a picture of two identical young girls with long flaxen hair, hazel eyes, and the widest, gappiest grins he had ever seen.

'You are a twin?' he asked in surprise.

Her answer came after a beat too long. 'Yes.'

He looked at her. Hannah's lips were drawn in. Her lightly tanned skin had lost a little of its colour.

'Why was she not out last night with you, celebrating your other sister's hen night?'

Her hands fisted into balls before she flexed them and raised her chin. 'Beth died a long time ago.'

His hand stilled.

'Please be careful with that. It's the last picture taken

of us together.' There was a definite hint of anxiety in her voice.

This was another clear-cut opportunity to convince her of his true self. All he had to do was rip the photo into little pieces and he guaranteed she would leave without a backward glance.

But no matter how much he commanded his hands to do the deed, they refused.

Hannah's voice broke through his conflicted thoughts. 'Can I have my stuff back now?' she asked, now speaking in her more familiar droll manner.

Without saying a word, he carefully slotted the photo back in its place, blinking to rid himself of the image of the happy young girls.

The last picture of them together?

His stomach did a full roll and settled with a heavy weight rammed onto it.

Getting abruptly to his feet, he dropped the bag by Hannah's seat. 'I need to speak with the crew. Put your seat belt on.'

Hannah expelled all the air from her lungs in one long movement, watching as Francesco disappeared through a door.

There had been a moment when she'd been convinced he was going to crush the photo in his giant hands.

If there was one thing she'd be unable to forgive, it was that.

But he hadn't. He'd wanted to, but the basic decency within him had won out. And he hadn't fired a load of questions about Beth at her, either.

It was very rare that she spoke about her twin. Even after fifteen years, it still felt too raw, as if vocalising it turned it back into the real event that had ripped her apart. People treated her differently. As soon as someone learned about it, she just knew that was how they would start referring to her. *That's the girl whose twin sister died.* She'd heard those very whispers at school, felt the curious glances and the eyes just waiting for the telltale sign of her suffering. She knew what her schoolmates had been waiting for—they'd been waiting for her to cry.

She'd cried plenty, but always in the privacy of her bedroom—the room she'd shared with Beth.

She'd learned to repel the curiosity with a bright smile, and ignore the whispers by burying herself in her schoolwork. It had been the same with her parents. And Melanie. She'd effectively shut them all out, hiding her despair behind a smile and then locking herself away.

When Francesco reappeared a few minutes later, she fixed that same bright smile on him.

'We'll be taking off in five minutes,' he said. 'This is your last chance to change your mind.'

'I'm not changing my mind.'

'Sicily is my turf. If you come, you will be bound under my directive.'

'How very formal. I'm still not changing my mind.'

His eyes glittered with menace. 'As I said earlier—on your head be it.'

'Gosh, it's hot,' Hannah commented as she followed Francesco off the steps of the plane. She breathed in deeply. Yes, there it was. That lovely scent of the sea. Thousands of miles away, and for a moment she had captured the smell of home. Her real home—on the coast of Devon. Not London. London was where she lived.

'It's summer' came the curt reply.

At least she'd had the foresight to change out of the leathers and into her sundress before they'd landed. Not that Francesco had noticed. Or, if he had, he hadn't acknowledged it, keeping his head buried so deep into what he was doing on his laptop she wouldn't have been surprised if he'd disappeared into the screen. The only time he'd moved had been to go into his bedroom—yes, he had a *bedroom on a plane!*—and changed from his own leathers into a pair of black chinos, an untucked white linen shirt, and a blazer.

A sleek grey car was waiting, the driver opening the passenger door as they approached. Another identical car waited behind, and Francesco's guards piled into it—except one, who got into the front of their own car.

The doors had barely closed before the guard twisted round and handed a metallic grey object to Francesco.

'Is that a gun?' Hannah asked in a tone more squeaky than anything a chipmunk could produce.

He tucked the object into what she assumed was an inside pocket of his blazer. 'We are in Sicily.'

'Are guns legal in Sicily?'

He speared her with a look she assumed was supposed to make her quail.

'I hope for your sake it's not loaded,' she said. 'Especially with you keeping it so close to your heart.'

'Then it's just as well I have a doctor travelling with me.'

'See? I have my uses.'

Despite her flippancy, the gun unnerved her. It unnerved her a lot.

Knowing on an intellectual level that Francesco was dangerous was one thing. Witnessing him handle a gun with the nonchalance of one handling a pen was another.

He's doing this for effect, she told herself. *Remember, this is an adventure.*

'Where are we going?' she asked after a few minutes of silence had passed.

'My nightclub.'

It didn't take long before they pulled up outside an enormous Gothic-looking building with pillars at the doors.

'This is a nightclub?'

'That's where I said we were going.'

In a melee of stocky male bodies, she followed him inside.

The Palermo Calvetti's was, she estimated, at least four times the size of its English counterpart. Although decorated in the same glitzy silver and deep reds and exuding glamour, it had a more cosmopolitan feel.

A young woman behind the bar, polishing all the hardwood and optics, practically snapped to attention at the sight of them.

'Due caffè neri nel mio ufficio,' Francesco called out as he swept past and through a door marked *Privato*.

Like its English equivalent, his office was spotless. Two of his men entered the room with them—the same two who'd been guarding the English Calvetti's when she had turned up just five short days ago.

Francesco went straight to a small portrait on the wall and pressed his fingers along the edge of the frame until it popped open as if it were the cover of a book.

'Another cliché?' she couldn't resist asking.

'Clichés are called clichés for a reason,' he said with a shrug of a shoulder. 'Why make it easy for thieves?'

Watching him get into his safe, Hannah decided that it would be easier to break into Fort Knox than into Francesco Calvetti's empire. The inner safe door swinging open, her eyes widened to see the sheer size of the space inside, so much larger than she would have guessed from the picture covering it.

Her stare grew wider to see the canvas bags he removed from it and she realised that they were filled with money.

Francesco and his two men conversed rapidly, all the

while weighing wads of notes on a small set of electronic scales and making notes in a battered-looking A4 book. When the young woman came in with two coffees and a bowl of sugar cubes, Francesco added two lumps into both cups, stirred them vigorously, then passed one over to Hannah, who had perched herself on a windowsill.

'Thanks,' she said, ridiculously touched he'd remembered how she liked her coffee.

Not that it would have been hard to remember, she mused, seeing as he took his exactly the same.

The same thought must have run through Francesco's head because his eyes suddenly met hers, a look of consternation running through them before he jerked his head back to what he was doing.

It amazed her that he would allow her in his inner sanctum when such a large amount of money was, literally, on the table. Then she remembered the gun in his jacket, which he had placed over the back of his captain's chair.

Peering less than subtly at his henchmen, she thought she detected a slight bulge in the calf of the black trousers one wore.

Unnerved by the massive amounts of money before her and the fact she was alone in an office with three men, two of whom were definitely armed, she reached for her phone to smother her increasing agitation.

Working through her messages, Hannah's heart sank when she opened an email from an excited Melanie, who had finally, after months of debate, settled on the wedding-breakfast menu. She could only hope the response she fired back sounded suitably enthusiastic, but she couldn't even bring herself to open the attachment with the menu listed on it, instead opening a work-related email.

It was the most significant event in her little sister's life and, much as Hannah wanted to be excited for her, all she felt inside when she thought of the forthcoming day was dread.

'What are you doing?' Francesco asked a while later, breaking through her concentration.

'Going through my messages.'

'Again?'

'I like to keep abreast of certain patients' progress,' she explained, turning her phone off and chucking it back into her bag.

'Even at weekends?'

'*You're* working,' she pointed out.

'This is my business.'

'And the survival and recovery of my patients is *my* business.'

She had no idea what was going on behind those chocolate-fudge eyes but, judging by the set of his jaw and the thinning of his lips, she guessed it was something unpleasant.

A few minutes later and it appeared they were done, the two henchmen having placed all the money into a large suitcase.

'Before you leave for the bank, Mario,' Francesco said, speaking in deliberate English, 'I want you to show the good doctor here your hand.'

The guns hadn't made any overt impression on her, other than what he took to be a healthy shock that he armed himself in his homeland. He felt certain the next minute would change her impression completely.

Mario complied, holding his hand with its disfigured fingers in front of her.

She peered closely before taking it into her own hands and rubbing her fingers over the meaty skin.

A hot stab plunged into Francesco's chest. He inhaled deeply through his nose, clenching his hands into fists.

She was just examining it like the professional she was, he told himself. All the same, even his mental teeth had gritted together.

'What do you see?' he demanded.

'A hand that's been broken in a number of places—the fingers have been individually broken, too, as if something heavy was smashed onto them.'

'An excellent assessment. Now, Mario, I would like you to tell Dr Chapman who broke your hand and smashed your fingers.'

If Mario was capable of showing surprise, he would be displaying it now, his eyes flashing at Francesco, who nodded his go-ahead. This was an incident that hadn't been discussed or even alluded to in nearly two decades.

'Signor Calvetti. He did it.'

Hannah looked up at Francesco. 'Your father?'

Deliberately, he folded his arms across his chest and stretched his legs out. 'No. Not my father.'

Her eyes widened. 'You?'

'*Sì*. I caught him stealing from my father. Take another look at his hand. That is what we do to thieves in my world.'

CHAPTER FIVE

FRANCESCO KEPT HIS gaze fixed on Hannah, waiting for a reaction other than her current open-mouthed horror.

See, he said with his eyes, *you wanted proof? Well, here it is.*

She closed her eyes and shook her head. When she snapped them back open, she gave Mario's hand another close inspection.

'These scars look old,' she said.

'Nearly twenty year,' Mario supplied in his pigeon English. 'Is okay. I ask for it.'

'What—you asked for your hand to be smashed?'

'What he means is that he did the crime knowing what his punishment would be if caught,' said Francesco.

Her eyes shrewd, she nodded. 'And yet, even after what you did to him and his so-called crime, he still works for you, is trusted enough to handle large quantities of money on your behalf, and, if I'm reading this right, carries a gun that he has never turned on you in revenge.'

How did she do it?

She'd turned it round on him *again.*

'Do not think there was any benevolence on my part,' he countered harshly, before nodding a dismissal at Mario, who left the office with his colleague, leaving them alone.

Hannah remained perched on the windowsill, her hair

now turned into a bushy beehive. She'd crossed her legs, her pale blue dress having ridden up her thighs. It was one of the most repulsive articles of clothing he had ever seen: shapeless, buttoned from top to bottom, clearly brought for comfort rather than style. And yet…there was something incredibly alluring about having to guess what lay beneath it.…

'What did he steal?'

'He was a waiter at one of my father's restaurants and made the mistake of helping himself to the takings in the till.'

'How much did he take?' she asked. Her former nonchalance had vanished. It pleased him to hear her troubled tone.

'I don't remember. Something that was the equivalent of around one hundred pounds.'

'So you maimed him for one hundred pounds?'

Francesco drew himself to his full height. 'Mario knew the risks.'

'Fair enough,' she said in a tone that left no doubt she meant the exact opposite. 'Why didn't you just call the police?'

'The police?' A mirthful sound escaped from his throat. 'We have our own ways of handling things here.'

'So if he stole from your father, why did *you* mete out the punishment?'

Francesco remembered that day so clearly.

He'd caught Mario red-handed. There had been no choice but to confront him. He'd made him empty his pockets. His father had walked in and demanded to know what was going on.

How clearly he remembered that sickening feeling in the pit of his stomach when Mario had confessed, looking Salvatore square in the eye as he did so.

And how clearly he remembered feeling as if he would

vomit when Salvatore had turned his laser glare to him, his son, and said, 'You know what must be done.'

Francesco had known. And so had Mario, whose own father had worked for Salvatore, and Salvatore's father before him. They'd both known the score.

It was time for Francesco to prove himself a man in his father's eyes, something his father had been waiting on for years. Something *he'd* been waiting on for years, too. A chance to gain his father's respect.

But how could he explain this to Hannah, explain that it had been an opportunity that hadn't just presented itself to him but come gift-wrapped? Refusal had never been an option.

And why did he even care to explain himself?

Francesco didn't explain himself to anyone.

He hadn't explained himself since he'd vomited in the privacy of his bathroom after the deed had been done, and only when he was certain he was out of earshot.

That was the last time he'd ever allowed himself to react with emotion. Certainly the last time he'd allowed himself to feel any vulnerability.

Overnight he'd put his childhood behind him, not that there had been much left of it after his mother had overdosed.

'I did it because it needed to be done and I was the one who caught him.'

She kept her eyes fixed on him. There was none of the reproach or disgust he expected to find. All that was there was something that looked suspiciously like compassion.... 'Twenty years ago you would have been a boy.'

'I was seventeen. I was a man.'

'And how old was he?'

'The same.'

'Little more than children.'

'We both knew what we were doing,' he stated harshly. 'After that night we were no longer children.'

'I'll bet.'

'And how many more hands have you mangled in the intervening years?'

'Enough of them. There are times when examples need to be made.'

Violence had been a part of his life since toddlerhood. His mother had tried to protect him from the worst of his father's excesses but her attempts had not been enough. His first memory was looking out of his bedroom window and witnessing his father beating up a man over a car bonnet. The man had been held down by two of his father's men.

His mother had been horrified to find him looking out and dragged him away, covering his eyes. Francesco had learned only ten months ago that the bruising he often saw on his mother's body was also from the hands of his father, and not the result of clumsiness.

Francesco had spent his entire life idolising his father. Sure, there were things he'd never been comfortable about, but Salvatore was his father. He'd loved and respected him. After his death four years ago, certain truths had been revealed about aspects of his father's business that had taken some of the shine off his memories, like discovering his drug importing. That in itself had been a very bitter blow to bear, had sickened him to the pit of his stomach. But to learn the truth of what he'd done to his mother… It had sent Francesco's world spinning off its axis.

The walls of the spacious office started to close in on him. The air conditioning was on but the humidity had become stifling, perspiration breaking out on his back.

Hannah stared intently into those beautiful chocolate eyes. Only years of practice at reading her patients allowed her to see beneath the hard exterior he projected. There was pain there. A lot of it. 'What is it about me that scares you so much?'

His lips curled into a sneer. Rising from his chair, he strode towards her like a sleek panther. 'You think you scare me?'

'What other reason is there for you to try so hard to frighten me off and go out of your way to try to make me hate you? Because that's what you're doing, isn't it? Trying to make me hate you?'

He stilled, his huge frame right before her, blocking everything else out.

She reached out a hand and placed it on his chest. 'I bet you've never treated a woman like this before.'

'Like what?' he asked harshly, leaning over and placing his face right in hers, close enough for her to feel the warmth of his breath. 'You're the one with the foolish, romanticised notions about me. I warned you from the start that you didn't belong in my world, and yet you thought you knew best.'

'So this is all to make me see the real you?'

'We had a deal, Dr Chapman,' he bit out, grabbing her hand, which still rested against his hard chest, and lacing his fingers through it. He squeezed, a warning that caused no physical pain but was undoubtedly meant to impress upon her that, if he so chose, he *could* hurt her. 'I made you a guarantee that by the end of our time together I would be the last man you would want to give your virginity to.'

Squeezing his fingers in return, her mouth filling with saliva, she tilted her chin a touch. His mouth was almost close enough to press her lips to....

'If you really want to prove it, then hurt me, don't just give me a warning. You're twice my size—it would take no effort for you to hurt me if you really wanted.' Oh, but she was playing with fire. She didn't need Francesco to point that out. But no matter what she had seen in the two hours she'd been in his country, deep in her marrow was the rooted certainty that he would never hurt her, not in any meaningful sense.

If eyes could spit fire, Francesco's would be doing just that. But there was something else there, too, something that darkened as his breathing deepened.

'See?' she whispered. 'You can't hurt me.'

'Where does your faith in me come from?' His voice had become hoarse.

'It comes from *here*,' she answered, pulling their entwined fingers to her chest and pressing his hand right over her heart. 'I've seen the good in you. Why do you have so little faith in yourself?'

'I have no illusions about what I'm like. You have dedicated your life to healing sick children, whereas my life revolves around power and money, and all the seediness they attract.'

'Your power and money mean nothing to me.'

A groan escaped from his lips and he muttered something she didn't understand before snaking his free hand around her neck and pressing his lips to hers.

All the air expelled from her lungs.

She'd had no notion of what kissing Francesco would be like, could never have envisaged the surge of adrenaline that would course through her veins and thicken her blood at the feel of his firm lips hard against hers, not moving, simply breathing her in.

Returning the pressure, she placed a hand to his cheek, kneading her fingers into the smooth skin as she parted her lips and flitted her tongue into the heat of his mouth.

Francesco's breathing became laboured. His hold on her neck tightened then relaxed, the hand held against her chest moving to sweep around her waist and draw her flush against him to deepen the connection. When his own tongue darted into her mouth, she melted into him, two bodies meshed together, kissing with a hunger that bloomed into unimaginable proportions.

He tasted divine, of darkness and coffee and something else Hannah could only assume was *him*, filling her senses.

Deep inside, the pulsations she had first experienced when he had touched her in his London office began to vibrate and hum.

To think she had gone for twenty-seven years without experiencing *this*.

Brushing her hand down his cheek to rest on the sharp crease of his collar, she stroked the tips of her fingers over the strong neck, marvelling at his strength and the power that lay beneath the skin.

It wasn't the power that came from his position in the world that attracted her so much, she thought dimly, it was the latent masculine power within *him*.

Before she could make sense of all the wonderful sensations rising within her, he pulled away—or, rather, wrenched apart the physical connection between them.

His chest rising and falling in rapid motion, Francesco took a step back, wiping his mouth as if to rid himself of her taste.

'I know my power and money mean nothing to you,' he said, virtually spitting the words out. 'That's why getting involved with you is wrong on every level imaginable.'

Trying to clamp down on the humiliation that came hot on the heels of his abrupt rejection, Hannah jumped down from the windowsill. 'I don't know how many times I have to say this, but I do *not* want to become involved with you, not in any real sense. All I want is to experience some of the life every other woman takes for granted but which has passed me by.'

'And you *should* experience it, but it should be with someone who can give you a future.'

'Medicine is my future.'

'And that stops you building a future with a man, does it?'

Not even bothering to hide her exasperation, she shook her head. 'I'm married to my work, and that's the way I like it. I want to make it to consultant level and I've worked too hard and for too long to throw it all away on a relationship that would never fulfil me even a fraction as much as my job does.'

'How can you know that if you've never tried?'

She pursed her lips together. A deep and meaningful debate about her reasons for not wanting a relationship had not been on the agenda. 'I just know, okay?'

'Your job will never keep you warm at night.'

'My hot-water bottle does a perfectly good job of that and, besides, what right do you have to question me on this? I don't see a wedding ring on your finger. If the internet reports on you are true, as you say they are, you seem to have a phobia towards commitment yourself.' Hadn't that been another tick on her mental checklist, the fact Francesco appeared to steer away from anything that could be construed as permanent?

His face darkened. 'I have my reasons for not wanting marriage.'

'Well, I have mine, too. Why can't you respect that?'

Francesco took a deep breath and slowly expelled it. Why could he not just take everything Hannah said at face value? *His* body was telling him to just accept it, to take her back to his villa and take her, just as she'd asked, until she was so sated she would be unable to think.

But even if he did take her words at face value and accepted that she wasn't asking for anything more than one night, it didn't change the fact that making love to her would taint her. She deserved better than Salvatore Calvetti's son, even if she couldn't see it herself.

He would make her see.

'Let's get out of here,' he said, unable to endure the claustrophobia being shut in four walls with Hannah Chapman induced a minute longer. 'I'm taking you shopping.'

'Shopping?'

'You need a dress for tonight.'

'Why? What's happening tonight?'

'We're going to my casino. There's a poker tournament I need to oversee. I'm not having you by my side dressed as some kind of bag lady.'

Her face blanched at his cruel words, but he bit back the apology forming on his tongue.

In truth, there was something unbearably sexy about Hannah's take-me-as-I-am, comfortable-in-my-skin approach to her appearance, and the longer he was in her company, the sexier he found it.

A bag lady.

Francesco looked at her and saw a *bag lady*?

Having been dumped in a designer shop, whereby Francesco had promptly disappeared, leaving at her disposal a driver with the words, 'I'll meet you at my villa in a few hours—buy whatever you want and charge it to me,' Hannah still didn't know whether she wanted to laugh or punch him in the face.

Trying on what was probably her dozenth dress in the plush changing room, she reflected on his words.

Okay, so her appearance had never been a priority, but did she really look like a bag lady?

Her clothes were mostly bought online when the items she already owned started wearing out. She selected clothes based on suitability for work and comfort. Clothes were a means of keeping her body warm.

Her hair... Well, who had the time for regular haircuts? Not hardworking doctors fighting their way up the food chain, that was for sure. And if the rest of her colleagues managed to fit in regular visits to a salon, then good for them. Still, she had to admit her hair had become a little wild in recent years, and racked her brain trying to remember the last time a pair of scissors had been let loose on it. She came up with a blank.

She could remember the first time her mother had let her and Beth go to a proper hairdresser rather than hack at their hair with the kitchen scissors. It had been their twelfth birthday and the pair of them had felt so grown-up. How lovingly they'd attended their hair after that little trip, faithfully conditioning it at regular intervals.

She tried to think of the last time she'd conditioned her hair and came up with another blank.

Was it really possible she'd gone through the past fifteen years without either a haircut or the use of a conditioner? A distant memory floated like a wisp in her memories, of her mother knocking on her bedroom door, calling that it was time for her appointment at the hairdresser's. She remembered the knots that had formed in her throat and belly and her absolute refusal to go.

How could she get a haircut when Beth wouldn't be there to share it with her? Not that she'd vocalised this particular reasoning. She hadn't needed to. Her mother hadn't pressed her on the issue or brought the subject up again. Haircuts, make-up, all the things that went with being a girl on the cusp of womanhood were banished.

How had she let that happen?

After selecting a dress, a pair of shoes and matching clutch, and some sexy underwear which made her blush as she fingered the silken material, she handed the items to the manager, along with her credit card.

'Signor Calvetti has made arrangements to pay,' the manager said.

'I know, but I can pay for my own clothes, thank you.'

'It is very expensive.'

'I can afford it.' And, sadly, she could. She didn't drink and rarely socialised—Melanie's hen do had been Hannah's first proper night out that year. After paying off her mortgage and other household bills every month, her only expenditure was food, which, when you were buying frozen meals for one, didn't amount to much. She didn't drive. Her only trips were her monthly visits to her parents' home in Devon, for which she always got a lift down with Melanie and her soon-to-be brother-in-law.

Her colleagues, especially those around the same age as her, regularly complained of being skint. Hannah, never spending any money, had a comfortable nest egg.

How had she allowed herself to get in this position?

It was one thing putting money aside for a rainy day but, quite frankly, she had enough stashed away that she could handle months of torrential rain without worrying.

Despite her assurance, the store manager still seemed reluctant to take her card.

'Either accept my card or I'll find a dress in another shop,' Hannah said, although not unkindly. She smiled at the flustered woman. 'Honestly, there's enough credit on there to cover it.'

'But Signor Calvetti...'

Ah. The penny dropped. It wasn't that the manager was worried about Hannah's credit; rather, she was worried about what Francesco would do when he learned his wishes had been overruled. 'Don't worry about him—I'll make sure he knows I insisted. He's learning how stubborn I can be in getting my own way.'

With great reluctance, the manager took Hannah's card. Less than a minute later the purchase was complete. Hannah had spent more in one transaction than she'd spent on her entire wardrobe since leaving medical school.

'I don't suppose you know of a decent hairdresser that could fit me in with little notice, do you?'

The manager peered a little too closely at Hannah's hair, a tentative smile forming on her face. 'For Signor Calvetti's lover, any salon in Palermo will fit you in. Would you like me to make the phone call?'

Signor Calvetti's lover... Those words set off a warm feeling through her veins, rather as if she'd been injected with heated treacle. 'That's very kind, thank you—I'll be sure to tell Francesco how helpful you've been.'

Five minutes later Hannah left the boutique with a shop assistant personally escorting her to the selected salon, her driver/bodyguard trailing behind them.

Having her hair cut was one of the most surreal events she could ever recall and, considering the dreamlike quality of the day thus far, that was saying something.

The salon itself was filled with women who were clearly the cream of Sicilian society, yet Hannah was treated like a celebrity in her own right, with stylists and assistants fawning all over her and thrusting numerous cups of strong coffee into her hands.

At the end, when she was given the bill, she made an admirable job of not shrieking in horror.

Oh, well, she told herself as she handed her credit card over for another battering, it would surely be worth it.

She was determined that, after tonight, Francesco would never look at her like a bag lady again.

CHAPTER SIX

HANNAH HAD BEEN shopping in Palermo for such a long time that Francesco started to think she'd had second thoughts and hopped on a plane back to London.

He could have found out for himself by calling the bodyguard he'd left to watch over her, but resisted each time the urge took him. He'd stopped himself making that call for almost two hours.

Thus, when the bulletproof four-by-four pulled up within the villa's gates late afternoon, he fully expected Hannah to get out laden with bags and packages, having gone mad on his credit card. Likely, she would have changed into one of her new purchases.

Instead, she clambered her way out and up the steep steps leading to the main entrance of his villa, still dressed in that ugly shapeless dress. All she carried was her handbag and two other bags and, to top it all off, she wore a navy blue scarf over her hair.

She looked a bigger mess than when he'd left her in the boutique.

Even so, his heart accelerated at the sight of her.

Taking a deep breath to slow his raging pulse, then another when the first had zero effect, Francesco opened his front door.

Hannah stood on the step before him. 'This is your home?' she asked, her eyes sparkling.

'*Sì.*'

'It's fabulous.'

It took every ounce of restraint within him not to allow his lips to curve into the smile they so wanted. 'Thank you.'

He took a step back to admit her. 'You were a long time.' Immediately he cursed himself for voicing his concern.

'The boutique manager—a fabulous woman, by the way—managed to get me into a hairdresser's.'

'You've had your hair cut?' He caught a whiff of that particular scent found only in salons, a kind of fragrant chemical odour. It clung to her.

'Kind of.' Her face lit up with a hint of mischief. 'You'll just have to wait and see—the hairdresser wrapped the scarf round it so it didn't get wind damaged or anything.' She did a full three-sixty rotation. 'I can't believe this is your home. Do you live here alone?'

'I have staff, but they live in separate quarters.'

'It's amazing. Really. Amazing.'

Francesco's home was a matter of pride, his sanctuary away from a life filled with hidden dangers. Hannah's wide-eyed enthusiasm for it filled his chest, making it expand.

'Who would have guessed being a gangster would pay so well?' Her grin negated the sting her words induced. 'I'm just saying.' She laughed, noticing his unimpressed expression. 'You're the one trying to convince me you're a gangster.'

'You really don't believe in beating around the bush, do you?'

Her nose scrunched up a little. 'Erm…I guess not. I've never really thought about it.'

'It's very refreshing,' he surprised himself by admitting.

'Really? And is that a good thing?'

'Most refreshing things are good.'

'In that case…excellent. It's nice to know there's something about me you approve of.' Despite the lightness of her tone, he caught a definite edge to it, an edge he didn't care for and that made him reach over and grab her wrist.

'When are you going to learn, Dr Chapman, that my approval should mean nothing to a woman like you?'

'And when are you going to learn, Signor Calvetti, that I may be a doctor but I am still a human being? I am still a woman.'

He was now certain the edge he had detected was the whiff of reproach.

Surely he should be delighted she was starting to see through the layers to the real man inside. So why did he feel more unsettled than ever?

'Believe me, *Dr* Chapman,' he said, putting deliberate emphasis on her title, 'I am well aware that beneath your haphazard appearance is a woman.'

A smile flitted over her face, not the beaming spark of joy he was becoming accustomed to but a smile that could almost be described as shy. Bright spots of colour stained her cheeks.

Shoving his hands in his pockets lest they did something stupid like reach out for her again, Francesco inclined his head to the left. 'If you head in that direction you will go through several living rooms before you reach the indoor pool, which you are welcome to use, although you might prefer the outside one. If you go through the door on the other side of the pool you'll find the kitchen. If you're hungry my chef will cook something for you, but I would suggest you keep it light as we will be dining in the casino.'

'We're eating out?'

'Yes. I'll show you to the room you will be sleeping in whilst you're here as my guest.'

'Which is only until tomorrow,' Hannah stated amiably, biting back the question of whether it would be *his* room she would be sleeping in, already knowing the answer.

Francesco's villa was a thing of beauty, a huge white palace cleverly cut into the rocks of the hillside. Walking up the steps to his home, the scent of perfumed flowers and lemons had filled her senses so strongly she would have been happy to simply stand there and enjoy. If she hadn't been so keen to see Francesco, she would have done.

She'd been aware he possessed great wealth, but even so...

It felt as if she'd slipped through the looking glass and landed in a parallel universe.

She followed him through huge white arches, over brightly coloured tiled flooring, past exotic furniture, and up a winding stone staircase to a long, uneven corridor.

'Was this once a cave?' she asked.

He laughed. *Francesco actually laughed.* It might not have been a great big boom echoing off the high ceilings, more of a low chuckle, but it was a start and it made her heart flip.

'Its original history is a bit of a mystery,' he said, opening a door at the end of the corridor. 'This is your room.'

Hannah clamped a hand over her mouth to stop the squeal that wanted to make itself heard. Slowly she drank it all in: the four-poster bed, the vibrant colours, the private balcony overlooking the outdoor pool...

'Wow,' she said when she felt capable of speaking without sounding like a giddy schoolgirl. 'If I didn't have to get back to work on Monday, I'd be tempted to claim squatters' rights.'

'You're still trusting I will get you back to London in time?'

She rolled her eyes in answer.

'Let us hope your faith in me is justified.'

'If I turn out to be wrong then no worries—I'll get my own flight back.'

'And what about your passport? You will need that to leave the country.'

'My passport's in my bag.'

'You are sure about that?' At her puzzled expression, Francesco leaned over and whispered into her ear, 'A word of advice, Dr Chapman—when in the company of criminals, never leave your bag open with your passport and phone in it.'

With that, he strolled to the door, patting his back pocket for emphasis. 'Be ready to leave in two hours.'

Hannah watched him close the door before diving into her handbag.

Unbelievable! In the short time she'd been in his home, Francesco had deftly removed her passport and mobile and she hadn't noticed a thing.

She should be furious. She should be a lot of things. He had her passport—effectively had her trapped in his country—but it was her phone she felt a pang of anxiety over.

She had to give him points for continuing to try to make her see the worst in him, but there was no way in the world he would keep hold of her stuff. She had no doubt that, come the morning, he would return the items to her.

The morning…

Before the morning came the night.

And a shiver zipped up her spine at the thought of what that night could bring.

Francesco sat on his sprawling sofa catching up on the day's qualifying event for one of the many motor racing sports he followed, when he heard movement behind the archway dividing the living room from the library.

Sitting upright, he craned his neck to see better.

He caught a flash of blue that vanished before reappearing with a body attached to it. Hannah's body.

Hannah's incredible body.

His jaw dropped open.

There she stood, visibly fighting for composure, until she expanded her arms and said, 'What do you think? Do I still resemble a bag lady?'

A bag lady? He could think of a hundred words to describe her but the adjective that sprang to the forefront of his mind was *stunning*.

Where the blue dress she had changed into on his plane had been a drab, ill-fitting creation, this soft blue dress was a million miles apart. Silk and Eastern in style with swirling oriental flowers printed onto it, it skimmed her figure like a caress, landing midthigh to show off incredibly shapely legs.

Whatever the hairdresser had been paid could never be enough. The thick mop of straw-like hair had gone. Now Hannah's hair was twisted into a sleek knot, pinned in with black chopsticks. There was not a millimetre of frizz in sight. If his eyes were not deceiving him, she'd had colour applied to it, turning her multicoloured locks into more of a honey blonde.

She wore make-up, too, her eyes ringed with dark smokiness that highlighted the moreish hazel, her lips a deep cherry-red...

She looked beautiful.

And yet...

He hated it.

She no longer looked like Hannah.

'No. You no longer resemble a bag lady.'

'Well, that's a relief.' She shuffled into the room on shoes with heels high enough to make her hobble—although not as high as many women liked to wear—and stood before him, her hand outstretched. Her short nails hadn't been touched, a sight he found strangely reassuring. 'Can I have my phone back, please?'

'You can have it back when you leave Sicily.'

'I'd like it back now.'

'For what reason?'

'I've told you—I like to keep abreast of what's going on with my patients.'

'And what can you do for them here?'

'Not worry about them. No news is good news.'

'Then it seems I am doing you a favour.'

'But how am I going to know if there is no news? Now I'll worry that bad news has come and I won't know one way or the other.'

Hiding his irritation, he said, 'Do all doctors go to such lengths for their patients?'

Her lips pressed together. 'I have no idea. It's none of my concern what my colleagues get up to when they're off duty.'

'What happened to professional detachment? I thought you doctors were trained to keep your distance?'

A hint of fire flashed in her eyes. 'Keeping a check on the welfare of my patients is at odds with my professionalism?'

'I'm just asking the question.'

'Well, don't. I will not have my professionalism questioned by you or anyone.'

It was the first time Francesco had heard her sound even remotely riled. He'd clearly hit a nerve.

Studying her carefully, he got to his feet. 'I think it will do you good to spend one evening away from your phone.'

Hannah opened her mouth to argue but he placed a finger to it. 'I did not mean to question your professionalism. However, I am not prepared to spend the evening with someone who has only half a mind on what's going on. Constantly checking your phone is rude.'

Her cheeks heightened with colour, a mutinous expression blazing from her eyes.

'I will make a deal with you,' he continued silkily. 'You say you want to experience all the world has to offer, yet it will be a half-hearted experience if you are preoccupied with worrying about your patients. If you prove that you can let your hair down and enjoy the experience of what the casino has to offer, I will give you your phone back when we return to the villa.'

For the first time since she'd met him, Hannah wanted to slap Francesco. Okay, keep her passport until it was time to leave—that didn't bother her. She knew she would get it back. She knew she would get her phone back eventually, too, but she needed it *now*. She needed to keep the roots the mobile gave her to the ward.

And how dared he imply that she had no detachment? She had it. But she refused to lose her empathy. Her patients were her guiding motive in life. Never would she allow one of her young charges to be on the receiving end of a doctor who had lost basic humanity. She wouldn't. She couldn't. She'd been at the other end and, while it hadn't made the pain of what she went through any worse, a little compassion would have helped endure it that little bit better.

Eventually she took a deep breath and bestowed Francesco with her first fake smile. 'Fine. But if you want me to let my hair down and enjoy myself it's only fair you do the same, too. After all,' she added airily, 'I would say that, of the two of us, you're the greater workaholic. At least I take weekends off.'

Calvetti's casino was a titanic building, baroque in heritage, set over four levels in the heart of Palermo. Hannah followed Francesco up the first sweeping staircase and into an enormous room filled with gambling tables and slot machines as far as the eye could see. It was like stepping into a tasteful version of Vegas.

Flanked by his minders, they continued up the next set of stairs to the third floor. There, a group of men in black parted to admit them into a room that seemed virtually identical to the second floor. It took a few moments for her to realise what the subtle differences were. The lower level was filled with ordinary punters. The third floor, which had around a quarter of the number of customers, was evidently the domain of the filthy rich.

Sticking closely to Francesco, Hannah drank everything in: the gold trimming on all the tables, the beautiful fragrant women, the men in tuxedos—which, she noted, none filled as well as Francesco, who looked even more broodingly gorgeous than usual in his. After a host of conversations, Francesco slipped an arm around her waist and drew her through a set of double doors and into the restaurant.

And what a restaurant it was, somehow managing to be both opulent and elegant.

'Are the customers on the second floor allowed to dine in here?' she asked once they'd been seated by a fawning maître d' at a corner table.

'They have their own restaurant,' he said, opening his leather-bound menu.

'But are they allowed to eat in here?'

'The third floor is for private members only. Anyone can join, providing they can pay the fifty thousand euro joining fee and the ten thousand annual membership.'

She blinked in shock. 'People pay that?'

'People pay for exclusivity—the waiting list is longer than the actual membership list.'

'That's mind-blowing. I feel like a gatecrasher.'

She only realised he'd been avoiding her stare when he raised his eyes to look at her.

'You are with me.'

The possessive authority of his simple statement set her pulse racing, and in that moment she forgot all about being mad at him for refusing to hand back her phone.

'So what do you recommend from the menu?' she asked when she was certain her tongue hadn't rooted to the roof of her mouth.

'All of it.'

She laughed, a noise that sounded more nervous than merry.

A waiter came over to them. *'Posso portarti le bevande?'*

Francesco spoke rapidly back to him.

'He wanted our drink order,' he explained once the waiter had bustled off. 'I've ordered us a bottle of Shiraz.'

'Is that a wine?'

'Yes. The Shiraz we sell here is of the highest quality.'

'I don't drink wine. I'll have a cola instead.'

A shrewdness came into his eyes. 'Have you ever drunk wine?'

'No.'

'Have you ever drunk alcohol?'

'I had a few sips of champagne at Mel's hen do.' Suddenly it occurred to her that Melanie's hen party had been just twenty-four hours ago.

Where had the time gone?

It felt as if she'd experienced a whole different life in that short space of time.

'And that was your first taste of alcohol?'

She stared at him, nodding slowly, her mind racing. After all, wasn't the whole point of her being in Sicily with Francesco to begin her exploration of life? 'Maybe I *should* have a glass of the Shiraz.'

He nodded his approval. 'But only a small glass. Your body has not acquired a tolerance for alcohol.'

'My body hasn't acquired a tolerance for anything.'

The waiter returned with their wine and a jug of water before Francesco could ask what she meant by that comment.

The more time he spent with Hannah, the more intriguing he found her. Nothing seemed to faze her, except having her professionalism cast into doubt. And having her phone taken away.

He watched as she studied the menu, her brow furrowed in concentration. 'Are mussels nice?' she asked.

'They're delicious.'

She beamed. 'I'll have those, then.'

A platter of antipasto was brought out for them to nibble on while they waited for their meals to be cooked.

'Is this like ham?' she asked, holding up a slice of prosciutto.

'Not really. Try some.'

She popped it into her mouth and chewed, then nodded her approval. Swallowing, she reached for a roasted pepper.

'Try some wine,' he commanded.

'Do I sniff it first?'

'If you want.' He smothered a laugh when she practically dunked her nose into the glass.

She took the tiniest of sips. 'Oh, wow. That's really nice.'

'Have you really never drunk wine before?'

'I really haven't.' She popped a plump green olive into her mouth.

'Why not?'

Her nose scrunched. 'My parents aren't drinkers so we never had alcohol in the house. By the time I was old enough to get into experimenting I was focused on my studies. I wasn't prepared to let anything derail my dream of being a doctor. It was easier to just say no.'

'How old were you when you decided to be a doctor?'

'Twelve.'

'That's a young age to make a life-defining choice.'

'Most twelve-year-olds have dreams of what they want to do when they grow up.'

'Agreed, but most change their mind.'

'What did you want to be when *you* were twelve?'

'A racing bike rider.'

'I can see you doing that,' she admitted. 'So what stopped you? Or did you just change your mind?'

'It was only ever a pipe dream,' he said with a dismissive shrug. 'I was Salvatore Calvetti's only child. I was groomed from birth to take over his empire.'

'And how's that going?'

Francesco fixed hard eyes on her. 'I always knew I would build my own empire. I am interested to know, though, what drew you to medicine in the first place—was it the death of your sister?'

A brief hesitation. 'Yes.'

'She was called Beth?'

Another hesitation followed by a nod. When Hannah reached for her glass of water he saw a slight tremor in her hand. She took a long drink before meeting his eyes.

'Beth contracted meningitis when we were twelve. They said it was flu. They didn't get the diagnosis right until it was too late. She was dead within a day.'

She laid the bare facts out to him in a matter-of-fact manner, but there was something in the way she held her poise that sent a pang straight into his heart.

'So you decided to be a doctor so you could save children like Beth?'

'That's a rather simplistic way of looking at it, but yes. I remember walking through the main ward and going past cubicles and private rooms full of ill children and their terrified families, and I was just full of so much... Oh, I was full up of every emotion you could imagine. Why her? Why not me too? Meningitis is so contagious....' She took a deep breath. 'I know you must think it stupid and weak, but when Beth died the only thing that kept me going was the knowledge that one day I would be in a position to heal as many of those children as I could.'

Francesco expelled a breath, the pang in his heart tightening. 'I don't think it's weak or stupid.'

Hannah took another sip of her water. The tremor in her hand had worsened and he suddenly experienced the strangest compulsion to reach over and squeeze it.

'My mother was hospitalised a number of times—drug overdoses,' he surprised himself by saying. 'It was only the dedication of the doctors and nurses that saved her. When she died it was because she overdosed on a weekend when she was alone.'

He still lived with the guilt. On an intellectual level he knew it was misplaced. He'd been fifteen years old, not yet a man. But he'd known how vulnerable his mother was and yet still he and his father had left her alone for the weekend, taking a visit to the Mastrangelo estate without her.

It had ostensibly been for business, his father and Pietro Mastrangelo close friends as well as associates. At least, they had been close friends then, before the friendship between the Calvettis and Mastrangelos had twisted into antipathy. Back then, though, Francesco had been incredibly proud that his father had wanted him to accompany him, had left with barely a second thought for his mother.

While Francesco and Salvatore had spent the Saturday evening eating good food, drinking good wine and playing cards with Pietro and his eldest son, Luca, Elisabetta Calvetti had overdosed in her bed.

To think of his mother dying while he, her son, had been basking in pride because the monster who fed her the drugs had been treating him like a man.... To think that bastard's approval ever meant anything to him made his stomach roil violently and his nails dig deep into his palms.

His mother had been the kindest, most gentle soul he had ever known. Her death had ripped his own soul in half. His vengeance might be two decades too late, but he would have it. Whatever it took, he would avenge her death and throw the carcass of his father's reputation into the ashes.

'I have nothing but the utmost respect for medical professionals,' he said slowly, unfurling the fists his hands had balled into, unsure why he was confiding such personal matters with her. 'When I look at you, Dr Chapman, I see a woman filled with compassion, decency, and integrity. The world I inhabit is driven by money, power, and greed.'

'You have integrity,' she contradicted. 'A whole heap of it.'

'On that we will have to disagree.' He nodded towards the waiter heading cautiously towards them. 'It looks as if our main courses are ready. I suggest we move on from this discussion or both our meals will be spoiled.'

She flashed him a smile of such gratitude his entire chest compressed tightly enough that for a moment he feared his lungs would cease to work.

CHAPTER SEVEN

THANKFULLY, FRANCESCO KEPT the conversation over the rest of their meal light, with mostly impersonal questions about medical school and her job. His interest—and it certainly seemed genuine—was flattering. In turn, he opened up about his love of motorbikes. It didn't surprise her to learn he owned a dozen of them.

When their plates were cleared and Hannah had eaten a dark-chocolate lava cake, which was without doubt the most delicious pudding she'd ever eaten—except hot chocolate-fudge cake, of course—Francesco looked at his watch. 'I need to check in with my head of security before the poker tournament starts. Do you want to come with me or would you like me to get one of my staff to give you a tour of the tables?'

'Are you entering the tournament?'

'No. This one is solely for members. It's the biggest tournament that's held here, though, and the members like to see me—it makes them feel important,' he added, and she noticed a slight flicker of amusement in his eyes, which made her feel as if she'd been let into a private joke. It was an insight that both surprised and warmed her.

'You don't have much time for them?'

'I always make time for them.'

'That's not what I meant.'

'I know what you meant.' His lips, usually set in a fixed line, broke into something that almost resembled a lazy smile. He drained his glass of wine, his eyes holding firm with hers. 'Do you know the rules of poker?'

'Funnily enough, I do. It's often on late at night when I'm too brain-dead to study any longer and need to wind down before bed.'

'You're still studying?'

'Yes. Plus there are always new research papers being published and clinical studies to read through and mug up on.'

'Doesn't sound as if you leave yourself any time for having fun,' he remarked astutely.

'It's fun to me. But you're right—it's why I'm here after all.'

'When you said you'd spent your whole adult life dedicating yourself to medicine, I didn't think you meant it in a literal sense.'

She shrugged and pulled a face. 'It's what I needed.'

'But that's changed?'

'Not in any fundamental way. Medicine and my patients will always be my first priority, but my accident… It made me open my eyes…' Her voice trailed away, unexpected tears burning the back of her eyes. It had been so long since she'd spoken properly about Beth.

Hannah carried her sister with her every minute of every day, yet it had felt in recent weeks as if she were right there with her, as if she could turn her head and find Beth peering over her shoulder.

Blinking back the tears, she spoke quietly. 'I don't know if heaven exists, but if it does, I don't want Beth to be angry with me. She loved life. We both did. I'd forgotten just how much.'

She almost jumped out of her seat when Francesco placed a warm hand on hers, so large it covered it entirely. A sense of calm trickled through her veins, while conversely her skin began to dance.

'Would you like to enter the poker tournament?'

'Oh, no, I couldn't.'

'Think of the experience. Think of the story you'll have to tell Beth.'

With a stab, she realised how carefully he'd been listening. Francesco understood.

The sense of calm increased, settling into her belly. 'Well…how much does it cost?'

'For you, nothing. For everyone else, it's one hundred thousand euros.'

If her jaw could thud onto the table, it would. 'For one game of poker?'

'That's pocket change to the members here. People fly in from all over the world for this one tournament. We allow sixty entrants. We've had a couple drop out, so there is room for you.'

'I don't know. Won't all the other entrants be cross that I'm playing for free?'

'They wouldn't know. In any case, it is none of their business. My casino, my rules. Go on, Hannah. Do it. Enjoy yourself and play the game.'

It was the first time he'd addressed her by her first name. Oh, but it felt so wonderful to hear her name spilling from his tongue in that deep, seductive accent.

Play the game.

It had been fifteen years since she'd played a game of any sort—and school netball most certainly did *not* count when compared to this.

Straightening her spine, she nodded, a swirl of excitement uncoiling in her stomach. 'Go on, then. Sign me up.'

* * *

Francesco watched the tournament unfold from the sprawling security office on the top floor of the casino, manned by two dozen staff twenty-four hours a day. Other than the bathrooms, there wasn't an inch of the casino not monitored. Special interest was being taken in a blackjack player on the second floor—a man suspected of swindling casinos across the Continent. Of course, there was the option to simply ban the man from the premises, but first Francesco wanted proof. And banning was not enough. Once his guilt was established, a suitable punishment would be wrought.

The first round of the tournament was in full swing. On Hannah's table of six, two players were already out. Her gameplay surprised him—for a novice, she played exceptionally well, her poker face inscrutable. Of those remaining, she had the second-largest number of chips.

The dealer dealt the four players their two cards and turned three over on the table. From his vantage point, Francesco could see Hannah had been dealt an ace and a jack, both diamonds. The player with the largest pile of chips had been dealt a pair of kings. One of the table cards was a king, giving that player three of a kind. The player went all in, meaning that if Hannah wanted to continue playing she would have to put *all* her remaining chips into the pile.

She didn't even flinch, simply pushed her pile forward to show she wanted to play.

There was no way she could win the hand. Lady Luck could be kind, but to overturn a three of a kind... The next table card to be turned over was an ace, quickly followed by another ace.

She'd won the hand!

It seemed that fifteen years of perfecting a poker face,

along with too many late nights half watching the game played out for real on the television had paid off.

Hannah allowed herself a sip of water but kept her face neutral. The game wasn't over yet. No one looking at her would know the thundering rate of her heart.

The look on her defeated opponent's face was a picture. He kept staring from his cards to hers as if expecting a snake to pop out of them. Her two remaining opponents were looking at her with a newfound respect.

If she wasn't in the midst of a poker tournament, she'd be hugging herself with the excitement of it all. It felt as if she were in the middle of a glamorous Hollywood film. All that was needed was for the men to light fat cigars and create a haze of smoke.

As the next hand was dealt she noticed a small crowd forming around their table and much whispering behind hands.

She looked at her two cards and raised the ante. One of her opponents matched her. The other folded, opting to sit out of the hand. The table cards were laid. Again she raised the ante. Again her opponent matched her. And so it went on, her opponent matching her move for move.

She didn't have the best of hands: two low pairs. There was every chance that his cards were much better. All the same, the bubble of recklessness that had been simmering within her since she'd followed Francesco off the dance floor the night before grew within her.

It was her turn to bet. Both she and her opponent had already put a large wedge of chips into the pot.

Where was Francesco? He'd said he would be there socialising with the guests.

He wasn't in the room, but somehow she just *knew* he was watching her.

Her heart hammering, she pushed her remaining chips forward. *Please* let Francesco be watching. 'All in.'

Her opponent stared at her, a twitch forming under his left eye.

She stared back, giving nothing away.

He rubbed his chin.

She knew before he did that he was going to fold, hid her feelings of triumph that she'd successfully bluffed him.

The big pile of poker chips was hers.

It would appear that her long-practised poker face had become a blessing in itself.

Francesco could hardly believe what he was witnessing over the monitors.

Hannah was a card shark. There was no other way to describe the way she played, which, if you were in a position to see the cards she'd been dealt, as he was, at times verged on the reckless. Not that her opponents could see how recklessly she played. All they saw was the cool facade, the face that didn't give away a single hint of emotion.

For a woman who had never played the game before, it was masterful. And yet…

Something deep inside his gut clenched when he considered why she'd been able to develop such a good poker face. Only someone who'd spent years hiding their emotions could produce it so naturally. He should know. He'd been perfecting his own version for years.

When she'd knocked her fourth opponent out… The way she'd pushed her chips forward, the clear *simpatico* way she'd said, 'All in…'

His gut had tightened further. Somehow he'd known those two little words meant more than just the chips before her.

It didn't take long before she'd demolished her final opponent. Only when she'd won that final hand did that beautiful smile finally break on her face, a smile of genuine delight that had all her defeated opponents reaching over to shake her hand and kiss her cheeks. The mostly male crowd surrounding her also muscled in, finding it necessary to embrace her when giving their congratulations.

They wouldn't look twice if they could see her in her usual state, Francesco thought narkily. They would be so blinkered they would never see her for the natural beauty she was.

'I'm going back down,' he said, heading to the reinforced steel door. For some reason, his good mood, induced by dinner with Hannah, had plummeted.

Striding across the main playing area of the third floor, he ignored all attempts from players and staff to meet his eyes.

With play in the tournament temporarily halted so the players who'd made it through to the second round could take a break, he found Hannah sipping coffee, surrounded by a horde of men all impressing their witticisms and manliness upon her.

When she saw him, her eyes lit up, then dimmed as she neared him.

'What's the matter?' she asked.

'Nothing.'

'Ooh, you liar. You look like someone's stolen your granny's false teeth and you've been told to donate your own as a replacement.'

Her good humour had zero effect on his blackening mood. 'And you look like you're having fun,' he said pointedly, unable to contain the ice in his voice.

'Isn't that the whole point of me entering the tournament? Didn't you tell me to enjoy myself?'

Francesco took a deep breath, Hannah's bewilderment

reminding him he had no good reason to be acting like a jealous fool.

Jealousy?

Was that really what the strong compulsion running through him to throw her over his shoulder and carry her out of the casino and away from all these admiring men was?

His father, for all his catting about with other women half his age, had been consumed with it. His mother had suffered more than one beating at his hands for daring to look at another man the wrong way.

Francesco had assumed that, in his own case, jealousy had skipped a generation. The closest he'd come to that particular emotion had been in his early twenties. Then, he'd learned Luisa, a girl he was seeing, was two-timing him with Pepe Mastrangelo, whom she'd sworn she'd finished with. That hadn't been jealousy, though—that had been pure anger, a rage that had heightened when he learned she'd tricked him out of money so she could hightail it to the UK for an abortion. So duplicitous had she been, she'd no idea if he or Pepe was the father.

He'd despised Luisa for her lies, but not once had he wanted to seek Pepe out. Instead, Pepe had sought *him* out, his pain right there on the surface. But the only bruising Francesco had suffered had been to his ego, and the fight between them had been over before it started.

To learn he was as vulnerable to jealousy's clutches as the next man brought him up short, reminding him that he had Calvetti blood running inside him.

Salvatore Calvetti would never have walked away from the Luisa and Pepe debacle as Francesco had done. If Salvatore had walked in his shoes, Luisa would have been scarred for life. Pepe would likely have disappeared, never to be seen again.

But he didn't want to be anything like Salvatore.

He never wanted to treat *anyone* the way his father had treated his mother.

Raking his fingers through his hair, a growl escaped from his throat. Whether he liked it or not, Calvetti blood ran through his veins.

Just one more reason why he should never touch her.

Hannah looked as if she wanted to say something, but the gong sounded for the second round. She was placed on table one. Her chips were passed to her. Francesco watched as she stacked them into neat piles, oblivious to the crowd forming around her table.

The strength of his possessiveness had him clenching his fists. Was she really so ignorant of the admiring glances and lecherous stares?

She raised her eyes to meet his glare and gave a hesitant smile. He looked away.

A discreet cough behind him caught his attention. He turned to find his general manager standing there.

'We have the proof—the blackjack player *is* cheating us,' he said, his lips barely moving.

'Give me a few minutes.' Francesco barely bothered trying to hide his impatience.

Hannah was still looking at him, a puzzled groove in her forehead.

'I can get the ball moving…'

'I *said*, give me a few minutes.' The blackjack cheat could wait. Francesco would not step a foot away from the room until Hannah was done with the tournament. His presence was the only thing stopping the fawning men from trying their luck that bit harder.

She was done much earlier than he'd envisaged. From playing the first round like a pro and with a good dollop of luck, her game fell to pieces and she was the first player out.

She shrugged, smiled gracefully, took a sip of water, and leaned back in her chair.

He was by her side in seconds. 'Come, it is time for us to move elsewhere,' he said, speaking into her ear, ignoring the curious stares of all those surrounding them.

'I want to watch the rest of the tournament.'

'You can watch it from my security office. There are things I need to attend to.'

Hannah turned to face him. 'Go and attend to them, then,' she said with a shrug.

'But I require your company.' Or, rather, he wanted to get her away from this room full of letches.

Swivelling her chair around with exceptionally bad grace, she got to her feet.

'What is the matter with you?' he asked as they swept through the room and out of the door.

'Me?' Incredulous, Hannah stopped walking and placed a hand on her hip. 'I was having a lovely time until you came in looking as if you wanted to kill me.' Seriously, how could anyone concentrate with Francesco's handsome face glowering at them? 'You totally put me off my game, and then you dragged me out before I could enjoy watching the rest of it.'

She glared at him. She'd had such a wonderful meal, had thought he'd enjoyed himself, too, the aloof, arrogant man unbending into something infinitely more human that warmed her from the inside out. But now he'd reverted, and was more aloof and arrogant than ever.

'It wasn't you that angered me.'

She folded her arms and raised a brow in a perfect imitation of him. 'Really?'

'Did you not see the way those men were looking at you? As if you were a piece of meat.'

'They were just being friendly.' Men *never* looked at her

in that way. Not that she ever met men outside the hospital environment, she conceded.

'Take a look in the mirror, Dr Chapman. You're a beautiful woman.'

His unexpected compliment let loose a cluster of fluttering butterflies in her belly.

'And I'm sorry for putting you off your game—you're quite a player.'

'You think?' His compliment—for it was definitely a compliment coming from him—warmed her insides even further, making her forget to be cross with him.

He smiled, an honest-to-goodness smile, and reached out to touch a loose tendril of her hair. 'If you were to give up medicine, you could make a good living on the poker circuit.'

The butterflies in her belly exploded. Heat surged through her veins, her insides liquefying.

Was it her imagination, or was the longing she could feel swirling inside her mirrored in his eyes…?

Dropping his hand from her hair, he traced a finger down her cheek.

She shivered, her skin heating beneath his touch.

'Come. I need to attend to business,' he said before steering her off to the top floor, not quite touching her but keeping her close enough that she was constantly aware of his heat, of *him*.

'What are we going up here for?' she asked once she'd managed to get her tongue working again. But, oh, it was so hard to think straight when the skin on her cheek still tingled from his touch.

'A player from the second floor has been caught cheating. Stealing from us.'

'Have you called the police?'

He looked at her as if she'd asked if the moon was made of chocolate. 'That is not how we do things here.'

'How do you do things…?' The strangest look flitted over her face. 'Oh. You break hands.'

The sadness in Hannah's tone cut through him. Francesco paused to look at her properly. 'The punishment is determined by the crime.'

'But surely if a crime has been committed then the police should be left to deal with it? That's what they're paid for after all.'

'This is Sicily, Dr Chapman. The rules are different here.'

'Because that's what you were taught by your father?'

Her question caught him up short. 'It's nothing to do with my father. It's about respect and following the rules.'

'But who makes the rules? This is *your* empire, Francesco. Your father isn't here anymore. You're an adult. Your actions are your own.'

The air caught in his lungs, an acrid taste forming in his throat. 'Do you have an answer for everything?'

'Not even close.' She looked away, avoiding his gaze. 'If it's all the same to you, I'd like to wait downstairs.' Her tone had become distant.

His stomach rolled over. 'Nothing will happen to the cheating thief on these premises.'

'I don't want anything to happen to him off the premises, either. I'm a doctor, Francesco. I can't be—won't be—a party to anything that harms another person. I know this is your life and what you're used to, but for me…' She shook her head. 'I could never live with myself. Can you get one of your men to take me back to the villa?'

'Wait in the bar for me,' he said. 'I'll be with you in ten minutes.'

Not smiling, she nodded her acquiescence and walked

back down the stairs, gripping onto the gold handrail as she made her descent.

Francesco's chest felt weighted, although he knew not why.

He never made any apologies for his life and the way his world worked. Hannah knew the score—he'd never hidden anything from her. He'd *told* her what it was like. He'd warned her. In fact, it was the only reason he'd brought her here, so she could see for herself that he was not worth wasting her virginity on. It was not his fault she hadn't listened.

So why was the only thing he could see as he pushed the door open the sad disappointment dulling her eyes?

He entered the manager's office. Mario and Roberto, another of his most trusted men, were already there, along with the cheat.

Up close, he could see the cheat was a young man in his early twenties, who looked as if he should be playing computer games with an online community of other awkward young men, not systematically ripping off casinos across the Continent. He sat in the middle of the room. He looked terrified.

There was a tap on the door and the manager walked in, handing Francesco a dossier on the blackjack player's activity. It made for quick reading.

Mario watched him, waiting for the nod.

This was the part of the job Francesco liked the least. When he'd first bought into this, his first casino, three years ago, he'd employed his father's old henchmen, knowing them to be reliable and loyal. Within months, he'd paid the majority of them off when it became clear they expected to continue using the methods enjoyed by Salvatore as punishment. While he had always respected his father, Francesco had always known that when the time came for him to take over, his methods would be different, less extreme.

Mario was Francesco's man and capable of great restraint. Apart from one drug dealer who'd frequented Francesco's Naples nightclub and who they'd discovered was pimping out vulnerable teenage girls, he never made the punishments personal and never caused damage that would not heal.

When he gave the nod, Mario and Roberto would take the young man somewhere private. They would teach him a lesson he would never forget—a lesson that rarely needed to be given, as most people were not stupid enough to try to cheat a Calvetti casino. Francesco's reputation preceded him. And, really, this was the perfect opportunity to rid himself of Hannah. It was clear this whole situation had unsettled her enough to at least consider getting a flight home. If he gave the nod, he could guarantee she would be on the first flight back to England....

Yet her insinuation that he was following in his father's brutish footsteps jabbed him like a spear.

He was *not* his father. If this young cheat had tried any such behaviour in any of Salvatore's businesses, he would have disappeared. For ever.

Rules were rules, even if they were only unwritten. They were there for a reason.

His father would never have dreamed of breaking them....

Hannah nursed her strong coffee, gazing absently at the huge flat-screen television against a wall of the bar showing music videos. She didn't want to think of what was happening on the floor above her. If she thought about it hard enough she might just scream.

But when she tried not to think about it, thoughts of Melanie's wedding filled the space instead.

How could she endure it? Every morning she woke knowing the nuptials were one day closer, the knot in her belly tightening another notch.

She would give anything to get out of going, but even if an excuse came fully presented on a plate she would not be able to take it. Melanie had appointed her maid of honour, a role Hannah knew she did not deserve.

The wedding was something she would have to find a way to cope with. Whatever it took, she would try to keep smiling so her little sister could walk down the aisle without her day being ruined.

'Due bicchieri di champagne.'

Francesco's sudden appearance at her side startled her.

'Hi,' she said dully, hating that her heart thumped just to see him.

'Ciao.' He nodded. 'I've just ordered us each a glass of champagne.'

'You said you would take me back to the villa.'

'And I will. Five minutes. You look as if you need a drink.'

'I need to get my phone and my passport, and go home. To England,' she added in case her meaning wasn't absolutely clear.

Francesco had been right from the start. She really didn't belong in his world, not even on a temporary basis.

The injuries to Mario had been inflicted a long time ago and were, in effect, history. Mario's loyalty to Francesco only served to reinforce this notion of a long-forgotten event, something that had no bearing on the present.

The person they'd caught stealing tonight... This was now; this *was* the present.

Hannah was a doctor. She had dedicated her life to

saving lives. She could never be a party to someone else's injury.

'Come, Dr Chapman. You are supposed to be living a little. You are here to see something of the world and experience the things that have passed you by. You hardly touched your wine at dinner.'

'I'm really not in the mood.'

Pressing his lips to her ear, he said, 'I called the police.'

Her head whipped round so quickly she almost butted his nose. 'Seriously?'

Two glasses of champagne were placed before them. Francesco picked them up and nodded at a corner sofa. Thoroughly confused, she followed him.

Sitting gingerly next to him, she would have ignored the champagne had he not thrust it into her hand.

'Drink. You need to relax a little—you're far too tense.'

'Did you really call the police?'

'As you implied, I make the rules.' A slight smile played on his lips. 'I thought about the prison system here. When I said I was calling the police, the thief begged for a beating.'

She couldn't contain the smile that spread over her face or the hand that rose to palm his cheek. 'See? I *was* right about you.'

At his quizzical expression, she added, 'I knew there was good within you. You proved it by taking care of me so well after my accident, and now you've reaffirmed it.'

He shook his head. 'It's just for this one time, okay? And only because I respect your profession and the oath you took.'

'If you say so.' A feeling of serenity swept through her. Stroking her fingers down his cheek, she took a sip of her champagne.

'Better?'

She nodded. 'Much. I'll feel even better when I have my phone back.' She felt lost without it.

'Finish your champagne and I will take you back.'

His eyes bored into her, *daring* her to drink it. The sip she'd had still danced on her tongue, tantalising her, just as Francesco tantalised her.

This was why she was here, she reminded herself. Not to involve herself in the intricacies of his life but to experience her *own*.

Putting the flute back to her lips, she tipped the sparkling liquid into her mouth and drank it in three swallows.

A grin spread across his face, somehow making him even more handsome, a feat she hadn't thought possible.

'Good for you.' He downed his own glass before rising to his feet. 'Come. It is time to take you back.'

Hannah grabbed her clutch bag and stood. Her body felt incredibly light.

Surrounded by Francesco's minders, who'd been waiting in the corner of the bar for them, they left. When they reached the stairs, he placed a hand on the small of her back, a protective gesture that lightened her even further.

CHAPTER EIGHT

FRANCESCO'S VILLA WAS in darkness, but as soon as his driver brought the car over the foot of the driveway, light illuminated it, bathing it in a golden hue. With the stars in the moonless night sky twinkling, it was the prettiest sight Hannah had ever seen.

'Can I get you a drink?' Francesco asked once they were alone inside, his minders having left for their own quarters. 'How about a brandy?'

The effects of the champagne had started to abate a little, but did she want to risk putting any more alcohol into her system?

'Only a small one,' he added, clearly reading her mind.

'Yes, please. A small one,' she agreed, hugging herself.

She followed him through the sprawling reception and into the living room, where Francesco swept a small white object from the windowsill. 'Catch,' he said, throwing it at her.

Luckily she caught it. Before she could admonish him for the reckless endangerment of her phone, he'd continued through the huge library, through the dining room, diverted round the indoor swimming pool, stepped through huge French doors and out onto a veranda overhanging the outdoor pool.

It was like stepping into a tropical-party area where the

only thing missing was the guests. A bar—a proper bar, with flashing lights, high stools, and everything—was set up at one end. Tables, chairs, and plump sofas abounded.

'I bet you have some fantastic parties here,' she said. The perfect setting for the playboy Francesco was reputed to be, yet, she reflected, not at all the man who she was learning he was.

'Not for a long time.'

'Why's that?'

'I have different priorities now.' He raised his shoulder, affecting nonchalance, but there was no doubting the 'I'm not prepared to discuss this' timbre in his voice.

That was fine by her. She doubted she wanted to know what his new priorities were anyway.

She spotted a long white board jutting through the trellis. 'Is that a diving board?'

He nodded. 'It beats walking down the steps to reach the swimming pool.'

'You should get a slide—that would be much more fun.'

He chuckled and slipped behind the bar. 'That's not a bad idea. Do you swim?'

'Not for years.'

'I would suggest a dip now but alcohol and swimming pools do not mix well. We will have time for a swim in the morning—that is, if you want to stay the night. Or do you still want to get a flight home?'

There was no mistaking the meaning in his quietly delivered words.

A thrill of excitement speared up her spine, making her shiver despite the warmth of her skin in the balmy night air.

Dimly she recalled saying she wanted to go home. The anger that had made her say those words had gone. All that lay within her now was a longing, wrapped so tightly in her chest it almost made her nauseous.

This was what she'd wanted. It was the whole reason she was here.

She shook her head. 'I don't want to go home. I want to stay.'

His eyes held hers, heat flashing from them before he reached for a bottle and poured them both a drink, topping the smaller measure with a splash of lemonade. He handed it to her. 'I've sweetened it for you, otherwise your untried taste buds might find it a little too harsh.'

Their fingers brushed as she took the glass from him. That same flash of heat sparked in his eyes again.

'*Saluti,*' he said, holding his glass aloft.

'*Saluti,*' she echoed, chinking her glass to his.

Francesco took a swallow of his drink. 'I thought you would have checked your phone by now.'

'Oh.' Disconcerted, she blinked. 'I should, really.' After all the fuss she'd made over it, she'd shoved it into her clutch bag without even checking the screen for messages.

For the first time since she'd gained her permanent place on the children's ward, the compulsion to check her phone had taken second place to something else. And that something else was gazing at Francesco.

The more she looked at him, the more the excited nausea increased. Was it even nausea she felt? She didn't know; she had no name befitting the ache that pulsed so, so low within her.

While she stood there rooted, helpless for the first time to know what to do, all her bravado and certainty from the night before gone, Francesco finished his brandy and laid the glass on the bar. 'Time for bed.'

Bed…

Immediately the butterflies inside her began to thrash about, her heart racing at a gallop.

It was late. She'd been awake the best part of two days

after a night of hardly any sleep, yet she didn't feel the least bit weary.

But sleep wasn't what Francesco was implying with his statement.

She gulped her drink down, completely forgetting it had alcohol in it. It had a bitter aftertaste that somehow soothed her skittering nerves a touch. She felt like grabbing the bottle and pouring herself another, this time without the lemonade.

Francesco must have read what was going on beneath her skin, for he stepped out from behind the bar and stood before her. He reached out a hand and pulled her chopsticks out. After a moment's suspended animation her hair tumbled down.

'That's better,' he murmured. Before she could ask what he meant, he inhaled deeply and took a step back. 'I'm going to my room. I will let you decide if you want to join me in it or if you wish to sleep alone.'

'But…'

'I can see you're nervous. I want you to be sure. I meant what I said last night—I will not take advantage of you. My room is two doors from yours. I leave the ball in your court.' With that, he bowed his head, turned on his heel, and strode away.

After a long pause in which all the blood in her body flooded into her brain and roared around her ears, Hannah expelled a long breath of air.

What had she expected? That Francesco would take charge, sweep her into his arms, and carry her manfully all the way to his bedroom as if she weighed little more than a bag of sugar? That he would lay her on his bed and devour her, taking command of every touch and movement?

Hadn't she known he was far too honourable for that?

How right she had been that he would never do anything

to hurt her—even taking her phone had been, according to Francesco's sense of logic, for her own good. Saying that, if he ever stole it from her again she certainly wouldn't be so forgiving…. Oh, what was she thinking? After tonight he would never have another opportunity to steal her phone. Once this weekend was over she would throw herself back into her work—her life—and Francesco would be nothing but a memory of one weekend when she'd dared embrace life in its entirety.

If she wanted Francesco to make love to her, she would have to go to him….

But could she do that? Could she slip into his room and slide under his bedcovers?

Could she not?

No. She couldn't *not* do it.

She would never meet another man like him—how could she when she'd spent twenty-seven years having never met *anyone* who made her feel anything?

It had all felt so different last night, though, when she'd practically begged him to make love to her. Before she'd spent time with him and discovered the complex man behind the cool facade, the man who could be both cruel and yet full of empathy. A man who was capable of both great brutality and great generosity. He was no longer some mythological dream figure. He was flesh and blood, with all the complexity that came from being human.

Francesco stood under the shower for an age, fixing the temperature to a much lower setting than the steaming-hot he usually favoured. If he kept it cold enough it might just do something to lessen his libido.

He pressed his forehead to the cool tiles.

Hannah was his for the taking. She'd been his for the taking since she'd first strolled into his nightclub carrying a bunch of flowers for him. All he had to do was walk two doors down and she would welcome him into her arms.

It unnerved him how badly he wanted to do that. How badly he wanted her.

Would she come to him?

He honestly could not guess.

She was not one of the worldly women he normally spent time with, for whom sex was a form of currency.

Hannah was a twenty-seven-year-old virgin who'd hidden the essence of herself from the world—from herself, even—for the best part of fifteen years.

He'd seen the hesitation in her eyes when he'd said it was time for bed. All the boldness from the night before had vanished, leaving her vulnerability lying right there on the surface.

He would not be the man to take advantage of that vulnerability, no matter how easy it would be and no matter how much she would welcome it.

Francesco could pinpoint the exact moment when the determination to keep her out of his bed had shifted. It had been when he'd looked at that cheating thief, a man so like all those other men who'd been fawning over her during the poker tournament. Now that Hannah's sexuality had awoken, it wouldn't meekly lie back down when she returned to London and return to its former dormancy. Eventually she would meet another man she wanted enough to make love to. It could be any of those men. It could be any man, not one of whom could be trusted to treat her with the tenderness she deserved.

Hannah wanted *him*.

And, *caro Dio*, he wanted her, too, with a need that burned in the very fabric of his being.

But he knew that this final step had to come from her

and her alone, however agonising the wait for her decision would be.

Stepping out of the shower, he towelled himself dry, brushed his teeth, and wandered naked through the doorway of the en suite bathroom into his bedroom....

While he'd showered, Hannah had crept into his room. She stood before the window, her eyes widening as she took in his nude form.

'You've taken your make-up off,' he said, walking slowly towards her. She'd showered, too, her hair damp, her body wrapped in the thick white bathrobe kept in the guest room.

She raised a hand to a cheek, which, even in the dim light, he could see had flushed with colour.

He covered her hand with his own. 'This is better. You're beautiful as you are.'

She trembled, although whether that was down to the hoarseness of his voice or a reaction to his touch he could not say.

Slowly he trailed a hand down the swan of her neck to the V made by the bathrobe, slipping a finger between the bunched material to loosen it, exposing the cleavage of her creamy breasts. Slower still, he slid down to the sash and, using both hands, untied it before pushing the robe apart, exposing her to him.

Hannah's breaths became shallow. Her chest hitched. She stood as still as a statue, staring at him with a look that somehow managed to be both bold and shy. He pushed the shoulders of the robe so it fell softly to the floor.

His own breath hitched as he drank her in.

Her body was everything he'd imagined and more—her breasts fuller and higher, her belly softly toned, her hips curvier, her legs longer and smoother.

He swallowed, the ache in his groin so deep it was painful.

He forced himself to remember that she was a virgin. No matter how badly he wanted to go ahead and devour her, he needed to keep the reins on himself.

Hannah had never felt so exposed—had never *been* so exposed—as she was at that moment. Her heart thundered, her blood surged, but none of it mattered. The hunger in Francesco's eyes was enough to evaporate the shyness and quell any last-minute fears, although, when she dared cast her eyes down to his jutting erection, she experienced a different, more primitive fear that was accompanied by a wild surge of heat through her loins.

Naked except for the gold cross that rested at the top of his muscular chest, Francesco was truly glorious. For such a tall, powerful man he had a surprising grace about him, an elegance to his raw masculinity that tempered the powerhouse he was.

Moisture filled her mouth. She swallowed it away, her eyes captured by the heat of hot chocolate fudge that gleamed.

She wanted to touch him. She wanted to rake her fingers through the whorls of dark hair covering his chest, to feel his skin beneath her lips.

Except she was rooted to the spot on which she stood, helpless to do anything but receive his study of her naked form.

'We'll take it very slowly,' he said, his words thick.

She couldn't speak, could only jerk a nod, aching for it to start, yearning for it to be over, a whole jumble of thoughts and emotions careering through her. Out of the fear and excitement, though, it was the latter that rose to the top.

This was it....

And then she was aloft, clutched against Francesco's hard torso as he swept her into his arms and carried her over to the enormous four-poster bed, her private fantasy coming to life.

Gently he laid her down on her back before lying beside her. He placed a hand on her collarbone—the same bone that had been broken during the moment that had brought him into her life—before slanting his lips on hers.

The heat from his mouth, the mintiness of his breath, the fresh oaky scent of him…sent her senses reeling. His kiss was light but assured, a tender pressure that slowly deepened until her lips parted and his tongue swept into her mouth.

Finally she touched him, placing a hand on his shoulder, feeling the smoothness of his skin while she revelled in the headiness evoked by his increasingly hungry kisses.

He moved his mouth away, sweeping his lips over her cheek to nibble at her earlobe. 'Are you sure about this?'

'You have to ask?' In response to the low resonance of his voice, her own was a breathless rush.

'Any time you want to stop, say.'

She turned her head to capture his lips. 'I don't want to stop.'

He groaned and muttered something she didn't understand before kissing her with such passion her bones seemed to melt within her.

His large hand swept over her, flattening against her breasts, trailing over her belly, stroking her, moulding her. And then he followed it with his mouth. When his lips closed over a puckered nipple she gasped, her eyes flying open.

Always she had looked at breasts as functional assets, understanding in a basic fashion that men lusted after them. Never had it occurred to her that the pleasure a man took from them could be reciprocated by the woman—by *her*. She reached for him, digging her fingers into his scalp, silently begging him to carry on, almost crying out when he broke away, only to immediately turn his attention to the other.

It was the most wonderful feeling imaginable.

At some point he had rolled on top of her. She could feel his erection prod against her thigh and moaned as she imagined what it would feel like to actually have him inside her, being a part of her…

Oh, but she burned, a delicious heat that seeped into every inch of her being, every part alive and dancing in the flames.

It was as if Francesco was determined to kiss and worship every tiny crevice, his mouth now trailing down over her belly whilst his hands…

Her gasp was loud when he moved a hand between her legs, gently stroking his fingers over her soft hair until he found her—

Dear God…

He knelt between her legs, his tongue *there*, pressed against her tight bud.

What was happening to her?

Never in her wildest imaginings had she dreamed that the very essence of her being could ache with such intensity. Nothing. Nothing could have prepared her.

Oh, but this was incredible—*he* was incredible…

Right in her core the heaviness grew. Francesco stayed exactly where he was, his tongue making tiny circular motions, increasing the pressure until, with a cry that seemed to come from a faraway land, ripples of pure pleasure exploded through her and carried her off to that faraway land in the stars.

Only when all the pulsations had abated did Francesco move, trailing kisses all the way back up her body until he reached her mouth and kissed her with a savagery that stole her remaining breath.

He lifted his head to gaze down at her. The chocolate in his eyes had fully melted, his expression one of wonder. 'I need to get some protection,' he said, sounding pained.

She didn't want him to leave her. She wanted him to stay right there, to keep her body covered with the heat of his own.

He didn't go far, simply rolling off her to reach into his bedside table. Before he could rip the square foil open, she placed her hand on his chest. Francesco's heart thudded as wildly as her own.

Closing her eyes, she twisted onto her side and pressed a kiss to his shoulder. And another. And another, breathing in his musky scent, rubbing her nose against the smoothness of his olive skin.

With trembling fingers she explored him, the hard chest with the soft black hair, the brown nipples that she rubbed a thumb over and heard him catch a breath at, the washboard stomach covered with a fine layer of that same black hair that thickened the lower she went, becoming more wiry...

She hesitated, raising her head from his shoulder to stare at him. How she longed to touch him properly, but there was a painful awareness that she didn't know what she was doing. How could she know what he liked, how he wanted to be touched? It wasn't that she had minimal experience— she had *no* experience. Nothing.

'You can do whatever you want,' he whispered hoarsely, raking his hands through her hair and pressing a kiss to her lips. 'Touch me however you like.'

Could he read her mind?

Tentatively, she encircled her hand around his length, feeling it pulsate beneath her touch. Francesco groaned and lay back, hooking one arm over his head while the other lay buried in her hair, his fingers massaging her scalp.

His erection felt a lot smoother than she'd expected, and as she moved her hand up to the tip, a drop of fluid rubbed in her fingers.

A rush of moist heat flooded between her legs, a sharp pulsation, the same ache she had experienced when Francesco had set her body alight with his mouth. To witness his desire for her was as great an aphrodisiac as anything she had experienced since being in his room.

So quickly she didn't even notice him move, he covered her hand with his. 'No more,' he growled. 'I want to be inside you.'

She couldn't resist wrapping an arm around his neck and kissing him, pressing herself against him as tightly as she could.

Hooking an arm around her waist, Francesco twisted her back down, sliding a knee between her legs to part them.

With expert deftness, he ripped the foil open with his teeth and rolled it on before manoeuvring himself so he was fully on top of her and between her parted thighs, his erection heavy against her.

He pressed his lips to hers and kissed her, his left hand burying back into her hair, his right sliding down her side and slipping between them.

She felt him guide the tip of his erection against her and then into her, and sucked in a breath. Francesco simply deepened the kiss, murmuring words of Sicilian endearment into her mouth. He brought his hand back up to stroke her face and thrust forward a little more, still kissing her, stroking her, nibbling at the sensitive skin of her neck, slowly, slowly inching his way inside her.

There was one moment of real discomfort that made her freeze, but then it was gone, her senses too full of Francesco and all the magical things he was doing to dwell on that one thing.

And then he was there, all the way inside her, stretching her, filling her massively, his groin pressed against her pubis, his chest crushing against her breasts.

'Am I hurting you?' he asked raggedly.

'No. It feels…good.' It felt more than good—it felt heavenly.

'*You* feel so good,' he groaned into her ear, withdrawing a little only to inch forward again.

His movements were slow but assured, allowing her to adjust to all these new feelings and sensations, building the tempo at an unhurried pace, only pulling back a few inches, keeping his groin pressing against her.

The sensations he'd created with his tongue began to bubble within her again but this time felt fuller, deeper, more condensed.

Her arms wrapped around his neck, her breaths shallow, she began to move with him, meeting his thrusts, which steadily lengthened. And all the while he kissed her, his hands roaming over the sides of her body, her face, her neck, her hair…everywhere.

She felt the tension increase within him, his groans deepening—such an erotic sound, confirmation that everything she was experiencing was shared, that it was real and not just a beautiful dream. The bubbling deep in her core thickened and swelled, triggering a mass of pulsations to ripple through her. Crying out, she clung to him, burying her face in his neck at the same moment Francesco gave his own cry and made one final thrust that seemed to last for ever.

CHAPTER NINE

FRANCESCO STRETCHED, LOOKED at his bedside clock, then turned back over to face the wall that was Hannah's back. When they'd fallen into sleep she'd been cuddled into him, their limbs entwined.

The last time he'd had such a deep sleep had been his birthday ten months ago. That had been just two days before he'd discovered his mother's diaries.

For the first time in ten months he'd fallen asleep without the demons that plagued him screwing with his thoughts.

Only the top of Hannah's shoulder blades were uncovered and he resisted the urge to place a kiss on them. After disposing of the condom, he'd longed to make love to her again. He'd put his selfish desires to one side. She'd had a long week at work, little sleep the night before, and her body was bound to ache after making love for the first time. Instead he'd pulled her to him and listened to her fall into slumber. It was the sweetest sound he'd ever heard.

He rubbed his eyes and pinched the bridge of his nose, expelling a long breath.

If someone had told him just twenty-four hours ago that making love to Hannah Chapman would be the best experience of his life, he would have laughed. And not with any humour.

To know he was the first man to have slept with her

made his chest fill. To know that he'd awoken those responses... It had been a revelation, a thing of beauty.

Francesco had never felt humble about anything in his life, yet it was the closest he could come to explaining the gratitude he felt towards her for choosing him.

Hannah hadn't chosen him for his power or his wealth or his lifestyle—she'd chosen and trusted him for *him*.

To think he'd dismissed her when she'd blurted out that she wanted him to make love to her. She could have accepted that dismissal. Eventually she would have found another man she trusted enough...

It didn't bear thinking about.

The thought of another man pawing at her and making clumsy love to her made his brain burn and his heart clench.

Suddenly he became aware that her deep, rhythmic breathing had stopped.

His suspicion that she'd awoken was confirmed when she abruptly turned over to face him, her eyes startled.

'*Buongiorno,*' he said, a smile already playing on his lips.

Blinking rapidly, Hannah covered a yawn before bestowing him with a sleepy smile. 'What time is it?'

'Nine o'clock.'

She yawned again. 'Wow. I haven't slept in that late for years.'

'You needed it.' Hooking an arm around her waist, he pulled her to him. 'How are you feeling?'

Her face scrunched in thought. 'Strange.'

'Good strange or bad strange?'

That wonderful look of serenity flitted over her face. 'Good strange.'

Already his body ached to make love to her again. Trailing his fingers over her shoulder, enjoying the softness of her skin, he pressed a kiss to her neck. 'Are you hungry?'

His lust levels rose when she whispered huskily into his ear, 'Starving.'

A late breakfast was brought out to them on the bar-side veranda. Their glasses from the previous evening had already been cleared away.

Wrapped in the guest robe, her hair damp from the shower she'd shared with Francesco, Hannah stretched her legs out and took a sip of the deliciously strong yet sweet coffee. Sitting next to her, dressed in his own dark grey robe, his thigh resting against hers, Francesco grinned.

'You are so lucky waking up to this view every morning,' she sighed. With the morning sun rising above them, calm waves swirling onto Francesco's private beach in the distance, it was as if they were in their own private nirvana.

Breakfast usually consisted of a snatched slice of toast. Today she'd been treated to eggs and bacon and enough fresh rolls and fruit to feed a whole ward of patients.

Yes. Nirvana.

'Believe me, this is the best view I've had in a *very* long time,' he said, his eyes gleaming, his deep voice laced with meaning.

Thinking of all the beautiful women she'd seen pictured on his arm, Hannah found that extremely hard to believe.

Her belly twisted.

It was no good thinking of all those women. Comparing herself to them would be akin to comparing a rock to the moon.

For the first time in her life she wished she'd put some make-up on, then immediately scolded herself for such a ridiculous thought. All those women who had the time and inclination to doll themselves up...well, good luck to them. Even after the make-up lesson she'd been given in the salon, painting her face for their night out had felt like wasted time. Looking at her reflection once she was done had been like looking at a stranger. She hadn't felt like *her*.

She supposed she could always look at it as practice for Melanie's wedding, though—a thought that brought a lump to her throat.

'You do realise you're the sexiest woman on the planet, don't you?' Francesco's words broke through the melancholy of her thoughts.

'Hardly,' she spluttered, taking another sip of her coffee.

'I can prove it,' he murmured sensually into her ear, clasping her hand and tugging it down to rest on his thigh. Sliding it up to his groin, he whispered, 'You see, my clever doctor, you are irresistible.' As he spoke, he nibbled into the nape of her neck, keeping a firm grip on her hand, moving it up so she could feel exactly what effect she was having on him.

A thrill of heady power rushed through her. Heat pooled between her legs, her breath deserting her.

They'd already made love twice since she'd awoken. She'd thought she was spent, had assumed Francesco was, too.

With his free hand he tugged her robe open enough to slip a hand through and cup a breast, kneading it gently. 'You also have the most beautiful breasts on the earth,' he murmured into her ear before sliding his lips over to her mouth and kissing her with a ferocity that reignited the remaining embers of her desire.

'What…what if one of your staff comes out?' she gasped, moving him with more assurance as he unclasped her hand and snaked his arm round her waist.

'They won't.' Thus saying, he slid his hand under her bottom and lifted her off the chair and onto the table, ignoring the fact that their breakfast plates and cups were scattered all over it.

Francesco ached to be inside her again, his body fired up beyond belief, and such a short time after their last bout. It was those memories of being in the shower with her, when she'd sunk to her knees and taken him in her mouth for the first time....

Just thinking about it would sustain his fantasies for a lifetime.

Dipping his head to take a perfectly ripe breast into his mouth, he trailed a hand down her belly and slipped a finger inside her, groaning aloud to find her hot and moist and ready for him.

Diving impatiently into his pocket, he grabbed the condom he'd put in there as an afterthought and, with Hannah distracting him by smothering any part of his face and neck she could reach with kisses, he slipped it on, spread her thighs wide, and plunged straight into her tight heat.

Her head lolled back, her eyes widening as if in shock.

Silently he cursed himself. Such was his excitement he'd totally forgotten that until a few short hours ago she'd been a virgin.

'Too much?' he asked, stilling, fighting to keep himself in check.

'Oh, no.' As if to prove it, she grabbed his buttocks and ground herself against him. The shock left her eyes, replaced with the desire he knew swirled in his own. 'I want it all.'

It was all he needed. Sweeping the crockery this way and that to make some space, he pushed her back so she was flat on the table, her thighs parted and raised high, her legs wrapped around his, and thrust into her, withdrawing to the tip and thrusting back in, over and over until she was whimpering beneath him, her hands flailing to grab his chest, her head turning from side to side. Only when he felt her thicken around him and her muscles contract did he let himself go, plunging in as deep as he could with one final groan before collapsing on top of her.

It was only when all the stars had cleared that he realised they were still in their respective robes, Hannah's fingers playing under the Egyptian cotton, tracing up and down his back.

She giggled.

Lifting his chin to rest it on her chest, he stared at her intently.

'That was incredible,' she said, smiling.

He flashed his teeth in return. 'You, *signorina*, are a very quick learner.'

'And you, *signor*, are a very good teacher.'

'There is so much more I can teach you.'

'And is it all depraved?'

'Most of it.'

She laughed softly and lay back on the table, expelling a sigh of contentment as she gazed up at the cobalt sky. He kept his gaze on her face. That serene look was there again. To think he was the cause of it...

A late breakfast turned into a late lunch. Francesco did not think he had ever felt the beat of the sun so strongly on his skin. For the first time in ten months he enjoyed a lazy day—indeed, the thought of working never crossed his mind. The rage he felt for his father, the rage that had boiled within him for so long, had morphed into a mild simmer.

In the back of his mind was the knowledge that at some point soon he would have to arrange for his jet to take Hannah back to London, but it was something he desisted from thinking about too much, content to make love, skinny-dip, then make love again. And she seemed happy, too, her smile serene, radiant.

Kissing her for what could easily be the thousandth time, he tied his robe around his waist and headed back indoors and to his bedroom for more condoms.

The box was almost empty. He shook his head in wonder. He'd never known desire like it. He couldn't get enough of her.

When he returned outside, Hannah had poured them both another cup of coffee from the pot and was curled up on one of the sofas reading something on her phone.

'Everything okay?' he asked, hiding the burst of irritation that poked at him.

This was the third time she'd gone through her messages since they'd awoken.

She's a dedicated professional, he reminded himself. Her patients are her priority, as they should be.

For all his sound reasoning, there was no getting around the fact he wanted to rip the phone from her hand and stamp on it. After all, it was the weekend. She was off duty.

She looked up and smiled. 'All's well.'

'Good.' Sitting next to her, he plucked the phone from her hand and slipped it into his pocket.

'Not again,' she groaned.

'Now you have satisfied yourself that your patients are all well, you have no need for it.'

'Francesco, give it back.'

'Later. You need to learn to switch off. Besides, it's rude.'

'Please.' Her voice lowered, all her former humour gone. 'That's my phone. And I wasn't being rude—you'd gone to the bedroom.' She held her hand out, palm side up. 'Now give.'

'What's it worth?' he asked, leaning into her, adopting a sensuous tone.

'Me not kicking you in the ankle.'

'I thought you didn't believe in violence.'

'So did I.' A smile suddenly creased her face and she burst out laughing, her mirth increasing when he shoved her phone back into the pocket of her robe. 'Now I get it— threats of violence really do work.'

He kissed her neck and flattened her onto her back. 'The difference is I knew you didn't mean it.'

Raking her fingers through his hair, she sighed. 'I guess you'll never know.'

'Oh, I know.' Hannah healed people. She didn't hurt them.

But he didn't want to think those thoughts. The time was fast approaching when he'd have to take her home, leaving him limited time left to worship her delectable body.

'I'm going to be in London more frequently for a while,' he mentioned casually, making his way down to a ripe breast. 'I'll give you a call when I'm over. Take you out for dinner.' With all the evidence pointing to Luca Mastrangelo still sniffing around the Mayfair casino, Francesco needed to be on the ball. If that meant spending more time in London, then so be it. The casino would be his, however he had to achieve it. He would secure that deal and nothing would prevent it.

Hannah moaned as he circled his tongue around a puckered nipple.

At least being in London more often meant he could enjoy her for a little longer, too.

It never occurred to him that Hannah might have different ideas.

Hannah opened the curtains and stepped into the cubicle, pulling the curtains shut around her. She smiled at the small girl lying in the bed who'd been brought in a week ago with encephalitis, inflammation of the brain, then smiled at the anxious parents. 'We have the lab results,' she said, not wasting time with pleasantries, 'and it's good news.'

This was her favourite part of the job, she thought a few minutes later as she walked back to her small workspace—telling parents who'd lived through hell that their child would make it, that the worst was over.

Clicking the mouse to get her desktop working, she opened the young girl's file, ready to write her notes up into the database. Her phone vibrated in her pocket.

She pulled it out, her heart skipping when Francesco's name flashed up.

Time seemed to still as she stared at it, her hands frozen.

Should she answer?

Or not?

It went to voicemail before she could decide.

Closing her eyes, she tilted her head back and rolled her neck.

Why, oh, why had she agreed to see him again? Not that she had agreed. At the time she'd been too busy writhing in his arms to think coherently about anything other than the sensations he was inducing in her....

She squeezed her eyes even tighter.

Francesco, in all his arrogance, had simply assumed she'd want to see him again.

An almost hysterical burst of laughter threatened to escape from her throat.

There was no way she could see him again. She just couldn't.

Their time together in Sicily had brought him, her dream man, to life—the good and the bad. Being with him had been the most wonderful, thrilling time imaginable. She had felt alive. She had felt *so much*.

She had felt *too* much.

All she wanted now was to focus on her job and leave Francesco as nothing but a beautiful memory.

She would carry on seeking out new experiences to share with Beth for when the time came that they were together again. But these experiences would be of an entirely different nature, more of a tick box—*I've done that, I've parachuted out of an aeroplane*—experience. Nothing that would clog her head. Nothing that would compromise everything she had spent the majority of her life working towards.

But, dear God, the hollowness that had lived in her chest for so long now felt so *full*, as if her shrivelled heart had been pumped back to life. And that scared her more than anything.

It was easier to shatter a full heart than a shrivelled one.

'Hannah, you should go home,' Alice, the ward sister said, startling her from her thoughts. Alice looked hard at her. 'Are you okay?'

Hannah nodded. Alice was lovely, a woman whose compassion extended from the children to all the staff on the ward. 'I'm fine,' she said, forcing a smile. 'I'll be off as soon as I get these reports finished.'

'It'll be dark soon,' Alice pointed out. 'Anyway, I'm off now. I'll see you in the morning.'

Alone again, Hannah rubbed her temples, willing away the tension headache that was forming.

She really should go home. Her shift had officially finished two hours ago.

The thought of returning to her little home filled her with nothing but dread, just as it had for the past three days since she'd returned from Sicily.

Her home felt so empty.

The silence…how had she never noticed the silence before, when the only noise had been the sound of her own breathing?

For the first time ever, she felt lonely. Not the usual loneliness that had been within her since Beth's death, but a different kind of isolation. Colder, somehow.

Even the sunny yellow walls of her little cubbyhole felt bleak.

Francesco's phone rang. *'Ciao.'*

'That young drug dealer is back. We have him.'

'Bring him to me.'

Francesco knew exactly who Mario was on about. A young lad, barely eighteen, had visited his Palermo nightclub a few weeks ago. The cameras had caught him slipping bags of powder and pills to many of the clubbers. As unlikely as it was, he had slipped their net, escaping before Francesco's men could apprehend him, disappearing into the night.

He rubbed his eyes.

No matter how hard he tried to remove the dealers, there was always some other cocky upstart there to fill the breach. It was like trying to stop the tide.

The one good thing he could say about it was that at least he was making the effort to clean the place up, to counter some of the damage his father had done.

Salvatore had been responsible for channelling millions of euros' worth of drugs into Sicily and mainland Europe. How he had kept it secret from his son, Francesco would never understand; he could only guess Salvatore had known it was the one thing his son would never stand idly by and allow to happen. If Francesco *had* known, he would have ripped his father apart, but by the time he'd learned of his involvement, it had been too late to confront him. Salvatore had already been buried when he found out the truth.

It occurred to him, not for the first time, that his father had been afraid of him.

Slowly but surely, he was dismantling everything Salvatore Calvetti had built, closing it down brick by brick, taking care in his selection of which to dismantle first so as not to disturb the foundation and have it all crumble on top of him. Only a few days ago he had taken great delight in shutting down a restaurant that had been a hub for the distribution of arms, one of many in his father's great network.

While he'd been paying off Paolo di Luca, the man who'd run the restaurant on his father's behalf for thirty years, he had seen for the first time the old man Paolo had become. A man with liver spots and a rheumy wheeze. The more he thought about it, the more he realised all the old associates were exactly that—old.

When had they got so ancient?

These weren't the terrifying men of his childhood memories. Apart from a handful who hadn't taken kindly to being put out to pasture, most of them had been happy to be paid off, glad to spend their remaining years with their wives—or mistresses in many cases—and playing with their grandchildren and great-grandchildren.

There was a knock on the door, and the handle turned.

Mario and two of his other guards walked in, holding the young drug dealer up by the scruff of his neck.

With them came a burst of music from the club, a dreadful tune that hit him straight in his gut.

It was the same tune Hannah had been dancing to so badly in his London club, when he'd threatened the fool manhandling her.

The same Hannah who'd ignored her phone when he'd called and, in response to a message he'd sent saying he would be in London at the weekend, had sent him a simple message back saying she was busy. Since then…nothing. Not a peep from her.

It wasn't as if she never used her blasted phone. It was attached to her like an appendage.

There was no getting around it. She was avoiding him.

He looked at the belligerent drug dealer, but all he could see was the look of serenity on Hannah's face when he'd told her of calling the police on the casino cheat.

Hannah saved lives. She'd sworn an oath to never do harm.

What was it she'd said? *Who makes the rules?*

'Empty your pockets,' he ordered, not moving from his seat.

He could see how badly the drug dealer wanted to disobey him, but sanity prevailed and he emptied his pockets. He had two bags of what Francesco recognised as ecstasy tablets and a bag full of tiny cellophane wraps of white powder. Cocaine.

A cross between a smirk and a snarl played on the drug dealer's lips.

Francesco's hands clenched into fists. He rose.

The drug dealer turned puce, his belligerence dropping a touch when confronted by Francesco's sheer physical power.

Who makes the rules?

'You are throwing your life away,' he said harshly before turning to Mario. 'Call the police.'

'The police?' squeaked the dealer.

It was obvious that the same question echoed in Mario and his fellow guards' heads.

First the stealing, cheating gambler and now a drug dealer? He could see the consternation on all their faces, could feel them silently wondering if he was going soft.

Naturally, none of his men dared question him verbally, their faces expressionless.

'Yes. The police.' As he walked past the dealer, Francesco added, 'But know that when you're released from your long prison sentence, if I ever find you dealing in drugs again, I will personally break your legs. Take my advice—get yourself an education and go straight.'

With that, he strode out of his office, out of his nightclub, and into the dark Palermo night, oblivious to the cadre of bodyguards who'd snapped into action to keep up with him.

CHAPTER TEN

HANNAH BROUGHT HER bike to a stop outside her small front gate and smothered a yawn. She felt dead on her feet. The Friday-evening traffic had only compounded what had been a *very* long week.

She dismounted and wheeled her bike up the narrow path to her front door. Just as she placed her key in the lock, a loud beep made her turn.

A huge, gleaming black motorbike with an equally huge rider came to a stop right by her front gate.

No way...

Stunned, she watched as Francesco strode towards her, magnificent in his black leathers, removing his helmet, a thunderous look on his face.

'What are you doing here?' Her heart had flown into her mouth and it took all she had not to stand there gaping like a goldfish.

'Never mind that, what the hell are you doing back on that deathtrap?'

He loomed before her, blocking the late sun, his eyes blazing with fury.

Hannah blinked, totally nonplussed at seeing him again. Only years of practice at remaining calm while under fire from distressed patients and their next of kin alike allowed her to retain any composure. 'I don't drive.'

Breathing heavily through his nose, he snapped, 'There are other ways of getting around. I can't believe you're still using this...thing.'

'I'm not. It's a new one.'

'I gathered that, seeing as your old one crumpled like a biscuit tin,' he said, speaking through gritted teeth. 'I'm just struggling to understand why you would still cycle when you nearly died on a bicycle mere weeks ago.'

'I don't like using public transport. Plus, cycling helps shift some of the weight from my bottom,' she added, trying to inject some humour into her tone, hoping to defuse some of the anger still etched on his face. Her attempt failed miserably.

'There is nothing wrong with your bottom,' he said coldly. 'And even if there were—which there isn't—it's hardly worth risking your life for.'

The situation was so surreal Hannah was tempted to pinch herself.

Was she dreaming? She'd had so little sleep since returning from Sicily five days ago that it was quite possible.

'Like every other human on this planet, I could die at any time by any number of accidents. I'm not going to stay off my bike because of one idiot.' She kept her tone firm, making it clear the situation was no longer open for discussion. She was a grown woman. If she wanted to cycle, then that was her business. 'Anyway, you're hardly in a position to judge—do you have any idea the number of mangled motorcyclists I had to patch back together when I was doing my placement in Accident and Emergency?'

A cold snake crawled up her spine at the thought of Francesco being brought in on a trolley....

She blinked the thought away.

'My riding skills are second to none, as you know perfectly well,' he said with all the confidence of a man who knew he was the best at what he did. 'In any case, I do not ride around on a piece of cheap tin.'

'You can be incredibly arrogant, did you know that?'

'I've been called much worse, and if being arrogant is what it takes to keep you safe then I can live with that.'

His chocolate eyes held hers with an intensity so deep it almost burned. Her fingers itched to touch him, to rub her thumb over the angry set of his lips.

No matter how...shocked she felt at his sudden appearance, there was something incredibly touching about his anger, knowing it was concern for her safety propelling it.

She looked away, scared to look at him any longer. 'I appreciate your concern, but my safety is not your responsibility.'

Suddenly aware her helmet was still attached to her head, she unclipped it and whipped it off, smoothing her hair down as best she could.

God, since when had she suffered from vanity? Last weekend notwithstanding, not in fifteen years.

And why did she feel an incomprehensible urge to burst into tears?

It was a feeling she'd been stifling since she'd walked back into her home on Sunday night.

'What are you doing here?' she asked again, her cheeks burning as she recalled the two phone calls she'd ignored from him.

'That's not a conversation I wish to have on your doorstep.'

When she made no response, he inclined his head at her door. 'This is the point where you invite me into your home.'

Less than a week ago she'd invited him into her house, only to have him rudely decline.

Then, her heart had hammered with excitement for what

the weekend would bring. Now her heart thrummed just to see *him*…

'Look, you can come in for a little while, but I've had a long, difficult week and a *very* long, *very difficult* day, and I want to get to bed early.' Abruptly, she turned away and opened the door, terrified he would read something of her feelings on her face.

The last word she should be mentioning in front of Francesco was *bed*.

She could hardly credit how naive she'd been in sleeping with him. Had she seriously thought she could share a bed with the sexiest man on the planet and walk away feeling nothing more than a little mild contentment that she'd ticked something off her to-do list?

What a silly, naive fool she'd been.

Francesco thought he'd never been in a more depressing house than the place Hannah called home. It wasn't that there was anything intrinsically wrong with it—on the contrary, it was a pretty two-bedroom house with high ceilings and spacious rooms, but…

There was no feeling to it. Her furniture was minimal and bought for function. The walls were bare of any art or anything that would show the owner's tastes. It was a shell.

Hannah shoved her foldaway bike in a virtually empty cupboard under the stairs and faced him, a look of defiance—and was that fear?—on her face. Her hair had reverted back to its usual unkempt state, a sight that pleased him immeasurably.

'I need a shower,' she said.

'Is that an invitation?' he asked, saying it more as a challenge than from any expectation.

She ignored his innuendo. 'I've been puked on twice today.'

He grimaced. 'So not an invitation.'

'Give me five minutes, then you can tell me whatever it is you came all this way to discuss. While I'm gone, you can make yourself useful by making the coffee.' Thus saying, she headed up the wooden stairs without a backward glance, her peachy bottom showing beautifully in the functional black trousers she wore....

Quickly he averted his eyes. Too much looking at those gorgeous buttocks might just make him climb into that shower with her after all.

Besides, a few minutes to sort their respective heads out would probably be a good idea.

Hannah's reception had not been the most welcoming, but what had he expected? That she would take one look at him and throw herself into his arms?

No, he hadn't expected that. Her silence and polite rebuff by text message had made her feelings clear. Well, tough on her. He was here and they would talk whether she wanted to or not.

Yet there had been no faking the light that had shone briefly in her eyes when she'd first spotted him. It had been mingled with shock, but it had been there, that same light that had beamed straight into his heart the first time she'd opened her eyes to him.

Then he'd ruined it by biting her head off over her bike.

He cursed under his breath. If it took the rest of his life, he'd get her off that deathtrap.

He heard a door close and the sound of running water. Was she naked…?

He inhaled deeply, slung his leather jacket over the post of the stairs, and walked into the small square kitchen. He spotted the kettle easily enough and filled it, then set about finding mugs and coffee.

As he rootled through Hannah's cupboards, his chest slowly constricted.

He had never seen such bare cupboards. The only actual food he found was half a loaf of bread, a box of cereal, a large slice of chocolate cake, and some tomato sauce. And that was it. Nothing else, not even a box of eggs. The fridge wasn't much better, containing some margarine, a pint of milk, and an avocado.

What did she eat?

That question was answered when he opened her freezer.

It wasn't just his chest that felt constricted. His heart felt as if it had been placed in a vice.

The freezer was full. Three trays crammed with ready meals for one.

The ceiling above him creaked, jolting him out of the trance he hadn't realised he'd fallen into.

Experiencing a pang of guilt at rifling through her stuff, he shut the freezer door and went back to the jar of instant coffee he'd found and the small bag of sugar.

No wonder she had wanted to experience a little bit of life.

He'd never met anyone who lived such a solitary existence. Not that anyone would guess. Hannah wasn't antisocial. On the contrary, she was good company. Better than good. Warm, witty… Beautiful. Sexy.

Before too long she emerged to join him in the sparse living room, having changed into a pair of faded jeans and a black T-shirt.

'Your coffee's on the table,' he said, rising from the sofa he'd sat on. He would bet the small dining table in the corner was rarely used for eating on, loaded as it was with medical journals and heaps of paper neatly laid in piles.

'Thank you.' She picked it up and walked past him to

the single seat, leaving a waft of light, fruity fragrance in her wake. She curled up on it, cradling her mug.

Now her eyes met his properly, a brightness glistening from them. 'Francesco, what are you doing here?'

'I want to know why you're avoiding me.'

'I'm not.'

'Don't tell me lies.'

'I haven't seen you to avoid you.'

'You said you were busy this weekend, yet here you are, at home.'

Her head rolled back, her chest rising and falling even more sharply. 'I've only just got back from work, as you well know, and I'm on the rota for tomorrow's night shift. So yes, I am busy.'

'Look at me,' he commanded. He would keep control of his temper if it killed him.

With obvious reluctance, she met his gaze.

'Last weekend... You do realise what we shared was out of this world?'

Her cheeks pinked. 'It was very nice.'

'There are many words to describe it, but *nice* isn't one of them. You and me...'

'There is no you and me,' she blurted, interrupting him. 'I'm sorry to have to put it so crassly, but I don't want to see you again. Last weekend *was* very nice but there will be no repeat performance.'

'You think not?' he said, trying his hardest to keep his tone soft, but when she dug her hand into her pocket and pulled out her phone, the red mist seemed to descend as if from nowhere. 'Do *not* turn that thing on.'

Her eyes widened as if startled before narrowing. 'Don't tell me what I can and can't do. You're not my father.'

'I'm not trying...'

'You certainly are.'

'Will you stop interrupting me?' He raised his voice for the first time.

Her mouth dropped open.

'It's a bit much feeling as if I'm in competition with a phone,' he carried on, uncaring that she had turned a whiter shade of white. He knew without having to be told that there was no competition, because the phone had won without even trying. Because as far as Dr Hannah Chapman was concerned, her phone was all she needed.

He rose to his feet, his anger swelling like an awoken cobra, his venom primed. 'You hide behind it. I bet you sleep with it on your pillow.'

His comment was so close to the mark that Hannah cringed inwardly *and* outwardly. Dear God, why had he come here? Why hadn't he just taken the hint and kept away?

She hadn't asked for any of this. All she'd wanted was to experience one night as a real woman.

She'd ended up with so much more than she'd bargained for.

'Do you really want to spend the rest of your life with nothing but a phone to keep you warm at night?'

'What I want is none of your business,' she said, her tongue running away as she added, 'but just to clarify what I told you in your nightclub, I do *not* want a relationship—not with you, not with anyone.'

He threw his arms out, a sneer on his face. 'Of course you don't want a relationship. Your life is so fulfilling as it is.'

'It is to me.' How she stopped herself screaming that in his face she would never know.

'Look at you. Look at this place. You're hiding away from life. You're like one of those mussels we ate in the casino—you threw yourself at me to experience some of what you'd been missing out on, got what you wanted, then retreated right back into your shell without any thought to the consequences.'

She didn't have a clue what he was talking about. 'What consequences? We used protection.'

'I'm not talking about babies—I'm talking about what you've done to me!' If he'd been a lion he would have roared those last few words, of that she had no doubt. Francesco's fury was a sight to behold, making him appear taller and broader than ever, filling the living room.

She should be terrified. And there was no denying the panic gnawing furiously at the lining of her stomach, but it wasn't fear of him…

No, it was the fear of something far worse.

And this fear put her even further on the defensive.

Shoving her mug on the floor, she jumped to her feet. The calmness she had been wearing as a facade evaporated, leaving her jumbled, terrified emotions raw and exposed. 'I haven't done *anything* to you!'

'You've changed me. I don't know how the hell you did it—maybe you're some kind of witch—but whatever you did, it's real. I let a drug dealer escape without a beating last night, had my men turn him over to the police.'

'And that's a bad thing?'

'It's not how I work. That's never been how I work. Drugs killed my mother. Drug dealers are the scum of the earth and deserve everything they get.' Abruptly he stopped talking and took a long breath in. 'You gave me the best night of my life and I know as well as you do that you enjoyed every minute of it, too. You can deny it until you're blue in the face but we both know what we shared was special. *You* forced that night on *me*. It was what *you* wanted, and it's me that's paying the price for it.'

'You knew it was only for one night.'

'A one-night stand is never that good. Never. Not even close. But now you're treating me as if I'm a plague carrier, and I want to know why.'

'There's nothing to tell. I just don't want to see you again.'

'Will you stop lying?'

'I can't have sex with you again. I just can't. You've screwed with my brain enough as it is.'

'*I've* screwed with *your* brain?' His tone was incredulous. 'Do you have any idea what you've done to *me*?'

'Oh, yes, let's bring it all back to you,' she spat. 'The poor little gangster struggling to deal with his newly found conscience while I...'

Hannah took a deep breath, trying desperately to rein all her emotions back in and under her control. 'After my accident, you filled my mind. You were all I could think about. When I met you it only got worse. I came to you partly because I thought doing something about it would fix it. I thought we would have sex and that would be it—my life would return to normal, I'd be able to go back to concentrating on my job without any outside influences...'

'Didn't it work out exactly as you envisaged?' he asked, his tone mocking.

'No, it did not! I thought it would. But you're still there, filling my head, and I want you gone. My patients deserve all my focus. Every scrap of it. I want to experience more of life, but not to their detriment. This is all *too much* and I can't handle it.'

'I warned you of the consequences,' he said roughly. 'I told you a one-night stand wasn't for a woman like you.'

Something inside Hannah pinged. Taking three paces towards him, she pushed at his chest. 'You are a hypocrite,' she shouted. 'How many women have you used for sex? Double figures? Treble? How many lives have *you* ruined?'

'None. All the women before you knew it would only ever be sex. It meant nothing.'

'Ha! Exactly.' She shoved him again, hard enough to knock him off balance and onto the sofa. 'The minute the tables are turned, your fragile ego can't deal with it...'

She never got to finish her sentence for Francesco grabbed hold of her waist and yanked her onto the sofa with him, pinning her down before she could get a coherent thought in her head.

'You know as well as I do that what we shared meant something,' he said harshly, his hot breath tickling her skin. 'And contrary to your low opinion of my sex life, I am not some kind of male tart. Until last weekend I'd been celibate for ten months.'

She wanted to kick out, scream at him to get off her, but all the words died on her tongue when his mouth came crashing down on hers, a hard, furious kiss that her aching heart and body responded to like a moth to a flame.

That deep masculine taste and scent filled her senses, blocking out all her fears, blocking out everything but him. Francesco.

Just five days away from him, and she had pined. Pined for him. Pined for this.

She practically melted into him, winding her arms around his hard body, clinging to him, pressing every part of her into him.

And he clung to her, too, his hands roaming over her body, bunching her hair, his hot lips grazing her face, her neck, every available bit of flesh.

Being in his arms felt so *right*. Francesco made the coldness that had settled in her bones since she'd returned from Sicily disappear, replacing it with a warmth that seeped through to every part of her.

In a melee of limbs her T-shirt was pulled over her head

and thrown to the floor, quickly followed by Francesco's. Braless, her naked breasts crushed against his chest, the last remaining alarms ringing in her brain vanished and all she could do was savour the feel of his hard strength flush against her.

His strong capable hands playing with the buttons on her jeans, her smaller hands working on the zip of his leathers, somehow they managed to tug both down, using their feet to work them off to join the rest of their strewn clothing, in the process tumbling off the sofa and onto the soft carpet.

Only when they were both naked did Francesco reach for his leathers, pull out his wallet and produce a now familiar square foil.

In a matter of seconds he'd rolled it on and plunged inside her.

This time her body knew exactly what to do. *She* knew exactly what to do. No fears, no insecurities, just pure unadulterated pleasure.

The feel of him, huge inside her, his strength on the verge of crushing her, Hannah let all thoughts fly out of the window, giving in to this most wonderful of all sensations.

Later, lying in the puddle of their clothes on the floor, Francesco's face buried in her neck, his breaths hot against her skin, she opened her eyes and gazed at the ceiling. Hot tears burned the back of her retinas.

'Am I squashing you?' he asked, his breathing still ragged.

'No,' she lied, wrapping her arms even tighter around him.

Francesco lifted his head to look at her. There had been a definite hitch in her voice. 'What's the matter?'

'Nothing.'

'Stop lying to me.'

To his distress, two fat tears rolled down her cheeks.

'I'm so confused. *You* confuse me. I'd told myself I would never sleep with you again and look what's happened. You turn up and I might as well have succumbed to you the moment I let you in the door.'

Rolling onto his back, taking her with him so she rested on his chest, he held her tightly to him. 'All it proves is that we're not over. Not yet. Neither of us wants anything heavy,' he continued. 'For a start, neither of us has the *time* for anything heavy. But we enjoy each other's company, so where's the harm in seeing each other? I promise you, your patients will not suffer for you having a life.'

There was no room for Hannah in his life. Not in any meaningful way. The more he got to know her, the more he knew that what they shared could never be anything more than a fling.

Ever since he'd reached adulthood he'd assumed he would never meet a woman to settle down with. Even before he'd discovered his mother's diaries and learned of his father's despicable behaviour towards her, he'd known how badly she struggled to cope with his father's way of life.

His mother had been a good woman. Kind and loving, even when she was doped to her eyeballs on the drugs his father fed her by the trough. Not that he'd known his father fed them to her—back then he'd believed his father to be as despairing and worried about her habit as he was.

Elisabetta Calvetti had no more fitted into his father's world than Hannah fitted in his.

The women who did fit into Francesco's world and thrived were like poison. The rarer women—women like Hannah who did not fit in—he'd always known should never marry into such a dangerous life. To marry into it would destroy them, just as it had destroyed his mother.

Deep down, he knew he should have accepted her rebuffs and left her alone, but the past few days…

How could he concentrate on anything when his mind was full of Hannah?

The wolves, in the form of Luca Mastrangelo, were circling the Mayfair casino and Francesco needed to be on the ball. Otherwise the deal that would symbolise above all others that Salvatore Calvetti's empire was over, his legacy shrivelled to dust, would be lost.

He wasn't ready to let her go. Not yet. Knowing Hannah was in his life meant he could focus his attention entirely on the purchase of the casino and not have his mind filled with her.

'Okay,' she said slowly, pressing a kiss to his chest. 'As long as you promise not to make any demands on my time when I'm working, we can see each other.'

His arms tightened while the constriction in his chest loosened. He ignored the fact that her condition for seeing him—a condition he was used to dictating to his lovers and not the other way round—made his throat fill with bile.

CHAPTER ELEVEN

THE MAYFAIR CASINO was a lot shabbier than the ones Francesco owned, but the decoration was not something that concerned him. That was cosmetic and easily fixed. Even the accounts, usually his first consideration when buying a new business, mattered not at all. All he craved was what the business symbolised.

Tonight, though, symbolism and everything else could take a hike. He'd finally managed to drag Hannah out for the night.

Naturally, she'd been too busy to buy a new dress and had changed into the same dress she'd worn three weeks before in Sicily, confessing with an embarrassed smile that it was the only suitable item in her wardrobe.

He'd bitten back the offer of buying her a whole new wardrobe. He knew without having to ask that she would refuse. He was man enough to admit that it had been a blow to his pride when he'd learned she'd paid for the dress herself in Palermo. And her haircut. It surprised him, though, how much he respected her for it. She'd had free rein in that boutique. She could have easily racked up a bill for tens of thousands of euros, all in his name.

Tonight she looked beautiful. In the ten minutes she'd taken to get changed, she'd brushed her hair, but all this had done was bush it out even more. She'd applied only a little make-up. All she wore on her feet were her black ballet slippers.

In Francesco's eyes she looked far more ravishing than she had three weeks ago when she'd gone the whole nine yards with her appearance. Now she looked real. She looked like Hannah.

An elderly man with salt-and-pepper hair ambled towards them, his hand outstretched. 'Francesco, I didn't know you would be joining us this evening.' There was a definite tremor in both his hand and voice.

'I wanted to show my guest around the place,' he replied, shaking the wizened hand before introducing him to Hannah. 'This is Dr Hannah Chapman. Hannah, this is Sir Godfrey Renfrew, the current owner of this establishment.'

'Doctor?' Godfrey's eyes swept her up and down, a hint of confusion in them.

'Lovely to meet you,' Hannah said, smiling. Did Francesco *have* to keep referring to her by her title?

'The pleasure is mine,' he said quickly, before fixing his attention back on Francesco. 'I have some of your compatriots visiting me this evening.'

So that was the reason for Godfrey's discomfort.

Francesco glanced around the room, homing in on two tall men leaning against a far wall drinking beer.

So his spies had been onto something when they'd reported that Luca Mastrangelo was trying to usurp the deal. And it seemed as if Pepe was in on it, too.

If Francesco was in Sicily, all he would have to do was whisper a few well-chosen words into Godfrey's ear and the casino would be his.

But he wasn't in Sicily. And Godfrey had already proved himself immune to Sicilian threats, and much worse.

'I see them,' Francesco confirmed, keeping his tone steady, bored, even. 'They're old acquaintances of mine.'

'Yes…they said you had…history.'

That was one way of describing it. Smiling tightly, he bowed his head. 'I should go and say hello.'

Now wishing he hadn't brought Hannah out with him, Francesco bore her off towards the Mastrangelo brothers.

'Who are we going to say hello to?' she asked, surprising him by slipping her fingers through his.

Apart from when they were lying in bed together, she never held his hand. Not that they'd ever actually been out anywhere to hold hands, all their time together over the past fortnight having been spent eating takeaway food and making love.

'Old acquaintances of mine,' he said tightly, although the feel of her gentle fingers laced through his had a strangely calming reaction.

By the time they stood before the Mastrangelo brothers, his stomach felt a fraction more settled.

'Luca. Pepe.' He extended his hand. 'So the rumours are true,' he said, switching to Sicilian.

'What rumours would they be?' asked Luca, shaking his hand with a too-firm grip. Francesco squeezed a little tighter in turn before dropping the hold.

'I'd heard you were interested in this place.'

Luca shrugged.

'I thought you'd got out of the casino game.'

'Times change.'

'Clearly.' Francesco forced a smile. 'Does your little wife know you're going back into forbidden territory?'

Luca bared his teeth. 'You leave Grace out of this.'

'I wouldn't dream of bringing her into it, knowing how much she hates me.' Here, he looked at Pepe. 'I do believe your sister-in-law hates me more than you do.' Not giving either of them the chance to respond, he flashed his own teeth. 'I suggest the pair of you rethink your decision to try to buy this place. The documents for my ownership are on the verge of completion.'

Pepe finally spoke. 'But they're not completed yet, are they?'

'They will be soon. And if either of you try anything to stop the sale going through, you will live to regret it.'

'Are you threatening us?'

'You sound surprised, Luca,' he said, deliberately keeping his tone amicable. 'You should know I am not a man to deal with threats. Only promises.'

Luca pulled himself to his full height. 'I will not be threatened, Calvetti. Remember that.'

Only the gentle squeeze of Hannah's fingers lacing back through his stopped Francesco squaring up to his old friend.

He shook himself. He didn't want to be having this conversation in front of her, regardless of the fact that they were speaking in their native tongue and not in English.

'Don't start a war you'll never win, Mastrangelo.'

'I remember your father saying exactly the same thing to me when my father died. Your father thought he could take control of the Mastrangelo estate.' Luca smiled. 'He didn't succeed in getting his way. And nor will you.'

Baring his teeth one last time, Francesco said, 'But I am not my father. I have infinitely more patience.'

'Are you okay?' Hannah asked as soon as they were out of earshot.

'I'm fine. Let's get out of here.'

'But we've only just arrived.'

Expelling air slowly through his nose, he stopped himself from insisting they leave right now. He could insist and she would have no choice but to follow, but to do so would upset her, and that was the last thing he wanted to do.

Strangely enough, Hannah's presence tempered the

angry adrenaline flowing through him—not by much, but enough to take the edge off it.

Having promised to teach her how to play Blackjack, he found seats at a table for them to join in. Unlike at the tournament in Sicily, where her remarkable poker face was her biggest asset, there was no bluffing needed when playing against the dealer. She still picked it up like a pro. At one point he thought she would finish with more chips than him.

Watching her have fun eased a little more of his rage, enough so that there were moments he forgot the Mastrangelos were there, trying to muscle in on his territory. It pleased him enormously to watch her drink a full glass of champagne. She really was learning to switch off.

His driver was ready for them when they left. As soon as they were seated in the back, the partition separating them from the driver, Hannah squished right next to him and reached for his hand. Pulling it onto her lap, she rubbed her thumb in light circular motions over his inner wrist.

The breath of air he inhaled went into his lungs that bit easier.

'How do you know those two men?' she asked after a few moments of silence.

He could only respect her reticence in waiting until they were alone before starting her cross-examination. 'Luca and Pepe?'

'Is that their names?' she said drily. 'You forgot to introduce us.'

He sighed. 'I apologise. They're old friends. Were old friends. At least, Luca was.'

'Was?'

'Their father used to work for my father. And then he quit.'

He felt her blanch.

'Don't worry. My father didn't touch him—they'd been

childhood friends themselves, which saved Pietro from my father's vengeance. But the fact my father didn't put a bullet through him didn't mean the perceived slur could be forgotten. Once their professional relationship finished, family loyalty meant any friendship between Luca and I was finished, too. It's all about respect.' In his father's eyes, everything had been about respect. Everything.

How he'd envied the easy affection the two Mastrangelo boys shared with their father. It was the kind of relationship he'd longed for, but for Salvatore Calvetti a sign of affection for his only child consisted of a slap on the back if he pleased him.

'Have you not seen Luca since then?'

'He came to my father's funeral.' He looked away, not wanting her to see the expression on his face reflecting what he felt beneath his skin whenever he thought of his father's funeral. While a tiny part of him had felt relief that he could break free from Salvatore's shadow, he'd mourned the man. Truly mourned him.

If he'd known then what he knew now, he would have lit fireworks by his open graveside in celebration.

'My father's death freed me. It freed Luca and me to resume our old friendship. When we were kids we often used to play cards together, and always said that when we grew up we would open a casino together. We opened our first one three years ago, but then last year he decided he wanted out.'

'Why was that?'

He met her eyes. 'His wife thought I was bad for him.'

Her forehead furrowed. 'He said that?'

'Not in so many words. But it was obvious. She hates my guts.'

Still her forehead furrowed. 'But why?'

'Because I'm a big bad gangster.'

'No, your father was a big bad gangster,' she corrected.

'Even after everything you've witnessed, you still refuse to see it.' He planted a kiss on the end of her nose.

'No, I *do* see it. You are who you are, but you're nowhere near as bad as you like people to think.'

She wouldn't say that if she could read the thoughts going through his mind. Thoughts of revenge, not just against his father but against Luca Mastrangelo. And Pepe.

He would not allow the Mayfair casino to fall into Mastrangelo hands. It was *his* and he would do whatever was needed to ensure it.

'Do I take it that those men are also interested in buying the casino?' Hannah asked, swinging her legs onto his lap.

'I'd heard rumours they were after it. Being there tonight confirmed it.'

'And do I take it you threatened them?' At his surprised glance, she grinned ruefully. 'I might not speak Sicilian, but I can read body language.'

'And you think I have *good* in me?' Rubbing his hand absently over her calf, he couldn't help but notice the little bags that had formed under her eyes. Those little bags made his heart constrict.

This was a woman who worked so hard for such a good purpose she hardly slept. And *she* saw good in *him*?

'You won't hurt them,' she said with simple confidence.

He didn't answer. The one thing he would never do was lie to her. He'd lived a lifetime of lies.

Before she could question his silence, her phone vibrated. Dropping his hand, she reached into her bag.

'Is it work?' he asked, trying hard to keep the edge from his voice. The only time Hannah lost her sweet humour was when he mentioned her excessive use of her phone. On those occasions her claws came out.

She shook her head absently. 'Melanie.'

'She's back from her work trip?'

'Yep. She wants to know if I'm free tomorrow for the last fitting. For my bridesmaid dress,' she added heavily.

'Are you not going to answer?' When it came to work she would fire off a reply the second she read them.

'I suppose I should.'

Before he could question her reluctance, they pulled up outside his hotel.

'Shall we have a bath together?' he asked once they were safely ensconced in his suite.

Hannah's nose wrinkled. She felt all…out of sorts. Right then she needed something sweet to counteract the acidity that had formed in her throat. 'Can we have chocolate-fudge cake first?'

'Hot?'

She smiled. Already he knew her so well. Especially with regard to her hot chocolate-fudge cake addiction, which was fast becoming usurped by her Francesco addiction.

Was this how drug addicts started out? she wondered. A little fix here, a little fix there, then swearing never to do it again? But then temptation was placed right under their nose and they were too weak to resist? Because that was how she felt with him. Unable to resist.

Why did she even need to keep resisting? Addictions were bad things. How could Francesco possibly be classed as bad for her? Her work hadn't suffered for being with him.

The only reason to resist now was for the sake of her heart, and she'd already lost that battle. In reality, she hadn't stood a chance.

She looked at him, her big bear of a man.

What would he say if he knew that, despite all her protestations over not wanting a relationship, she'd fallen for him?

She'd watched him square up to those two men in the

casino and she'd wanted to dive between them and kung fu them into keeping away from him.

The strength of her protectiveness towards him had shocked her.

It was how she used to be with Beth. If you messed with one twin you messed with the other.

And like it had been with Beth, when she was with Francesco she felt safe. She felt complete. It was a different completeness but every bit as powerful.

'Will you come to Melanie's wedding with me?' She blurted out the words before she'd even properly thought of them.

Her heart lurched to see the palpable shock on his face.

'Sorry. Forget I said anything,' she said quickly. 'It's a silly...'

'You took me by surprise, that's all,' he cut in with a shake of his head. 'You want me to come to your sister's wedding?'

'Only if you're not too busy. I just...' She bit her lip. 'I just could do with...'

Francesco didn't know what she was trying to tell him, but the darting of her eyes and the way she wrung her hands together pierced something in him.

'Will there be room for me?' he asked, stalling for time while he tried to think.

A sound like a laugh spluttered from her lips. 'If I tell them I'm bringing a date they'll make room, even if it means sitting one of the grandparents on someone else's lap.'

'Okay,' he agreed, injecting more positivity than he felt inside. 'I'll come with you.'

The gratitude in her eyes pierced him even deeper.

It wasn't until midmorning they got into the enormous bath together. After a night of making love and snatches of tortured sleep, Hannah was happy to simply lie between Francesco's legs, her head resting against his chest, and enjoy the bubbly water.

Her phone, which she'd placed on the shelf above the sink, vibrated.

'Leave it,' he commanded, tightening his hold around her waist.

'It might be important.'

'It will still be there in ten minutes.'

'But…'

'Hannah, this can't continue. You're using your phone as an emotional crutch and it's not good for you.' There was a definite sharpness to his tone.

Since they'd started seeing each other properly, she'd been acutely aware of his loathing for her phone. Not her work, or the research papers or her studying; just her phone.

'I think it's a bit much you calling it an emotional crutch,' she said tightly. 'If one of my patients dies when I'm not on shift, then I want to know—I don't want to get to work and come face-to-face with bereaved parents in the car park or atrium or café or wherever and not know that they've just lost the most precious thing in their lives.'

The edge to his voice vanished. 'Is that what happened to you when Beth died?'

She jerked a nod. 'When Beth was first admitted, the doctor was very clinical in his approach, almost cold.' She fixed her gaze on Francesco's beautiful arms, adoring the way the water darkened the hair and flattened it over the olive skin. 'Beth died in the early hours of the morning, long after that first doctor had finished his shift. Luckily, she was in the care of some of the loveliest, most compassionate doctors and nurses you could wish for. They let us stay with her body for hours, right until the sun came up. I remember we had to go back to the children's ward as we'd left Beth's possessions there when she'd been taken off to Intensive Care. We got into the lift and that first doctor got in with us.'

She paused, swallowing away the acrid bile that formed in her throat.

'He looked right through us. Either he didn't recognise us as the family of the young girl he'd been treating twenty-four hours before, or he did recognise us and just didn't want to acknowledge us. Either way, I hated him for it. My sister was dead and that man didn't even care enough to remember our faces.'

'Do you still hate him?'

She shook her head. 'I understand it now. There are only so many times you can watch a child die before you grow a hard shell. We all do it. The difference is, he let his shell consume him at the expense of the patient. I will *never* allow myself to become like that. I never want any of my patients or their loved ones to think I don't care.'

'That must take its toll on you, though,' he observed. Francesco had only watched one person die: his mother. He'd made it to the hospital in time to say goodbye, but by that point the essence of *her* had already gone, her body kept alive by machines.

It had been the single most distressing event of his life.

To choose a profession where you were surrounded by illness and death... He could hardly begin to comprehend the dedication and selflessness needed to do such a job.

She shrugged, but her grip on his arms tightened. 'We send hundreds more children home healed than we lose. That more than makes up for it.'

He found himself at a loss for what to say.

Hannah had suffered the loss of the most precious person in her life—her twin—and she'd turned her grief into a force for good.

Hadn't he known from the start that she was too good for him? He still knew it, more than ever.

'Beth's death broke something inside me,' she said quietly. 'My parents tried very hard to comfort me, but they were grieving, too, and in any case I pushed them away. Melanie was desperate to comfort me, but I pushed her away, too. Since my accident I can see how badly I've treated my family. I've kept myself apart from them. I've kept myself apart from everyone…until you.'

His chest tightened. 'Your family was happy for you to isolate yourself?'

'No.' Her damp hair tickled his nose. 'They weren't happy. But what could they do about it? They couldn't *make* me.' Her voice became wistful. 'I think I wanted them to force the issue. I was so lost but I couldn't find the way out.…'

There was so much Francesco wanted to say as her words trailed away. None of it would help.

'You're probably right about my phone,' she muttered. 'I guess I have been using it as a crutch. It's easier for me to interact with an object than a human. At least that was the case until I met you.'

She turned her head, resting her cheek on his shoulder as she stared at him. 'I'm so glad you're coming to the wedding with me.'

The very mention of the *W* word was enough to make his stomach roil.

'I've been dreading it for so long now,' she confessed.

'Is Beth the reason you're so anxious about it?' He dragged his question out. 'Because she can't be there?'

Her nails dug into his arms. 'This is the first real family event we've had since she died.' She placed a kiss to his neck and inhaled. 'With you by my side, I think I can endure it without ruining Melanie's day. The last thing I want is to spoil things for her, but I don't think even my poker face will be able to hide my feelings.' She swallowed. 'It's all feeling so raw again.'

Francesco cleared the sourness forming in his throat.

He hadn't bargained on this. None of it was part of his plan, whereby he would see her whilst spending lots of time in London finalising the Mayfair deal, after which they would head their separate ways.

None of this was in the script.

He hadn't for a minute imagined she would start needing him, not his self-sufficient doctor who didn't rely on anyone but herself.

Something gripped at his chest, a kind of panic.

If it wasn't for the tears spilling down her cheeks and the confidences she'd just entrusted him with, he would have dreamed up a good excuse not to go there and then.

But Hannah crying? In his mind there was no worse sight or sound. He would promise her anything to stop it.

Francesco slammed his phone down in fury.

The purchase agreement he'd spent months working on had been blown out of the water, with Godfrey Renfrew admitting he wanted time to 'consider an alternative offer'.

The Mastrangelos were standing in his way.

He picked the receiver up and dialled his lawyer's number. 'I want you to arrange a meeting between me and Luca Mastrangelo,' he said, his words delivered like ice picks. 'Tell him that unless he agrees to meet tomorrow, he will only have himself to blame for the consequences.'

The second he put the phone down, his mobile rang. It was Hannah. *'Ciao,'* he said, breathing heavily through his teeth.

'What's the matter?' she asked, picking up on his tone even though she was in London and he in Palermo.

'Nothing. I'm just busy. What can I do for you?' Looking at the clock on his wall, he could see it was lunchtime. She must be calling him on her break.

'I haven't heard from you in a couple of days. I just wanted to make sure you're okay.' There wasn't any accusation in her voice. All he heard was concern.

'I'm busy, that's all.'

Silence, then, 'Any idea what time you'll be over tomorrow?'

He rubbed his eyes. He'd promised he'd be back in London early Friday evening so they could head straight down to Devon. She'd even booked him a hotel room.

'I'll confirm tomorrow morning,' he said, wishing he could relieve the sharp pain digging in the back of his eyes. He would ensure his meeting with Luca and Pepe took place in the morning. That would give him plenty of time to get to her.

More silence. 'Are you sure you're okay?'

'Go back to your patients, Dr Chapman. I'll see you tomorrow.'

Hannah checked her watch for the umpteenth time. Her bags were all packed, butterflies playing merry havoc in her belly.

She felt sick with nerves and dread. Knowing Francesco would be by her side throughout it all dulled it a little but not as much as it should.

He'd sounded so distant on the phone. The plentiful text messages from him had whittled away to nothing.

Something niggled in her stomach, a foreboding she was too scared to analyse.

Twitching her curtain, relief poured through her to see the large black car pull up outside.

Her relief was short-lived when she opened the door

and saw the serious look on his face. 'You're not coming with me, are you?'

He stepped over the threshold and pushed the door shut behind him. 'I apologise for the short notice, but I have to meet with Luca and Pepe Mastrangelo tomorrow lunchtime. The sale of the Mayfair casino is under threat.'

For long moments she did nothing but stare at him. 'You bastard.'

He flinched, but a cold hostility set over his features. 'I do not have the power to be in two places at once. If I could then I would.'

'Liar,' she stated flatly, although her chest had tightened so much she struggled to find breath.

This could not be happening.

'You could have arranged the meeting for any time you like. Your life doesn't revolve around a set schedule.' Francesco's time was his to do as he pleased. One of the very things she'd been so attracted to had turned around and bitten her hard.

Francesco could do as he liked, and what he liked was to avoid her sister's wedding.

He was asking her to face it alone.

After everything she had confided and all the trust she'd placed in him, he was leaving her to face the wedding on her own.

'It has to be tomorrow.' He raked his hands through his hair. 'I wanted to organise it for today but tomorrow is the only day the three of us can be in the same country at the same time. Time is of the essence. I won't allow the Mastrangelos to steal the casino away from me. I've worked too long on the deal to let it slip through my fingers—it's far too important for me to lose. I've arranged for Mario to drive you to Devon.'

'Don't bother. I'll make my own way there.' She'd

rather cycle on her pushbike. She'd rather walk. 'You can leave now.'

'Hannah, I know you're disappointed. I've gone out of my way to tell you personally—'

'Well, that makes everything all right, then,' she snapped. 'You're blowing me out of the water so you can kneecap some old friends but, hey, no worries, *you told me to my face.*'

'I have spent the best part of a year demolishing my father's empire, eradicating the streets from the evils he peddled,' Francesco said, his voice rising, his cool facade disappearing before her eyes. 'The only business he wanted that he couldn't have was this casino. He did everything in his power to get it, including abducting Godfrey's son, and still he didn't win. But *I will.* It's taken me *months* to gain Godfrey's trust and I will not allow the Mastrangelos to snatch it away from me.'

His father? Hannah had known his relationship with his dead father had been difficult, had seen the way he tensed whenever Salvatore was mentioned, but she'd never suspected the depths of Francesco's animosity towards him.

He paused, his eyes a dark pit of loathing, his malevolence a living, breathing thing. 'You live your life imagining Beth watching over you. Well, I imagine mine with my father watching over me. I like the thought of him staring down watching me destroy everything he built, but more than anything I want him to see me succeed where he failed. I want him turning in his hellish coffin.'

Hannah didn't think she had ever witnessed such hatred before, a loathing that crawled under her skin and settled in the nauseous pit of her belly.

This was the Francesco he had warned her about right at the start. The Francesco she had refused to see.

And now she did see, all she felt was a burning anger that made her want to throw up.

'Go and take your vengeance. Go ruin your old friends. Go and show your dead father how much *better* you are than him by purchasing the very casino he could never have. Let it symbolise how *different* you are to him.'

Shoving him out of the way, she opened the front door. 'Now leave, and don't you *ever* contact me again.'

His chest heaving, he stared at her before his nostrils flared and he strode past her.

'Enjoy your vengeance, Francesco,' she spat. 'Try not to let it choke you.'

He didn't look back.

CHAPTER TWELVE

HANNAH FIXED THE back of her pearl earrings into place, trying desperately hard to contain her shaking hands. Since that awful confrontation with Francesco the night before, it had been a constant battle to stop the tremors racking through her. The long last-minute train journey to Devon had been a constant battle, too—a battle to stop any tears forming for the bastard who'd abandoned her when she needed him most.

She didn't want to think about him. Not now. Not when she was minutes away from leaving for the church to watch her little sister get married.

There was a tap on the door, and Melanie walked into the room carrying a small box.

'How do I look?' she asked, putting the box on the floor, extending her arms and giving a slow twirl.

'Oh, Mel, you look beautiful.' And she did, an angel in white.

'You look beautiful, too.' Careful not to crease each other's dresses—Hannah wore a baby-pink bridesmaid dress—they embraced, then stepped back from each other.

'The cars are here and our bouquets are ready,' Melanie said. Her eyes fixed on Hannah's bedside table, on which rested a photo of Hannah and Beth, aged eight. 'I've got a bouquet for her, too.'

'What do you mean?'

'Beth. I've got her a bouquet, too.'

Hannah had to strain to hear her sister's voice.

'If she was still here she'd be a bridesmaid with you.' A look of mischief suddenly crossed Melanie's face. 'The pair of you would probably follow me down the aisle trying to trip me up.'

A burst of mirth spluttered from Hannah's mouth. She and Beth together had been irrepressible. 'We were really mean to you.'

'No, you weren't.'

'Yes, we were. We hardly ever let you play with us and when we did it was to torment you. I remember we convinced you to let us make you into a princess.'

'Oh, yes! You coloured my hair pink with your felt tip pens and used red crayon as blusher. You treated me like a doll.'

'I'm sorry.'

'Don't be. I was just happy you wanted to play with me.'

'It must have been hard for you, though,' Hannah said, thinking of all the times Melanie had been desperate to join in with their games, how their mum would force them to let her tag along and they would spend the whole time ignoring her. Unless they found a good use for her.

Melanie didn't even pretend not to understand. 'It was hard. I was very jealous. You had each other. You didn't need me.'

Silence rent the room as they both stared at the photo. Despite all her vows, hot tears stung the back of Hannah's eyes. How desperately she wished Beth was there. And how desperately the pathetic side of her wished Francesco was there, too....

Thank God Melanie hadn't grilled her about the latest sudden change to the seating plan, simply giving her a quick hug and a 'No problem.'

Melanie cleared her throat. 'We should get going before we ruin our make-up.'

Looking at her, Hannah could see Melanie's eyes had filled, too, a solitary tear trickling down her cheek.

She reached over to wipe it away with her thumb, then pressed a kiss to her sister's cheek. 'You do look beautiful, Mel. Beth would be insanely jealous.'

Melanie laughed and snatched a tissue from the box on Hannah's bedside table. She blew her nose noisily, then crouched down to the box she'd brought in and removed the lid. 'Here's your bouquet, and here's the one for Beth. I thought you might like to give it to her.'

Hannah sniffed the delicate fragrance.

She looked at her sister. Melanie had been nine when Beth died. A little girl. Now she was a woman less than an hour away from marriage.

How had she missed her own sister growing up? It had happened right before her eyes and she'd been oblivious to it. Melanie had followed Hannah to London. She had been the one to keep the sisterly relationship going—she'd been the one who'd kept the whole family going. Unlike their parents, who still took Hannah's reclusiveness at face value, Melanie at least tried. It was always at her suggestion that they would go out for lunch. It was always Melanie who organised their monthly visits back to Devon, carefully selecting the weekends Hannah wasn't on shift. Melanie, who had never wanted anything more than the company of her big sister.

Her sister. The same flesh and blood as herself and Beth.

Hannah took another sniff of the flowers. 'Do you want to come with me and give them to her?'

'Really?' Melanie was too sweet to even pretend to fake nonchalance.

When it came to visiting Beth, Hannah preferred solitude. Alone, she could chat to her and fill her in on all the family and work gossip.

Since the funeral she had never visited with anyone else.

She had done far too many things alone.

All those wasted years hiding herself away, too numb from the pain of her broken heart to even consider letting anyone in—not her parents, not her sister. No one. And she hadn't even realised she was doing it, pretending to be content in her little cocoon.

She hadn't meant to let Francesco in. If she'd known the risk to her heart, she would have taken his advice at the first turn and found a safer method to start living her life.

But she had let him in. In return he'd dumped her in the cruellest of fashions.

She didn't care about his reasons. He'd left her to face this day alone and she would never forgive him.

Except she wasn't alone....

Her heart had opened for him, but it had also opened for her poor neglected family, who wanted nothing more than to love her. All those years spent hiding her heart from them had been wasted years, she could see that now.

She didn't want to hide any more. She couldn't. She needed them. She *loved* them.

Ironically, Francesco's rejection had helped in an unexpected fashion. She would *not* allow Melanie's big day to be ruined by *him*.

Fixing her old practised smile to her face, she took Melanie's hand in her own and gave it a squeeze. 'Why don't we leave now? We can do it before the ceremony starts.'

Melanie's eyes shone. 'I would really like that.'

'Beth would, too. And so would I.'

* * *

Francesco checked his watch. It was bang on half past one.

In thirty minutes Melanie Chapman would walk down the aisle, followed by her doctor sister.

He swatted the thought away.

Now was not the time to be wondering how Hannah was holding up.

Now was the time for action.

With Mario and Roberto by his side, he strolled through the lobby of the neutral hotel both parties had agreed upon and headed up in the lift to the private suite hired for the occasion.

Two men, equally as large as his own minders, guarded the door.

'Wait here,' he said to his men.

This conversation was private.

Sweeping past them, he stepped into the room and shut the door.

He could taste the malice in the air in his first inhalation.

Luca sat at the long dining table, his black eyes fixing on him.

Pepe leant against a wall, his arms folded.

Hannah would be on her way to the church...

Where had that thought come from?

He'd successfully pushed Hannah out of his mind since he'd left her home. He'd cut her out. He would *not* allow himself to think of her. Or the pain on her face. Or the words she'd said, her implication that he was exactly like his father.

He was not like his father.

If he was anything like his father, Luca and Pepe would both be long dead by now—Pepe when he'd tried to fight him all those years ago, Luca when he'd broken their partnership. He hadn't just broken their partnership, he'd severed their friendship, too.

'Well?' said Luca, breaking the silence. 'You're the one who wanted this meeting. What do you want, Calvetti?'

He'd thought he'd known. The casino. The final piece in the obliteration of Salvatore Calvetti's legacy.

His revenge against the man Francesco had learned too late had used his mother as a punchbag.

As hard as he tried to push her out, the only image in his head was Hannah, lying on the cold concrete and opening her eyes, that serene smile that had stolen his breath.

Stolen his heart.

'Well?' Luca's voice rose. 'What do you want?'

Francesco looked at the two brothers. His old friends. He looked at Pepe, the man whose girlfriend he'd stolen all those years ago. He hadn't known she was still seeing him, but he'd known damn well Pepe had been serious about her.

No wonder Pepe hated him.

He looked back at Luca. His oldest friend. A man who'd found that rare kind of love he would do anything to keep.

The rare kind of love he could have with Hannah.

Could have had if he hadn't abandoned her on the one day she needed him.

He'd known the second she'd asked him to go to the wedding with her that she'd fallen for him.

And he, stupid fool that he was, had thrown it back in her face so cruelly, and for what?

Vengeance against a man who was already rotting in hell.

His heart beat so loudly a drum could have been in his ear.

Hannah wasn't his mother. She wasn't a young, suggestible girl. She was a professional woman with more backbone than anyone he knew.

More important, he wasn't his father, something she'd known from the off.

Only two people in his entire life had looked at him and seen *him*, Francesco, and not just Salvatore's son. One of those had given birth to him. The other was at that very moment bleeding with pain for her dead twin who couldn't be there to celebrate their sister's marriage.

What had he done?

He took a step back and raised his hands. 'It's yours.' At their identical furrowed brows, he allowed the tiniest of smiles to form on his lips. 'The casino. If you want it so badly, you can have it.'

They exchanged glances, their bodies straightening.

'I'm serious. It's all yours. I'll call Godfrey and withdraw my offer.' When he reached the door he looked straight at Pepe. 'I was very sorry to hear about the loss of your baby.'

Pepe's eyes flickered.

Turning back to Luca, Francesco continued, 'Send my regards to Grace. She's far too good for you, but I think you already know that.'

He turned the handle of the door.

'Calvetti.' It was Luca's voice.

Francesco turned one last time.

'The casino's yours. Not ours.'

'Sorry?'

A rueful grin spread over Luca's face. 'Grace and Cara were already furious at us for looking at buying a casino, and they're just about ready to kill us for instigating a war with you. We've already told Godfrey to accept your offer.'

In spite of the agonies going on within him, Francesco managed a grin. 'See? I said Grace was too good for you.'

Just as Hannah was too good for him.

He looked at his watch again. At any moment the bridal party would start their slow walk down the aisle.

'I need to be somewhere.'

Hannah followed Melanie up the aisle, trying very hard to keep a straight face, a hard job considering the train of Melanie's dress was streaked with grass and mud.

Beth was buried in the cemetery attached to this very church, and the pair had left the rest of the bridal party to say a few words to her and leave the bouquet by her headstone.

All those years when she'd refused to visit Beth's grave with anyone... How selfish she'd been.

How glad she was that Melanie had found a man who put her first, who loved her enough to compensate for all the neglect she had suffered at the hands of her big sister. Not that Melanie saw it as neglect. Bless her heart, Melanie understood. It hadn't been said, not in so many words, but it didn't need to be.

In all the years Hannah had been grieving the loss of her twin, she had neglected to recognise there was another person in her life grieving, too—a young woman who was a part of her, just as Beth was. Sure, it wasn't exactly the same—how could it be? But then, what two relationships were ever the same? Their parents loved them equally but the relationships between them all were different. Hannah's relationship with them couldn't be any more different.

She looked at her father, walking with Melanie's arm tucked inside his. She might not be able to see his face but she could perfectly imagine the radiant smile on his face. And there was her mother, on her feet in a front pew, still a beautiful woman, looking from her beloved husband to her two surviving daughters, tears already leaking down her cheeks.

And there was the groom, his legs bouncing, his nerves

and excitement palpable. When he knelt before the priest by the side of his fiancée, titters echoed throughout the church at the *HE* written in white on the sole of his left shoe, and the *LP* on the right.

So much love. So much excitement for a new life being forged together.

As they exchanged their vows, the tears she'd successfully kept at bay since that terrible argument with Francesco broke free.

According to Francesco's satnav, the route from London to Devon should take three hours and forty-five minutes by car. By motorbike, he estimated he could make it in two hours.

What he hadn't accounted for was stationary traffic as hordes of holidaymakers took advantage of the late English summer to head to the coast.

This was a country of imbeciles, he thought scathingly as he snaked his way around motionless cars. Why couldn't they all be sensible like Hannah and travel down on the Friday night when the roads were empty?

The ceremony would be over by now, the wedding breakfast in full swing.

Hannah needed air. Her lungs felt too tight.

She'd tried. She really had. She'd smiled throughout the ceremony and wedding breakfast, held pleasant conversations with countless family members and old friends she hadn't seen in years. The number-one question she'd received was a variant of 'Have you met a nice man yet?' While she'd answered gracefully, 'Not yet, but I'm sure I will one day,' each time she was asked it felt as if a thorn were being pressed deep into her heart.

Now all the guests had congregated at the bar while the

function room was transformed for the evening bash, she saw her opportunity for escape.

She stepped out into the early-evening dusk and sat on a bench in the hotel garden. She closed her eyes, welcoming the slight breeze on her face.

Five minutes. That was all she needed. Five minutes of solitude to clamp back down on her emotions.

'Can I join you?'

Opening her eyes, she found her mother standing before her.

Unable to speak, she nodded.

'It's been a beautiful day,' her mum commented.

Hannah nodded again, scared to open her mouth lest she would no longer be able to hold on.

How could Francesco have left her alone like this?

How could she have got him so wrong?

She'd been so convinced he would never hurt her.

She'd been right about the physical aspect. In that respect he'd given her nothing but pleasure. Emotionally, though... he'd ripped her apart.

For the first time in fifteen years she'd reached out to someone for help. He'd known what a massive thing that was for her and still he'd abandoned her, and for what? For revenge on someone who wasn't even alive to see it.

Had she been too needy? Was that it? How could she know? She had nothing to compare it to. Until she'd barged her way into his life, she'd had no form of a relationship with anyone. Not even her family. Not since Beth...

'Why did you let me hide away after Beth died?' she asked suddenly. Francesco's probing questions about her relationship with her parents had been playing on her mind, making her question so many things she'd never considered before.

She felt her mother start beside her.

A long silence formed until her mum took Hannah's hand into her own tentatively, as if waiting for Hannah to snatch it away. 'That's a question your father and I often ask. When Beth died, we knew, no matter the pain we were going through and Mel was going through, that it was nothing compared to what you were living with. You and Beth… you were two peas in a pod. She was you and you were her.'

Hannah's chin wobbled.

'When you said you wanted to be a doctor, we were happy you had something to focus on. When you first hid yourself away, saying you were studying, we thought it was a good thing.' She rummaged in her handbag for a tissue and dabbed her eyes. 'We should have handled it better. We were all grieving, but we should never have allowed you to cut yourself off. At the time, though, we couldn't see it. It was so gradual that by the time we realised how isolated you'd become, we didn't know how to reach out to you anymore. To be honest, I still don't. I wish I could turn the clock back to your teenage years and insist you be a part of the family and not some lodger who shared the occasional meal with us.'

'I wish I could, too,' Hannah whispered. She gazed up at the emerging stars, then turned to look at her mother. 'Mum, can I have a hug?'

Her mum closed her eyes as if in prayer before pulling Hannah into her embrace, enveloping her tightly in that remembered mummy smell that comforted her more than any word could.

Hannah swallowed the last of her champagne. The bubbles playing on her tongue reminded her of Francesco. The optics behind the bar reminded her of Francesco. The man who'd just stepped into the function room, where the dancing was now in full swing, also reminded her of Francesco.

Unable to bear the reminder, she turned her attention back to the party surrounding her. The women from Melanie's hen party had hit the dance floor, dragging her dad up there with them. She couldn't stop the grin forming on her face as she watched his special brand of dad dancing. At least she knew where she got her rhythm from.

Why wasn't she up there with them?

Why was she hiding by the bar, observing rather than joining in?

She'd made it through the day with what was left of her shattered heart aching, but she'd *made* it. She'd come through the other side and she was still standing. She hadn't fallen apart at the seams.

A record that had been hugely popular when she was a kid came on. Her grin widening, Hannah weaved through the tables to the dance floor and grabbed her father's hands. His answering smile was puzzled, shocked, even, but delighted all the same.

Their special brand of nonrhythmic dancing took off, a crowd quickly forming around them, the bride and groom hitting the floor, too.

She could do this. She could be a part of life. She didn't have to sit alone on the sidelines.

One of her sister's hen party tapped Hannah on the shoulder. 'Isn't that the man from Calvetti's?' she yelled above the music, pointing across the room.

Following the pointing finger, Hannah's heart jolted to see the tall figure she'd spotted leaning against the wall watching the dancing. Watching *her*.

She gave an absent nod in response, tuning out everything around her—everything except him.

Francesco.

Her stomach lurched heavily, feeling as if it had become detached from the rest of her.

He began to move, snaking his way round the packed tables, revellers parting on his approach in a manner that evoked the strongest sense of déjà vu.

Her heart flipped over to see him so groomed and utterly gorgeous in a snazzy pinstriped suit, the top buttons of his crisp blue shirt undone, exposing the top of his broad chest and the cross he wore around his neck....

Up close he looked in control and terrifying, the intent in his eyes showing he could eat her alive if she refused him anything.

Francesco crossed the dividing line onto the dance floor. After the road trip from hell, he'd finally made it to her.

Nothing had come easy that day, the puncture on his tyre the last straw. By the time the helicopter had illegally landed to collect him, he'd been ready to rip someone's head off.

At last he stood before her. She'd frozen on the spot, her eyes big hazel pools of pain and bewilderment.

What had he done to her?

He had no idea what was being played by the DJ and nor did he care. When he placed his hands on Hannah's hips and pulled her to him, the sound tuned out and he moved her in a rhythm all their own.

She looked so vulnerable in her traditional bridesmaid dress. She trembled in it, rigid in his arms yet quivering.

He could feel eyes from all directions fixed on them.

'What are you doing here?' she asked, not looking at him.

'I want us to talk.'

'I don't want to be anywhere near you.'

'I know.' He breathed her scent in. 'But *I* need to be near *you*.'

She moved to escape his arms but he tightened his hold, continuing to move her around the floor. 'I'm not letting you go anywhere, not until you've given me the chance to speak.'

'I'm not speaking to you here,' she hissed into his ear, her warm breath sending completely inappropriate tingles racing over his skin. 'This is my sister's wedding. These guests here are my family and my sister's friends.'

'And I should have been with you today, getting to know them, instead of leaving you to face it on your own, but I'm the bastard who let his thirst for revenge cause pain to the one person in the world he loves.'

He stopped dancing and looked at her. The pain in her eyes had gone, only stark bewilderment remaining.

'*You*,' he emphasised. 'I love *you*. I should have trusted fate when it brought you to me.'

'I don't want to hear it.' Her voice was hoarse, her cheeks flushed.

Her resistance was nothing less than he deserved. He released his tight hold and stepped back, keeping his hands on her arms so she couldn't run.

'Remember when I gave you five minutes of *my* time?' he said, reminding her of that time a month ago when she'd first begged for five minutes. If he'd known then what those five minutes would lead to, he would have locked himself away in his office without a second thought. What an arrogant fool he had been. 'Now I am asking for five minutes of *your* time.'

Had it really only been a month ago that she'd propositioned him?

How could his entire world transform in such a small timeframe?

'Believe me, if I could have that time again I would do everything differently,' she said, wriggling out of his hold. 'Let's go sit in the garden. But only because I don't want to have a scene in front of my family.'

* * *

The breeze had picked up since Hannah had sat in the garden with her mother. Now the evening party was in full swing, the peace she'd found then had gone, music and laughter echoing through the windows.

She sat on the same bench. A bunch of kids had escaped the party and were having a game of football with an empty can.

Francesco sat next to her, keeping a respectable distance. All the same, she could feel his heat. How she wished she didn't respond to him so physically. Her emotional reactions to him were bad enough without her treacherous body getting in on the act, too.

'Go on, then, what did you want to talk about?' she said, making a silent vow to not say another word for the duration of the next five minutes. If he started spouting any more nonsense about loving her she would walk away.

If he loved her he would never have let her face this day on her own.

'I want to tell you about my father,' Francesco said, surprising her with his opening thread.

Despite her vow to remain mute, she whispered, 'Your father?'

He breathed heavily. 'I always knew what a bastard he was, but he was my father and I respected him. God help me but I loved him. All I ever wanted was his respect. I turned a blind eye to so many of his activities but turned the blindest eye to what was happening right under my own roof.'

His eyes held hers, the chocolate fudge hard, almost black.

'I always knew my father was a violent man. To me that was normal. It was our way of life. I knew he craved respect. Again, that was normal. What I did not know until after his death four years ago was that he was one of mainland Europe's biggest suppliers of drugs. That was a blow, enough to make me despise him, but not enough to destroy all my memories of the man. But what I learned just a year ago when I discovered my mother's diaries was that he beat her throughout their marriage, cheated on her, and fed her the drugs that eventually killed her.'

When he reached for her hand she didn't pull away, not even when he clasped it so tightly she feared for her blood supply.

'She was seventeen when they married, an innocent. He was twenty-three years older and a brute from the start.' He practically spat the words out. 'He forced himself on her on their wedding night. He beat her for the first time on their honeymoon. I wish I'd known, but my mother did everything in her power to protect me from seeing too much. As a child it was normal for my mother to be bruised. We would laugh at how clumsy she was, but it was all a lie.'

He shook his head and dragged his fingers through his hair. 'I spent three days reading her diaries. When I finished I was filled with so much hate for the man. And *guilt*—how could I have been so blind? The man I hero-worshipped was nothing but a drug-peddling wife beater. He *wanted* her hooked—it was a means to control her. I swear if he hadn't been dead I would have killed him myself using my bare hands.'

Hannah shivered. Oh, poor, poor Francesco. She'd known he hated his father, but this? This was worse than she could ever have imagined.

Suddenly he let go of her hand and palmed her cheeks. 'I have spent the past eleven months eradicating everything that man built. Everything. The parties stopped, the womanising stopped. All I wanted was vengeance for my mother and, even though my father was rotting in hell, I was determined to destroy what was his. I'd already closed his drug dens, but I resolved to annihilate everything else—the armouries, the so-called legitimate businesses that were in fact a front for money laundering—every last brick of property. The one thing I wanted above all else, though, was the Mayfair casino.'

Here, his eyes seemed to drill into hers. 'Years ago, my father tried to get that casino. It was the only failure of his life. He tried everything to get his hands on that place, but Godfrey Renfrew refused to sell it to such a notorious gangster. That failure was a large thorn in my father's side. For me to purchase that same property would mean I had succeeded where he had failed, proof that I was a better man than him.'

'So you've won,' she said softly. 'You've got your vengeance.'

'No.' He shook his head for emphasis. 'I walked into that room with the Mastrangelos today and knew I had lost. I had lost because I had lost *you*. How could I be a better man than him when I had let the most important person in my world down for the sake of vengeance?'

He brushed his lips against hers, the heat of his breath filling her senses, expanding her shrivelled heart.

'After speaking with the Mastrangelos, I called Godfrey earlier and withdrew my offer for the casino,' he whispered. 'I don't want it anymore. It's tainted. All I want is you. That's if you'll have me. I wouldn't blame you if you didn't.' He sighed and nuzzled into her cheek. 'You asked me once if you scared me. The truth is you did—you scared me because you made me feel, and because I knew I wasn't worthy of you. The only real relationship I have as a reference is my parents', and witnessing that was like living in one of Dante's circles of hell. You deserve so much better.'

'Not all marriages and relationships are like that.'

'Intellectually, I know that. Emotionally, though, it's

taken me a lot longer to accept it. I wanted to protect you from me. I looked at you and saw the innocence my mother had before she married my father. I didn't want to taint you.'

'How could you do that? You are not your father, Francesco. You're a mixture of both your parents and the uniqueness that is *you*. You're just you. No one else.'

He almost crushed her in his embrace. 'I swear I'll never hurt you again. Never. *You* make me a better man. Even if we leave here and head our separate ways, I will still be a better man for having known you.'

Tears pricked her eyes. Her heart felt so full she now feared it could burst.

Head their separate ways? Was that really what she wanted?

'I know how important your work is to you and I would never want to get in the way of that. Medicine is your life, but what I want to know—*need* to know—is if you can fit me into your life, too. Forget what I said about you not fitting into my world—it's *your* world *I* need to fit into. Let me in, I beg of you. I'm not perfect, not by any stretch of the imagination, but I swear on my mother's memory that I will love and respect you for the rest of my life.'

Hannah's chin wobbled. But she kept it together, refusing to let the tears fall. All the same, her voice sounded broken to her own ears. 'I love that you're not perfect.'

He stilled and pulled away to look at her. His eyes glittered with questions.

'Neither of us is perfect but...' She took a deep breath, trying to keep a hold of her racing heart. If Francesco, her big, arrogant bear of a man, could put his heart and pride on the line... She cupped his warm cheek. 'I think you're perfect for me.'

She'd barely got the words out before his mouth came

crashing down on hers, a kiss of such passion and longing that this time the tears really did fall.

'Don't cry, *amore*. Don't cry.' Francesco wiped her tears away and pressed his lips to her forehead. He wrapped his arms around her and she nestled her cheek against his chest.

He gave a rueful chuckle. 'I can't believe I worried about *you* getting burned. I should have known from the start— deep down I think I did—that, of the two of us, I was the more likely to be.'

'Oh, no, but you were right,' she confessed. 'And I'm glad I was so blasé about your concerns because if I'd known how badly you *would* burn me I would have run a mile.'

She tilted her chin back up to look at him. She felt light, as if the weight that had been compressing her insides for what felt like for ever had been lifted. 'You've brought me back to life and let colour back into my world. You make me whole and I want to be in your life, too. Your past, everything you've been through has shaped you into the man you are today and that's the man I've fallen in love with.'

'You really love me?'

For the first time Hannah saw a hint of vulnerability in Francesco's cool, confident exterior.

'More than anything. I didn't think I needed anyone. You've shown me that I do. Not just you, but my family, too.' She kissed his neck then whispered into his ear, 'You've also weaned me off my addiction to my phone. I've only checked it three times today.'

He threaded his long fingers through her hair, a deep laugh escaping his throat that deepened when he snagged a couple of knots. 'If I could trust myself not to break every bone in his body, I would pay another visit to that bastard who knocked you off your bike and thank him.'

'For bringing us together?'

'The stars aligned for us that morning.'

'Shame about my broken collarbone and concussion.'

'Not forgetting your poor finger.'

She giggled. She hadn't thought of her finger in weeks. 'I'm surprised you let him walk away without any injury.'

'He took one look at me in his doorway and virtually wet himself. I didn't need to touch him. If the same thing were to happen to you now, I doubt I would be so restrained.'

'Yes, you would,' she chided, rubbing her nose into his linen shirt.

'And you know that how?'

'Because you would never hurt me, and to cause physical injury to another human, especially in my name, would be to hurt me.'

'You still believe that? After what I did to you last night, you still believe in me?'

'I believe it more than ever.' And she did. She, more than anyone, knew the hold the past had on the present. All that mattered was that they didn't allow the past to shape their futures. 'In any case, I bet he'll spend the rest of his life having nightmares that you'll turn up on his doorstep again.'

'Good. He deserves it.' He gave a humourless chuckle. 'We should invite him to our wedding.'

'Why, are we getting married?'

'Too right we are. I love you, Dr Chapman, and I will love you for the rest of my life.'

'I love you, too, Signor Calvetti.'

He kissed her again. 'Dottore Hannah Calvetti. It has a nice ring to it.'

'Hmm...' Her lips curved into a contented smile. Francesco was right. It had a wonderful ring to it.

EPILOGUE

HANNAH WALKED CAREFULLY up the steep steps to the front door of the villa, happily inhaling the scent emitted by the overabundance of ripe lemon trees.

Francesco opened the door before she got to the top.

'*Buonasera, Dottore Calvetti,*' he said.

'Good evening, Signor Calvetti,' she replied, before slipping into fluent Sicilian-Italian. 'How has Luciano been today?'

'An angel. Well, he's been an angel since I relieved the nanny. I think he might have given her an extra grey hair or two today. He's definitely worn himself out—he fell asleep fifteen minutes ago. But enough of the small talk—how did you do?'

She couldn't hide the beam that spread across her face. 'I got the job!'

Francesco's face spread into an identical grin. He drew her to him and kissed her, then rubbed his nose to hers. 'I knew you could do it, you clever lady. In fact, Tino is at this moment preparing your favourite meal to celebrate.'

'Mussels in white wine?'

He nodded with a definite hint of smugness. 'Followed by hot chocolate-fudge cake.'

'I love you!' Tino, their chef, made the best chocolate-fudge cake in the world.

He laughed and tapped her bottom. 'Go shower and get changed. I'll open a bottle of wine.'

This time it was she who kissed him, hard.

'Before I forget, Melanie messaged me earlier,' she said. 'They can definitely come for the weekend.'

'Great. Let me know the times and I'll get the jet over to England for them.'

With a spring in her step, Hannah climbed the stone staircase and headed down the uneven corridor to their bedroom. As she passed their eighteen-month-old son's nursery, she poked her head through the door to find him in deep sleep. He didn't stir when she lowered the side of the cot to press a gentle kiss to his cheek. 'Night, night, sleep tight,' she whispered before slipping back out.

She opened her bedroom door and there, on her dressing table, was the most enormous bunch of roses she had ever seen, huge even by Francesco's standards.

His faith in her never ceased to amaze her.

Luciano had come into their lives more quickly than either had anticipated. Within two months of their marriage she'd fallen pregnant, which hadn't been all that surprising considering the laissez-faire approach to contraception they'd adopted.

When it came time for Hannah to take maternity leave, they'd uprooted to Sicily. It had been agreed that when her maternity was up they would move back to London. Except...she'd fallen in love with Sicily, with the people and the language. Besides, it was easier for Francesco to run his empire from there, so she saw more of him during the week than she had in London, and they hated having to spend nights away from each other.

Full of determination, she'd set about learning the language. She'd employed a tutor and within weeks had refused to answer Francesco or any of his staff unless they spoke in their native tongue. She had been determined to master it. And they had all been determined to help her.

'I got the job, Beth,' she said, speaking aloud in English, just in case Beth hadn't bothered to learn Italian with her. Now that she couldn't visit her grave so regularly, she had taken to simply talking to her whenever the mood struck. Sometimes, in her dreams, her twin spoke back. 'I'm going to work at the hospital on the children's ward here in Palermo and train for my consultancy here, too.'

All the pieces had come together.

She could not be happier.

* * * * *

A TOUCH OF
TEMPTATION

TARA PAMMI

To the man who started it all, my father, for giving me my love of books, for never holding me back, for always believing that there was nothing I couldn't do if I set my mind to it.

CHAPTER ONE

KIMBERLY STANTON STARED at the white rectangle of plastic on the gleaming marble counter in the ladies' bathroom. Terror coated her throat as though it might come to life and take a bite out of her. It looked alien, out of place amidst the lavender potpourri, the crystal lamp settings and the glossy chrome fixtures.

The few minutes stretched like an eternity. The quiet lull of voices outside was exaggerated into distorted echoes.

Her heart beat faster and louder. A painful tug in her lower belly stole her breath. She clutched the cold granite vanity unit and clenched the muscles in her legs, willing herself to hold on.

The scariest word she had ever encountered appeared on the stick.

Pregnant.

No confusing colors or symbols that meant you had to peek again at the box discarded in terrified panic.

Simple, plain English.

Her heart leaped into her throat. Her legs shaking beneath her, she leaned against one of the stalls behind her, dipped her head low and forced herself to breathe past the deafening whoosh in her ears.

Her one mistake, which technically she had committed twice, couldn't haunt her for the rest of her life, could it?

But she couldn't change the consequences. She had never been naïve or stupid enough to wish it either.

She flicked the gleaming chrome tap open and dangled her fingers under the ice-cold water. The sound of the water hitting the sink drowned out the sound of her heartbeat, helping her focus on her breathing.

In, out. In, out...

She closed the tap. Straightening up, she was about to reach for the hand towel when she looked at the mirror and froze.

She stared at her reflection, noting the dark circles under her eyes, the lack of color in her face, the skin pulled tautly over her bones. Drops of water seeped through the thin silk of her blouse to her skin beneath.

She looked as if she was on the brink of a nervous break-down. And maybe she was. But she didn't have time now. The breakdown had to wait. She touched the tips of her fingers to her temple and pressed. The cold from her almost numb fingers seeped into her overheated skin.

She had no time to deal with this now. She had to compartmentalize—set it aside until she was alone, until she was equipped to think logically, until the shock making her jittery all over faded into nothing more than a numbing ache.

And when it did she would assess the situation again with a clear head, take the necessary action to equip herself better to handle it. It wasn't as if she didn't have any experience with dealing with shock and pain.

Although why she had chosen this particular moment to take the test when the pregnancy kit had been burning a rectangular hole in her handbag for more than a week was anybody's guess. Or maybe she was having another momentary collapse of her rational thinking circuits.

She had been having those moments a lot lately.

She pulled her lip-gloss out of her clutch and reapplied

it with shaking fingers. She ran a hand over her suit. The silky material under her fingers rooted her back to reality.

She needed to get back out there. She needed to circulate among the guests—a specially put together group of investors she had researched for more than six months. Investors who had shown interest in her web startup *The Daily Help*.

She had a presentation to give. She had to talk them through the financial outline she had sketched for the next five years. She had to convince them to invest in *her* startup when there were a million others mushrooming every day.

She had to convince them that the recent scandal about her, Olivia and Alexander had nothing to do with the way she did business. It was a sign of how strong her business proposal was that they had even showed up, despite the scandal.

She straightened her jacket and turned toward the exit. And paused midstride.

Turning back, she picked up the plastic tube, wrapped it carefully in the wrapper she had left on the sink and threw it into the trash. She fumbled when she turned the corner, struggling to breathe past the tight ache in her gut. She placed her hand on her stomach and drew in gulps of air, waiting for the tidal wave of pain that threatened to pull her under to pass.

Striding out of the restroom, she plucked a glass of sparkling water from a passing waiter and nodded at an old friend from Harvard. She was glad she had booked this conference hall in one of the glitzy hotels in Manhattan, even though her tightfisted CFO had frowned over the expense.

Kim didn't think an evening in her company's premises—a large open space in the basement of a building in Manhattan, unstructured in every way possible—would encourage confidence on the investors' part.

She checked her Patek Philipe watch, a gift from her

father when she had graduated from Harvard, and invited everyone to join her in the conference room for the presentation.

She felt an uncharacteristic reluctance as she switched on the projector. Once she concluded the presentation she was going to be alone with her thoughts. Alone with things she couldn't postpone thinking about anymore.

It happened as she reached almost the end of her presentation.

With her laser pointer pointed at a far-off wall, instead of at her company's financial forecast on the rolled-out projector screen, she lost her train of thought—as though someone had turned off a switch in her brain.

She searched the audience for what had thrown her.

A movement—the turn of a dark head—a whisper or something else? Had she imagined it? Everything and everyone else faded into background for a few disconcerting moments. Had her equilibrium been threatened so much by her earlier discovery?

The resounding quiet tumbled her out of her brain fog. She cleared her throat, took a sip of her water and turned back to the chart on the screen. She finished the presentation, her stomach still unsettled.

The lights came on and she smiled with relief. Several hands came up as she opened the floor to questions. She could recite those figures half-asleep. Every little detail of her company was etched into her brain.

The first few were questions she had expected. Hitting her stride, she elaborated on what put her company a cut above the others, provided more details, more figures, increasing statistics and the ad revenue they had generated last year.

Even the momentary aberration of a few minutes ago couldn't mar the satisfaction she could feel running in her veins, the high of accomplishment, of her hard work bearing fruit.

She answered the last question, turned the screen off and switched on the overhead lights.

There *he* was. The reason for the strange tightening in her stomach. The cause of the prickling sensation she couldn't shed.

Diego Pereira. The man who had seduced her and walked away without a backward glance. The man whose baby she was pregnant with.

She froze on the slightly elevated podium, felt her gut falling through an endless abyss. Like the time her twin sister had dragged her on a free-fall ride in an amusement park. Except through the nauseating terror that day she had known that at some point the fall would end. So she had forced herself to sit rigid, her teeth digging painfully into the inside of her mouth, while Liv had screamed with terror and laughter.

No such assurance today. Because every time Diego stormed into her life she forgot the lesson she had learned long ago.

Her hands instinctively moved to her stomach and his gaze zeroed in on her amidst the crowd. She couldn't look at him. Couldn't look into those golden eyes that had set her up to fall. Couldn't look at that cruel face that had purposely played with her life.

She forced herself to keep her gaze straight, focused on all the other curious faces waiting to speak to her. It was the most excruciating half hour of her entire life. She could feel Diego's gaze on her back, drilling into her, looking for a weak spot—anything that he could use to cause more destruction.

At least he'd made it easy for her to avoid him, sitting in one of the chairs in the back row with his gaze focused on her.

She slipped, the heel of one of her three-inch pumps snagging on the carpet as she moved past him. Just the dark scent of him was tripping her nerves.

Why was he here? And what cruel twist of fate had brought him here the very same day she had discovered that she was pregnant?

Diego Pereira watched unmoving as Kim closed the door to the conference hall behind her, her slender body stiff with tension. She was nervous and, devil that he was, he liked it.

He flicked through the business proposal. Every little detail of her presentation was blazing in his mind, and he was impressed despite his black mood. Although he shouldn't really be surprised.

Her pitch for investment today had been specific, innovative, nothing short of exceptional. Like her company. In three years she had taken the very simple idea of an advice column into an exclusive, information-filled web portal with more than a million members and a million more waiting on shortlists for membership.

He closed his eyes and immediately the image of her assaulted him.

Dressed formally, in black trousers that showed off her long legs and a white top that hugged her upper body, she was professionalism come to life—as far as possible from the woman who had cried her pleasure in his arms just a month ago.

He had even forgotten the reason he had come to New York while he had followed her crisp, confident presentation. But the moment she had realized he was present in the audience had been his prize.

She had faltered, searched the audience. That seconds-long flicker in her focus was like a nervous scream for an average woman.

But then there was nothing average about the woman

he had married. She was beautiful, brilliant, sophisticated. She was perfection personified—and she had as much feeling as a lump of rock.

A rock he was finally through with—ready to kick out of his life. It was time to move on, and her little nervous sputter at the sight of him had gone a long way toward pacifying his bitter resentment.

He walked to an elevator and pressed the number for the tenth floor. When he reached her suite he pulled the gold-plated keycard he had bribed from the bellboy from his coat packet.

He entered the suite and closed the door behind him.

The subtle scent of lily of the valley assailed him instantly. It rocked him where he stood, dispensing a swift punch to his gut more lethal than the ones he had taken for half his life.

His lungs expanded, drawing the scent of her deep into him until it sank once again into his blood.

His body pulsed with remembered pleasure. Like a junkie getting his high.

He studied the suite, with its luxurious sitting area and mahogany desk. Her files were neatly stacked on it, her sleek state-of-the-art laptop on top of them. Her handbag—a practical but designer black leather affair—lay near the couch in the sitting area.

The suite was everything its owner was—high-class, flawless and without an ounce of warmth.

He turned at the sound of a door on his right.

Closing the door behind her, she leaned against it. A sheen of sweat danced on her forehead.

He frowned, his curiosity spiking.

Her glistening mouth trembled as she spotted him, her hands moving to her midriff.

There was a distinct lack of color to her skin. Her slender shoulders quivered as she ran the back of her hand over her forehead.

He looked at her with increasing curiosity. Her jacket was gone. A V-necked sleeveless white silk blouse showed off her toned arms. The big steel dial of her designer watch highlighted her delicate wrist. A thin gold chain dangled at her throat.

The shadow of her breasts beneath the thin silk drew his gaze.

He swallowed and pulled his eyes up. The memory of her breasts in his hands was cutting off his breath more effectively than a hand choking his windpipe. The feel of her trembling with pleasure in his hands, the erotic scent of her skin and sex—images and sensations flooded through him.

He could no more fight the assault than he could stop breathing.

Her eyes flared wide, the same heat dancing in those chocolate depths.

She was the very embodiment of perfection—always impeccably dressed, exuding the sophistication that was like a second skin to her. Yet now she looked off-balance.

He reached her, the slight sway of her lithe figure propelling him toward her. "Are you okay, *gatinha?*"

She ran her palm over her face, leaving pink fingerprints over her colorless skin. Stepping away from him, she straightened the already immaculate desk. Her fingers trembled as she picked up a pen and moved it to the side.

She was more than nervous.

"No, I'm not," she said, shrugging those elegant shoulders. The frank admission was unusual. "But that's not a surprise as I just saw *you,* is it?"

He raised a brow and sliced the distance between them. "The sight of me makes you sick?"

Her fingers clutched the edge of the desk, her knuckles

white. "The sight of you reminds me of reckless stupid behavior that I'd rather not remember."

He smiled. "Not even the good parts, where you screamed?"

Pink scoured her cheeks. The slender set of her shoulders straightened in defense. She moved to the sitting area and settled into a leather chair. "Why are you here, Diego?"

He watched with a weird fascination as she crossed her legs and looked up at him.

The nervousness he had spied just moments ago had disappeared. She sounded steady, without a hint of anger or upset. Even though the last time they had laid eyes on each other she had been half-naked in his bed, her face bereft of color as he had dressed and informed her that he was done with her.

There was no reproach in her tone for *his* behavior a month ago.

Her calm composure grated on him like the edge of a saw chipping away at wood.

She drove him to be the very worst of himself—seething with frustration, thrumming with desire—whereas she remained utterly unaffected.

He settled down on the coffee table in front of her and stretched his legs so that she was trapped between them. He flipped open the file next to him against his better instincts, to finish what he had come for. "Your proposal is brilliant."

"I don't need you to tell me that," she threw back, her chin jutting out.

He smiled. The confidence creeping back into her tone was not a surprise. When it came to her company his estranged wife was a force to be reckoned with. "Is that your standard response to a potential investor?"

She snorted, and even that was an elegant movement of her straight nose. "It's my standard response to a man who I know is intent on causing me maximum damage."

Diego frowned. "Really? Have I done that?"

She snatched the proposal from his hands and the scent of her wafted over him. He took a breath and held it fast, the muscles in his abdomen tightening.

Droga, two minutes in her company and he was…

He expelled it with the force of his self-disgust. Pleasure was *not* the reminder he needed.

"You already had your revenge, Diego. After I walked out on our marriage six years ago you refused to divorce me with the express purpose of ruining my wedding to Alexander. Then you seduced me and walked out four weeks ago. Isn't that enough?"

"Seeing that you went back to your life, didn't even falter for a second, I'm not sure."

Something flickered in her molten brown gaze as she spoke. "I propelled my sister and Alex into a scandal, putting everything Alex has worked for at risk."

"Again, *them*—not you. From where I stand nothing has gotten to you. Apparently nothing *ever* gets to you."

She ran her fingers over her nape, her gaze shying away from him. Sudden tension pulsed around her. "You left me utterly humiliated and feeling like a complete fool that morning. Is that better?"

He had wanted her anger, her pain, and it was there in her voice now, thrumming with force. But it was too little, too late. Even now it was only the prospect of her precious company having caught his interest that was forcing any emotion from her.

"Maybe," he said, shrugging off his jacket.

Her gaze flew to his, anxious. "Tell me—what do I need to say so that you'll leave my company alone? What will save it from the utter ruin you're planning?"

"I thought your confidence in your company was unshakeable? Your strategy without pitfalls?"

"Not if you make it your life's mission to destroy it," she

said. Her voice rang with accusation, anger, and beneath it all, a curious hurt. "That's what this is all about, isn't it? Anyone who crosses you, who disappoints you, you ensure their ruin. Now it's my turn."

She straightened, her hands folded at her middle. The action pushed her small breasts into prominence. He trained his gaze on her face as though his life depended on it. Maybe not his life, but his very sanity relied on his self-control.

He didn't plan to lose it again.

"Six years ago you were obsessed with revenge, driven by only one goal—to ruin your father. You didn't care who you hurt in the process. You took his small construction company and expanded it into an empire—encompassing energy generation, mining. If I were to believe the media—and knowing you personally I'm very much inclined to—you are called a bastard with alarming frequency. You crushed anything that got in your way. Including your own father." She shot up from the seat and paced the length of the room. "I don't believe in wasting precious time fighting the inevitable. So whatever you're about to do—do it. But I won't go down without a fight. My company—"

"Means everything to you, right? You should be held up as an example to anyone who doubts that women can be as unfeeling and ruthless as men," he interjected smoothly, feeling that flare of anger again.

She stared at him, her gaze puzzled. "Why do I get the feeling that that's not a compliment?"

"It's not."

Her fingers tightened on the windowsill behind her. "We're even now, Diego. Let's just leave it at that."

He moved closer. He could see his reflection in her eyes, her slender shoulders falling and rising with her rapid breathing. Her gaze moved to his mouth and he felt a roar of desire pummel through his blood. It was impossible not to remember how good she had felt, how she had wrapped her legs around him and urged him on with soft little growls.

If he kissed her she wouldn't push him away. If he ran the pad of his thumb over the pulse beating frantically at her throat she wouldn't argue. She would be putty in his hands.

Wasn't that why he felt such a physical pull toward her? Because when he touched her, when he kissed her, it was the one time he felt that he owned this woman—all of her. Her thoughts, her emotions, the core of her.

He fisted his hands. But it would prove nothing new— to him or to her. Self-disgust boiled through him for even thinking it. He had let her get to him on the island, burrow under his skin until the past six years had fallen away and he'd been standing there with her letter in hand.

Never again.

He needed a new beginning without being haunted by memories of this woman. He needed to do what he had come for and leave—*now.*

"I realized what I had done wrong the moment I left the island," he said, unable to stop himself from wringing out the last drop of satisfaction. He had never claimed to be a great man. He had been born a bastard, and to this day he *was* one. "I've come to rectify that mistake."

Kim trembled all over, an almighty buzz filling up her ears.

"A mistake?" Her throat ached as it pushed that word out.

His golden gaze gleamed, a knowing smile curving his upper lip. "I forgot a tiny detail, although it was the most important of all."

He plucked a sheaf of papers from his coat pocket and slid them on to her desk. Every inch of her tensed. The words on those familiar papers blurred.

"I need your signature on the divorce papers."

She struggled to get her synapses to fire again, to get her lungs to breathe again.

The innocuous-looking papers pierced through her defenses, inviting pain she had long ago learned not to feel. This was what she had wanted for six long years—to be able to correct the mistake she had made, to be able to forget the foolish dream that had never stood a chance.

Her palms were clammy as she picked up the papers.

"My staff at the villa were never able to locate the copies you brought."

She shivered uncontrollably at the slight curiosity in his words. *Because she had torn them up after that first night when Diego had made love to her.*

No, not *love*. Sex. Revenge sex. The this-is-what-you-walked-away-from kind. For a woman with an above average IQ, she had repeated the same mistake when it came to Diego.

She turned the papers over and over in her hands. *This was it.*

Diego would walk out of her life. She would never again have to see the foolishness she had indulged in in the name of love. What she had wanted for so long was within her grasp. Yet she couldn't perform the simple task of picking up the pen.

"You could have sent this through your lawyer," she said softly, the shock and confusion she had held in check all evening by the skin of her teeth slithering their way into her. Her stomach heaved. "You didn't have to come yourself."

He leaned against the table, all cool arrogance and casual charm. But nothing could belie the cruel satisfaction in the curve of his mouth. He wanted blood and he was circling her like a hungry shark now that he could smell it.

"And miss the chance to say goodbye for the final time?"

"You mean you wanted to see the fallout from your twisted seduction?"

"Seduction?" he said, a dark shadow falling over his features. The force of his anger slammed into her like a gale.

"Why don't you own it, like you do everything else? There *was* no seduction." He reached her before she could blink. "What does it say about us that even after six years it took us mere hours after laying eyes on each other to end up in bed? Or rather against the wall…"

Her stomach somersaulted. Her skin sizzled. He was right. Sex was all she could think of when he was close. Hot, sweltering, out-of-control, mind-blowing, biggest-mistake-of-your-life-*that-you-made-twice* sex.

She would die before she admitted how much truth there was in his words, how much more he didn't know.

She grabbed her pen and signed the first paper, her fingers shaking.

She lifted her chin and looked up at him, gathering every ugly emotion simmering beneath the surface and pouring it into her words. "It's nothing more than a stimulus and response—like Pavlov's dog. No matter how many years pass, I see you and I think of sex. Maybe because you were my first. Maybe because you are so damn good at it."

The papers slithered to the floor with a dangerous rustle. She felt his fury crackling around them. He tugged her hard against him, his body a smoldering furnace of desire.

She had angered him with her cold analogy. But it only made the void inside her deepen.

His mouth curled into a sneer. "Of course. I forgot that the cruise, those couple of months you spent with me, were nothing but a rich princess's wild, dirty rebellion, weren't they?"

She felt a strange constriction in her chest, a tightness she had nothing to fight against. A sob clawed its way up her throat.

She hated him for ruining the most precious moments of her life. For reducing them to nothing. She hated herself for thinking he had loved her six years ago, for losing her mind the moment she had seen him again four weeks ago.

For someone who had been emotionally stunted for so long, the upsurge of emotion was blinding—pulling her under, driving reason from her mind.

She bunched her fingers in his jacket, his heart thundering beneath her touch. "It's good that you're so greedy you came back for more. Because I have news for you."

CHAPTER TWO

"YOU HAVE NEWS…?" He frowned, his fingers locked in a tight grip over hers. "What, *princesa?* Do you have a new man lined up now that your sister has stolen the last one? Do you think I give a damn?"

"I'm pregnant."

He didn't move. He didn't blink. Not even a muscle twitched in his mobile face.

Hot satisfaction fueled her. She had wanted to shake his infuriating arrogance. *She had.* On its heels followed raking guilt.

Her knees buckled under her. Only Diego's hold on her was keeping her upright.

God, she hadn't meant to blurt it out like that. She hadn't even dealt with what it meant to *her,* what it implied…

What did it say about her that the only positive thing she felt about the pregnancy was that it could shock Diego like nothing else could?

After the way he had treated her she owed him nothing. And yet keeping him in the dark required a price higher than she was willing to pay.

He had provided her with the best opportunity to tell him, to get it done with. For all she knew he wouldn't even care. He had wanted revenge, he'd got it—with little scruples—and now he had divorce papers ready. And he would keep on walking.

His gaze sliced to her, searching her face. Her composure unraveled at his silence.

The roguish arrogance was gone from his face, replaced by a resolute calm. Every inch of her quaked.

"Is it mine?"

Her gut started that dangerous fall again. She needed to get herself under control. Because Diego was a master at reading her. Whatever she wished, he would do the opposite. Just to make her life harder.

She needed to play it cool. "Why do you think I'm giving *you* the good news?"

"You slept with me mere *hours* after laying eyes on me again," he said, his golden gaze betraying his fury, "while the man you were ready to marry still had his lapdog out looking for you and your twin was being your damned *placeholder* in his life."

She trembled as he walked away from her, as though he couldn't bear to breathe the same air as her.

"And you went back to him as soon as I left you. Except he was two-timing *you* just as you were doing him. So I repeat: is the baby mine?"

"That's not true. Alex and I—"

She shut her mouth with a snap, leaned back against the soft leather, trembling from head to toe. Guilt hung heavy in her stomach. The media, her father—the whole world had crucified Liv, while Kim was the one responsible for it all.

Except Diego knew where she had been and what she had been up to while Liv had pretended to be her. And of course Diego thought Kim had quietly crawled back to Alex, that nothing had changed for her. That she had jumped into his bed from Alex's and then jumped straight back.

That was untrue on so many levels.

Even before Diego had made his true intentions known

Kim had broken it off with Alexander. Only Diego didn't know that.

Her next breath filled her with his scent—dark and powerful. Her eyes flew open.

He raised a brow, watching her with hawklike intensity. "It's a simple question, *gatinha,* and sadly one only a woman can answer."

There was nothing in his tone—no nuance of sarcasm, no hint of anger or accusation—nothing that she could latch onto and feed her fury, her misery.

"Alex and I…" she whispered, feeling heat creep up her skin. "We—"

"All I need—" his words came through gritted teeth "—is your word. Not a day-by-day update on your sexual activity."

Mortification spread like wildfire inside her. Really, she needed to get a grip on herself—needed to stop blurting out things Diego had no need to know.

More information on her non-existent sex-life fell into that category without a doubt. She already had a permanent reminder of how scandalously she had behaved. And now Alex and Liv, her father—*the whole world* was going to find out…

Her gut churned again with a vicious force. "Of course it's yours."

His jaw tight, he nodded. His easy acceptance, his very lack of a reaction, sent a shiver running down her spine. She had expected him to burst out, had braced herself for an attack.

Why did he trust her so easily? He had every right to demand a paternity test. Every right to question the truth of her claim. That was what she wanted from him. That was what she expected from him.

Instead his self-possession—something she usually prided *herself* on—grated on her nerves. She was still panicking. She had blurted out the news in a petty fit of pique. Whereas he didn't even blink.

She laughed, the sound edging toward hysteria. "What? No accusations? No demands for proof? No talk of DNA tests? Just like that, Diego?"

He turned away from her to lean against the wall and closed his eyes. He ran his hand over the bump on his nose. Tension overflowed from him, filling up the huge suite, rattling like an invisible chain, reaching for her. His eyes flew open and her gaze was caught by his.

"DNA tests are for women to whom being pregnant with a rich man's child means a meal ticket to a better life. An accusation my father threw at my mother every time she showed up with me on his doorstep, begging for support."

His words vibrated with emotion. His very stillness, in contrast to the loathing in his words, was disquieting in the least. "However, with our history, I don't think that's what you're going for."

Kim tucked her head in her hands, wondering what she had started. A lump of something—she refused to call it gratitude—blocked her throat, making it harder for her to speak. He could have turned this into something ugly if he wished. *He hadn't.*

Everything within her revolted at being obligated to him for even that small display of honor. It made her weak, plunged her into useless wishing.

She couldn't let him put her in the wrong. She couldn't forget that the very reason she was in this situation was because he had orchestrated payback.

She felt the hard wall of heat from his body and stiffened.

"For a woman who fairly blazes with confidence in every walk of life, your hesitation would be funny if it wasn't the matter of a child. Are you not so sure who the father is yourself?" he whispered softly, something deadly vibrating in his tone.

"There's no doubt," she repeated.

Thinking with a rational mind, she knew she should just tell Diego the stupid truth. That she had never slept with Alexander. But then Diego would never leave the truth alone.

"Now that we have solved that particular puzzle, what do you need from me?"

It took her a moment to realize that he was waiting for an answer. A chill began to spread over her skin. "I…I don't need *anything* from you."

"Of course not." An edge crept into his tone, his gaze devouring her. Something stormy rumbled under that calm now. "Then why tell me?"

"Honestly? I wasn't thinking," she said, wondering if she was destined always to make mistakes when it came to him. "You were gloating. You were…"

"Nice to know something touches you," he said, a fire glinting in his gaze. She opened her mouth to argue and shut it just as quickly. "And if I hadn't been here to gloat? Would you have called me then?"

"That's a question I don't have to answer, because you *are* here. And stop pretending as though this means something, Diego. You were ready to walk out of my life, and I say keep on walking."

"Your arrogance in thinking that you know me is astounding, *querida*. Did I teach you nothing four weeks ago?"

His words rumbled around her, and images and sensations tumbled toward her along with them. But she refused to back down. "You take risks. Your business tactics are barely on this side of the law. The last thing you need in your life is a baby. If I had hidden this from you you would have only found more reason to hate me."

"To think for a moment I assumed that you weren't doing

this for purely selfish reasons but for the actual wellbeing of the child you're carrying…"

She flinched, the worst of her own fears crystallized by his cutting words. Her earlier dread intensified. That was what she should have immediately thought of. *The child's welfare.* "I want nothing but a divorce and an exit from you."

His laughter faded and shadowed intent filled his face. He grabbed the papers she had signed not five minutes ago and shredded them with his hands.

His calm movements twisted her gut. "Then what do you have in mind? We'll kiss each other and make up? Play happy family—"

He came closer—until she could see the gold specks in his eyes, smell the dark scent of him that scrambled her wits.

"I'm not turning my back on my child."

Panic unfurling in her stomach, she shot up from her seat. "You're out of your mind. This is not what I planned for my life—"

"I'm sure you had a list of requirements that needed to be met in order to produce the perfect offspring," he said, his words ringing with bitter satisfaction, "but it's out of your hands now."

"It is. But what I *can* control is what I do about it now. Being a mother is going to be hard enough. Dealing with you on a regular basis will just tip me over into…"

Perverse anger rose within her—perverse, irrational and completely useless. He could walk away from this. She *needed* him to walk away from this. But *she*…she had no such choice. She had a lifelong commitment. She was supposed to love this baby. She was supposed to…

"You don't want this baby?"

"Of course I don't. I'll even go so far as to say it's the

worst thing that has ever happened to me!" she shouted, the words falling off her trembling lips.

Shock flickered in his gaze, but she didn't have the energy to wish them unsaid.

"This baby is going to be a walking, talking reminder of the biggest mistake of my life. You've achieved what you wanted, Diego. You've done your worst. You have changed my life in a way I can't control. Now, please, leave me to get on with it."

Diego breathed out through his teeth and hit the punching bag again with renewed force. His right hook was beginning to fall short again. The injury to the muscle in his bicep was making itself known. The same injury that had forced him to withdraw from financially lucrative streetfights. The injury that had forced him to reach out to his father for help when he had been sixteen and unable to pay for his mother's treatment.

But he wouldn't stop now. He breathed through the vicious pain, hating himself for even remembering.

The clock on the wall behind him chimed, reminding him he'd been at it for more than two hours now.

Sweat poured down from his forehead and he shook his head to clear it off. His T-shirt was drenched through and the muscles in his arms felt like stones. Adrenaline rushed through him in waves and he was beginning to hear a faint thundering in his ears. Probably his blood whooshing. But he didn't stop.

Because even trying to drown himself in physical agony he couldn't block out Kim's words.

Stimulus and response!

Meu Deus, the woman reduced him to the lowest denominator with her infuriating logic. No one had ever got under his skin like she did. And she was carrying his baby.

The resentment that had glittered in her brown eyes pierced even the haze of his pain.

Punch.

Of course it's yours.

Thump.

It's the worst thing that has ever happened to me.

Punch.

This baby is going to be a walking, talking reminder of the biggest mistake of my life.

Thump.

Nausea whirled at the base of his throat, threatening to choke him with its intensity. He'd had enough rejection from his father to last him several lifetimes. He would be dead before he did the same to his child or became a stranger.

He took one last punch and pulled his gloves off. He picked up a bottle of water, guzzled half of it down and dumped the rest over his head. The water trickled over his face into his eyes. The biting cold did nothing to pacify the crazy roar in his head.

Because Kim had been right. He didn't want to be a father.... He wasn't fit to be a father...

He let a curse fly and went at the punching bag again, shame and disgust boiling over in his blood. Pain waves rippled up his knuckles. His skin started peeling at his continued assault.

He had no good in him. All he had was hatred, jealousy. He didn't possess a single redeeming quality that said he should even be a *part* of a child's life. He had chosen to walk the path he had with full clarity of thought—to take everything from his father that he deserved. He had known exactly what he was doing when he'd reached for that goal.

And that was what he wanted to do now, too. He wanted to take his child from Kim and walk away. Every nerve in him wanted to ensure he had full custody.

But he could not sink so low again.

He had let his hatred for his father lead him to destroy his half brother's life in the process. If not for Diego's blind obsession Eduardo would have been…

He shivered, a chill swamping him.

He couldn't risk that happening with his child. If, because of his obsession with Kim, he hurt his child in any way he wouldn't be able to live with himself. He couldn't let his anger at her drive him into making a mistake again—not anymore. Not when it could hurt his own child.

Playing happy family with Kim, seeing her every day, when she was the one weakness he had never conquered—every inch of him revolted at the very thought.

And yet he couldn't escape his responsibility. He couldn't just walk away and become a stranger to his own child.

He had a chance to change the vicious cycle of neglect and abuse he and Eduardo had gone through.

He would move mountains to make sure his child had everything he'd never had—two loving parents and a stable upbringing. Even if that meant tying himself to the woman who brought his bitterest fears to the surface.

CHAPTER THREE

KIM PULLED THE satin pillow over her head and groaned as her cell phone chirped. She hadn't gotten into bed until three in the morning, after going over the new feature on *The Daily Help* with the design architect and writing her own feature for the career advice section she did every Tuesday.

Pushing her hair out of her eyes, she looked at the digital clock on the nightstand. It was only seven. She felt a distinct lack of energy to attack the day. When her phone rang for the third time in a row she switched the Bluetooth on.

"Kim, are you okay?"

Liv.

Tension tightened in the pit of her stomach at the concern in her twin's voice. She had been putting Liv off for two weeks now.

She pushed herself up on the bed and leaned against the metallic headboard. "I'm fine. Is everything okay with you and Alex?"

"We're fine. I'm just…" Liv's uncharacteristic hesitation hung heavily between them. "God, Kim—is it true? Why the hell didn't you *tell* me?"

Kim swallowed, fear fisting her chest. "What are you talking about?"

"You've made front page headlines. Not just the scandal rags, like I did, but even the business channels on television."

"What?"

"It says you're pregnant. Are you?"

Diego.

Kim closed her eyes and breathed huge gulps of air. Obviously her refusal to have anything to do with him, her refusal even to answer his calls, meant Diego had begun playing dirty.

"Yes."

"When were you going to tell me? Are you…? I mean, are you okay with this? Does Diego know? What are you planning to *do?*"

They were all perfectly valid questions. Kim had just shoved them down forcefully.

"I'm perfectly fine, Liv. I don't have the time right now to process what it means. Once this upcoming milestone for my company has passed I'll make a list of the things I need to do." She closed her eyes, fighting for composure. "I'll even have a few sessions with Mommy Mary."

"Who is Mommy Mary?"

"The expert on all things maternal on my team."

"On *what?*"

"On what I need to learn to be the perfect mother. It's not like *we* had a good example, is it?"

"And until then you're just going to put it on the back burner?"

What else was she supposed to do? Focus on the relentlessly clammy feeling in her stomach every time her thoughts turned to the baby growing in her womb?

The stark contrast between the terrifying emptiness *she* felt and her newly pregnant CFO's glorious joy was already a constant distressing reminder that something vital was missing in her own genetic make-up.

"I can't botch this opportunity for my company by losing my focus."

"I don't know what to…" Olivia's tone rang with the

same growing exasperation Kim had sensed in their recent conversations. "Let me know if you need anything, okay?"

Kim tucked her knees close as Liv hung up. She wanted to reach out to Liv. Liv's love came with no conditions, no judgment.

But Kim—she had always been the strong one. She had had to be in order to protect first her mother and then Liv from their father's wrath.

She couldn't confide her fears in anyone. Least of all to her twin, to whom loving and caring and nurturing came so easily.

Whereas Kim had trained herself so hard to not care, not to let herself be touched by emotions. She'd had to after she had learned what her mother had planned...

Only had she accomplished it so well—just as she had everything else in life—that she felt nothing even for the child growing in her womb?

Because even after a week all she felt was utter panic at the thought of the baby. She had spent a fortune buying almost a dozen more pregnancy test kits, hoping that it had been a false positive. And every time the word "pregnant" had appeared her stomach had sunk a little lower.

Or was it because of the man who had fathered her baby? Could her anger for Diego be clouding everything else? Was this how their mother had felt? Beneath her fear of their father, had she felt nothing for her children?

Without crawling out of bed, she pulled her reading glasses on and powered up her iPad. Her heart thumped loudly. She clicked on to one of her favorite websites—one she could count on to provide news objectively.

The Daily Help's pregnant CEO Kimberly Stanton's best kept secret—a secret marriage or the identity of her unborn baby's father?

It was the first time she wasn't in the news being lauded for one of her accomplishments.

The article, for all its flaming header, didn't spend time speculating on the answer to either of the questions it posed. But suddenly she wished it did. Because the speculation it *did* enter into was much more harmful than if they had spawned stuff about her personal life.

The article highlighted the way any woman—especially one who was pregnant and with her personal life in shambles—could expect to expand her company and do it successfully.

Should investors be worried about pouring their money into a company whose CEO's first priority might not be the company itself? One who has been involved in not one but two major scandals? Could this pregnancy herald the death of the innovative startup *The Daily Help* and its brilliant CEO Kimberly Stanton's illustrious career?

She shoved the tablet away and got out of bed, her mind whirling with panic. She ran a hand over her nape, too restless to stay still. It might have been written by Kim herself, for it highlighted every little one of her insecurities—everything she had made a list of herself.

For so long she had poured everything she had into first starting her company and then into making it a financial success. She had never stopped to wonder—never had a moment of doubt when it came to her career.

She opened the calendar on her phone. Her day was full of follow-up meetings with five different investors. By the end of the day she intended to start working on putting the plans she had outlined about the expansion of her company into full gear.

She couldn't focus on any other outcome—couldn't

waste her mental energies speculating and in turn proving the contentious article right.

Only then would she deal with Diego. There was no way anyone else would have known or leaked the news to the media. She had confided in only one person.

Wasn't this what Diego had intended all along? She was a fool if she'd thought even for a moment that he wanted anything but her ruin.

Kim clicked End on her Skype call and leaned back in her chair. Her day had only gotten worse since Liv's phone call. That had been her fifth and last unsuccessful investor meeting. Not one investor was ready to wire in funds.

Whereas the invoices for the new office space she had leased, for the three new state-of-the-art servers she had ordered, for the premium health insurance she had promised her staff this year mocked her and the vast sum of numbers on the papers in front of her was giving her a headache.

She leaned her head back and rubbed the muscles knotting her neck. Her vision for her company, her team's livelihood, both were at stake because she had weakened.

Hadn't she learned more than once how much she could lose if she let herself feel?

The number of things she needed to deal with was piling up. Panic breathed through her, crushing her lungs and making a mockery of the focus that she was so much lauded for. She forced large gulps of air into her lungs.

Breathe in...out...in...out... She repeated it for a few minutes, running her fingers over the award plaques she kept next to her table, searching for something to tune out the panic.

Pull yourself together, Kim. There are people counting on you.

It was the same stern speech she had given herself at thirteen, when she had discovered her mother's packed bag one night. And the note to her father that had knocked the breath from her.

She had survived that night. She could survive anything.

She had to go on as before—for her company's sake and for her own sake. If she lost her company she had nothing. She *was* nothing.

She picked up her cell phone and dialed Alex's number. He was someone with whom she had always tossed around ideas for her business, someone she absolutely trusted. And someone she had been avoiding for the past month...

But she needed objective, unbiased advice, and Alex was the only one who would give it to her. She would exhaust every possibility if it meant she could go on with the plan for expanding her company.

Diego cursed, cold fury singing through his blood as he stared at the live webcast on his tablet. Reporters were camped with cameras and news crews in front of Kim's apartment complex in Manhattan.

He rapped on the partitioning glass and barked her address at his chauffeur.

His gaze turning back to the screen again, he frowned at a sudden roar in the ruckus. And cursed again with no satisfaction as he recognized the tall figure. Her ex had arrived. Diego could almost peek into how the press's mind would work.

The news about her pregnancy on top of the scandal last month, when her twin had been found with Kim's ex—the press would come to only one conclusion.

That the unborn child—his child—was Alexander King's.

This was not what he had intended when he'd had his head of security leak the news of her pregnancy to the media.

He stared at the tall figure of Alexander King as he

walked into the complex without faltering, despite the reporters swarming around him. Acrid jealousy burned through him. He slammed his laptop shut, closed his eyes and sought the image of Eduardo's frail body.

Which was enough to soak up the dark thoughts and send some much-needed reason into his head.

He had done this before—let his obsession consume his sense of right or wrong. He had let it blind him to the fact that Eduardo had needed his help, and instead he'd turned on him.

He couldn't do that again. This was not about what Kim could drive him to. It was about what was right for their child.

Kim took a sip of her water as Alex finished a call. She had emailed him her proposal and set up the appointment. Now she wished she had waited for the weekend. Stupid of her not to expect how much the media would make of Alex visiting her *alone* on a Friday evening at her apartment.

She had never been more ashamed of herself. It had taken everything in her to ask Alex for his help but she had no other options. A flush overtaking her, she plucked up the daily statistics report her website manager had sent her.

Based on the turnover of her company in the last quarter, and on her expansion proposal, investing in her company was a sound opportunity for any shrewd businessman. Except for the scandal she had brought on herself.

Their daily numbers, the number of questions that came into their portal and the website hits, had spiked well above average today.

But she knew, as was pointed out by the breakdown in front of her, that this was because twenty percent of the questions had been about her pregnancy, whether she was married and—worst of them all—whether she was married to the father of her baby.

She needed to make a statement soon.

Tucking his phone into his pocket, Alex turned toward her. "I'm sorry, Kim. You know how much I trust your business savvy. But, as brilliant as your plan and forecast is, I can't invest in it right now."

Her stomach turning, Kim nodded. It was exactly as she had expected: the worst.

She blinked back tears as he wrapped an arm around her. "With everything going on out there right now I just... As much as I hate to admit it, my association with your company in the current climate would only damage your credibility."

Kim nodded, the comfort he offered making her spectacular failure even harder to bear. "I know. And I'm so sorry for putting you and Liv through this—for everything. If I could I would go back to that day and do everything differently." She smiled and corrected herself. "Well, except for the part where I left you with Liv."

He laughed, and her mounting panic was blunted by the sheer joy in that sound. "You don't have to go through this alone, Kim. You should come and stay with—"

"She's not alone to deal with this. And I would think twice, if I were you, before touching my wife again."

Kim jerked around so quickly that her neck muscles groaned.

Diego stood leaning against the door of her apartment, a dark, thundering presence, and he looked at them with such obvious loathing that her mouth dried up.

Next to her, Alex stayed as calm as ever as he turned around. Just like her, he knew who was behind the leak to the media. But, gentleman that he was, he hadn't asked her one personal question.

The very antithesis of the man smoldering with anger at the door.

Mortification heating her cheeks, she met Diego's gaze.

"Don't do this, Diego. Don't make me regret ever knowing you."

He shrugged, the movement stretching the handmade grey silk tight over his muscular frame. "Don't you already? Aren't you going to introduce your husband to your ex, *querida?*"

Alex moved at her side, reaching Diego before she could blink. Her breath hitched in her throat as they both looked at each other.

"Call me anytime, and for any kind of help, Kim," Alex said.

Without another word he strolled out, closing the door behind him. The silence pulling at her stressed nerves, Kim walked past the sitting area to her kitchen, the open layout giving her an unobstructed view of Diego. She pulled a bottle of orange juice out of the refrigerator and poured it into a glass.

Diego leaned against the pillar that cut off the kitchen from the lounge. She raised the glass to her mouth and took a sip. His continued scrutiny prickled her skin. Every time she laid eyes on him she felt as if she was one step closer to a slippery slope.

"What is this? A lesson in caveman behavior?"

"I don't understand your relationship with that man."

She blinked at his soft tone. "Don't turn this around on *me*. Were you going to beat your chest and drag me to your side by my hair if he hadn't left?"

He smiled, his gaze moving to her hair. He flexed his fingers threateningly. "I've never done that before...but if anyone can push me to it, it's you."

Her mouth open, she just stared at him.

"You like throwing my background in my face, don't you? I'm not ashamed that my life began on the streets of Rio de Janeiro, that I used my fists for survival."

She glared at him, insulted by his very suggestion. "It's

got nothing to do with your background and everything to do with how you are acting now."

"True. This one's my fault. I should have expected you to go to him for help."

It was the last thing she'd expected him to say.

Calling her a few names, maybe challenging her word about the paternity of the baby as the whole world was hotly speculating—sure. But this? No. His continuing trust in her word threw her, kept her off-balance.

Or was that what he truly intended?

The doubts assailing her, the real possibility of her company falling apart, filled her veins with ice. "As you have made it your mission to destroy my life, I went crawling for help to the man whom I deceived dreadfully by sleeping with you. *Satisfied?*"

Diego let his gaze travel lazily over Kim. A long-sleeved white cotton top hugged her slim torso and the flat of her stomach, followed by tight blue jeans that encased her long legs. Her short hair was pulled back with a clip, leaving shorter tendrils teasing her cheekbones.

He believed her that the baby was his. She had nothing to gain by lying to him and everything to lose.

Except he didn't understand how, having been almost literally dragged from the altar by Diego, away from a man who was now *apparently* happily married to her twin, Kim could still share a relationship with Alexander that wasn't the least bit awkward.

Was she still pining after him? After all, she had gone to him for help. That in itself was revealing.

"I gave you a week, *gatinha*. I refuse to be ignored. I refuse to let you put your company before the baby and—"

She put her glass down with a force that splashed the juice onto her fingers. Her posture screamed with barely contained anxiety. "The baby's not going to be here for nine months. Do you expect me to sit around twiddling my thumbs until then? I'm not going to give up something I have built with sheer hard work just because I'm pregnant."

There it was again. Her complete refusal to accept that things were going to change.

"I expect you to slow down. I expect you to return my calls. I expect you to stop working sixteen-hour days." She didn't look like perfection put together today. She looked tired and stressed out. Guilt softened his words. "You look like you're ready to fall apart."

"And whose fault is that? I've been trying to minimize the damage you've caused with your dirty tricks."

"You have no idea *how* dirty I'll fight for what I want. Propelling you toward *him* wasn't what I intended, however. But I had forgotten how stubbornly independent you are."

"Careful, Diego. You sound almost jealous. And yet I know you don't give a hoot about me."

"Remember I'm an uncivilized, dirty thug," he said, with a slanted look at her. "A street-fighting Brazilian, *pequena*. Of course I'm jealous."

Kim wiped her fingers on a hand towel, feeling a flush creep up her neck.

Of course she remembered. She remembered every moment of her short-lived marriage with crystal-clear clarity. She had called him that the week before she had left him, her misery getting the better of her. It wasn't where he had come from that had bothered her. It was what he represented to him because of it that had shattered her heart.

"Why? Even *you* can see, after everything you have set in motion, how much Alex loves my sister."

He circled the pillar and neared her, frowning. "And this doesn't bother you at all?"

"What?"

"That the man you had been about to marry is now married to your twin."

"I'm incredibly happy for them. If there's one good thing that's come out of this whole debacle it's Liv and Alex."

"Only one good thing? Still not sure, then?" he queried silkily, his gaze instantly moving to her stomach.

Her spine kissed the steel refrigerator as he suddenly swallowed her space. "Any child who's the product of you and me is of course not a good thing."

"You make it sound like it's a product we designed together."

His words were soft, even amused, and yet they lanced through her. "Excuse me if I'm not the perfect vision of maternal instinct you were expecting."

He stared at her, his gaze searching hers. "Your genes needed a bit of diluting anyway, and you need a bit of softening up. All work and no play makes Kimberly a crabby girl."

"Yes, well—look where all that playing has landed me."

She sucked in a deep breath, sheer exhaustion finally catching up with her. Trust Diego to force her to face the one thing she didn't want to think about.

"We can't even have a conversation without jumping at each other's throats, Diego." Every dark fear she was trying to stay above bled into her words. "How do you think it bodes for the…the child?"

Without looking away from her he pulled her hands from behind her and tugged her gently. Stupefied, she went along, for once lacking the energy to put up a fight. With a hand at her back he guided her to the lounge and pushed her onto the couch.

He settled down on a chair opposite.

She felt the force of his look down to her toes. "You might not want this baby, but you want to do the right thing by it—right?"

She swallowed and nodded, a fist squeezing her chest. It was the only thing she was capable of at this point.

"Good. And, as much as you were hoping that I would walk away, I won't." His gaze was reassuring, his tone comforting. "Believe me, *gatinha,* that's a whole lot more than most kids ever have."

Was it?

Maybe if her mother hadn't left that night…and even when she had maybe if she had at least included Kim… would her life have been different, better, today? No, there was no point in imagining a different past or present. Being weak, trusting her heart, only led to unbearable pain. She had learned that twice already.

"Why are you jealous of Alexander?" The moment the question fell off her lips she regretted it.

His long fingers on his nape, Diego closed his eyes and then opened them slowly. His resentment was clear in the tight line of his mouth. "Alexander King has your confidence. I don't. And, having crawled out of the gutter, I find my first reaction is to hate any man who has what I want."

His stark admission pulled the rug out from under her. "You want my confidence?" She sighed. "How about you stop trying to destroy me for a minute and then we can talk?"

He leaned forward, his elbows on his knees, his expression amused. "Isn't it interesting how your company being in crisis means I'm destroying your life, but when I ruined your wedding you didn't have a word to say? So, did he agree to save your company and thus your *life?*"

His absolutely accurate assumption that her life revolved around her career and her company was beginning to grate on her nerves. She had always prided herself on her unemotional approach. It had been a factor that had put her in direct competition with ruthless businessmen like him.

"No."

He plopped his ankle on his right knee. "Is it because

you deceived him? Have you noticed how you leave *all* the men in your life with less than nice impressions?"

"Not everyone in the world is as concerned about pay-back as you are."

His gaze glittered for a second, but the next he was a rogue, savoring the mess he was making of her life. "So why did Mr. King refuse to be your savior?"

"Because—thanks to your tricks and my own stupid-ity—my image is in tatters. My company is based on the idea of a panel of experts giving women advice on any topic from health, career and fashion to politics, finance and sex. The operative word being *experts*. And, as unfair as it is, a woman who seems to *not* have her personal life together without blemish is not someone others—even other women—want advice from. It doesn't matter that nothing has changed in the way I think or in my brain matter since I learned about my pregnancy. It just is."

"But eventually the news would have come out. I just accelerated it."

He was right. It was something she would have had to face in a couple of months anyway. The sooner she dealt with all this, found a way to resolve this situation with her company, the better.

She still needed an investor, but she was not as worried about running her company as the whole world was. She could do it with her hand tied behind her back.

It was the pregnancy that was the near-constant worry scouring through her.

She had succeeded in everything she had taken up in her life. Pregnancy had to be the same, right?

If she prepared enough, if she was willing to work hard, she could do a good job at being a mother, too. She refused to think about it any other way—refused to give weight to the worry eating away at her from inside.

"What's was the point of all this, Diego?" she said, feeling incredibly tired. "Would it make you feel better if I begged you for help? Leeched money off you in the name of child support?"

"Yes."

She blinked at the vehemence in his answer.

"What I wanted was to scare away all your other investors so that you have no one else to turn to but me."

"Why?"

"It seems putting your company in crisis is the only way for me to get your attention."

Her temper flared again. "That's the second time you have mentioned my success, my company, as though it's something to be sneered at—when you pursued your *own* success with ruthless ambition. And wasn't that why you married me six years ago? Because I was smart, ambitious? Now that I'm pregnant you're asking me to put all that aside and suddenly morph into your vision of everything maternal? I never thought *you* would tout double standards."

Diego ran a hand over his nape. Just the mention of their short-lived marriage was like throwing a punch in his face. She was doing it again—getting under his skin. And it would end in only one way.

"Do you really want to go down the rabbit hole of the past, *gatinha?*"

He didn't want to argue with her. He could see very well that something about her pregnancy was stressing her out. So why didn't she make it easy on herself? If she didn't know how to, he would do it. He would drag her kicking and screaming back into his life and force her to slow down if that was what he had to do to take care of her.

He stepped over the coffee table and joined her on the couch. She scooted to the other corner. He sighed. It seemed either they argued or they screwed, and neither was what he wanted to do. Even if one option had infinitely more appeal than the other.

"I'm not asking you to give up your work. I'm asking you to acknowledge that pregnancy changes things."

Her feet tucked under her, her arms wrapped around herself, she scrunched farther into the corner. She looked absolutely defeated. "And what does *that* entail? Throwing myself a conception party and inviting the whole world?"

"You have no friends, you don't talk to your sister and you're a workaholic. You live in a fortress isolated from anyone else. That cannot continue."

"Keeping myself idle for hours on end with nothing to do is not going to turn me into *mother of the year* when the baby comes. In fact it would just…"

His patience was thinning, but there was something in her voice—a note of desperation—that snagged his attention. "Just what?"

Her stubborn silence was enough to drive his control to the edge again. Was this what he was signing up for a lifetime of?

"I will invest in your company."

Her gaze widened. Her head shook from left to right. "I'll bounce back from this."

"No, you won't." He leaned toward her, and the scent of her caressed him. "Things are different from what they were a week ago."

"Because you manipulated them to your advantage."

"I would have been dead in a ditch years ago if I didn't push things to my advantage." He smiled, enjoying her stupefied silence. "Now I've got you hooked, haven't I? I can see the gears already spinning in your head."

"What's the catch?"

"Aah… Look at us, *gatinha*. We're like an old married couple, reading each other's minds without words. If that's not a true, abiding love, then I don't know what is."

"Stop it, Diego. Why the investment now?"

"Perhaps I don't want to see your hard work go to waste?

Or I'm overcome by a consuming need to help you? I still have a soft spot for my wife?"

Kim shivered as though someone had trickled an ice cube over her spine. His taunts were painful reminders of things she had cherished once and then realized to be false. He was mocking feelings she held close to her heart, emotions she had locked up forever.

"Not funny." With each cheeky retort her anxiety spiraled higher and higher. There *had* to be a huge price to pay for this. "What do you want from me?"

"We make our marriage work. For good."

She jumped from the couch, a chill descending into her veins. He couldn't be serious. It was a twisted joke. That was all it had to be...

She swallowed at the calm in his gaze. "Now I get it. No one is allowed to say no to you, to walk away from you, without you going all *revenge of the ninja* on them. I'm not a task you failed at once and are determined to conquer."

"Let's be very clear about something, *princesa*." The dark humor faded from his gaze, replaced by something hard and flinty. "Putting up with you, tying my life to yours again, is like signing up for a lifetime of torment. But it's a *sacrifice* I'm willing to make for my child. To provide a stable home, to give it everything I didn't have. *Nothing more.* I plan to be a hands-on parent and I will accept nothing less from you."

Bile snuck up Kim's throat. Everything within her rebelled at the thought of being tied to him. It was no better now than it had been six years ago. Then she had been his prize, his trophy, to parade before his father in his victory over a horrible childhood. Now her significance was the fact that she was going to be the mother of his child.

It shouldn't hurt. But it did. And the hurt was followed by the same raking guilt that had taken up permanent residence in her gut.

She couldn't think about what this meant for her. She had to think of the baby. She had to do what was right.

Whether she wanted to be a mother or not, whether or not she felt anything for the life growing inside her, it didn't matter. Unconditional love. She had never received it, she didn't know it, but responsibility and being strong for someone else—that she understood.

"Is this another trick so you can taunt me for the rest of my life? I won't let you use the child as some kind of pawn."

"Every inch of me wants to walk away from you. Every cell in me regrets sleeping with you. I told myself I would not waste another minute on you. But what we did has had consequences. All this is motivated by the fact that we're having a child together. A child who will have a proper father—not one who will just drop in for birthdays and pose for pictures—and a proper mother. A family. I will do everything in my power to ensure my child has everything I never had."

She swallowed, the emptiness she felt exaggerated by his words. In that moment she didn't doubt him.

Diego would do everything for their child. She could see the resolve burning in his eyes. If only he had felt a little of that toward her when they had been married. If only she felt one tenth of the emotion he felt for their child.

"We don't have to be married for that. We could share custody."

"My child is not spending half its life traveling between you and me like a soccer ball. We will be a family—a proper one."

"I'm not sleeping with you."

He laughed—the first sound he'd made that was filled with genuine amusement. "Afraid you won't be able to resist? Don't worry, Kim. I've learned that there are some things in life that can damage even dirty-fighting and wicked me. Like sleeping with you."

"Finally something we agree upon," she said loudly, trying to drown the thundering of her own heart. It figured that now he had caused maximum damage Diego had no interest in her. Why that should bother her of all the things that had happened today was beyond her.

Really, she was becoming a regular passenger on the cuckoo train.

She slid into the couch again, her knees shaking beneath her, trying to grasp the rollercoaster she was signing up for.

"So—a sexless, everlasting marriage to a man who hates me, who owns the biggest share of my company and who will no doubt find unadulterated joy in telling me what a horrible mother I make for the rest of my life? Sounds like a perfect recipe for happily-ever-after."

"Happily-ever-after? Is that what you want, *princesa?* Would you even know it if it bumped you on your over-achieving head?"

Hulking over her, he surrounded her, his gaze drilling holes into her.

"For the last time—your company is just a bargaining chip for me. I only ask that you do your best for our child. And as to sex—" his voice lowered to a sinuous whisper, his breath tickling her lips "—if you really want to change that part of the equation we can revisit it—say in a couple of years?" Dark enjoyment slashed the curve of his mouth.

She pulled her gaze upward. The whole situation she found herself in was absurdly comical. If only it wasn't her life. "A reward system? *Great.* Sex for good behavior?"

His mouth curved again, in a smile that dimpled his cheek, pure devilish amusement glittering in it. Her breath stuck in her throat. She had always loved that dimple. On any other man it would have looked effeminate. On Diego it touched his ruthless masculinity with a mischievous charm.

"See—just the way you like it. Everything reduced to a simple business transaction. Be a good little wife and you can have all the sex you want."

CHAPTER FOUR

STANDING IN FRONT of the elevator on her floor, Kim studied herself in the gleaming doors and breathed in gulps of air. So much for her hope that she might be one of the women that Mommy Mary mentioned, who had breezy pregnancies, nesting instincts and glowing skin.

Right.

What she had was nausea, exhaustion, acne—and mood swings as though she had just gotten off of antidepressants. And nothing but an unrelenting detachment at the sight or talk of anything baby-related.

Only a ninety-hour work week, with the added stress of handling PR about the new investment and the expansion of her company, had kept her from spiraling further down.

Two days after he had cornered her in her apartment Diego's legal team had contacted her own. She refused to feed her curiosity by asking where *he* was. Negotiations had been completed in a day and she now had two million dollars to sink her teeth into. It was more than she had expected in her wildest dreams.

She should be overjoyed—she had the investment and she was being awarded the prestigious Entrepreneur of the Year award by the Business Bureau Guild tonight.

But she couldn't turn her mind from thoughts of Diego. It was like a rerun of six years ago, when she had returned to New York, her heart in pieces, wondering if he would call her, if he would come after her...

Not even a month since he'd come back into her life and he was already reducing her to that pitiful self—to someone who signed up for getting hurt so easily.

Maybe she should have accepted Liv's offer to attend the awards ceremony with her and Alex. But she was still avoiding Liv and her well-meaning questions, and arriving with them would only give rise to more of the speculation that was beginning to mess with her head.

Running her company meant she always worked sixteen to eighteen hour days, and that didn't leave time for abiding friendships—or anything else for that matter. It was how she had tailored her life. And she loved it just that way.

Except for the strange tightness in her chest at the thought of the evening ahead, *alone*.

She stepped into the elevator and heard the swish of the doors closing behind her. Leaning her head against the cool mirrored surface of the wall, she fought the tears clogging her throat, a volatile rush of emotion flooding her.

In a way, the threat to her company's expansion had taken her mind off the pregnancy. Now there was nothing to do except face the void inside her. What she wouldn't give to feel one positive thing about this pregnancy...even if it was something as trivial as relief that the nausea was abating.

She reached the front lobby and asked the doorman to hail a taxi. She walked out behind him and pulled her wrap tighter around her shoulders. A black limo came to a smooth stop at the curb.

She stepped out of the way as a chauffeur opened its door. And felt Diego's presence behind her, emerging from her building.

"Ready to go?"

Her heart kicking against her ribcage, she turned around

so quickly that she almost lost her balance. Diego's hand shot out to hold her before she stumbled to the ground.

His arm around her waist, he pulled her to him, enveloping her in a purely masculine scent and hard muscles that made her feel soft all over.

Warmth flooded her, flushing out the inexplicable loneliness of a minute ago. She breathed in a big gulp of air, expanding and contracting her lungs.

Her stomach lurched in an altogether different, pleasurable way. *Why couldn't he make her nausea worse?*

Dressed in a gray Armani suit that hugged his broad shoulders, with his hair slicked back from his forehead, she wondered if he had materialized right out of her thoughts. He exuded raw magnetism, sliding her heartbeat ratcheting up and her already active hormones into overdrive.

His bronzed skin gleamed with vitality in the streetlights, his slightly bent nose and glittering eyes adding to his allure. Languid sensuality cascaded from him.

Even in the chilly New York evening she felt the heat of his perusal on her skin.

"Careful, *pequena,*" he whispered.

A frisson spread in ripples from where his big palm stayed over her back. His grip on her waist tightened as he felt her shiver, the heat from his callused palm singeing her skin through the silk material.

"I know those heels are part of your image but you need to be careful."

She raised her gaze to him, tingling everywhere he touched her. She searched his face hungrily. After his absence for a week she had started believing he regretted his commitment to her—at least the personal part of it.

The moment she found her balance he let her go. As though he didn't want to touch her unless absolutely necessary. Whereas she still tingled everywhere from the briefest of contacts.

"What are you doing here?" she said loudly, trying to speak past the continued boom of her heart.

"I'm coming with you to the awards ceremony."

She closed her eyes and counted to ten, hating herself for the excitement sweeping through her. This was the result of depriving herself of basic human company. This stupid, dangerous thrill at the prospect of an evening with Diego. "Why?"

His smile seemed feral. "To see the whole world praise my wife and fall at her feet for her brilliance."

"Yeah, right. Where exactly did you come from?"

His gaze devoured her, swift and dismissive. "The penthouse."

"The penthouse? What were you doing in the penthouse?" she shot at him, regretting the question the moment she'd said it.

Was he visiting a woman up there? Did she really want to know what Diego got up to in his free time? It had been hard enough to resist gobbling up information about him in the past six years.

"Moving in," he said, with an exaggerated patience that wound her up a little more. "As will you. It will be our home. Until we figure out something more permanent."

"You moved to New York? When? Why?" She refused even to acknowledge the other suggestion he'd slipped in. Equal parts of dread and hope thrummed through her. Because, despite every protest she made with Diego close, the knot in her stomach about her pregnancy relented just a little.

"Why do you think I've moved here?" His mouth twitched. "Have you noticed your brilliance deserts you when I'm around?"

"There's nothing new about that, is there?" She sighed. Really, it was better to accept it than fight it. "For every inch you move closer it's like my IQ drops a few points.

My brain works *sooo* much better with a continent separating us."

He took a step closer and she could smell the scent of his soap and skin combined. Her heart raced. She made a *ca-ching* sound. "Down five points."

His gaze alight with laughter, he ate up a little more of the space between them. She felt the heat of his body tease her skin, tug lower in her belly.

She made another sound with her mouth. Only it emerged croaky and faint this time. "Down five more."

He neared her, tugged at her wrap, which was trailing toward the ground, and tucked it neatly around her bare shoulders. Encompassed by his wide frame, she felt the world around her fall away. His fingers grazed her nape in the barest of touches and lingered. Need rippled across her, every inch of her hyper-sensitive to his nearness.

She wet her lips. "Annndddd…I'll probably spell my own name wrong if you ask me now."

Throwing back his head, he laughed. It was such a heart-felt sound that she couldn't help but smile, too. And marvel at the breathtaking beauty of the man. She felt the most atavistic thrill, like a cavewoman—the very thing she had accused him of being—that he was choosing to spend the evening with her.

He moved away from her, his mouth still curved. "We want you functioning with your normal brilliance tonight, right?"

She should be glad he had some kind of control, because apparently she had none when it came to him. Swallowing her body's frustrated groan, she looked away from him. "Have you really moved to New York?"

He studied her with a lingering intensity. The laughter waned from his face. "Aah…you thought I wasn't coming back."

"I went by your past record." She gave voice to the

thought that wouldn't leave her alone. "Of course I forgot that this time you have something precious to come back for."

He closed his eyes for an infinitesimal moment, his posture throwing off angry energy. When he spoke, his gaze was flat, his voice soft with suppressed emotions. "Are you accusing me of something, *pequena?*"

She shook her head. She was too much of a coward to hear what she already knew—that she hadn't mattered enough for him to come after her six years ago.

With his hand at her back, he nudged her toward the waiting limo.

She settled into the seat, scrambling to get her wits together. Acknowledging that her common sense went on a hike when he was close was something; mooning over him was another. She crossed her legs. Her dress rode up to her thighs and she tugged the fabric down, heat tightening her cheeks. Watching her like a vulture, Diego didn't miss anything. She pulled her wrap tighter and sat straight, like a rigid statue.

One glance in the tinted windows was enough to throw her further equilibrium.

She was due for a haircut, which meant her hair didn't have the blunt look she preferred but curled around her face in that annoying way. And she hadn't had the strength, for once, to straighten it to its usual glossy look. She had applied a little foundation and her usual lip gloss. But she looked pale after another sleepless night. She plumped her hair with her fingers on one side, so that a curl covered it.

She fidgeted in her seat and pulled the edges of her wrap together. *Again.* She should have changed, even if it had meant she would be late. Because the dress just…*clung* too much. The fabric cupped her breasts tight. One could probably even make out the shape of her…

Damn it. Nothing about the evening felt right.

Diego's attention didn't waver from her for a second.

She looked at him and uttered the first thing that came into her head. "Do I look okay?"

"Excuse me?"

"It's a simple question, Diego."

"Really? I didn't think you needed assurance in any walk of life."

"Well, you're wrong. I have lots of moments where I think I might just break," she said, with a catch she couldn't hide, "and this pregnancy is bringing out the worst in every way possible—mood swings, nausea. And you're not making it easy by…"

He pulled her hand into his and squeezed. His touch anchored her—a small but infinitely comforting gesture. "Tell me how I can help."

"For starters you can tell me—" she sucked in a deep breath "—how I look."

His gaze flicked to her, roguish amusement glinting in it. "Okay. Take off that wrap."

Her mouth clamped shut, Kim sat rigid, her hands fisted in her lap.

"Do you want my opinion or not?"

"Yes."

He grabbed the edge of her cashmere wrap and pulled it.

His gaze traveled over her slowly, methodically, from her hair to her shoulders, left bare by the strapless beige silk dress which hugged every curve. She sucked in her breath as it hovered over her midriff.

It felt like forever before it moved to her bare legs and her feet clad in Prada pumps.

He cleared his throat. "You look *different*," he finally said.

Of course he was going to squeeze the moment for everything. "What kind of different?"

Amusement glinted in his gaze. "Are you fishing for a compliment, *minha esposinha?*"

"Maybe… And stop calling me your wife." She smoothed her hands over her thighs. The soft, lush silk only heightened her anxiety. "This is not me. I much prefer—"

"Conservatively cut clothes that say 'look at my brain, not at my breasts.'"

Did he miss *anything?* "I have to present the right image, work harder than a man for the same level of respect. Not everyone in the business world is as forthcoming as you are with their confidence in my capabilities—much less their…money…" she finished slowly, realizing how much truth there was in her words.

She knew firsthand how ruthless a businessman he was, that the only allowances he made were for hard work. He might have invested in her company in the most twisted way possible, but he hadn't had to. If he'd truly wanted to leave her with no options he could have really let it all go down the drain…

"Thank you for your investment—for your trust in me," she said, trying to breathe past the tightness in her chest.

He shrugged. "Only a fool would doubt your company's success, or your ability to run it whatever your personal life." His gaze moved over her again quickly. "Although I have to tell you it doesn't really work."

She blinked, her skin tingling at his appraisal. "What doesn't?"

He smiled, apparently finding her stupidity very amusing. "Whatever you wear—even those trousers and shirts that you are so fond of—it doesn't hide the fact that you're hot."

Something latent uncoiled in his gaze—a spark—but was gone before the meaning of his words even sank in. How did he do that? How was he so effortlessly able to look at her with so much desire in his eyes and in the next bank it down to nothing?

She stared at his dark head as he powered up his tablet.

She had thought nothing had changed in him in six years. She was wrong. A lot had—and not just his success.

The man she had married had been a passionate twenty-one-year-old, quick to anger and to love. His emotions had simmered on the surface almost like a glow, a blaze of un-diluted energy that lured everyone toward him.

His drive to succeed, his determination to squash any-thing that lay in his way—she had understood *that* ambi-tion. But this new, refined man...he had a disconcerting calm, a control to him, that gave no clue as to what was simmering beneath the surface. Unless he told her with that piercing honesty.

She had expected him to question her about the preg-nancy. He hadn't. She had expected him to walk away with-out a backward glance. He hadn't. And on top of that he was really here, in New York. Because he wanted to give their marriage a real try.

She couldn't get the measure of him because everything she had taken for granted before was now hidden beneath a veneer of sophisticated charm, of polite courtesy.

But she knew the man beneath it, and she didn't buy that façade for a second. If she lowered her guard, if she let him into her life any more than she absolutely had to, she had a feeling he would only strike again. And this time she wouldn't be able to walk away unscathed.

A scowl on his face, he flicked the tablet off. He leaned forward in a sudden movement, his jaw tight. "So, why the change in how you dress?"

She had a feeling he'd meant to say something else—as if he was working to control himself first. "It's a friend's design. I agreed to do her a favor and wear it tonight. Except she tricked me and didn't deliver it until an hour ago. She knew I wouldn't—"

"You wouldn't wear it otherwise? Smart woman," he said. "She knows that the only way to get you to do something for others is to trick you or to manipulate you."

His words pricked her with quiet efficiency. "Is this what you mean by creating a happy environment to raise a kid? Throwing continuous barbs at me? Because I've seen that marriage. I'm a product of that marriage. And, believe me, it only screws up the kids."

She leaned back against the seat, feeling as fragile as a piece of glass. How stupid had she been to believe even for a moment that there could be truce between them? Six years of separation wasn't enough to thaw this anger between them. Or the attraction, for that matter.

"I had…I *have* every intention of making this work."

His words weren't bereft of emotion now. On the contrary, they vibrated with a dark intensity that gave her goosebumps.

"Except you make it so hard to be civilized with you."

"What are you talking about?"

He raised the tablet toward her. "I just watched the coverage of your press statement."

"And?"

"You left out the most important part. *Again.*"

"I don't know what you're talking about. My statement was concise. I followed the details of the investment contract, just as your legal team dictated, and I stopped it from downgrading into Twenty Questions about my personal life."

"Your personal life," he said softly, "is not just yours anymore."

She waited for him to elaborate. Unknown dread pooled in her gut.

The limo came to a stop in front of the plush New York

Plaza Hotel, where the awards ceremony was being held. She could hear the hushed roar of the crowd outside.

Before she could blink he opened a small velvet box.

Drawing a painful breath, she tucked herself farther into her seat, her heart pounding behind her ribcage. He'd done this on purpose—waited until the last minute.

The diamond twinkled in the dark, every cut and glitter of it breathtaking in its princess setting. There was an accompanying band of white gold, exquisitely simple in contrast to the glittering diamond.

Alarm twisted her stomach into a knot. That simple band might very well be an invisible shackle, binding her to him. And it could unlock every impossible hope, every dangerous dream she had so ruthlessly squashed to survive. "I don't want to wear it. I don't know what you think this achieves…"

Her words faltered as he gently tugged her hand into his and slipped the rings on her finger. They were cold, heavy against her skin, yet she felt branded.

"It puts a stop to the dirty speculation about you…about my child."

"What does it matter what the world thinks?"

"Do you know when the first time my mother took me to see my father was?"

Every other thought fled her mind. She just stared at him. She knew he didn't like talking about his childhood. And she hadn't pushed him six years ago.

"I was six. We stood outside his house for three hours before he even met with us. Then she took me again when I was seven. Every year she would drag me to his doorstep, hoping this time he would accept me as his son. I grew up hearing the neighborhood's taunts—*bastard* and so much more. She wanted a different life for me, a better one, but I never cared. I didn't think he owed me anything. Until she ended up in the hospital."

A cloud of dark anger surrounded him in proportion to the incredible cruelty of his father's treatment. A knot twisted in her own gut. Could she blame him for how much he had hated his father? Because she knew, firsthand, what a parent's negligence, even indifference, could do to a child. "How old were you?"

He blinked as though suddenly realizing she was there. "Sixteen. Her body was weakened by years and years of hard labor and not enough food. I couldn't pay for her treatment, and she'd made me promise I wouldn't go back to the street gangs. So I went to see him. By myself for the first time."

Her gut churned, the subdued violence in him raising the hairs on her neck. Sixteen years old—he had been nothing but a child himself. Suddenly she had a feeling where this was going. She understood what had angered him so much. Guilt spiraled through her.

"I went to the offices of his construction company. I begged him to pay for her treatment. I told him I would work for him for the rest of my life. He had his bodyguard drag me by my collar and throw me out. She died that night. And I swore I would take everything from him. I didn't stop until I destroyed him."

"Diego, how would I—?"

"There is very little I have asked of you or will ever ask of you. But when it comes to our child I won't settle. I will never be that boy who was denied his rights ever again." He shrugged—a casual movement, in complete control of himself. "I want my child to be recognized as mine. You had the perfect chance to do that at your press statement. You didn't. So now we will do it my way."

Diego let his fingers linger around Kim's as she stepped out of the limo and joined him on the red carpet in front of the New York Plaza.

He felt her fingers stiffen in his, her body already taut as a tightly wound spring.

For a minute everything around him, all the ruckus, faded away as he let himself indulge in the gloriously sensuous figure she made by his side.

The cream-colored dress drew a straight line, covering her breasts, but it was the sexiest sight he had ever seen. His fingers fanned out of their own volition over her back. The cut of the dress was such that it didn't begin again until the upper curve of her buttock.

Everything in him that was barely restrained roared at the silky feel of her skin.

Desire was a hard knot in his belly, messing with his thinking. As it had been in the limo. It was hard enough to resist her when she dressed in trousers and jackets, even though they didn't hide the sensuality of the woman beneath.

At least *he* had never been able to buy into the frosty business façade. Maybe because he knew the passion that lurked beneath her composed, perfect exterior.

But dressed as she was now, every curve and dip delineated so sexily, her long legs in those heels… He had a better chance of stopping breathing than controlling his hunger for her.

Her wrap slipped and a creamy shoulder glistened in the camera flashlights. A simple chain with a teardrop diamond pendant glittered at the juncture of her breasts. He swallowed, heat flexing in his muscles, pumping him for action, and pulled his gaze away.

A roar erupted around them as they turned together and mounted the carpeted steps. Flashes exploded in their faces, a frenzy of questions in the air around them.

Her press statement about a new investor for her company, against all the odds, had been sensational enough. The fact that it was him hadn't gone unnoticed by the media.

But of course she hadn't answered their questions. Which meant the task was left to him. More fool him that he had believed even for a minute she would do the right thing. That she would give him what he deserved without him having to fight for it.

It was good that he'd fought his whole life for every little thing—from the roof over his head, to every single morsel of food.

He had fought for his mother, he had fought for himself, and now he would fight for his unborn child.

He tightened his grip around Kim as she faltered, her mouth stiff with the smile she'd pasted on, her chin tilted high. It was but a momentary fracture in her perfection, not noticed by anyone but him.

The media were like bloodhounds after her, rejoicing in even a little crack in the pedestal of perfection that Kimberly Stanton stood on.

Nothing would give him more satisfaction than fracturing that pedestal, breaking the woman, so that all of her was undone at his hands. Except it would require a price from him, too, a piece of his soul, and he was damned if he'd let her take anything more from him.

"Ms. Stanton, is it true that you were still married when you were engaged to your twin's husband?"

"Who is the father of your child?"

"Are you seeing Mr. Pereira now?"

Diego heard her startled gasp amidst the rumble and forced her to stop beside him. Had she not expected this? Had she no idea how hungry the media was for a story—*any story*—about her?

He leaned over the thick rope that contained the press, toward the microphones thrust into his face. "It is Mrs. Pereira," he said, and paused, waiting for his words to sink in. He turned toward Kim and smiled. He bent and kissed her cheek. The shock in her gaze was visible only to him.

The softness of her skin burned an imprint on his mouth and he turned toward the flashing cameras again. "And we're very happy to begin our life together again, with our baby on the way."

The crowd went ballistic. He hadn't expected any less.

"You guys are married?"

"Reunited after six years."

He pulled her tighter toward him, every action hungrily raked over by the crowd. She felt like a ticking bomb that could go off at any minute.

"My wife realized her mistake and came back to me on the eve of her wedding."

"You are happy to be together?"

"Incredibly happy," he said, tongue in cheek. "Like we've never been apart."

Kim turned to him, her face devoid of any color. "You bastard," she hissed at him.

He deftly pulled her away from the uproar his statement had caused, dark satisfaction heating his blood. His arms around her slender waist were literally keeping her upright as he and his wife climbed the stairs.

An incredible high buzzed through his veins. Possessive triumph sang in his blood.

His wife.

He had waited for this moment for a long time. To be able to shout to the world that Kim was his wife and have her accept it.

The fact that he had arrived at it through foul means and six years late didn't diminish his victory one bit.

He'd learned a long time ago that playing fair would give him nothing but a bruised body and a broken heart.

CHAPTER FIVE

IT WAS THE worst evening of Kim's life.

It shouldn't have been.

The awards ceremony was being held in the huge banquet hall at the Plaza, the food was delicious and she was rubbing shoulders with great business minds.

Yet in between avoiding Liv's curious gaze, fielding congratulations from her peers, which were *not* over her being chosen for the prestigious award, Kim had never wanted to escape more.

She had realized two minutes after they had walked in that Diego's infuriating statement to the press had given new meaning to the term fairy-tale ending. It wasn't enough that the incredible mockery of his statement—something she would have cherished in an alternative life—haunted her, pricked her.

With the news of his two-million-dollar investment in her company coupled with his revelation that he was the father of her child *and* that they were married, he'd suddenly become her knight in shining armor.

No matter that the same crowd—the same media—had called him a monster just days ago, for his predatory tactics when it came to new businesses, for the way he had recently used a man's gambling losses to take ownership of an island off of Brazil's coast. An ecological paradise, no less, which he was allegedly going to mine and destroy for its precious metals.

Her mouth hurt from the contented smile she forced to her lips as more people congratulated her for the fact that she had landed on her feet with Diego.

She didn't know what infuriated her more—Diego's charming smiles and the intimate glances he threw her way in the face of everyone's prurient curiosity about them, or the educated crowd's insulting joy that she finally had her act together.

As if Diego's very presence in her life could somehow make her brain work better. She laughed at the irony of it.

By the time the awards presentation was over and her speech delivered—which had left a sour taste in her mouth—all she wanted was to escape the crowd, sink into her marble bathtub and lose her mind in a crossword puzzle.

But her torment was nowhere near over yet.

His grip on her wrist unyielding, Diego pulled her onto the dance floor. His hands around her waist, he enveloped her in a hard wall of heat until he filled her vision and the invigorating scent of him was all she could breathe.

He had held her at arm's length ever since she had blurted out the news of her pregnancy. The sudden intimacy of his embrace now toppled her equilibrium, and her flesh sighed against his hardness.

Her skin tingled when his callused fingers moved over her back at images and sensations she'd rather not remember: the feel of those calluses on the sensitive skin of her thighs, the muscles in his back bunching under her fingers... Her body reveled in the memories his nearness evoked.

She sucked in a sharp breath, willing herself not to melt into his arms, not to enjoy it so much. Because all this was for show. He was playing to the media, leaving no doubt in anyone's mind about them, leaving her no way out.

At least no way out with her life still intact.

He studied her, curious amusement playing on his mouth. "You're not enjoying the evening?"

She pulled her head back and glared at him. "I've never been more disappointed in my entire life. I'm the same person with the same faculties I had yesterday. And yet *you* get lauded for sweeping me off my feet."

A smile curved his lush mouth, and infuriated her further.

"You weren't this upset even when I trapped you at the island."

"I don't like being thought an incompetent idiot," she said, gritting her teeth.

His mouth narrowed with displeasure. "You mean you don't like even the *illusion* that you're in love? You have your investment, your company's reputation is intact and you have my total support with the pregnancy. I don't see what's bothering you so much."

Put like that, she sounded the very epitome of selfishness. But she couldn't quiet the increasing panic that things were slowly but surely slipping out of her control. That Diego was stripping away everything she needed to survive. Whatever his intentions, the truth was that he would bring her down to her knees, plunge her into the same whirlpool of crippling hope, if she wasn't on guard.

"There's no need for this pretense that we're living a happily-ever-after. As if this is *Romeo and Juliet Reunited*."

"No? Have you thought of how this might have affected your sister and her life? Being continually mobbed by the media speculating on how she felt about her sister carrying her husband's child?"

Her mouth fell open. "Liv always knew the truth."

"Does it mean it doesn't bother her? Hurt her? Cast a dirty shadow on her marriage? What about Alexander King? You went straight to him for help, and you claim guilt for having deceived him, but did you think for a minute what this twisted speculation might do to him? Do you care that you've asked them to pay a high price just because it raises your hackles to be tied to me?

Shame flooded her within, and her gaze wavered away from him. God, every word out of his mouth was true. She had been avoiding Liv, worried she would know that Kim was barely keeping it together.

"Did you give a moment's thought to me? Or have you, in your usual selfish fashion, neglected to think of anyone else but you?"

"How would I know how you felt about this? Until a couple of hours ago I didn't know how cruelly your father had treated you, or how your mother died. You never told me anything. Once we were off that ship you kept me in a bubble, as if…" She met his gaze, the disbelief spiking there halting her words.

But would she have behaved differently even if she had known?

He frowned, and she had a feeling he was thinking the same.

"The truth is that it scrapes at you that you're not able to reduce this pregnancy and my involvement in it into something tangible." Frustration glimmered in his gaze. "Anything that makes an average woman happy breaks *you* out in hives."

"Your fault if you thought me average."

"No, I didn't think you average—or this warped either. You cover it all up with your perfection."

She mocked a pout, her heart crawling into her throat. Only Diego could reach the horrific truth with a few careless words. The muscles in her face hurt with the effort to keep the smile intact, even though inside everything had crumbled under his attack.

But she couldn't let him or their marriage mean anything

to her. He had already proved her worst fear true once. If she let her guard down, if she let herself care, she would just break this time. "Does that mean you don't want a perfect wife anymore?"

His fingers tightened over her hipbones, a fierce scowl bunching his forehead. "You're the one obsessed with perfection. Not me. And I never wanted a perfect wife either."

"You mean *now?*"

"What?"

"Now that you've achieved all this status, this wealth, now that you've proved yourself to your father and the whole world, you don't need a trophy wife for an accessory *now.* Not like you did six years ago."

His hand stole up her back, his fingers curling possessively around her nape. Her skin seared as though branded. The entire world around them fell away in that moment. As did the veneer of his sophistication. A curse fell from his lips and she colored. Even her little grasp of Portuguese was enough for her to understand.

"You don't want to wear my ring. You didn't want to acknowledge the baby as mine. However much I want to give this marriage a try, you're determined to make this warfare. Maybe working sixteen-hour days with no social life is beginning to fry your brain and corrupt your memories."

He whispered in her ear. It was a low growl, every word pulsing with the slow burn of his anger.

"Because I was not the one that walked away. You knew when you married me what I came from. When we got off the cruise, when the dirty reality of my roots, my life, began to creep in, you didn't want me anymore. So don't you *dare* blame me for the past."

Diego set Kim away from him, his muscles pumping with furious energy. He needed to walk away right that moment, before he did something stupid.

Like kissing her senseless or driving his fist into the nearest wall.

This was the woman who had looked back at him calmly after he'd slept with her and then discarded her as if she was garbage. This was the woman who had then quietly slunk back to her life, to her waiting fiancé, calmly dismissed any thought of him and gone on with her life.

Nothing touched her—not the fact that he was back, not the fact that she was carrying his child. How many times did he need to learn the same lesson?

How *dared* she place the blame for their failed marriage at his feet?

And yet he could swear he had seen sadness lurking in her eyes as she had called herself a trophy wife, felt her shiver as if her words were leaching out the warmth.

He was about to walk out of the hall, away from the crowd, when someone tapped him on the shoulder. He turned around, his control razor-thin.

Beautiful brown eyes—open, smiling, similar to Kim's and yet so different—greeted him. *Olivia King.*

She wore a red knee-length dress. A ruby pendant hung at her neck. Where Kim's hair was cut into a sophisticated blunt style, Olivia's hair was long and curly and wild. There was nothing drastically different from the way Kim was dressed, especially tonight in a dress uncharacteristic of her. And there was the same sensuous vitality to Olivia that was muted but so much more appealing in Kim.

"Hello, Diego," she said, with very little hesitation in her expression.

He raised a brow at her familiarity. She waved a hand at him and moved closer. The gesture, her very movement, lacked the grace and the innate poise he expected from that face. It stunned him into a moment's silence.

"Sorry to be crowding you on the dance floor like this, but I have to take my chance now. You're the father of my niece or nephew—" a smile split her mouth "—and I only have a few moments before Alexander chews my head off for butting in."

His anger thawing, Diego took the hand she offered boldly.

Where Kim wore her sophistication, her brilliance, like an armor that no one could pierce, Olivia's irreverence, her open smile, was the pull. Her emotions were right there in her smiling gaze.

A man wouldn't look into those eyes and wonder if she was his salvation or his purgatory. He wouldn't have to spend a lifetime wondering if he was banging his head against a rock.

They looked exactly the same and yet were so different. He found it highly disconcerting and illuminating. Because he didn't feel the least bit of attraction toward her.

He frowned. "A chance at what, Mrs. King?"

Her gaze twinkled. "Call me Liv. My chance to talk to you. Everyone's talking about your statement to the press, and Kim hasn't been very…forthcoming about you."

"No?" Just like that his ire rose again. "Let's just say I'm your perfect sister's dirty little secret."

His gaze sought the woman in question and found her immediately. Kim was standing at a table, talking to Alexander.

They were peas in a pod, those two. So similar in everything. And yet Alexander King had walked away from Kim, entrenched himself in scandal for Olivia.

"Which you've made sure is not a secret or dirty anymore," Olivia said, with the initial warmth fleeing from her words.

He flicked his gaze back to her. "Waiting for your sister to do the right thing was a futile exercise."

A little frown appeared in her brow. "My sister…" She

hesitated, as though choosing her words carefully. "She's always kept her feelings and her fears to herself."

"You mean she *has* any under that brilliance?"

Her brow furrowing, Olivia continued, "Kim always had to be the strong one—for my mother and for me. It was the only way to survive—the only way she could protect me."

"From whom?" he said, before he could stop himself. He rubbed his nape, feeling tension curl into his muscles. Damn his wife and his ever-spiraling curiosity about her. "You know what? All I care about is that she does the right thing by my child."

He couldn't keep his resentment out of his words.

Olivia nodded. "Look, all I wanted to say was that I'm glad you and Kim are working things out."

"Do you know, if looks could kill, I would have died a few times from your husband's wrath in the past few minutes?"

She glanced to where they stood—her husband and his wife. "Please ignore Alexander." She bent toward him, and though she stood at a perfectly respectable distance to someone standing on the other side of the room, it looked as though she was too close to Diego. "He's a bit possessive when it comes to me."

She had sidled closer to him just to get a rise out of her husband. On cue, the frown on the other man's brow deepened across the banquet hall. Diego smiled despite everything. "He doesn't like me very much."

She smiled. "My husband has a very rigid sense of right and wrong."

"*Really?* And yet he carried on with you while pretending to be married to her? Traded her for you without a moment's—?"

Her gaze flashed with anger. "Alexander and Kim—what they shared was not a real relationship. Even before she knew about us, after her time with you on the island, she broke it off with him. I mean, they never even—"

Kim had broken it off with Alexander? When? He felt as though he'd had his breath knocked out of him. "Never even what, Olivia?"

Olivia's look was more calculated now, gauging if he was trustworthy. "Did you mean what you said to the press? About a new beginning with Kim?"

"Yes."

"Alexander and Kim never had a physical relationship."

Diego felt as if a curtain was falling away from his eyes. Primal satisfaction filled his veins even as he wondered why his perfect wife would hide something like that from him. Especially when he had accused her of being unemotional and unaffected by how easily she had gone back to Alexander.

But of course Kim offered nothing of herself. Truth or anything else. Frustration erupted through him.

True, he had given her the perfect reason to believe him the enemy. And that had to change if their marriage had a chance of being anything but a battleground.

He looked up at Olivia just as she stiffened next to him. Within seconds the color fled from her animated face and her gaze was stricken with fear. Diego turned to see where her gaze was trained.

Their father, Jeremiah Stanton, was shaking hands with someone.

His gaze instantly zeroing on his wife, Alexander cut his way across the crowd toward them, his stride purposeful.

Even Diego felt a flash of anxiety at the fear that filled Olivia's eyes. "Olivia? Are you all right?"

She glanced up at him, her gaze glittering with pain. "Sorry. Old habits die hard." She bent toward him, the very picture of anxiety. "You have to find Kim immediately— okay?"

"What are you talking about?"

"My father," she said, glancing at him and turning away quickly. "I know his wrath when he's displeased better than anyone. He won't like what the media's been saying about her."

"I don't either."

"You don't understand. He will rip into her for this. Whatever issues you have with her, tonight just...just take care of her."

Her muscles quivering, Kim paced the quiet corner of the banquet hall.

Every inch of her wanted to confront Diego, challenge every arrogant word he had uttered about six years ago. She could take anything he tossed at her—his tactics to control her company, his manipulations. But she couldn't stand his latest accusations. His background had never bothered her—not then, not now. As if she had *ever* assumed that she was better than him, as if she hadn't given it *everything* she had in her—until he had turned her into his prize trophy.

She turned toward the banquet hall, determined to have it out with him right there. And then she saw her father at the edge of the crowd, walking toward her, wearing the fiercest scowl she had ever seen.

With her father being out of country for the past month she had almost forgotten about him. They hadn't had their twice-weekly lunch, and of course he had only flown in today. Which meant this was the first he'd be hearing about everything.

She smiled as he neared her, a feeling of failure threading through her. She ran a hand over her stomach, unable to stop herself. Anger fell off him in dark waves. Which wasn't unusual—except before it had always been targeted at Liv.

She bent her cheek toward him as she always did, but he

didn't kiss it. Straightening up, she met his gaze. The fury pulsing in it curled into dread in her stomach.

"Have you lost your goddamned mind, Kimberly?" His words were low and yet his wrath was a tangible thing around them. "I'm gone for a month and not only have you screwed up your life, but your company too?"

She drew a sharp breath in. "Dad, I understand how awful this must sound to you, but I'm trying my best to control the damage. I'm so sorry you had to hear about it like this."

"Are you? Wherever I turn I'm smacked in the face with news that both my daughters are indiscriminate…" His gaze flicked to her. "Are you really no better than Olivia?"

She shook her head, hating the disappointment in his words. "For the last time—Liv did nothing wrong. And, yes, I know that I've messed up, but the truth is that I—"

"Unless you can tell me that everything I've heard so far is false there's nothing you can say."

His gaze flayed her, eroding her already thin composure.

"You run away from your wedding, you get yourself pregnant by God-knows-who… After everything I taught you you've proved that you're no better than the trash your mother was. These are *not* the actions of the daughter I raised—the daughter I've always been proud of."

Her heart sinking to her feet, Kim clutched at his hands. She was *not* like her mother. She was *not* weak. "He's not just someone I picked up, Dad," she said, for the first time acknowledging that very fact to herself, too. She had walked away from the hurt Diego had caused her six years ago, given up on a foolish dream, but it didn't mean she was impervious to his sudden reappearance in her life.

"Is it true, then?"

"What?"

"You married him six years ago? He's the father of your…*child?*"

She nodded. "Diego is the baby's father. And, yes, our marriage is valid."

"Then you'd better work it out with him and clean up this mess. The last thing I want is a bastard grandchild."

She flinched at his cutting words. "I will, Dad. I promise. Will I see you—?"

He shook his head, his denial absolute. "Don't call me until you've kept yourself out of the news for a while. And if you can't clean it up you're just as dead to me as your sister is."

Nodding, Kim sagged against the wall as he walked away without a backward glance. She exhaled a long breath, tears prickling behind her eyes. It had to be the damned hormones again. Because her father's reaction should not be a surprise. She had seen it enough times with Liv.

She had let so many people down recently—Liv, Alex, her father *and* herself. Apparently Diego was the only one who didn't care about the consequences. She turned her head and saw him standing there, watching her father go, rage mirrored in his golden gaze.

Diego couldn't believe his own eyes. His ears rang with those softly delivered yet harsh words. It was nothing a father should ever say to his child, and Diego himself had had more than his share of nasty words from his own father.

His temper frayed to the edge. Every inch of him wanted to turn around, find Jeremiah Stanton and pound his fists into the older man.

In another lifetime he wouldn't have given it another thought. He would have worked through his fury the only way he knew how. But he was not that man anymore. He had promised his mother that he would remove the violence that had been part of his life for so long as a member of a street gang.

Even though keeping his promise was the hardest thing at moments like this.

Kim looked frazzled. Her dress had more color than her face. He wrapped a hand around her shoulders and the shocking thing was that she let him. He felt her shiver and a curse fell from his lips. "Are you okay?"

Her brown eyes drank him in silently. The very absence of hurt in them jarred through him. "I'm perfectly fine."

"You were apologizing to him while he uttered the foulest words and yet you flay me for lesser sins?"

He felt her smile against his arm. Holding her like this was pure torture but he couldn't let go.

"That's just the way my father is."

He reared back, frowning. "He laid into you in the middle of a crowd. For what? Because you slept with me? Because you're pregnant? Because you let your control slip for one night? You're twenty-five, you're the CEO of your own company." He frowned as another thought came bursting in. "Are you saying he's always been like this?"

"Yes, but it was usually aimed at my mother and then Liv."

His breath left him in a sharp hiss. "But not you? Ever?"

"I never gave him the chance—never let him find fault with me. I did everything he asked me to and I excelled at it."

"So you're not upset?" he said, disbelief ringing through him.

"I'm upset that I gave him any reason. But you already know that I regret my actions four weeks ago."

"You're *defending* him?"

"My father is responsible for all the success I have achieved. If he hadn't continually pushed me, I would have—I would *be*—nothing. This is his way of warning me to not let it all go down the drain."

"You make one mistake—*if* it can be called that—and he tears you apart? Don't you see—?"

"You're reading too much into this, Diego."

Her mouth was a study in resignation that mocked his anger.

"I've always known that his approval comes with conditions."

"I saw fear in Olivia's eyes. Are you saying he didn't put it there?"

She glanced past him, her gaze riddled with anxiety. "Yes, he did," she said. "Do you know where she is?"

Fisting his hands, Diego reined in another curse. She wasn't upset for herself but for her twin. "Alexander's with her."

"I always tried my best to protect Liv," she said, with a hint of pleading in her tone, as if she needed to explain herself. "The only way to do that was to play peacekeeper by not giving him any more reason to lose it."

Why was it her job to protect Olivia? He kept those words to himself through sheer will. "So of course you had to become everything perfect?"

"Why do you say that like it's a—" she glared at him "—curse? How is he any different from you?"

"Your father is a bully of the worst sort," he said through gritted teeth. "I fought in street-gangs, yes, but I used my fists for survival. If that's what you think about me—"

"No. I didn't mean that you're a bully." She looked at him, her expression pleading. "I meant he's no different from anyone else in his expectations of me. He's just upfront about it. My accomplishments, my capabilities, are the things that draw people to me. Nothing else..." She swallowed, as if she found it hard to speak the words. "It's why you married me six years ago, it's why Alex picked me for his wife and it's what my father's approval of me is based on."

There it was again—that accusation. As though he hadn't...

She swayed and he caught her, questions tumbling through his head.

His throat felt raw at her matter-of-fact admission. But buried beneath it there had been...*hurt.* Her attachment to her company, her isolated lifestyle... Suddenly his perspective shifted, as though he had been looking at her until now through a dirtied window.

"I think I've had enough excitement for the night," she said softly, puncturing his thoughts. Her fingers clasped his arm. "Can we leave?"

He nodded and guided her toward the exit, his palm staying on her back. He couldn't tear his gaze from her, however.

She looked breathtakingly beautiful, every curve and dip of her sexy body outlined in that damned dress, every step she took grace embodied.

Whether it was her disconcerting statement, or the weary look in her eyes, he didn't see the aggravatingly prickly woman she had become.

Instead she reminded him of the night he had met her, on the cruise ship six years ago. The memory stole through him like an insidious drug, catching him unawares.

She had been standing alone on the deck, away from the rest of the crowd. Wind had been whipping her hair; her green knee-length dress had been molded against her slender figure.

None of the usual festivities that attracted a nineteen-year-old—dancing or drinking—had grabbed her interest. She had looked utterly alone, heart-wrenchingly alluring, driving every dormant instinct of his to the surface. He had observed her for over an hour before he had approached her.

They had done no more than exchange their names that night, but he had spent over two hours teasing a smile from her. And when she had smiled he had found the most thrilling, satisfying joy in it. He had felt on top of the world.

That was how she looked now.

Infinitely fragile and unraveled, as if the tiniest pressure might splinter her perfection apart. She *was* hurt by her father's outbursts, though for the wrong reasons.

That flash of vulnerability shredded the anger and scorn with which he had covered up his desire. He had only deceived himself that it was all gone. Need and something more sinuous glided through his veins.

He wanted to grab her by those dainty shoulders and shake her until she realized she didn't need her father's approval, conditional or otherwise. He wanted to kiss her just as much as he wanted to provoke her, until her beautiful eyes sparkled with that infuriating combination of logic and desire. But he couldn't—not if he wanted to keep his sanity intact.

He couldn't fight the feeling that he knew very little about the woman he had married six years ago. Her statement that what she'd represented to him was the reason why he had wanted her pricked like a thorn in his side.

What if there was more to why she had left him? Was he culpable too? And, if he was, why didn't the aggravating woman call him on it?

CHAPTER SIX

KIM SLID FROM the luxurious bed in Diego's spare bedroom—
or one of the *six* spare bedrooms. She cast a glance toward
the digital alarm clock on the nightstand. It was only five
minutes past seven.

Diego's housekeeper, Anna, had mentioned a pool out
on the terrace. She needed to burn off some of her restless energy.

Walking into the closet, which was the size of her living
room, she searched for her swimsuit. By the time Kim had
returned from work the day after she had moved in, Anna
had unpacked everything for her.

Spotting the trendy one-piece she had bought recently,
Kim tugged off her pajamas and tank top.

She knew why she felt so restless. Coordinating her
move into Diego's penthouse to be when he was out of the
country had felt like the best idea. Except now she couldn't
dwell on anything else.

Would he be pleased? What if he had changed his mind?
She had been on tenterhooks for days after the awards ceremony, waiting for him to manipulate something, anything,
in order to get her to move.

But he had surprised her with a strangely disappointing silence.

His words at the awards ceremony wouldn't leave her
alone, though. Neither had she been able to get Liv's face,

when she had waylaid her on the steps of the Plaza, out of her head. Liv had clutched at Kim's hand, concern pinching her mobile mouth.

Her every action, every word, since she had learned of her pregnancy had been directed by the selfish need to protect herself, to make sure she didn't reveal the slightest weakness in front of Diego. She had conveniently pushed Liv away, refused to share anything, uncaring of how worried she might be.

When had she stopped caring about everyone else's feelings along with her own? When had the lines between being strong and selfishness blurred? Would she continue to push Diego away because he was the one man who had the power to hurt her, to drive her to weakness?

Would she do that when she had the child too? Would she put her own well-being first always? Would she put herself before her child as her own mother had done?

The questions had tied her up in knots. So before she lost her nerve and remembered the million reasons why it was a bad idea she had called Anna and informed her she was moving in.

She pulled her robe on and pushed her feet into comfy slippers. It took her a few minutes of walking through the long corridor to reach the lushly carpeted foyer.

She reached the grand salon and sighed. Huge pillars stood in the room, supporting high ceilings. The room could have housed her entire apartment. Pristine white marble floors gleamed beneath her slippered feet, and the glass walls all around offered three-hundred-and-sixty-degree views of midtown Manhattan and the southern end of Central Park.

Contemporary art graced the walls. She smiled as she recognized a couple of artists native to Brazil.

It was the spectacular luxury she had expected from a man with Diego's assets, and yet it was different. There was no ostentation here or anywhere else in the penthouse. Just a quiet, simmering elegance—a flash of bright red here and there, a candid portrait of a street-fighter on the streets of Rio de Janeiro reflecting Diego's passionate nature.

The best feature, however, was that it was so big she needn't ever see Diego unless required.

Feeling a lightness that had been missing for several weeks, she walked through the salon toward the terrace.

She stepped into the covered part of the L-shaped space and a shape emerged from the shadows. She had expected it to be only Anna and her for another night.

A quiet gasp escaping her, she stepped back. A teenager, his bulging biceps inked with elaborate tattoos, one of which looked eerily familiar, met her gaze. Her mouth fell open as he moved toward her and the light from the salon behind her illuminated his face.

The left side of his rugged face was covered in blue and purple bruises. His hair was cropped close to his scalp. A naughty smile split his severely cut mouth, which had blood crusted on it. "You are Diego's wife?"

Between his thick accent and his swollen lip Kim was barely able to understand him. She nodded, a different kind of shiver overtaking her now.

He stepped in front of her when she moved, leaving only just enough space between them. His gaze traveled over her leisurely in a defiant, purposeful scrutiny that she assumed was meant to make her nervous.

With every inch of her headspace taken up by thoughts of Diego, she wasn't.

"I'm Miguel," he said, still sporting that smile, which was just short of lascivious. "If you get...*bored* with Diego..." He finished his sentence with a wink and a subtle thrust of his hips that left no doubt in her mind. "Call me. I will treat you right."

She stood stiffly without blinking. "Nice to meet you,

Miguel," she threw at him, refusing to show how much his presence had spooked her.

She stepped onto the rooftop terrace, her head spinning with questions—which fled her mind at the sight in front of her.

The vast terrace was illuminated with little solar lights lined up against the floor. The rest of the light came from the spectacular skyscrapers of Manhattan around them. The effect was breathtakingly simple and just the peace she wanted.

There was a fire pit with comfy-looking recliners to her left, and a small bar with a glass top. But it was the perimeter of the pool that caught and held her attention.

A hot tub was on one side, with a couple of loungers on the other.

She walked toward the pool like a moth drifting to light—until the splish-splash of long, powerful strokes punctured the silence.

It took her a moment to realize that half the pool stretched past the terrace, overhanging the streets of New York. Her heart thudded like a tribal drumbeat, her gaze searching for the powerful figure in the water.

Not that she needed to see him to know that it was Diego. Only *he* could find swimming in a pool that edged twenty stories into the sky relaxing.

She was about to turn around, ready to flee, when he swam to the edge of the pool facing her and stood.

His wet hair clung to his scalp, outlining the strong angles of his face. Water sluiced enticingly over biceps that flexed while holding him up. His gaze ran over her, sweeping thoroughly from the top of her mussed hair to the opening of her robe and her bare legs. "Is everything okay?"

She folded her arms around her midriff. "Yes, everything's fine. I just…"

"Did you come up for a swim?"

"What? No. I…." She clasped the sash of her robe, moving to the balls of her feet, ready to run.

She sighed. This was her reality now. Seeing Diego in all his glorious forms, apparently counting up her points on his weird reward system for sex. She smiled at the absurdity that she was actually keeping count.

How desperate was she?

"I did come for a swim," she said, trying hard to keep her gaze on his face. And not trail down his wet, sexy body. "But not from my own apartment."

He pushed at the water dripping from his forehead with his hand. His frown grew. "From where, then?"

"Didn't Anna tell you? I moved in when you went to… Well, wherever it is that you went."

Luckily he didn't seem to have noticed the curiosity in her words.

With an agility that was a beauty to watch he pulled himself up in a single movement. And of course he was naked.

She gasped and closed her eyes. But the sight of his chest and midriff, velvet skin rippling over toned muscles, was etched into her mind. A twang shot through to her sex. She squeezed her thighs—which didn't help at all.

The man was knock-your-knees-out-from-under-you sexy. Was it any wonder he'd always been able to scramble her senses as easily as he did?

"You can open your eyes now."

She did.

A white towel was wrapped low on his hips. He walked around the pool, reaching the bar on her right in silence. The muscles in his back moved sinuously as he poured himself a drink and quickly guzzled it down.

A faint hum began thrumming over her skin. Even the thin silk of her robe felt oppressive.

The tattoo on his back, right under his shoulderblades, glimmered under the low lights. A memory rose to the sur-

face, heating her already warm skin. She had traced that
ink with her fingers first and then with her tongue, fascinated by the ripple and play of his muscles at her actions.

Six years on she shivered as sensations from that long-
forgotten night touched her just as powerfully.

She moved without realizing it to where he stood, and
ran a finger over the wing of the eagle.

He jerked, the muscles in his back bunching tight. As if
she had touched him with a hot poker. He faced her before
she could blink, his scowl fierce.

She jerked her hand back. "That tattoo…" She licked
her lips, her cheeks tightening, "That eagle shape… The
teenager I just met—he has—"

Suddenly he was so close that she could smell the scent
of him, see the evening stubble on his jaw, feel the warmth
of his body. His scowl deepened. "Miguel?" He looked
back inside. "Did you run into him? Did he say anything
wrong to you?"

"Not really," she said, hurrying to reassure him. "I just
didn't spot him until he stepped out of the dark. I didn't
know anyone else was here, or that you were back."

His frown grew. He moved away from her, his movements edgy. "Anything more?"

She shook her head belatedly.

Heat unfurled in the pit of her stomach as he turned to
the side, dropped his towel casually and pulled up a pair
of black sweatpants. She caught a glimpse of tight butt and
rock-hard thighs.

Her heart raced. The stretchy fabric of her swimsuit was
chafing everywhere it touched. She needed that swim even
more than before.

He turned around to face her, his expression serious.
With his glorious rippling chest close enough to touch, it
was hard to focus on his face.

"I'll arrange something else for him. He's already upset

Anna in the few hours he's been here. Probably why she forgot to mention you were here. He won't harm you, but I know how nervous you get around people from that background."

Hurt splintered through her, knocking the breath out of her. Maybe it was because she hadn't been prepared to see him tonight. Maybe it was her hormones again. She glared at him, finding it hard to speak. "Did I say that?" Her words rang in the silence. "I wouldn't even have mentioned him if you weren't flashing that tattoo. I knew this was a bad idea. You might have the best intentions, but you'll never—"

"Wait." His long fingers clasped her wrist and pulled her to him.

She fell into him with a soft thump that made her sigh. Her fingers landed on his chest. The thump-thump of his heart was as loud as her own. He was hard and hot and all she wanted to do was curl into him. Even when he flayed her with his words.

She closed her eyes, lacking the strength not to care about his opinion.

"I didn't mean to upset you." He pulled her chin up and she opened her eyes. His hands on her waist were a languid weight, searing her. "This is our home and I want you to feel safe and be happy here."

Something warm and gooey bloomed inside her chest. She took a deep breath as if she could capture it there. A tingling warmth spread through her—something she remembered from the cruise. For the first time in her life she had felt cherished.

His fingers lingered on her cheek. "The last time our marriage fell apart it was just us." Just as easily he took the warmth away. "This time we have someone else to think of... Do you understand?"

She nodded, swallowing her disappointment. She strove to sound just as casual as he did. "It doesn't bother me. This place is so huge anyway I don't have to even see you if I don't want to, right?" His expression didn't relax. "And… thanks for thinking of me."

He was right. This wasn't about what either of them wanted.

At his quick nod, she grabbed his wrist. The hair on his forearms tickled her fingers. "I appreciate your support since I…since we found out about the—" she needed to stop choking on the word *baby* "—the pregnancy. You've been…great about it, and I…well, I haven't."

His gaze moved to her mouth and lingered. The need to feel his mouth on hers, the need to touch him, rose inside her.

It wasn't the blaze of lust that had driven reason from her head a few weeks ago. Now it was more of a slow, soft burn that always smoldered beneath her skin. It was an insidious longing more dangerous than pure lust.

He extracted his hand from hers as though he couldn't wait to get away. Her heart sinking to her toes, she suddenly realized she wanted his company. Just for a few more minutes. Even if it meant prolonging her own torment.

So she said the first thing that popped into her head. "What happened to Miguel's face?"

He stopped and turned around, surprise flickering in his gaze. Was her interest in the teenager, in what went on in Diego's life, so shocking? *Really,* she wasn't the one with corrupt memories of their short marriage.

"It was his initiation into a street-gang last week. With everything else going on I wasn't able to stop it."

Because he had been dealing with *her.* "He's got the same tattoo as you do. Is it the same street-gang you were a part of?"

For a second the same sensuous memory of that long-ago night flared in his gaze, the pupils turning molten gold. "Yes," he said, in that clipped *whatever* tone of voice.

Turning away from her, he grabbed a white tee shirt and pulled it on. It was a silent version of *show over, move on.*

Something within her rebelled. His calm dismissal was beginning to annoy the hell out of her. Before he could walk away she moved closer to him, effectively blocking him.

"So you got him out of the street-gang?"

"Yes—kicking and screaming."

"He didn't want to come with you?"

He shook his head. "What I forced him to leave behind is the only life he knows. And I need to keep an eye on him. Like I said, he won't harm you. But he's got a grudge against me."

She slid to a lounger and crossed her legs. "Now it all makes sense."

He plunked down on the one next to her. "What do you mean?"

She felt him still and hid a smile. Perverse satisfaction filled her. He wasn't as unaffected by their situation as he made out. "Of course at first I thought it was…you know…the appeal of the *sexy older woman* and all," she said, tongue-in-cheek. She was rewarded by his begrudging grunt. "But now I see it was partly to get back at you. Although I have to admit even with half his face covered in bruises he's quite the looker. He made me a very interesting offer."

He pounced on her like a predator on his prey. One minute they were sitting on two separate loungers, the next he was on hers, his muscular thighs on either side of her, trapping her neatly. His broad shoulders filled up her vision. The very air she breathed was filled with the scent of him.

"You said he didn't say anything." His words were a low growl.

"I meant he didn't say anything threatening."

"What *did* he say to you?"

Diego had been like this with her before, too. And, for

all the time she had spent learning to be self-sufficient, his protective attitude had had her melting like butter under the sun. She smiled, just enjoying the moment. "Stop acting all grouchy caveman over the fact that he talked to me and I will tell you."

Diego closed his eyes, gripped the edge of the lounger and counted to ten. On two he remembered her laughing face. Five—her long, bare, toned legs. On eight the silk robe clinging to her skin, ending several inches above her knees. The luscious picture she made was etched onto his retinas.

Meu Deus, the temptation she presented—walking around his home, making his space her own—was more than he could handle tonight. Even though it was exactly what he had asked her to do.

His trip to Rio de Janeiro, seeing his half brother in the clinic—just a shell remaining of the boy he had once been—it beat down on him like a relentless wave determined to drown him. He knew what to expect, and yet every time the sight of Eduardo kicked him in the gut.

Now he had Miguel to contend with, too. He really couldn't afford to make mistakes in handling the teenager.

And throw in his enticingly sexy wife—parading in a swimsuit, no less—he knew where he would slip up.

He must have truly misplaced his marbles to have suggested that she move in, to think that he could keep his libido in check with her under the same roof.

He would see her in the mornings, all mussed up and unraveled, the way he liked her best. And before he went to bed. The sensuous scent of the woman would be absorbed into every inch of his living space. He hoped his child appreciated the torture he was going through for his or her sake.

"Diego?"

Her voice in front of him was tentative, testing, her fingers on his infinitely tempting. He swallowed a groan. The mischievous note in her voice was gliding like velvet over his skin.

Drawing another bracing breath, he opened his eyes. "Tell me what he said."

"Something about calling him if I ever got bored with you."

"It's not a joke, *gatinha*. Women, like bikes and land, are possessions jealously guarded in that world. Coming onto you is a challenge thrown at *me*."

She frowned, studying him with interest. "But you were from the same background and you never treated me like that. In fact it was the oppo…" Her gaze flickered to him, wary.

Something tightened in his chest. "How *did* I treat you?"

The slender line of her shoulders trembled. "Like I was a princess."

"And yet you…?"

No. He didn't want to turn this into a battle again.

"That was my mother's doing," he said. "Any little good I have in me, she gave it to me. By the time I was ten I had seen how horribly my father treated her, as if life wasn't hard enough for her as a single mother. She would have peeled my hide if I was anything but respectful toward a woman."

Laughter lit up her eyes. "I would have loved to see that."

Her smile wound around him. He couldn't breathe for a second. "And *you*… I could never…"

"What?" She scooted closer and clutched his hands. "Please tell me."

He brought her hand to his mouth and kissed the palm. The scent of her tickled his nostrils. "That cruise… I went on it to amuse Eduardo. You were like this exquisite gift that somehow landed in my lap. That first week I was even afraid to touch you. I was terrified that I would somehow mar you."

She shied her gaze away from him, but not before he saw the incredulous look in her eyes.

"Is that why you took forever to kiss me?" she asked with a laugh.

He didn't buy it. She was struggling under the weight of what he had said. *Why, when she had known how much he had loved her?*

"I mean, I might as well have been wearing a T-shirt that said Take My Virginity that first week."

Laughter barreled out of him. "I don't remember you coming onto me that hard."

"That's not a surprise. Every woman on that cruise ship wanted a bite of the GMM. I had very stiff competition—especially from that hot dancer."

Wasn't *she* full of surprises? "What's GMM?"

A blush dusted her cheeks pink. "Glorious Man Meat."

"Aah…I'm very honored."

"Liv's term. Two minutes after meeting you I finally got what she meant." A naughty smile—a very rare sight—split her mouth. "Though now, what with you all old, out of shape and with this whole daddy-in-the-making thing—" her gaze caressed his body in a swift sweep, belying her words "—I think we can pass the title of GMM on to Miguel," she finished with a dreamy sigh.

The little cat was needling him on purpose. But it was this cheeky, smiling side of her that got to him. He leaned into her and clasped her face with his hands.

Before he could think better of it, he touched his mouth to hers.

The barest of contacts was enough to spread a wildfire of need inside him. With a groan that was torn out of him, he pulled her close and devoured the lushness of her mouth.

Her fingers dug into his arms. She mewled against his

mouth, a sound made deep in her throat that slithered over his skin.

He half dragged her into his lap, his hands spanning her thin waist, seeking and searching the curve of her breasts.

Droga, but she was all soft and warm, the stretchy fabric of her swimsuit no barrier. He closed his hands over her covered breasts, felt the tightened nipples grazing his palms. He rubbed his palms up and down and her mouth opened on a soft moan.

"*Meu Deus,* I touch you and you blow up like TNT…"

He plunged his tongue inside her mouth and licked the inseam. He felt lightheaded with desire, every drop of blood flowing south.

He pressed wet kisses down to her neck—just as the two floodlights on the opposite sides of the terrace came on, drowning them in bright light.

With a gasp, Kim slid off his lap. Her lips were swollen and pink, her hair all mussed up. Their gazes met in silence for a second, before both of them burst out laughing.

"I'm thinking that was Miguel, right?" she said, her smile still in place.

Her taste lingering on his mouth, he nodded. "Sorry."

"No, it's good he stopped us when he did. Of course I *did* earn my kiss, but you don't want to give me too many points."

He raised a brow.

A teasing glint appeared in her eyes. "Remember? Sexual points for good behavior? You kissed me because I moved in, right? Like a dutiful little wife? Or was that just you forgetting your own—?"

He made a quick lunge to catch her, but she was too fast this time. With lithe grace she moved to the other side of the lounger. Her robe half dangled around her elbows, giving him a perfect view of her swimsuit-clad body.

Holding his stomach tight, he sucked in a sharp breath. His wife was hot. There was no other word for it.

Like everything else she wore, the swimsuit was modest, a one-piece in hot pink. But it showcased the swell of her high breasts, the dip of her dainty waist…which would soon be rounded…the slight flare of her hips and long legs that went on forever. The memory of how she had wrapped them around him while he had thrust into her, her tight heat clenching him. He was rock-hard just thinking about it.

Which meant it was time to walk away, however painful the simple act was.

She tied the sash on her robe, stepping back as he reached her. He raised his hands. "Stay and have your swim," he said. "I need to have a talk with Miguel anyway."

She waylaid him again. If she kept touching him like that, one of these days he wasn't going to be able to walk away. "I forgot to ask—how is Eduardo?"

Just hearing his half brother's name felt as if someone had stuck a knife in his side. He stilled, the ball of guilt around his neck threatening to choke the life out of him. He had lived through busted kneecaps, broken bones and so much more, but this clawing, crippling guilt—it was going to gouge him alive from inside out.

"I'm surprised he's not still following you around. He worshipped you."

Every word out of her mouth was true, and every single word dug into his skin like the sharp end of a knife.

"Diego?"

He jerked back from her. "He's in a rehabilitation clinic in Sao Paulo."

"What? Why?"

Eduardo was the best kind of reminder as to how far Diego could go when he was obsessed with something—when he let something he wanted have control over him.

Then, it had been pursuit of his wealth. Now it could be the woman in front of him, waiting for an answer.

"He's receiving treatment for a cocaine addiction."

"Eduardo used cocaine? But he used to be so… That's awful. He was always so sweet and kind to me."

Kind and sweet. They were the perfect words to describe Eduardo.

Fisting his hands, Diego rocked on his heels, bile filling his throat.

His half brother had been a nice kid, weak at heart, forever bullied by the man who had fathered them—which Diego had learned too late. Diego should have protected him. Instead Diego had been the one who nudged him that last step toward his own self-destruction.

But he wouldn't give up. He would never give up on him. If Eduardo didn't have the will to fight for his life anymore Diego would fight for him. He would use every cent he had, would wield all his power, if it meant he could get his half brother back.

CHAPTER SEVEN

KIM SCRUNCHED HER eyes closed and tried to recall all the literature she had been reading over the past month. With little Jennie wailing in her arms and that image from her afternoon appointment flashing before her eyes it was all a blur. *There were two. She wasn't even equipped for one.*

Telling Laura, her company's design architect, that she would look after little Jennie for a couple of hours had seemed like a good idea. She had been reading all about how to take care of a baby for almost a month. So of course she was ready for a ground test, right?

Wrong.

Sweat beaded her brow. Her arms were starting to ache a little bit.

She bent her knees and picked up the cheat sheet she had made out of Laura's instructions, even though she knew them by heart.

She had warmed the pumped milk to precisely the exact temperature, tested it on her wrist, had fed Jennie and even tried to burp her. And then she'd put her down for a nap. Not a minute early or late.

The nap had lasted ten minutes, ending in a loud wail. According to Laura's schedule Jennie should have napped for at least an hour.

Tucking the baby tighter against her chest, she swung a little from side to side, imitating what she had seen Laura do when she had brought the baby to the company's premises a couple of times.

Her chubby cheeks scrunched up tight, Jennie wailed louder. The muscles in Kim's arms quivered until she shook all over. Even her head was beginning to pound now.

She increased the pace of her walk, tension tugging her skin tight. She should call Laura and take Jennie back to her. Every hysterical inch of her wanted to. *Will you desert your child when it gets hard?* the annoyingly logical part of her asked.

No, she couldn't accept failure—yet.

She heard the door open and turned around. Why hadn't she thought of Anna?

Diego stood in the doorway, frowning.

Her heart sank to her feet, dismay making her weak-kneed.

His gaze amused, he checked his watch.

"Was I gone *that* long?"

"You said you were going to Sao Paulo."

They both spoke at the same time.

His mouth tightened. As it did every time their conversation skated anywhere near Eduardo. "My trip got postponed."

Her shoulders felt as if there were metal rods tied to them, crushing her with their weight. The last thing she needed was for Diego to see her abysmal failure.

"What's with the baby?"

"She's—"

"Laura's. I know. She had her with her last week."

She nodded, insecurities sawing at her throat. Of course he remembered Jennie from that one visit—while Kim had always scrambled even to remember her name.

He had picked her up one evening last week from work—a strangely domestic but comforting gesture—and she had been forced to introduce her staff to him. All forty of them—from their sixty-year-old office manager Karen to nineteen-year-old intern Amy—had mooned over him. *And* informed her with a sigh the next morning that they understood her actions perfectly.

"Kim?"

She sighed. Jennie's little mewls were picking up volume again. "I offered to look after her for a few hours."

A single eyebrow shot into his hairline. "Why?"

She raised her voice to be heard over the infant's cries. "I decided to take myself on a test drive, and Laura's the only one with a baby."

"You're *practicing* because you're pregnant?"

"Something like that."

"Isn't that a little extreme?"

"I believe in being prepared."

"Prepared for what?"

She pushed her hair out of her face with her free hand, trying to ignore his gaze drilling into her.

"I...I don't know what's wrong with her. She won't calm down." Hitching Jennie up with her one hand, she wiped her forehead. "I've fed her, changed her and tried to burp her. I'm running out of ideas except to take her back."

She looked around the cozy sitting area she had taken over for the evening, taking in the untouched protein shake, the dirty diaper on the rug, Jennie's blanket trailing over the edge of the designer leather couch...

But it was the clawing urge to take Jennie back to Laura and pretend the evening had never happened that gutted her.

Tears burned in the back of her throat, gathering momentum like a storm.

Dear God, how was she...?

Diego's hard frame in front of her pulled her to a stop.

Jennie's wails were becoming incessant, her little face scrunched up tight. Kim's heart sank to the floor. She was ready to bawl her *own* eyes out.

She raised her gaze to Diego, her neck stiff, her forearms strained to the point of shaking. "She won't stop crying, Diego."

He took Jennie from her, his movements infinitely gentle. The little girl fit on his forearm with room to spare.

Kim's heart lurched into her throat.

With curious ease he held Jennie high in the cradle of his arms, her pink dress contrasting against his rough, large hands. "Might be because you're holding her too tight and she can feel your tension."

"That's not true. She was crying long before I picked her up…"

The infant immediately stopped crying, as though confirming Diego's statement. He swung the cradle of his arms left to right, gently, his gaze never moving from Jennie.

Kim froze as he cooed to her. It was the most wonderful sight she had ever seen.

"Babies are very sensitive to our own moods and personalities."

His soft words landed like a slap on her. "What the hell does *that* mean?"

The look he threw her, puzzled and doubting, pierced through the last shred of her composure.

"It means that she can sense that you're nervous—*wound up*." His gaze drilled into her. "*Overwrought, stressed out…* do you want me to go on? What *you* feel is setting *her* off. If you just—"

"I get it—okay!" she said, practically shouting.

Every muscle in her trembled, and her chest was so tight that it was an effort to breathe. As long as it had just been in her head it had still been bearable. Given voice like that, it tore through her.

"She can sense that I don't care, that I want to be doing anything but looking after her. That's it, right?"

* * *

Diego lowered the sleeping infant into the tiny bassinet and tucked her in tight. The little girl settled in without a whisper, and he rubbed his thumb over a plump cheek.

A soft, sleepy gurgle erupted from the baby's tiny mouth.

Whatever his past sins, the new life that was coming was a precious gift. If only he could figure out what was worrying Kim.

Familiar frustration spiked through him. The past few weeks they had fallen into a somewhat torturous routine of sorts. With each passing day and every single minute they spent in each other's company—and this was with both of them avidly trying to keep it to a minimum—he had realized how hard it was to keep his hands to himself. Especially when he had begun to see glimpses of the girl he had fallen in love with so long ago.

She still hadn't cut down her work hours, but she *had* spent the last Sunday home watching a soccer game with him and Miguel. Who, interestingly, had said more to her than he had to Diego.

He might even say she was slowly letting her guard down with him. Except when Anna or he brought up the pregnancy.

Then she immediately retreated behind that shell of hers. She refused to share what was on her mind. And yet more than once he had seen her reading articles on motherhood on her tablet, lost in deep thought.

And tonight she had borrowed a baby. Because she had known he would be out for the night.

Foreboding inched across his skin. Once he had been too involved in his own world and had neglected Eduardo when he had needed him. He wasn't going to make the same mistake again. He was going to get to the root of what was bothering her tonight.

He eyed her across the room. She was plumping the

same pillow on the couch, her shoulders stiff with tension, her punches into it increasing steadily, until her jabs were vicious and accompanied by soft grunts.

He reached her quickly, meaning to catch her before she buried whatever was troubling her under grating self-sufficiency. With a hand on her shoulder, he turned her around. "If you're imagining that to be my face," he said, "let me…"

She let him look at her for only a second before she pushed away from him. But what he had seen in that second was enough to stun Diego.

Tears filled her huge brown eyes.

His breath felt as if it had been knocked out of him—as if someone had clocked his jaw. He had never seen her tears. Not when he had humiliated her, not when he had threatened her company, not even when her father had shredded her.

With an arm thrown around her waist he tugged her hard against him and locked her there. She was plastered to him from shoulder to thigh. Her soft flesh shuddered and rearranged itself against him.

"Let me go."

"Shhh…" he whispered near her ear, knowing that she was extra-sensitive to any touch there. "I just want to look at you."

Her hands against his chest, she glared at him, her tears unshed.

Every inch of her was taut, like a tightly wound spring, and a slow tremor was inching through her. Something had shaken her up badly. He tightened his arms around her, waiting for the tremors to pass.

Dark blue shadows danced under her huge eyes. Her hair was not the sleek polished silk that gleamed every time she moved her face in that arrogant, thoroughly sexy way of hers. Instead it curled around her face, lending a false vulnerability to the sharp angles of her face.

But the fact that she was close to exhaustion was written in the dull pallor of her skin, in the pinched look stamped upon her features.

His ire rose to the surface again, and he didn't fool himself that he was worried for his unborn child. The anxiety that he couldn't purge from his system, the anger that had his muscles quivering for action, was all for *her*.

Despite his best intentions he just couldn't *not* care about her.

He moved his hand up from her waist to her nape and dug his fingers into her hair, held her tight.

His grip didn't hurt her. He knew that. But he needed that hold on her for a second—the deceptive illusion of control over her, over her emotions.

Because she reduced him to what he'd been born to.

All the trappings of wealth, all the polish he had acquired in the past six years, fell away, reducing him to what he was at his core. Someone who had been born into the gutter and craved a better life that had remained out of his grasp for so long.

There was always a part of her that remained unreachable, unattainable to him, as though he still didn't make the cut.

He trailed his gaze over her, from the well-worn Harvard T-shirt that hugged her breasts to the low slung sweatpants that left a strip of flesh bare at her midriff.

"You can't stop shivering. You look awful," he said.

Pushing away from him, she glanced down over herself. Distaste marred her brow. "I spent last night at work and I didn't have time for a shower when I came back."

"Aren't you working enough without taking on baby-sitting?"

She glanced at Jennie and trembled again. "I just... I

wanted to see if I could handle her for a few hours." The resigned curve of her mouth tugged at him.

"*Meu Deus,* what is the matter with you?"

Silence.

He frowned, resisting the urge to shake her by her shoulders. He had never seen her so defeated, never heard that self-deprecating tone in her words. He picked her up and settled down into the recliner with her in his lap. The fact that she sagged into him without a protest alarmed the hell out of him.

"You look like you're ready to tip over. Answer my question, *pequena.* What's going on?"

She tucked her knees in closer. Tears rolled over her cheeks. "There are two, Diego."

He raked his mind. "Two... *Two what, gatinha?*"

"Two heartbeats."

He pushed her chin up none too gently. *"What?"*

A shadow descended on her face, her skin a tight mask over the fine bones. "I went to see the doctor today for a routine checkup. She thought it best to do an ultrasound. There are two... Diego, there are twins."

His mouth slack, Diego couldn't believe her words. Incredible joy flushed through him. He was going to be a father to not one but two babies. He had no breath left in him. He felt lightheaded, as if nothing could mar his happiness anymore. He was going to have a family—a proper one—with *two* babies looking to him for everything.

He shivered at the magnitude of what it meant.

It had been a shock when he had first learned of the baby, but now all he felt was exceptionally blessed. As if for the first time in as far as he could remember he had a chance to be something good, to build something good—as if life had finally handed him a good turn.

Gathering Kim tight in his arms, he pressed a kiss to her upturned mouth and tasted her tears.

He pulled back from her, the worry etched into her pinched mouth, the sheer terror in her gaze, puncturing his own joy.

"That's why you brought Jennie over? Why you're practicing?"

He cupped her jaw, forcing her to look at him. His mouth felt dry. Words were hitching in his throat. He palmed her back, up and down, looking for words to do this right.

Because he had never been in this position of offering comfort or strength to her—ever. She had never leaned on him for anything. Her unwavering strength was both incredibly amazing and annoying at the same time.

"This is not something where we practice for perfection, *gatinha*," he said softly, anxious to remove anything negative from his words. "We just try to do our best."

"But that's not enough, is it? Good intentions and effort can't make up for what's missing. You told me once your mother had never been able to scrape enough money to feed you properly, but you didn't care, did you? Because you knew that she loved you."

"As will you love our children. I told you before—we don't have to be perfect parents; we just have to love them enough—"

She fought against his grip again, a whimper escaping her. That pained sound sent a shiver racing up his spine.

"Whatever is paining you, I swear I will help you through it, *gatinha*. Tell me, what is—?"

"I'm not good with babies." Her words sounded as if they were tortured, as if they were ripped from her. "I'll never be, so it's a good thing you're here. Or else our kids might never stop crying—might turn out just like me, hating their mother."

Something squeezed in his chest and he released a hard breath, shoving aside his own conflicted emotions for the minute.

"And the fact that you're exhausted has nothing to do with it?"

She bit her lip. Her uncertainty—something he had never seen—was a shock to his system.

"How do you feel about being a full-time stay-at-home daddy?"

He smiled even as stark fear gripped him. "And what will *you* do?"

"I'll do everything else." She ran her tongue over her lips, her brow tied into that line that it got when she was in full-on thinking mode. "I'll work, I'll clean, I'll cook. I'll even—" She stopped, as though she had just caught on to the desperation in her words. Her tears spilled over from her eyes, her slender shoulders trembling under the weight of perplexing grief. "I don't feel anything, Diego."

His heart stopped for a minute, if that was possible. "What does that mean?"

"For the babies. I don't feel *anything*."

He sucked in a breath, the anguish he spied in her gaze sending waves of powerlessness hurling through him.

"Except this relentless void, there's nothing inside of me when I think of them," she said, rushing over her words as though she couldn't stop them anymore. "I should look forward to it now, at least. I should be used to it by now. At first I thought it was because I was angry with you. Because you were the father. It's not. *It is me.* All I can think is how I wish it was anyone but me. *Every waking moment.* I can't bear to look at myself because I'm afraid I will see changes I don't want to. My team is more excited about this than I am. The ultrasound technician was more excited than I was when we looked at them. *And now there are two.* What if I never feel anything for them? What if all these years of…? What if I never love them? They'll realize that, won't they? God, I would just curl up and die if they—"

"Shh…" Diego swallowed past the tears sawing at his throat and hugged her tight, pouring everything he couldn't say into the embrace. He couldn't bear to see her like this. This pain—her pain—it hammered at him with the quiet efficiency of a hundred blows.

How blithely had he assumed she didn't give a damn about anything but herself? How easily had he let her rejection of him color everything else? How easily had he let his own hangups blind him to her pain?

Her cutting indifference every time she had mentioned the pregnancy had been the perfect cover for this terrifying panic beneath. Regret skewered through him.

He pressed his mouth to her temple and breathed her scent in. He had no idea if it was for his or her benefit. "You built a million-dollar company from nothing but your talent and your hard work. Don't tell me your failure with Jennie tonight means you won't love our children."

Her upper body bowed forward, her forehead coming to rest on his shoulder as though the fight was literally deflating her. "I've spent years cauterizing myself against feeling anything. I think I did it so well that nothing can reach me now."

"That's nonsense." Diego wrapped his hands around her and tucked her closer to him. "You care about your sister. You told me you tried your best to protect her from your father's wrath. I'm sure once the babies come you—"

"I'm the reason Liv suffered so much at my dad's hands. It was my responsibility to protect her. Nothing else."

"What are you talking about?"

"You think you're the only one who has a monopoly on guilt?"

Frustration boiled through Diego as defiance crept back into her tone. Her shields fell back into place, the pain shoved away beneath layers and layers of indifference. His hold over her was just as fleeting as always.

* * *

Feeling Diego stiffen against her, Kim slid out of his reach. Her knees threatened to collapse under her, but anything was better than the cocoon of his embrace.

It had felt so good. The temptation to buy into his words that everything would be fine, the need to dump the bitterest truth in his lap, had been dangerous.

Except she was sure there would be nothing but distaste left on his face if she did that. She would take his anger anytime.

That was what living with him was doing to her—slowly but surely eroding everything she had learned to survive.

"How come you're so good at it?" she threw at him, the pain dulling to a slow ache.

For now there was nothing to do but wait. That was the part that was slowly driving her crazy. There wasn't a way to *make* herself feel. There was no switch to turn it on.

"I'm not. But Marissa always has a baby attached to her hip, and I think I've picked up a thing or two in all these years."

An image of a laughing, petite brunette flashed in front of Kim's eyes. Her mouth burned with the acidic taste of jealousy. Until now she had held on, pretended even to herself that he didn't matter to her, that falling into his bed four weeks ago had been nothing but a mistake.

"Marissa?"

He nodded slowly, a flat, hardened look replacing the tenderness she had seen seconds ago, as though he resented Kim even uttering her name. Not as though. *He hated it.* It was there in the way his stance stiffened, in the way he turned away from her.

"You were...?" Kim swallowed, forcing the lump in her throat down, that acidic taste burning her mouth. "You've been with *her* all these—?"

He shrugged. "Over the years Marissa and I have always

drifted toward each other. In between deserting spouses, deaths and even…" His gaze fell to Jennie and his mouth curved into a little smile. "She's nothing if not maternal."

The last sentence was like driving a knife into her already torn-up gut. "But you're not with her anymore because of me?"

His gaze collided with her. "Because you're pregnant with my child."

Kim flinched.

"When I learned of your wedding I was furious. Marissa didn't like my reaction. She gave me an ultimatum. I had to finish things with you if I wanted a life with her."

"But that means you…" She blinked. "You didn't come to the island to sed…to sleep with me?" She corrected herself at the last minute.

The arrogant resolve in his eyes dissolved and she sucked in a sharp breath.

"No. I wanted to see you one last time, to show you what I had become. To throw the divorce papers in your face and walk away. Instead I saw you and lost my mind again."

Bitter disappointment knuckled her in the gut. How pathetic was it that she felt cheated because Diego hadn't come to find her for some elaborate revenge scheme? That she hadn't merited even that much of his energy?

Exactly as she hadn't with her own mother.

She bit out a laugh. It was either that or dissolve into tears. "And I fell pregnant and ruined your plans…and hers."

He shot up from the couch and materialized in front of her. "It would be so much easier if I could blame you, but we were both there."

"Oh *please*. Will you stop with the whole honorable act? I would much prefer seeing the hatred in your eyes than looking for things that are not there."

"*I* hurt her, Kim. Not you. The one thing she asked of me was to finish things with you. Because of my insane obsession with you, because of my refusal to leave you alone—" every word out of his mouth reverberated with bitter disgust, and the depth of it slammed into her "—I...I broke her heart, and there's no way to fix it. I have to live with that guilt my entire life."

He stepped away from her as though he couldn't bear to be near her now Marissa had been mentioned, as though even looking at her compounded his guilt.

"I'll send Anna down. She will look after Jennie," he said, halting with his hand on the doorhandle. "Make sure you eat something and get some sleep. Think of the babies, if nothing else."

She sank to the couch as he closed the door behind him. She had hated him for setting her up, for ruthlessly walking away, but he had paid the price for their reckless passion just as she had.

She wished with every cell in her being that he was the ruthless man she had thought him. Because the man he was underneath—kind and thoughtful—how was she supposed to resist him?

He could have thrown her ineptitude in her face, laughed at her fears. Wasn't that why she had been stewing in it by herself? But he hadn't.

He had held her, hugged her, tried to make her feel better. He had been genuinely concerned for her. He could make it so easy for her to depend on him, to bask in his concern, to fall deeper and deeper...

That was if she wasn't *already* in exactly the situation she had fought so hard against.

Her legs shook as she hugged herself. She needed Diego in her life. No, she *wanted* Diego in her life. But the gnawing, terrifying truth was that nothing but his honor was keeping him there.

Nothing about *her* was keeping him there.

CHAPTER EIGHT

IT WAS, WITHOUT doubt, a sex party.

Diego had no other name for it. His thoughts had swung from mild curiosity to full-blown agitation when a six-foot bouncer had checked his ID at the entrance and announced that admittance cost ten thousand dollars.

He had spent the better part of the evening trying to find Kim. It was half past ten now, and this was where her colleague had finally directed him to.

The party was in full swing in a two-floor Manhattan loft that had taken him several phone calls to locate. He scowled and moved past a waitress dressed in a French maid's costume serving hors d'oeuvres.

Soft, sultry music streamed through the richly carpeted foyer from cleverly hidden sub-woofers. Pink neon lights strategically placed on the low ceiling bathed the lounge, illuminating the retro-style furniture and a bar. It was very elegantly done, with a high-class Parisian feel to it.

The lower floor was dotted with futons against the retro chic walls, and in the corner a thin, exotically dressed woman was working massage oil into a naked man's back. On the other side of the full bar was a huge dance floor, where at least twenty men and women were softly bumping into one another.

He gritted his teeth and loosened his tie. What the hell was Kim doing *here*? Was this to compensate for the vulnerability she hadn't been able to hide yesterday? Or was it an act of defiance to rile him up because he had organized her day today?

He glanced up the curving staircase toward the more expansive upper floor. Every muscle in him tightened as his gaze fell on more than one couple getting hot and heavy up there, their moans adding to the soulful music downstairs.

A sudden chill hit Diego. Which floor was Kim on?

Running a hand over his nape, he moved toward the dimly lit lounge. He had no idea what he would do if he didn't find her on the lower floor. Already every base instinct in him was riled up at the very fact that she was here, of all places.

If he found her with… No, that thought didn't even bear thinking.

He reached the outer edge of the dance floor, searching for her. He froze at the edge of the crowd as he finally located her. She was right in the center of the crowd, her hands behind her head, moving in perfect rhythm to the music, while a smartly dressed man had his hands around her waist.

His blood roared in his veins. *Mine,* the barely civilized part in him growled.

She was only dancing, he reminded himself, before he gave in to the urge to beat the crap out of the man touching her. A caveman—just as she had called him.

He slowly walked the perimeter of the crowd.

Her eyes closed, her legs bent, she was moving with an irresistible combination of grace and sensuality that lit a fire in his blood. Every muscle in his body tightened with a razor-edged hunger.

Her hair shone like raw silk. Her mouth was painted a vivid dark red, almost black, like nothing he'd ever seen on her before. Usually her lips shimmered with the barest gloss. A black leather dress hugged every inch of her—

cupping her breasts high, barely covering her buttocks. The dress left her shoulders bare, and the exposed curves of her breasts were the sexiest sight he had ever seen.

She'd done the rest of her face differently, too, heavier make-up than he had ever seen. Usually the lack of make-up only served to heighten the no-nonsense, made-of-ice vibe she projected.

It was the opposite today—that outfit, her make-up, everything signaled sexual availability, grabbing attention and keeping it there. Was that why she was here? What had prompted this out-of-character interest in a sex party, of all things?

She looked like his darkest fantasy come true.

Lust knuckled him in the gut. All he wanted to do was pull the dress down until her breasts fell into his hands, past her hips until she was laid bare for him, and then plunge into her until neither of them could catch their breath, until the roar in his blood stopped.

He moved closer to her without blinking, his heart pounding in his ribcage, his skin thrumming with need. Her gaze lit upon him and shock flashed in it. Good—she'd recognized him.

He stepped on the raised platform and roughly collared the guy dancing with her, moved him out of the way. He palmed her face and tilted it up roughly. "Are you high?"

"What?" Even her question sounded uneven. "Of course not."

He sniffed her. Nothing but the erotic scent of her skin met his nostrils. His jeans felt incredibly tight. It was all he could do to stop from pressing into her. If he did, he didn't think he could stop. "Are you drunk?" he said, noting a hoarse note in his own words.

She shook her head, something dangerous inching into her gaze. She ran a hand over her midriff, drawing Diego's gaze to the dress again. "If you're just going to spoil my fun…"

He blocked her as she turned away from him, the forward momentum pushing her breasts to graze against his chest. He clamped his fingers around her arm and tugged her.

She turned to face him. A strip of light illuminated the lush curve of her mouth, leaving the rest of her face in shadow. "What are you doing?"

He bent his head and tugged her lip with his teeth. Molten heat exploded in every nerve. His cock ached hard. Her hissing breath felt like music to his ears. "Taking you home."

She dug her heels in and he loosened his hold. "I'm not ready to leave yet."

"Yes, you are."

To hell with all his rules, and with sanity and with whatever crap he had spun to keep things rational between them.

She was *his*—whether she knew it or not, whether she liked it or not. And not just because she was going to be the mother of his children.

Kim pulled the flaps of Diego's leather jacket tighter around her and stepped out of the limo. A gust of wind barreled into her. She folded her hands against her midriff, her mouth falling open as she realized why the drive from the party had taken so long. Diego had been talking non-stop on his cell phone, effectively silencing any questions she had.

They were at a private airstrip. The ground crew was finishing up its prep, and the aircraft was being revved up. A tremor traveled up and down her spine.

She walked toward Diego, who was still talking on his phone.

His gaze traveled the length of her once again, intractable.

"What's going on?"

He clicked his phone shut. "I have something urgent to take care of."

Her stomach tightened. "So go. I'll even bid you goodbye with a smile."

"You're coming with me. You can laze in a spa, swim in a beach, shop for maternity clothes…among other things."

Her skin sizzled at the double intonation on the last bit.

"Everything you *should* be doing."

Her breath hitched in her throat at the resolve in his gaze. "You like lording it over me, don't you? I'm not going anywhere with you."

He took a step toward her and backed her against the limo. He pulled her hand into his and twined their fingers. She felt his touch to the tip of her toes.

"I was worried about you. I am still. So shut up and accept it."

Her heart thumped inside her ribcage. Gooey warmth flooded through her. No one had ever worried about her. *Ever.* It had been her job to worry for as long as she could remember.

She had worried about her mom first, shielded her from her father. And after she had walked out she had tried her best to protect Liv from her dad's wrath. No one had ever seen past the veneer of her perfection to the emptiness beneath—even Liv, who cared about her….

With his thumb and forefinger he rubbed over her forehead. "Stop thinking so much. You will stay with me so that I can keep an eye on you."

"Why?"

"You didn't seem yourself last night. Or just now."

"Last night I was hormonal. Tonight I'm horny."

Liquid fire blazed in his gaze.

"Those are the only colors on my rainbow lately."

He laughed, the sexy dimple in his cheek winking at her.

"Hormonal and horny women *need* looking after."

It had been a very strange day on so many accounts.

Once the janitor had locked her out of her company's premises she had returned to her apartment, fuming with disbelief. Because for the past six years she had worked every Saturday except the day she had gone to her wedding.

By the time she had finished every last scrap of the delicious sandwich Anna had given her, taking away her laptop in the process, and with her usual intelligence deserting her, Kim had realized too late that everything had been orchestrated by Diego.

Total lack of sleep last night meant she had zonked out for the rest of the day.

"I came to check on you twice and you were sleeping. Anyone with a little sense can see your body needs rest. Why do I have to force you to it?"

She flushed, unbidden warmth spurting in her. He had checked on her. *Twice.* She should resent his high-handed attitude; she should at least offer token resistance. But she couldn't muster a protest past the warm fuzzies filling her up.

When had anyone ever checked on her? This was the same strangely weakening, cared-for sensation that had driven her to marry him six years ago. She had stupidly wanted that feeling to last forever.

"And what were you doing *there,* of all places?"

He sounded so aggravated that she smiled. "I was going crazy after sleeping straight through the day. So I made a list of all the things I need to get ready before the babies come. Then I—"

He tapped her temple with one long finger. "I'm going to cure you of your overthinking if it's the last thing I do."

"Then I got thinking of all the things I won't get to do anymore *when* the babies arrive."

"And going to a sex club was one of them?" His frown deepened into a full-fledged scowl. "What else was on it?"

The flare of interest in his gaze goaded her. Last night had been terrifying on so many levels. Right at that moment she would do anything to see what he felt for her reflected there. Even if it was just lust.

"Sex with a stranger was number two and sex in a public place number three. I thought I could shoot two birds with one—"

He tilted forward, all two hundred pounds of hulking, turned-on, prime male focused on her. A tingle started deep in her lower back and began inching its way all over. Her palms slapped onto his chest as he angled his lower body closer.

"You're pushing me on purpose, *pequena*. Are you ready for the consequences?"

His rock-hard thigh lodged in between her thighs, sparking an ache in that exact spot. A whimper clawing out of her, she pushed at him. The feel of hard muscles and the thundering of his heart under her fingers was just as torturous.

The heat uncoiling in his gaze made mincemeat of her. "Okay, fine. I made that up," she said, cupping his jaw. "I…I didn't know what to do with myself. But if you're going to rearrange my everyday life the least you can do is…"

His gaze locked on her mouth and he relented the pressure of his thigh just a little. "What?"

"Let me enjoy it the way I want to."

"Coward."

A slow smile—one that should come with a health warning—curved his mouth, digging deep grooves into his face. Glorious warmth unraveled inside her. She loved it when he looked at her like that, when he smiled like that. As if she was the only one in the world who could put it there.

It was wishful thinking at best, dangerous indulgence at worst, but she couldn't fight the feeling.

"It kills you to ask, doesn't it? To admit, even if only for a second, you wanted to see me?"

She smiled, incapable of resisting him at that moment. "I did call your secretary. She had no idea when you would be back. So I took Carla's offer."

"The sex expert on your team? Carla was there too?"

She smacked his chest with the back of her hand at the exaggerated interest in his words.

A car pulled up alongside their limo, the headlights illuminating the airstrip.

Miguel stepped out of the dark sedan. He opened the trunk and pulled out a pretty pink suitcase which, even in the low light, looked familiar.

Her jaw hit her chest. "That's mine."

"I had Anna pack some of your things." He nodded at Miguel, who disappeared back into the car without a word to Kim. "Let's go."

He was serious. He was taking her away on a holiday. She shouldn't be so happy about it, but she was. "But I—"

"You're taking a few days off. Do you want to spend it alone? Maybe interview some more nannies? Borrow another baby? Dodge more calls from Olivia?"

Heat tightened her cheeks. She was getting more than a little obsessive in her *Planning for Pregnancy* phase. As if she could somehow make up for lacking the most necessary part of it. And, judging by the way Diego was looking at her, he knew that she was slowly going insane.

For the first time in her life she didn't want to be alone. She didn't have any strength left.

"I can't just leave like that, Diego. I run a company. My laptop—"

He turned around. "It's in there," he said, with a nod toward another bag she hadn't noticed before.

Her laptop case. She hated it when anyone touched it. Her most precious possession was in there.

She moved to take it from him but he held it behind him.

"I'm warning you again. This is a vacation. Mary and Amber have already been informed."

Her assistant and her VP of Operations.

"I will send this back with Miguel unless you agree that your time on it will be limited."

"*Limited?* What does that mean?" she said, hurrying behind him.

He paused at the foot of the plane's stairs, one hand extended toward her. "You'll be allowed one hour every day on that laptop."

Reaching him, she paused. "What am I supposed to do for the rest of the day?"

His hand clasping hers, he smiled, the very devil lurking in his gaze. "I'm sure we will find something enjoyable."

She waited until they were settled into the flight and she had picked at her dinner before she started looking around her seat.

Without asking, Diego knew what she was looking for. He couldn't believe it. The woman really was a workaholic.

"Where's my laptop case?" she threw at him, meeting his gaze.

"It should be somewhere here." Her expression anxious, she unbuckled her seat belt and stood up.

He leaned forward and grabbed her hand, stopping her. "This is what I'm talking about. What is so important that you need it *now?*"

With her other hand she pushed at his hold. "I don't." She looked almost panicky. "I just... I want to make sure it doesn't get misplaced."

He stared at her for a few seconds before replying, "It's in the rear cabin."

After a few minutes he followed her there, unable to keep his mind on anything else.

She knelt by the small side table next to the bed and unzipped the case. Smiling, he hunkered down on his knees next to her.

"What are you looking for?"

Her gaze wide, she froze with her hand inside the case. "Oh, just a…an old CD of songs I made a while ago. I want to upload it to my iPod and I…" She swallowed as he didn't budge. "I would prefer to do it alone."

He laughed. "Send me on my way so that you can work? *No.*"

"Never mind." She began zipping it closed. "I don't think the CD's in here anyway."

He grabbed the leather case from her.

Her hand shaking, she tugged it back. "No, Diego… Don't…"

"You are acting *really* strange," he murmured, and tugged the zipper open.

A bulging envelope fell out—a faded one, with a logo he instantly recognized. It was from a photo studio in Rio where he'd used to have his pictures developed long ago.

Where she had gone to have the pictures developed from the disposable cameras she and Eduardo had carried on that cruise.

She grabbed it and tucked her hand behind her jerkily.

He met her gaze, his chest incredibly tight. The last thing he wanted was to remember the pain he had felt when she had walked out. Not when they were finally starting over again, even if not with a clean slate.

The memory brushed his words with a harsh edge. "I'm surprised you didn't burn them all a long time ago."

Hurt flashed in her gaze. Still on her haunches, she moved away from him, as though she was shielding a precious commodity. "They're catalogued under 'Mistakes Never to Be Repeated.'"

"Why do you have them in your laptop case?"

Her answer was extremely reluctant. "When I packed my stuff to be moved I put them in there, to keep at work."

So that he didn't see them even by accident.

Anger burning through him, he made a quick move. The envelope fell from her arms, scattering pictures all around him. Every one of them showed Kim and him, happy, smiling, the world around them faded to nothing.

He grabbed a couple and crumpled them in his hand.

She gasped and plucked at his hand, her fingers digging into his bunched fist. "No... What are you doing?"

"I'm going to do what you should have done—tear them and trash them."

She was trembling. "Don't you dare."

He grabbed another one, seething inside. He was about to rip it in half, when she clamped his wrist, her grip strong as a vise.

She shook her head, hot anger burning in her eyes. "Stop it, Diego."

He let the picture go and pulled her toward him. "Why did you leave?"

"What?"

"It's a question I should have asked years ago."

"Believe me, the answer won't make you happy."

With a grunt, she tried to pry his fingers open. Her nails, even though blunt, dug into his knuckles. He didn't care, and apparently neither did she.

"Let it go, Diego."

"No. Not unless you answer my question. And truth this time."

"I've never lied to you."

"You've never told me the truth either. Like the fact that you never slept with Alexander."

Her gaze flashed to him even while her fingers still jabbed at his. "Is that it? You want to know how many men I've slept with in my life? Two—you first, and then this other guy a year after I left you, because I couldn't forget you. But it was horrible. There—are you happy?"

A red haze descended in front of his eyes. "What is supposed to make me happy? The fact that you would do anything to wipe me from your mind? Everything you give me—whether your word, or your promise, or even a damn kiss—I have to fight you for it. But you know what? I've fought for everything in my life and I fight dirty. So, unless you want me to rip up every picture I see here…"

Her efforts doubled. She scooted closer to him on her knees, stretched to her full height and then tilted her head to see the picture he was holding. "God, Diego, don't you dare—"

He pulled away from her and raised his hand, looked at the picture, too.

His stomach churned with a vicious force.

This one had been taken the night after he'd had sex… no, had made love to her. However much he tried, it was a night he couldn't cheapen. Not even in his thoughts.

Did she feel the same? Was that why the picture was so important to her? He was sick and tired of second-guessing.

He held it with both his hands. There was a small tear in the picture already.

She slammed into him as she tried to reach it. "Give it back, Diego…"

"No."

"Fine."

She didn't shout. And yet her words vibrated with raw pain and utter desolation.

"I left because you turned me into a prize to parade before your father—into some trophy that was a victory over your childhood."

"You said I treated you like a princess."

"Yes—a princess dressed up in glittery clothes and exhibited for the status she provided. Anyone who asked, you recited my accomplishments as though it was my résumé. You were obsessed with taking over your father's company. You spent every waking minute devising ways to get more access, more information. I...I loved you, and you broke my heart."

"How is that possible? I was ready to move so that you could go to Harvard. I wanted to give you everything you had before I—"

"I didn't want money or a grand life. I didn't want to go back to Harvard. I wanted to stay with you."

Diego's head swam with each word she uttered. "What?"

"I tried to tell you that last week. All I cared about was being with you. You didn't spend a single minute with me. We spent every evening at some gala or charity event. During the day you disappeared to God knows where. You made all these plans for how we would live our lives in New York....I didn't want that life. When I met you I was running away from that life. Liv was gone and I felt so utterly alone. I went on that cruise on an impulse and I met you. No one's ever looked at me like you did that fortnight, like there was something to me beyond... But in the end, you were the same as anyone else."

Diego forced himself to breathe past the heaviness in his throat. She clamped his wrist again, but her grip was slippery, her fingers shaking. She breathed in slowly, softly, as though it took a lot of effort.

"That picture..." Her words were low, heavy, desolate. "It represents the happiest time of my life, Diego. The only happy time. So, *please,* give it back."

His heart crawling into his throat, Diego dropped the picture. She picked it up from the floor, and the others with it, and tucked them back into the envelope hurriedly, as though she didn't trust his temper.

He had done everything she had blamed him for and more. He had come to his own conclusions about why she had left him, let it fester inside. He had let his own insecurities color her actions. He had destroyed his happiness with his own hands...

All in pursuit of the very wealth and status that had robbed him of the two people who had truly loved him, who had cared about him.

He lifted her chin, his hands shaking with impotent rage. That familiar guilt clawed through him. Another person he'd hurt, another black mark on the increasing roster of his sins.

He palmed her cheek, tracing the jutting angles of her cheekbones with his fingers. Words rushed out of him on a wave of powerlessness that pricked his muscles.

"I did love you. I couldn't bear the thought of not seeing you again once we were off that ship. That's why I married you. I...I was obsessed with defeating my father, yes, but I never meant to hurt you. But of course neither of us had enough faith in the other, did we? You didn't have enough to tell me the truth, and I didn't have enough to drag you back to me."

"Why didn't you?"

Fury such as he had never heard, rattled in her words. But she didn't wait for his answer.

He should have gone after her. But he had been able to see nothing past what he had termed as her rejection of him. He had driven himself to new, ruthless heights, manipulated and eventually driven Eduardo over the cliff.

All because she had made him realize the bitter truth that he had shoved beneath his fight for survival—that he would never be enough.

CHAPTER NINE

KIM STEPPED OUT of the shower stall in the luxurious rear cabin. She loved the circular space with its vanity lighting, but the hot water hadn't helped.

Tugging on satin shorts and a matching silk top, she put her robe back on and tied the sash. She eyed the huge bed anxiously. She trailed her fingers over the soft Egyptian cotton.

Were they going to share a bed when they couldn't even bear to look at each other?

She put a trembling hand to her forehead. Her racing thoughts were giving her a dull ache. The only time someone had put her first and she had run away from it. She wanted to go out and… What? Apologize for being a coward who had ruined their lives?

Her cell phone chirped an alarm. It was time for her multi-vitamin. She pushed at the strange sparkly bag that sat on top of her handbag with a little grunt. The bag slipped, its contents slipping onto the lush carpet at her feet. It was the goody bag from the sex party earlier that night.

She stared, aghast, at the tasteful assortment of favors scattered against the elegant rug.

Pink fur handcuffs, what were surely painful nipple clamps, two bottles of strawberry and chocolate-flavored massage oil, a contraption in shocking pink made in the shape of a…

It was a vibrator.

A sound—a cross between a gasp and a moan—escaped her. Heat pumped to her cheeks. Excitement dried her mouth. She stared at the doorway, a wild idea taking root in her.

She had had enough of his stupid rewards system. She was going to go for the jackpot.

She picked up the vibrator and settled on to a small settee facing away from the entrance to the main cabin. The smooth silicone was soft and yet hard in her hand. Sucking in a quick breath, she clicked the small button on the side.

A soft whir filled the cabin.

She didn't know what drove her to it. Maybe it was the horny part of her that she had no control over. Maybe it was the self-loathing running through her veins because she was still a coward who, instead of walking up to Diego and kissing him, as every cell in her wanted to, only dared to sit in here and play sexual peekaboo with him.

She didn't care.

She leaned against the wall, tugged her robe open and pushed it back over her shoulders.

Her PJs were nothing to write a Victoria's Secret catalog about, but at least the spaghetti strap top and the shorts were satin, in a cute shade of peach with little bows. They were not dull or boring, as Diego had said.

Her shorts exposed her legs which, thanks to Carla, she had gotten waxed for the party. Her toenails, painted the same sexy pink as the vibrator, gleamed against the cream leather couch.

The grooved velvet handle offered a sturdy grip as she held the vibrating head of it against her smooth calf. It tickled her skin and a giggle escaped her.

Laughing, she dragged the vibrating head upward from her calf. The thump-thump of her heart as she heard movement in the main cabin gobbled up the calming whir of the device.

She stalled as she reached her knee and pulled it back down. Up and down she moved it, covering a little more ground on the way up every time.

A tingle started sweeping up the base of her neck, across her face, spreading all over her skin. A shocking wetness dampened her panties. Even her palm felt slippery on the handle.

Her mouth dried up.

Because her clammy palm had nothing to do with what the device in her hand was doing to her body and everything to do with the thundering presence of the man looming at the entrance to the cabin, looking down at her from behind.

She could feel his gaze on her, daring her to raise her head and meet his gaze.

She could feel his hardened breathing in the way oxygen was swiftly depleted around her.

She could feel his arousal in the way her body reacted to his presence, in the way it was feeding off the desire he was emanating, even if she couldn't hear it or see it.

Her heart hammered. Her legs shook. Every muscle in her body trembled with an almost feverish chill. It was a good thing she had sat on the couch or she would have melted into a puddle of longing at his feet.

Bending her head, she moved the vibrating tip up past her knee this time. Her already sensitized skin vibrated with a thrumming awareness.

She reached the halfway point up her thigh.

He didn't interrupt her.

She let her boneless right leg collapse to the side, opening up her inner thigh to her hand. Her breathing quickened, the scent of arousal filling the scant air in the cabin.

He didn't make a sound.

The vibrating head reached the sensitive skin of her inner thigh. Heat crept along every inch of her skin as she moved the head a little more. Heat pooled at her sex.

He didn't move in his stance.

Her boldness had a shelf life of a few minutes at best, and it was fast running out. Sitting there, open in front of him, even with her shorts covering her aching flesh, she felt the most erotic thrill begin in her lower belly.

Over the past few seconds this had morphed into a battle of wills. He was calling her bluff, daring her to continue. And she was damned if she'd give in. She wanted his hands on her body, his fingers on her aching flesh, and she would settle for nothing less.

Refusing to look up, she moved her wrist another inch, up under the hem of her shorts. It was nowhere near where she wanted it.

She threw her head back, closed her eyes and imagined it to be his long fingers crawling up her thigh, propelling her toward ecstasy. A moan began inching its way up all the way from her lower back and she let it out.

The sound was erotic, thrilling to her own ears.

Rough hands seized the vibrator from her boneless fingers. Her eyes fell open, her body whimpering with unfulfilled desire.

His golden gaze glittering dark with fire, he loomed over her, color bleeding into his cheeks.

The desire uncoiling in his gaze was enough to scare her back into her shell—where it was safe, where she didn't risk anything.

No.

A muscle jumped in his jaw as he flipped off the vibrator and threw it across the cabin. It landed with a thud.

She pulled herself to a kneeling position. The robe slid from her arms. "You better have a good reason for throwing that away."

Tension smoldered around them, tightening every muscle in her into a quivering mass of anticipation.

"What the hell do you think you're doing?" His accent was thickened, his words rolling over each other.

She ran a hand over her throat. His gaze followed the movement hungrily. "With the *blast from the past* episode we've just had, I figured it would be forever before you wanted to touch me again, so I was taking matters—"

He pulled her flush against him, until her breasts were crushed against the solid musculature of his chest. It was heaven. It was hell. It was everything she wanted with crystal-clear clarity.

"Do you want me to touch you?"

"Yes." She dragged his hand to her chest, her heart racing. Her breasts cried out for his touch. "Here." She dragged it down to her stomach. "And here." She pulled it farther down to the juncture of her thighs. "Everywhere. Nothing but your touch will erase this pain—"

He plundered her mouth with his, swallowing her words. His lips were hard against her, grinding into her with savage need, forcing her to open up to him.

With a moan that never left her throat she gripped his shoulders and opened her mouth. He plunged his tongue into her—fast, ardent strokes that sent arrows of need shooting lower.

Molten desire pooled between her legs and she tried to squeeze them closer.

But his thigh was lodged between hers. And, God, he was so deliciously hard. She rubbed against his rock-hard muscles, groaning, whimpering.

She wanted him so much, needed him so much, and she was going to let him fill her inside out, fill every inch of her, with him, with his scent, with his touch, until the regrets gouging holes inside her were gone.

Because she wanted another chance at this. She wanted another chance with Diego.

Diego had never felt such all-consuming desire as he did for this woman. Need prickled along his skin, making his erection an instrument in self-torture. Seeing her with that blasted vibrator in her hand, her legs open in sinful invitation, was enough to push him to the edge of his control.

And he had never had much to begin with. Not when it came to her.

He plunged his tongue into her mouth with all the finesse of an impatient teenager. He licked the inseam, nipped at the sensitive flesh.

There was no tentativeness in her either. In fact the bold strokes of her tongue against his own had him thrusting his hips into her soft stomach like a randy animal.

Meu Deus, she tasted like sunshine and strawberries and the decadent promise of wild, hot sex. A hint of lily of the valley clung to her skin and filled his nostrils.

A loud whimper emanated from her when he sucked on her tongue. Her hands crawled up his nape into his hair. When she tugged his lower lip between her teeth he shuddered violently, jerking his lower body into hers.

The groove of her legs cradled his erection perfectly as she rubbed herself against him. Heat gathered low at the base of his back, balling up into unbearable need in his shaft.

How could anything that felt so good be bad?

He wanted to take her right there. Because she was his and she wanted him, and it was the one place where there was only truth between them.

He slipped his hands under the flimsy satin of her top. Her skin, silky soft and warm to the touch, slithered like velvet under his rough palms. Her breathing was harsh; her soft gasps and groans were goading him on.

He was about to tug the silky strap off her shoulder when she shook her head and pulled back.

He growled instantly, like a wild animal denied its prey at the last moment.

The next minute her hands were on the fly of his jeans. He groaned—more of a request this time than a demand— as she undid the button.

His teeth were on edge as his jeans gave in. And she wrapped her long fingers around his shaft.

With a guttural groan, he pushed into her hand, blood roaring in his veins.

His eyes flicked open when her hand stopped its mind-bending caresses.

Sweat gleaming on her brow, she was trying to tug her shorts down, but her fingers kept slipping on the satin hem. She tugged a little more and the sight of black panties peeking out from under the hemline sent his blood pressure skyrocketing.

Every inch of his body was coiled tight, anticipating the pleasure, remembering how tight and wet and good she had felt around him the last time. She tugged her top off and lust blinded him.

But it was the sight of her stomach that cleared his vision. She wasn't showing much yet, but her midriff wasn't flat either. And it stopped him in his tracks.

He didn't want to force her against the wall and be done in a minute, which he was very close to doing. This could not be about slaking his lust. He didn't want to lose control as he had done the last time. Not now. Not ever again.

Because once they did this he wouldn't stop with tonight. He wanted her in his bed for the rest of their lives. If he kept control of his sanity, if he held himself back, maybe there was hope for a civilized relationship with her after all. That was what it had to be, for the sake of his children.

He wanted *her* to lose control, he wanted *her* mindless

with pleasure and he wanted her begging for release. This time he wanted to savor every inch of her, wanted to linger over her body. This time he wanted all of her revealed to him.

"I want you inside me *now*, Diego. Please…" she said, her words a sensuous whisper.

Gritting his teeth, he clasped her wrists and stopped her. "No."

Kim blinked, felt a tightening in her throat.

It was the cruelest word in the English language. She sagged against him, her breath coming in choppy little puffs. It was a good thing his hard body was still supporting her or she would have sagged to the floor. She hid her face in his rising and falling chest, loath to reveal the tears burning at the backs of her eyelids.

He lifted her into his arms. Only when he lowered her onto the bed, on top of the covers, did she open her eyes again. He stood over her, his tight features set into a stony mask of spine-tingling…*resolve*. That was the only word for it.

What she saw in the tight set of his mouth, in the lingering heat in his hungry gaze, set all her internal alarms ringing.

His jaw set, he trailed his gaze over her slowly, from the top of her hair to her pink toenails, without missing an inch in the process. Something flitted into it and a flutter began in the pit of her stomach.

She was still clothed, even though the upper curves of her breasts were visible over her bra and her shorts were bunched up against her upper thighs.

He disappeared and then reappeared on the bed in the blink of an eye. With something in his hand. "Take off your clothes."

Her breaths came quick and rushed. The pink handcuffs

looked absolutely flimsy in his large hands. An unrelenting throb, a tremble, started in her. Pushing back with her heel, she tried to roll away from him. He didn't let her.

With her ankle in his free hand, he flicked his wrist and she slid down the bed, her legs now trapped between his knees.

A dark smile full of sinful promises curved his mouth. The handcuffs dangled in the air above her. "I want to see every inch of you, lick and kiss every inch of your skin. I want you incoherent with pleasure."

She shook her head, her mouth dry as a desert. His words had the most arousing effect on her. A slow, wicked pull began pulsing at her sex and she clutched her thighs together.

It wasn't enough that she had surrendered. She had to surrender *everything*. His words and her thoughts collided, her mind and her body clashed, even as an illicit thrill shot through her.

"No."

He shrugged, sitting back on his haunches. "My way or no way. Last offer, *gatinha*. Give up your control or I'm walking out the door."

There was a savage satisfaction, a grating pride in his words, that irked her.

She wanted to say, *Fine*. Slide off the bed and walk away. The word trembled on her lips. The sensible part of her was screaming at her to walk away. But what had all these years of being careful and logical brought her?

A crushing loneliness and nothing else.

She nodded, unable to give words to her acceptance.

His teeth were bared in a smile, gleaming with unabashed hunger.

Sliding back on the bed, trembling with a host of conflicting emotions, she unhooked her bra and shrugged it off.

A hungry groan was torn out of Diego and it shuddered around them.

He seemed to freeze right in front of her, drinking her in. Need knotted her nipples and moved incessantly lower. Gritting her jaw, she lay back against the bed and slowly peeled off her shorts in one movement.

He leaned forward and she drew in a sharp breath, her fingers halting on the edge of her panties. He clasped her wrists and tugged her arms upward. His shirt grazed her nipples, setting her skin ablaze. The hem of his jeans rubbed against her belly. She groaned and almost bucked off the bed, the delicious friction setting her skin on fire.

He neatly clamped her wrists with the handcuffs and moved back to his knees. "Turn around and lie facedown," he threw at her roughly, before sliding off the bed.

She bristled at his command, even though the hoarse note in his words, the way he moved away from her as though he didn't trust himself, sent a wave of feminine power rippling through her.

CHAPTER TEN

"CHOCOLATE OR STRAWBERRY?"

The question from across the room was fraught with unsatisfied hunger, mirroring her own. The soft Egyptian cotton chafed against her breasts and her skin. She let out a shaky breath.

"I have a choice?"

Silence—waiting, threatening—met her.

She shut her eyes, clutched the sheets with her fingers and mumbled "Chocolate..." Every second he didn't touch her was reducing her into a mindless state of anticipation and need.

She didn't know what she had expected—didn't know what his question even meant. It was definitely *not* the hot slide of his oil-slick palms over her back.

The massage oil.

She groaned as he rubbed at the knots in her shoulder. The scent of dark chocolate combined with his own, infiltrating every pore of her. His calluses abraded her skin, sparking tiny pinpricks of pleasure all over.

Done with the knots in her shoulders, his hands moved down, over her lower back, lower still to her buttocks. She closed her eyes and savored the sensation as they traveled over her buttocks, her thighs, her calves and even her feet.

They pulled and kneaded, rubbed and stroked, until every muscle in her was pliant and boneless. Her throat was raw with the sounds she made. She felt as if she was floating on clouds.

But he didn't stop.

And suddenly the tempo of his touch changed.

A different kind of pleasure slithered over her skin. Her mouth dried up. Her breath hitched in her throat.

Even his breathing seemed different, shallower, the strokes of his fingers more calculated.

A heat flush was overtaking every inch of her as he pushed her thighs the tiniest inch apart.

His slick hands molded over her thigh muscles. With new tension replacing old knots, she breathed hard. He tugged her panties down. She shuddered and struggled to move.

"Relax, *pequena*."

His command was gruff, curt.

She felt the slide of his hot mouth, open and scorching against the base of her spine. She moaned—a guttural sound that filled the cabin.

He scraped his teeth over one buttock. She clenched her thighs, trying to catch the ache there. With his huge palm between her thighs, he didn't give her that satisfaction.

She whimpered, ready to beg. "Please, Diego...just—"

"No, *gatinha*. Remember—my rules, my way."

His words elicited an erotic thrill from her that she had no way to control. Sliding his left hand beneath her tummy, he pulled her up a little, while his right hand steadily but slowly crept toward her sex.

An electric current sizzled along her nerves. She bit her lower lip hard, striving to catch the groan that was tearing out of her.

"Let go of your lip," he ordered, his voice guttural.

She shook her head in denial, or something like it.

He snuck a finger into her sex. Millions of nerve endings flared to life.

She flinched from the pleasure and then shivered all over, her toes curling into the bed.

Dear God, what was he doing to her?

She was draped over his hand like a rag doll, *everything* open and visible to him. She had never felt so vulnerable and so out of control. And yet she couldn't wait for him to do whatever he wanted with her.

His hand reached her curls, delved through her folds. She was aching for his touch, for the pressure that would send her over.

"*Droga,* but you're so wet and ready."

A scream built in her chest and she trembled from head to toe. "Please, Diego…" she whispered on a sob.

Another finger joined the first inside her sheath. She rubbed herself into his touch and heard his groan.

His fingers reached finally and stroked her clitoris. "Come for me, *gatinha.*"

She opened her mouth and breathed in jerkily. Pleasure built as he moved his fingers faster, inside and out, the heel of his palm rubbing against her with every movement. She closed her eyes, heat gathering momentum in her pelvic muscles, her groans sounding erotic.

Until he pressed down with his thumb and forefinger and set fire to that aching bundle of nerves.

She cried out as she orgasmed violently, white lights exploding behind her eyes, her breath hitching somewhere between the base of her throat and her lungs, her body fraying with the assault of pleasure, her mind utterly soaked with satisfaction.

The sound of her climax, rasping and throaty, wrenched a tormented answering shudder from Diego. He placed his palm on her lower back as the tremors in her body slowly subsided and then pulled her up to her knees gently. The scent of her arousal was thick in the air he breathed. Her skin was warm to the touch, with a faint sheen of sweat on it. Her locked hands lay in front of her. Her neck was thrown back against his shoulder.

His erection nestled into the curve of her buttocks. He rubbed himself against her and groaned, his shaft aching with need.

She felt so breakable in his rough hands, and the receding shudders in her slender body, her nudity, revealed a fragility that she hid under her perfection.

He pressed an open-mouthed kiss just above the indent of her buttocks and she tautened like an arrow. She tasted of chocolate and sweat. He trailed kisses upward, tasting and licking her, until he reached the graceful curve of her neck.

He opened his mouth and bit the tender flesh there. A moan rumbled out of her. She struggled against the handcuffs.

"Unlock them, Diego."

Her words were a raw, needy whisper. His stomach muscles tightened into hard rocks.

"I like you like this, *minha esposinha*," he said, uncaring that he sounded like the dirty thug he was. He pushed her hair away from her face and licked the seam of her ear.

Her response was a delicious tremble. "You're still fully dressed."

He moved his right forearm until his palm lay flat against her belly. She sucked in a sharp breath. He pushed her back onto the bed and joined her, lying on his side. She went without a sound. He laughed.

A delicate pink dusting her cheeks, she tried to cross her arms over her breasts and the triangle of curls that stole his breath.

She glared at him. "What?"

"I really like you all pliant and naked like this. All mine to do whatever I want with."

"Undo the cuffs, Diego," she said, with a hint of pleading in her words now.

He smiled and slid his palm up toward one breast, kneaded the soft flesh.

She closed her eyes on a long exhale and twisted to the side. As if she would deny him access. He stood up from the bed and eyed the dips and valleys of her body, need yanking relentlessly at his groin.

He shed his clothes quietly and rejoined her on the bed.

"Are your breasts already fuller, *gatinha?*" he asked, his words slurring around his tongue. "You're not quite showing, but I see the signs." He kissed the curve of her hip. "Here." He planted another one on her stomach. "Here."

Her gaze flew open, stroked over his naked body with a swift greed that set his teeth on edge. "You're still punishing me for walking away, aren't you?"

"I'm not. I adore seeing you naked, searching for the small little changes in your body that my children might already be causing."

She swallowed visibly, her gaze filled with a dark fear.

"I prefer to lie in bed with you and savor every inch of you instead of screwing you against the wall."

A single tear rolled out of her eye and he caught it with his mouth. It knocked the breath from his lungs. He palmed her face and forced her to look at him. "If you want me to stop—?"

She shook her head, the remaining unshed tears making her eyes twinkle like precious stones. "I'm...*glad* that it's your children inside me, Diego."

He felt a strange tightness in his chest as he captured her mouth again. Even the erotic pull of her mouth wasn't enough to dilute the disappointment that slashed through him. He'd had the feeling she had meant to say something else. But, as usual, she had kept it to herself.

And why the hell was he hanging on to each word of

hers like a faithful little dog? He needed to keep this on *his* terms.

He palmed her breast and felt a shudder go through him as the pebbled tip rasped against his palm. Her moan, almost bordering on a sob, filled his ears. His fingers looked worse than rough around the puckered nipple. He flicked it with the pad of his thumb and she pushed herself into his hand.

He kept his gaze on her, the sounds she made at the back of her throat, the lust that she couldn't hide from him, bleeding into the air around him, giving him unparalleled satisfaction.

She was his wife. She was going to be the mother of his children. This strong, brilliant, stubborn woman, who was worried that she didn't care about the babies in her womb, she needed him, needed something only he could give her.

In that moment she was unraveled at his touch, a hair trigger away from exploding with pleasure again.

Desire was a feral pounding in his veins. He hardened a little more, heat billowing from his very skin.

Nothing but her short gasp could have stopped him, so intent was he on losing his mind in her body and its softness.

"What is it, *pequena?*"

Her gaze took a few seconds to focus on him. She wiggled her handcuffed wrists and scrunched her nose. "They're beginning to hurt now."

He unlocked them instantly.

The next moment was a blur to his lust-soaked brain. As soon as he took the handcuffs off her she rolled away from him.

But he was in no mood for games or smiles. Somewhere between rubbing oil onto her body and seeing her naked he had begun losing control of himself again, started losing a small part of himself again. And he was damned if he'd let her take anything he wasn't willing to give.

"Come here, Kim," he said arrogantly.

Her gaze widened. She hadn't obviously missed the dark edge to his words. But of course she didn't heed his warning. She never did. It was always a battle of wills with her.

"Make me."

Kim squealed as Diego trapped her neatly on the bed. She threw punches. Not one fazed him. She even aimed her leg for a swift kick. It was too late.

He held her beneath him, his body a blazing furnace of tightly controlled desire.

He bent his mouth and took her nipple in his mouth. She lost the capacity for all coherent thought. He suckled at it—deep, long pulls that instantly sent pangs of need arrowing down to her sex—while his erection throbbed against her thighs.

She bucked off the bed, a throaty moan ripped from her throat. She snuck her hands into Diego's hair and held him there. He softly blew on the nipple and turned his attention to the other one. He rolled it between his fingers, rasped his stubble against the sensitive underside. She was ready to climax again.

She moved her legs restlessly and the rasp of his hair-roughened leg against hers sent sensations spiraling inside her. He closed his lips on the nipple and tugged it between his teeth. It was beyond bearable, bordering on pain-pleasure.

"I want to touch you, Diego," she pleaded, pushing him back, her hands on his shoulders. He didn't budge an inch.

He continued the assault with his mouth, trailing hot, wet kisses between her breasts, toward her stomach. Every inch of her skin that he kissed felt as if it was waking up from a long slumber.

The minute she felt his breath on her thighs she decided enough was enough. She rolled to slip from under him, a smile stretching her mouth from ear to ear.

Before he could stop her, she pushed him back on the bed and lay atop him from head to toe, her breath shaking in and out of her. Their mingled groans filled the silent cabin.

The rasp of her skin against his, the friction, was incomparable. Her breasts rubbed against his chest. His erection pressed into her belly. Her legs tangled with his.

Without giving him a moment to breathe, she pressed her mouth to his.

And she didn't do it tenderly. She gave the kiss everything she had in her, infusing her touch with every little emotion she had never been able to put into words and never could. She traced his lush lower lip with her tongue, nipped the moist inside, sucked his tongue into her mouth, rubbing herself against him like a cat.

God, whatever she did, she couldn't stop rubbing against him.

He breathed out on a hiss, his muscles shifting and pressing into her.

"You're going to be the death of me," he whispered as she dragged her mouth down to his neck.

He sounded utterly on edge, and she liked him like that. She bit his nipple and his fingers tightened on her arms.

She moved down and the friction of their sweat-slick bodies threatened to drive her crazy. She rubbed herself over his erection. He growled.

She dragged the tip of her tongue over the hard ridges of his stomach. He roared.

She clasped her fingers around his shaft and slid her fist up and down. Sweat shimmered on his brow. He jerked his hips into her touch, his stuttering breathing filling her ears. She bent and licked the swollen head, the taste and scent of him sending pulsing tingles straight to her wet core.

She laid her palm flat against his flinching abdominal muscles and licked the head again.

His upper body shot up off the bed, and before she could blink he'd tugged her boneless body until she was straddling him.

He grabbed her hips and entered her—slowly, hotly, precisely—until all she could feel was his possession. She clamped her arms around him so his face burrowed into her breasts as he pulled himself up.

A billion nerves jumped into life as their hips bumped into each other.

She dug the tips of her fingers demandingly into his rock-hard shoulders. She opened her eyes, ready to beg for more—and froze.

His gaze was studying her raptly, glittering with raw intensity, as though he saw into her very soul and found her disappointingly wanting. It was a sensation she couldn't shed, a feeling she couldn't shake.

But she was damned if she'd let it spoil the most precious moment of her life.

She kissed his mouth and moved swiftly off him.

And pushed herself back onto him.

They both groaned, the sounds needy, desperate, on edge.

She bent her head and bit his shoulder, digging her teeth into the muscle none too gently. It was all the signal he needed, apparently.

With a rough groan he reversed their positions, until he was on top of her. Throwing her legs over his shoulders, he thrust into her, harder, faster, until neither of them could see clearly, until neither could even breathe properly, until their bodies were ready to jump out of their shells.

She came with an unchecked scream that was torn out of her on a surge of need. Pleasure rocked through her—

waves and waves of unrelenting pressure that splintered and spread through every inch of her.

With one final thrust, Diego collapsed over her.

Eventually, even though it felt like forever, the pleasure waves receded, bringing in their wake painful realization. As though there was always a price for such life-altering joy as she had found in his arms.

She was in love with Diego. She always would be.

Had she ever been out of love with him really? It was a simple truth, as simple and soul-wrenching as the babies growing inside her.

Every inch of her wanted to retreat, hide, until she could come to terms with the terrifying truth. She needed to prepare herself, needed to set expectations for herself. She couldn't let it make her weak.

She couldn't let her love for him define her existence.

Diego felt Kim stiffen even before he pulled out of her. But he refused to let her hide from him. Not after the most intense orgasm of his life.

But when had it been anything less than explosive with her?

Still joined with her, he tumbled onto his back and pulled her with him until they were both lying sideways. He cupped her breast and kissed the upper curve of it, unable to resist the urge.

She opened her eyes with a helpless moan, dark chocolate pools swimming with desire. And yet there was a shadow of retreat, too.

"No, no, no," he whispered, putting his free hand on her temple and pressing.

She half smiled, every bit of it reluctant and torn from her. "No, what?"

He tapped her temple with his finger. "No thinking."

The shadows disappeared from her gaze and her mouth curved into a wide smile. He felt something loosen in his gut.

"No thinking, huh? That's like asking you…"

He raised his brow, urging her on.

"Like asking you to not be *sexy*." She raked her nails over his abdomen and he sighed with pleasure. "Although if you are naked like this I can't *actually* think."

He laughed. He really liked her like this. And not just because she was naked and sexy and it drove him crazy with desire. But because an inherent part of her—a side of her he rarely if ever saw—was exposed to him when they made love.

This intimacy, he realized slowly, was something she guarded closely—as she did all her feelings. It was something she had shared only with him. Primal satisfaction beat through him at the realization.

"Then we will be naked all the time. I mean, if that's what it takes to have a happy marriage I'm up for it."

She laughed, and the rich sound surrounded him.

He moved his hands toward her breasts and cupped them. "You were right. All this sophistication—it's just on the outside. Beneath it I'm an old-fashioned, chauvinistic man."

"Yeah?" she said, challenge glinting in her gaze. But her gaze dropped as he flicked a hard nipple with his fingers, her breathing becoming sharp.

"Yeah. I would like my wife to not think too much— even if she *is* one of the most brilliant women I have ever met. I would like to protect my wife from the big, bad world—even though she's the strongest woman I have ever met. I would like to be the only man—or the only *equipment*," he amended quickly, and she laughed, "that is allowed to touch her. I would like to be the only one who can—"

"Tie her up in knots? Make her forget right or wrong?

Turn her world upside down and generally plunge her life into chaos?"

His heart pounded so hard in his chest that he wondered if it would burst out of him.

"You already do all that and more to me, Diego."

Before he could pull in his next breath she pushed him onto his back and straddled him. With sure movements she wrapped his fingers around him and guided him inside her wetness as though she had blurted out too much...as though she didn't want him to linger over her words.

Once she started to move over him, her high breasts moving softly with her movements, her eyes drooping to half-mast with need, he forgot everything but the lust driving him to the edge.

He thrust upward in rhythm with her movements, he pulled himself up as her tempo increased. He pulled her nipple into his mouth and tugged at it with his teeth.

And she exploded around him, her muscles contracting and pulling at him. He thrust one more time into her and hit his own orgasm. He jerked his hips into her for every inch of pleasure she could give him, but something else was fueling the pleasure breaking out all over him.

CHAPTER ELEVEN

Sitting on the terrace overlooking the Brazilian coast, Kim ran her hands over her bare arms. The evening sky glittered with stars and the breeze carried a hint of the exotic flowers that were native to the island, which was an ecological paradise.

The past ten days she had spent here had flown by in a whirl, and they had been the best days of her life.

She saw Diego most days, except when he made trips to Rio di Janeiro. He made a lot of those—even though he was often back before she'd realized he was gone.

He didn't inform her about his schedule and she was still too new at this…whatever *this* was—to ask him to share. But the time they did spend together was becoming more and more precious to her.

Two days into their stay she had taken a trip around the island with Miguel, who had joined them a day after they arrived. She had met four young men, ranging from Miguel's eighteen-year-old best friend to a hulking brute of a boy whose age was indeterminate. And that was when she'd realized the truth.

Diego was doing everything he possibly could to get as many kids out of the street gang he himself had been a part of and bring them here. He was giving them honest work to do, showing them a different way of life. Some came willingly in search of a something better, and some, like

Miguel, who had seen too much violence already, didn't believe a better world existed.

She had thought Diego obsessed with wealth, determined to take everything he thought the world had denied him. She couldn't have been more wrong. She'd felt an insane urge to shout to the world what an honorable man he was, how wrong the media's perception of him was. So she had started a project with Miguel's help, excited to be doing something for Diego.

He might think himself damned, but with each passing second Kim could only see the good, the honor in Diego. And fall deeper into love with him.

Only being in love was just as horrible as she remembered it to be.

Not that she didn't enjoy the attention he showered on her. She had never been so pampered in her life. Forget pampered—no one had ever even so much as cooked a meal for her.

She walked on white beaches every day, swam in the infinity pool that edged from the villa into the ocean, napped for an hour every afternoon. The third day after their arrival Diego had even taken her on a hot air balloon ride over the island. It had been the most wonderful time she'd had.

He had shown her the exotic flora on the island, the place where construction had begun on a house for the teenagers he was bringing over. They had even seen Miguel and the other kids playing soccer on a vast expanse of untouched land.

Anything she asked for, she had it in a few hours—like the state-of-the-art camcorder she had requested.

He even had Miguel watch over her when he was busy, and the little punk seized her laptop every day after an hour, as though she was on the clock.

It had taken a couple of days but she had gotten over her panic about her company. Her staff were experts at what they did; of course they could manage without her for a couple of weeks.

She should feel on top of the world. And she did in those split seconds when she could stop obsessing and let the tight leash she kept on herself go.

Her day, from dawn to dusk, was spent wondering why he didn't kiss her again, what was stopping her from crawling into his bed—wherever it was that he slept. She was tired of waiting for him to make a move when all she wanted was to surround herself with him.

She wanted him, and she was pretty sure, from the way his hungry gaze ate her up, he wanted her. Tonight she would...

All her intentions disintegrated into dust when he walked onto the terrace. With his BFF in tow.

Jealousy burned like a blaze in her chest. She trembled from head to toe. The strength of it was feral. It pummeled her muscles into action and she got up in a sudden movement that made her lightheaded. She clutched at the wrought-iron railing.

Just the sight of him with Marissa was enough to burn a hole through her heart.

For the first time in over a week Kim had no appetite for dinner. Even though Anna had prepared everything the way Kim liked.

She smiled and nodded, answered with yes or no for the first half hour, pushing her food halfheartedly around on her plate. The other woman—or *was* she the other woman in this case?—was nothing but polite, inquiring after Kim's health, how she was enjoying her stay on the island.

There was only so much Marissa could do to squelch the awkwardness while Kim stayed resolutely mute. But what could she say?

She felt such an influx of emotions—jealousy roped

with guilt that she had destroyed this woman's life with one single action, a hot rush of anger toward Diego for subjecting them all to this—she was literally stupefied into speechlessness.

Eventually Marissa switched to Portuguese, and Kim was almost grateful for the snub. She waited another ten minutes before she excused herself and fled back to the terrace.

Loneliness churned through her and she suddenly missed Liv with an ache. She needed her irrepressible twin so much right now. Because her life was in tatters if *this* was how being in love was going to feel.

A soaring high one minute and a gut-wrenching low the next.

It was early evening the next day when Diego found Kim walking along the beach, a couple of miles from the villa. He made a quick call.

This part of the island was even more untouched than the other side. Pristine white sands, turquoise waters—he loved this view. This island was the one thing he owned that gave him the utmost satisfaction and joy at what he had achieved in life.

It was a place with nothing but sky and acres of land around him. The one thing he had craved for so long. Somewhere that wasn't a ditch to call his own. Now Miguel, and others like him, could enjoy the freedom that came from knowing their very lives *didn't* depend on their ability to throw punches and fight dirty.

Not that he had ever stopped. Now it was just for different things.

Today the view didn't hold his interest. And he had a feeling the quiet contentment he had felt over the past week or so had been more to do with the solitary figure half a mile in front of him than his success in purchasing the island that he had wanted for so long.

To break that spell he had brought Marissa. He could have caught up with her on his next trip to Rio. But he knew she'd wanted to see the island. And he was loath to change anything in his life just because Kim was in it now.

That was the only way to keep this in check. Only Kim had looked as if he had slapped her last night.

It had taken everything he'd had in him to not chase after her when she had left for the terrace halfway through dinner. Instead he had spent the evening with Marissa, going over the last few legalities. Even her update that visa issues were now taken care of for two more boys like Miguel hadn't been enough to keep his mind from Kim.

And yet he had fought the pull.

He didn't even have a clear idea why. As each day passed with her he had felt an increasing sense of uncertainty creeping into his thoughts. As to how much he enjoyed her company, how much he looked forward to seeing her in the morning, how much he enjoyed it when she pored over a financial report with him and came up with a solution in two minutes flat.

He had learned early on that anything that felt that good always came with a high price.

He tucked his hands into the pockets of his trousers and came to a standstill, watching her. Not his heart, though. It pounded extra hard in his chest.

The utter silence, punctured only by the ocean's waves, cocooned them, weaving its own magic.

She stood barefoot in the sand, the ocean lapping at her feet.

Her slender back, skin glowing in the sun, was pure temptation marred only by two yellow strings tied at the neck and then down lower. His gaze followed the curve of

her back to the dip. A sarong-style wrap hugged her pert behind. Her long legs were only visible again from her knees.

He released a shaky breath. He had purposely pulled
himself back these past few days, held back through sheer
will. He didn't want to fall headlong into his desire for
her again, to forget the right and wrong of the situation—
forget himself.

He wanted the comfortable camaraderie they had slipped
into to last. He wanted something stable for his children,
and for the first time since she had told him that she was
pregnant, for the first time on this island, he felt the good-
ness of what they had in his bones.

This felt right. This felt good. And he would do anything
to keep it like that.

The line of her shoulders tightened infinitesimally. Her
hands wrapped around herself and she stiffened, holding
herself aloof from the world.

It was enough to burst the bubble of tranquility he had
felt just a second ago. Tension curled his muscles and his
mind geared up for whatever fight she was going to throw
his way, his body exulting in the thrill shooting through
his blood.

She turned and met his gaze.

He felt the intensity of her look as if she had run those
long fingers over him. His muscles were flexing and rear-
ing for her touch. Lust rocketed through him, tightening
every muscle with fiery need.

Her lustrous hair slapped across her face. Her bikini top
cupped her breasts just as he wanted to. He couldn't deny
they were looking rounder. She had put on some weight,
was losing that gaunt, over-worked look. And she had that
first blush of pregnancy he had overheard Anna mentioning to her.

It was in the slight flare of her hips, in the fullness of
her breasts, in the healthy flush of her skin. Her stomach,

though not yet round, was beginning to grow. He trailed his gaze over her, enjoying the sheer eroticism of looking at her.

She was the sexiest woman he had ever seen, and her innate modesty made her even more appealing. Even now she was oblivious to her effect on him, on his self-control, as her overactive mind whizzed through something.

"Do you miss being with her?"

Diego blinked. For a second he didn't understand her question. "*Droga,* I knew I shouldn't have left you alone for so long. You're ripe for a fight, aren't you?"

"That's ridiculous."

"You are much more comfortable when we're fighting, when you can peg me into whatever box you can. We have been laughing, generally enjoying each other's company, for over a week now. So of *course* it's time to draw the lines again."

"I…I'm serious, Diego."

He didn't miss whatever it was he had once shared with Marissa. It had been a comfortable relationship they had both fallen into whenever something had gone wrong in their lives—the one good thing that had stood firm despite every hardship they had faced.

He just wished he had realized sooner that it had meant so much more to Marissa than it had to him. What he felt for Kim—a crazy obsession that knew no right or wrong— he had never had with any other woman in life.

Nothing like the fizzle of anticipation roaring in his blood as she came closer, nor the tightening in his gut every time he thought he had finally reached the core of her and then she retreated behind her shell again.

She came to a halt right in front of him. Her scent teased his nostrils. Hot arousal was inching across his skin.

"You don't have to spare my feelings. I can take it," she said.

Curiosity blazed like a forest fire through him. "Does that mean it would hurt you if I said I do miss her?"

"Yes," she replied, her mouth a tight line.

Was it downright sadistic of him to *enjoy* the fact that she could be hurt by his actions? That he had a hold over her, however tenuous?

"I couldn't trust myself to not lose it right in front of her. That's why I left. I will understand if you...want me to leave."

He cursed—a filthy word his mother would have washed out his mouth for. "What the hell does that mean?" At her grating silence, he answered. "I don't miss her."

"Then why is she here? Who are you trying to punish by pushing us all together? Yourself or me?"

He frowned. "You want me to cut her out of my life? Tell her she has no part in it now that you are here? She's the one person who has stood by me my whole life. Whether I was a success or a failure, whether I was being a sanctimonious bastard or not. What do you expect me to do? Tell her—?"

Kim shook her head, feeling sick to her stomach. She got it now. Marissa was the *constant* whereas Kim was the *variable*—the one who could disappear from his life any minute.

Maybe even the one he could leave behind when he didn't want her anymore?

"I don't know," she said, her anxiety spilling into her words. "All I want to know is whether you'll give this... us...a real chance or not."

"And bringing a friend of mine here means I won't?" He smiled. "Is this you being jealous, *gatinha*?"

Kim flinched. "I'm sorry. I don't know what came over me. I have no right to—"

He tugged her around. "Yes, you do. You have every right to ask me whatever you want to. You might not always like the answer. It could be worse than what you lose by keeping silent. Why do you *do* that?"

"What?"

"Walk away silently."

She tried to shy her gaze away from him. "I don't know what you're talking about."

"Yes, you do. Even last time on the island, when I said I was done with you, you didn't utter a word. You should have called me a bastard right then. Instead you left without a word. You fight more for your company than you do for yourself."

"If I don't ask anything of you, don't expect anything of you, you can't hurt me."

He shook his head. "It is never that simple."

"It's the only way to survive."

"Who hurt you?"

She tried to turn away from him but he wouldn't let her. This was not a conversation she wanted to have. "No one hurt me, Diego. However, you will be disgusted by the depths of selfishness I can fall to."

His hands locking her in place, he looked into her eyes. "Nothing you do or have done will ever make me despise you. Make me angry, yes. Drive me crazy, yes... But disgust me...? *No.* Haven't I showed you that already?"

"The night before my mother left I found her note."

"A note?"

Every inch of her shook just remembering that night. "It was one line. Addressed to my father. She was leaving him and taking Liv with her."

Leaving her behind.

She had gone to her mother's room to check on her, to inform her of what her father had planned for the next day, to tell her that she had taken care of everything needed for a small party at their house.

Instead she had found a small bag sitting on the floor

of the closet. It had contained her mother's jewelry, cash, her passport and—the thing that had sent a shiver down Kim's spine—Liv's passport. For a frantic minute she had emptied the bag, looking for her own passport, her lungs constricting painfully.

It hadn't been in that bag.

Wondering if her mother had made a mistake, her head reeling from what it meant, she had walked to the bed and found the note scribbled on her mother's stationery.

It had been the worst moment in her life—sitting there, wondering what she had done wrong, how she could have acted any different, why her mother would choose to take Liv but not her...

Her vision blurred. The same confusion, the same utter desolation sprang inside her at the memory. The words she hadn't dared to speak aloud, the thoughts that wouldn't leave her alone even after all these years, the fears she hadn't shared with another soul, poured out of her on a wave of uncontrollable pain.

"For as long as I can remember I did everything I could to shield her from my father. I always stayed strong for her. I stayed by her bed when she was ill. I never once asked her for anything, Diego. And in the end she—" her voice broke, her insides twisting into a mass of pain.

Diego's rough palms on her cheeks, the familiarly comforting scent of him, pulled her out of the depths of despair. He forced her to look at him.

"Tell me you confronted her, Kim. Tell me you demanded to know why."

"No. And I didn't beg her to take me, too, if that's what you want to hear." Her throat felt as if pieces of glass were stuck in it. "I threatened to go to my father with the note if she went anywhere near Liv. I stayed awake by Liv's side all night. And my mother...she...left sometime during the night. But you're right. I *am* an unfeeling, selfish bitch."

"You did nothing wrong." His words were a frustrated growl.

"No? You see, I was determined to not let her rob the one person who loved me from my life. Except you know what...?"

His stomach churning with a vicious force, Diego watched Kim. She walked away from him, trembling from head to toe, her words vibrating with pain.

"Liv paid for it. With our mother gone, my father turned his corrosive, controlling attention to *her*."

"You can't blame yourself for that. You were a child."

"He made her life miserable every single minute of every single day, Diego," she said, her fists locked by her sides. "There—are you disgusted now?"

How could he hate her for surviving when he would have done the same? She'd lived her life with the cards she had been dealt and made no excuses for it.

She slipped from him before he could tell her how much he understood, how that kind of hurt never died down.

She could have hated Olivia after her mother left. But she had been strong for both of them, had tried to shield her from their father when she had been nothing more than a teenager herself. And she thought there was nothing in her that felt...

He tugged her closer and wrapped his hands around her. She didn't relax immediately. He tightened his hold.

She smelled of the ocean and lemons and something undeniably *her*.

He stood holding her like that, running his fingers over her back. So many things rushed through him. Utter amazement at her strength robbed him of his ability to speak.

Walking away from her mother, from her father, from him—it was the only way she had survived.

A lump in his throat cut off his breath and he relaxed his hold on her.

Handling her was no different from handling a hurt teenager like Miguel, really. Miguel lashed out at the world in order to live through his pain, whereas Kim internalized everything to survive—pushed her own feelings and desires so deep inside she had pretty much cauterized herself against any hurt.

If his childhood had been hell, hers had been no better. Just a different kind of hell.

"You remind me of Miguel," he whispered, breathing her scent deep into his lungs.

She looked up at him, reluctance filling her gaze. "I don't know what to make of that."

"Whenever I see him in pain I want to hunt down everyone that's hurt him. It's the same way I feel right now. Instead of protecting you, your mother used you and Olivia as shields against her husband. She was not fit to be a mother. And I will throttle you if you compare yourself to her again."

Tears glazed her eyes.

He moved his palm to her stomach and felt his heart kick inside his chest. "Except I've never wanted to kiss Miguel, as I want to do you, every waking minute."

Kim blinked back the tears that prickled behind her eyes. His tenderness was unraveling her and she was terrified she would never be whole again, never be strong again.

Day by day, word by word, he had slowly peeled away all her armor. Her emotions were spilling and overflowing. It was both terrifying and exciting.

She shivered and scrunched closer to him. His arms were steel bands around her, his body a furnace of need and want. And for the first time in her life she felt wanted. As if her wishes mattered, as if *she* mattered. And not for her brains, for her accomplishments, but for the person she was beneath all that—scared and hurt and frozen.

She moved in his embrace and pressed her mouth to his chest. He rumbled beneath her touch.

"Come with me," he whispered.

Her smaller hand encompassed by his, she let him tug her whichever way he wanted.

They walked for about five minutes, the sand crunching under their feet.

She came to a sudden halt, dragging Diego to a stop along with her. Dusk was beginning to streak the sky orange above them and a custom-made cabana, its dark oak gleaming in the fading sunlight, stood about two feet from them, big enough to accommodate two people.

And narrow enough to squish them together.

Pristine white cotton sheets covered the opening, contrasting richly against the dark oak. Heat uncurled low in her belly, her legs threatening to collapse under her.

And that wasn't all.

A small table was set up in front of the cabana, with candles and dinner for two. A pink cardboard box with a small bow also sat on it. The curly "A" on top of it looked very familiar...

His hard body shifting behind her, Diego wrapped his arms around her, his strong legs supporting her own.

"That's a box from Angelina's in Paris." It was her favorite patisserie on the Champs d'Elysées.

Suddenly she knew what was in it. She turned to him, laughter bubbling out of her.

"Anna told me you've mentioned their pastries once or twice."

She met his laughing gaze. "How about a million times?"

"Happy Anniversary, *minha esposinha.*"

Her breath hitched in her throat. It was the first thing that had hit her when she'd woken up this morning—the reason why she had wandered away so far from the villa.

It was the one date she had always taken off and spent at her apartment, reliving that day.

She nodded, struggling to speak past the lump cutting off her breath. Stretching on her toes, she pressed into him until his erection rubbed against her bottom.

He groaned and hugged her tighter.

"I don't want the pastry."

He licked the seam of her ear. Her skin was too fraught with need to contain her.

"What *do* you want, *querida?* Whatever it is, I will bring it to you."

"You," she said clearly, loud enough for anyone in the vicinity to hear. It wasn't all she actually wanted to say, though. "I want *you,* Diego."

Without waiting for his answer she dragged him toward the cabana, intent on showing him with her actions everything she still wasn't brave enough to put into words.

They tore off each other's clothes with frenzied movements, as though they were both aware of how fragile, how precious this moment of perfection was.

Pushing her back into the soft mattress, Diego stretched out on top of her, his taut muscles a heavenly weight over her. His mouth, his tongue, his caresses, *he* was everywhere—kissing her, licking her, tasting her, generally reducing her body to a writhing mass of sensations and needs. He didn't give her a minute to breathe.

She cried out loud, the raw sound clawing its way out of her throat, when he pulled her nipple deep into his mouth and suckled at it. His rough fingers tweaked its twin, and twangs of hot pleasure shot down between her legs.

He smelled of the ocean, his muscles taut and shifting under her touch. She sobbed incoherently when he rubbed her aching core with the heel of his palm while his mouth trailed wet kisses around her navel. Pleasure coiled low in her belly, tugging every nerve-ending inside her along for the ride. Her whole body was unfolding mindlessly in tune with his erotic strokes.

His hair-roughened legs rubbing against hers, he reversed their positions with one smooth movement until she was straddling him.

Her sex quivered with need as his erection rubbed against her folds, and a shiver inched its way all over her skin.

Putting her weight on her thighs, she resisted.

His face was all severe planes and rough angles in the fading light. His choppy breath bounced off of her skin, giving her goosebumps.

His mouth was tight, his gaze drugged with desire. "This is not the time for one of your arguments, *gatinha*."

She smiled at the way his words rolled over each other, his accent creeping into his words. She placed her palms on his thighs and the rock-hard muscles clenched under her touch.

He groaned—a guttural, painful sound—as she drew her palms upward a little, until the pads of her fingers were idly tracing the length of his erection.

Her mouth dry, she forced herself to put her thoughts into words. "I want you on top of me." Pushing her hands into her hair, she stretched innocently.

His gaze moved to her breasts. Naked hunger was etched into his face. "Why?"

She slid off him and stretched alongside him. He immediately turned toward her. "I'm going to start showing in a little while." He moved his palm to her stomach. "And I…we…in the coming months it's going to be awkward."

He frowned. "So you won't want to have sex anymore? Because being near you and not having it will kill me."

She laughed. God, she would never have enough of his piercing honesty. "I will. But today I want your weight over me as you enter me. I want to feel every inch of you plastered to me."

He didn't say anything. He just pulled her wrists up with one hand and kissed her mouth, plundering her. Kneeled between her legs. Pulled one leg over his shoulder. Covered every inch of her with him as he thrust into her.

She was already wet and ready for him. But something more than pure lust sang in her veins. Her breasts shifted against his chest as he moved inside her. Her stomach groaned under the weight of his muscles. Sweat beaded over his forehead and she licked his shoulder when he thrust again.

It was hard and crushing. Her breathing was ragged, her skin ablaze with need. The delicious friction of his thrusts awakened a billion nerve-endings in her groin muscles.

Sharp bursts of pleasure crested over her. Desire pooled low and intense in her pelvis. She sensed his control slipping, his desire taking over, just as hers did, and each thrust was more desperate and less measured. Each sound he made was rougher and filled with a delicious lack of control.

When they hit their climaxes and pleasure broke out all over her she knew nothing was going to protect her heart now. How stupid she had been to think she still had control over this—that she could withstand it without losing herself.

Her heart was Diego's now—*whatever* he wanted to do with it. And she couldn't help but hope, after everything they had been through together, that he wouldn't trample it.

CHAPTER TWELVE

IT HAPPENED WHEN they had almost reached the villa. The fact that it had been near midnight by the time they had finished with each other, *and* with dinner at the secluded spot, meant that the loud, strident peal from his cell phone shattered the peace, the moment of perfection.

Diego froze next to her, bringing them both to a grinding halt even before he picked it up. He literally froze—his body next to her and his hand around hers going from delicious warmth to dreadful cold in a second. The jarring tune blared again, and Kim realized why she had felt a shiver go down her spine that first time.

That ringtone was different from his usual one. Which meant he had set it up for a particular call. And he seemed to expect the worst.

He shifted to the side, almost as though hiding himself from her, and picked up his phone.

The conversation lasted two minutes—tops.

A curse flew from his mouth and Kim flinched. With a growl that had the little hairs on her neck standing, he hurled his cell phone. It fell into the ocean and sank in seconds with a little gurgle.

Leaving the most deafening silence around them.

His emotions floated over him like a dark cloud that cut off the intense physical connection she had felt with him only a few minutes ago. Like a signal of extreme danger to anyone who dared approach him.

Foreboding inched over her, her skin chilly in the balmy night air.

He stared into the ocean, his shoulders rattling.

She reached him quietly where he stood, with tension and aggression pouring out of every sinew of him. "Diego, what's going on?"

"He's dead."

The words landed around them with the intensity of an earthquake that shook everything. She swayed for a second, her gut trembling. She dug her toes into the sand, blindly seeking to root herself. "Who?" she asked, wishing her instincts could be wrong.

"Eduardo."

The anguish in him wound itself around her. "I'm so sorry, Diego."

"Multiple organ failure killed him."

"I—"

"But they are wrong."

Her tongue wouldn't move to form the words she wanted to ask. She was so terrified of everything crumbling. "What do you mean?"

"*I'm* the one who killed him. As surely as if I put my hands on his throat and choked the life out of him."

Kim gasped. The self-loathing in his words was unbearable to hear. The need to comfort him pounded in her blood. "What are you talking about? Eduardo loved you."

"And I used his love, his trust in me, to my advantage. He was already crumbling under the weight of my father's expectations. And you know what I did? I befriended him under false pretenses, gained access to the company's information and pulled it out from under him. My father had no choice but to hand it over to me. I told myself Eduardo was barely keeping it together anyway. And then, when you left, I wanted blood. I went from driven to obsessed. Instead of helping him, I pushed him into his own destruction. I should have known Eduardo was already using—should have known how close he was to breaking. By the time I did it was already too late. Are you *still* glad that it's my children you're carrying, *gatinha?*"

The words dug their claws into her.

"I am. Because you're not that man anymore, Diego. You never were. I see how you are with Miguel, what you've gone through to pull him from that life. Whatever culpability you have in Eduardo's death—if you have any—you have paid for it a million times over."

She moved toward him and folded her arms around his middle from behind. A tremor shook him and it crashed into her, his raw anguish churning her stomach.

Innocence. They had both never had it. And even without realizing it they had been drawn to each other. For the first time she felt the loss of it as keenly as he did.

She pressed her mouth to his shoulders, felt him shudder under her touch, felt his rock-hard muscles relax against her. Felt him pull in a breath with the utmost effort.

She wanted to do everything she could to ease his pain. The intensity of how much she wanted to rocked through her. For a second she thought he might let her share his pain—for once let *her* support *him*.

"You have to forgive yourself. If you don't you'll—"

He walked away from her without a word.

His silence whipped at her hope. The weight of his guilt was a crushing weight on her own shoulders, even if he said it wasn't her fault.

Kim stood there watching him go, her hold on him just as slippery as the sandbanks holding the ocean at bay.

Kim didn't see Diego over the next couple of days. It was Miguel who informed her that he had gone to Sao Paulo to bury Eduardo, and that Marissa was by his side. It was Miguel who didn't leave her side for a minute, as though he could understand her mounting confusion.

Marissa was the one person Diego hadn't shut out of his grief. His friend had stayed by his side while Kim had watched from afar.

It hurt like nothing else in her life had—like a nail stuck under her skin, gouging into her flesh. And there was nothing she could do to change it

Would it be like this forever? She hated that feeling from the depths of her soul—hated that her happiness, her very state of mind, was dependent on whether Diego would ever smile at her again.

It was the same vicious circle of hell she had gone through when she had found her mother's note. What could she have done differently? What could she change within herself? It was a powerless, clawing feeling she couldn't shed.

She blinked back tears, disgusted by the feeble feelings. She missed him every minute of every day with an intensity that stole the breath from her lungs.

How could she live like this forever? Wanting to be more, needing to be more to him, but knowing that she could never change it?

She knew they had formed a bond in the past days. She knew, for all that her life had been an emotional desert, that what they shared had been special. But he would never love her. She would never amount to anything other than the mother of his children.

It was a truth she had already known, except now it felt excruciatingly unbearable.

Pain constricted her chest. Her lungs were collapsing under its crushing weight. She sank to her knees on the hardwood floor in her bedroom and hugged herself.

She couldn't live with him like this—forever wondering, waiting for the moment he decided she wasn't worth it, the moment he decided he was done with her.

Because he would. Sooner or later he would decide he only wanted his children. She would go mad waiting for that moment.

She had wanted this chance with him, but she didn't want it at the cost of losing her sanity, her will.

Diego couldn't believe the evidence of his own eyes. His gut kept falling lower and lower as he methodically checked each room through the villa. He left her room for last—like a coward postponing the moment of truth.

She has gone.

Miguel had texted him almost two hours ago. Because Miguel, unlike his pilot and the rest of the staff, had known something was wrong, had known her swift departure was something Diego wouldn't have agreed to if his life had depended on it.

Lost in his own world on the other side of the island, pushing himself through another rigorous workout, Diego had seen it too late.

His heart, if it was possible, felt as if it had come to a screeching halt. Because he had instantly known it wasn't a work emergency, as she had claimed to everyone else, or a tantrum because he had been avoiding her since he had heard Eduardo's news.

Kim didn't throw tantrums. She didn't argue, and she didn't fight back—she left quietly, as though he wasn't even worth a goodbye.

His helicopter was gone, his pilot was gone and Kim was gone. And yet he couldn't crush the fleck of hope holding him together.

It was the most pathetic feeling that had ever run through him. Right up there with the hope that had fluttered every time his mother had trotted him down to his father's house to beg for his help.

He arrived at the suite she had been using. The sheer curtains at the French windows flew in the silence. Crickets chirped outside on the veranda.

She hadn't left the room as spotless as she usually did. A couple of paperbacks were still on the bed.

The scent she used, lily of the valley, fluttered over the breeze toward him. Knocked him in the gut like a kick to his insides. He breathed deeply, trying to get the knot in his belly to relent.

A strange sense of déjà-vu descended on him. He looked at the bathroom, his heart in his throat, waiting for her to emerge from it as she had in the hotel suite that day. She would come out and turn her nose up at him. Challenge him. Rile him. And kiss him.

Breathing through the pain, he reminded himself that it would crest soon. It had to.

It didn't.

He rammed his fist into the nearby wall and roared a pithy curse.

Despite his best efforts, he was right where she had left him six years ago—he still wasn't enough for her. Why else would she leave without a word?

In the wake of that crushing realization came waves of roaring fury and unrelenting pain. He was damned if he'd let her go.

He would move heaven and earth to drag her back into his life. He would spend every last dollar he had and more on suing her for custody, using any legal means he had to tie her to him. He would destroy everything he had built— destroy himself if that was the price to make her his again.

He wanted her back in his life. And he would fall as low as needed.

* * *

He had just hung up with his lawyer when Miguel entered his office. He cast a long look at Diego, threw a file on his table, switched on the flatscreen TV and left.

Diego was about to turn off the TV when a familiar sight stopped him in his tracks. The pristine white beaches, the turquoise waters as a background, with Miguel in the fore-front, were *here*—on the island.

Stunned, he settled into the couch.

The documentary started with Miguel being asked questions about his past life. Diego could see the resentment in his face, past hurt playing shadows in his dark gaze, the effort it cost him to answer those questions.

He shivered as he realized it was Kim answering the questions. She walked Miguel through every tough question, her tone gentle as he revealed his horrible past

The questions then focused on his current life. His chest tightened and a warm energy flew in Diego's veins as she probed Miguel on how Diego had taken Miguel out of the street gang in Rio di Janeiro, how Diego had worked long days to get through to Miguel that violence wasn't the an-swer, how Diego had brought him to this island…

Tears burned in Diego's eyes as the short feature went on. As Kim interviewed the other two kids who had joined them last week.

And then it was her smiling face that filled his huge screen.

"The world should know of Diego Pereira's efforts to get these kids out of violent street gangs and toward a bet-ter life."

Her statement reverberated within him, shaking the rigid fear at the core of him loose.

He switched the television off, his heart pounding. She thought the world should know what he was doing. But he had never wanted the world's applause, the world's validation.

He had wanted it from *her,* had craved it. He had wanted to be worthy of the strong, brilliant, beautiful woman she was.

Feeling as though he was coming apart, he opened the file that Miguel had tossed at him.

The contents of the file blew him away. There were detailed plans for the infrastructure required to run a shelter for kids recovering from drug problems. There was a list of healthcare workers who had expertise in working with kids like Eduardo. A list of legalities and forms that needed to be fulfilled in order to begin such a program right there on the island.

It was detailed, precise and exactly what he had had in mind when he had bought the island. He had never revealed his plans to her. She couldn't have created a file that made her loss more apparent.

Every inch of him ached at the emptiness he felt. Had she been horrified by what he had driven Eduardo to?

Seeing Eduardo's body, seeing his own father, whom he had hated for so many years, his hatred blazing just as ever, had broken the hold he had kept on himself—had shown him what he couldn't achieve through wealth or power, however hard he fought.

All his life he had fought for everything he had. But he hadn't been able to make his mother happy before she died, he had never received his father's acknowledgment or praise and he hadn't been able to save Eduardo.

If he did anything to manipulate Kim now, if he fell any lower—even if it was because he loved her—he would probably only destroy her, as he had done Eduardo, and she had already suffered enough.

He closed his eyes and threw his head back. Grief

scratched at his throat, and his muscles were burning with the need to fight, to bring her back into his life.

But he couldn't.

He couldn't force her to love him—not as he loved her. With every breath in him. With every cell in him. And letting her go meant letting go of the dream he had looked for with her and his children.

He had no doubt she would love their babies, whatever her fears.

In the end, after everything he had done to get to this stage in life, he was terrifyingly powerless again—and alone with it all.

CHAPTER THIRTEEN

"ARE YOU GOING to avoid me for the rest of our lives?"

Kim drew a sharp breath, her fork freezing midway to her mouth, as Liv's words flew across the lounge like loaded missiles. She had been back in New York for a week now and had been dreading confrontation. But this wasn't one she had prepared herself for.

She had forgotten that Liv still had a key to her apartment. And she had been so lost in her own thoughts that she hadn't even heard the front door being opened.

Liv joined her at the dining table, her gaze brimming with concern—and something else. *Almost fear.*

"Hey, Liv."

She lifted her fork to her mouth and took a bite of pasta. She chewed on it, forcing herself to keep at bay the nausea that had been threatening all day. It had become worse the moment she had returned—as though her body had gone into fully fledged revolt the minute she had got off the plane from the island.

Away from Diego.

Liv pulled a chair out, sat down at the table and studied her.

"You look like hell, Kim. You shouldn't look like this."

Kim nodded, and ran her palm over her midriff. She raised her head and met Liv's gaze. "I just haven't been sleeping well. I have been taking good care of myself, Liv," she said guiltily. "I've cut down my hours. I've been eating lots." She pushed her chair back and hugged Liv. Hard. "*You* look wonderful, though."

Liv's arms tightened around her. "Please tell me this is just you being hormonal. Because you're scaring me."

Kim bit her lip, striving to hold back the raw ache in her throat. "You and Alex okay?" she said softly. Every time she saw one of them she felt the knot of guilt in her stomach relent a little. As different as they were, Alex was the perfect man for her sister.

If Diego hadn't stopped her Alex wouldn't have fallen in love with Liv, and *she* wouldn't have the babies growing in her womb... A shiver went over her.

"I'm not here to talk about Alexander and me."

Kim laughed and pulled back from her. "That means you're fighting again?"

Liv shrugged. "He's angry that I forged his signature on Emily's parental release form so that she can screen-test for a movie role," she replied, a guilty blush stealing into her cheeks.

"*You forged his...?* God, Liv. I know how he is about his sister. How *could* you?"

"Acting's in her blood, Kim. She was going to do it whether he agreed or not. And Alexander...*when he loves someone*...it's just so..." She hesitated, a little shiver spewing into her words. "Emily doesn't realize how easily she can hurt him. And I would rather he be pissed off with me than—"

"Than be hurt by her?" Kim finished for Liv, her gut folding in on itself.

She stared at her twin, a fog falling away from her eyes. They looked similar, yet they were so different on the inside. Even before their mother had left Liv had always somehow understood their mother's pain.

Hadn't that always been the difference between them?

Liv's ability to put everything she loved before herself? To take that leap again and again, even if it pained her? To risk everything for love?

Kim had always assumed that *she* was the stronger one—the one in control, the one with no weaknesses. What if her strength had only been a self-delusion? Was she a coward after all? A coward who didn't believe herself worthy of being loved?

She had been so sure she loved Diego, but apparently only if there were no risks involved, only if she was sure that he would return her feelings.

"I'm worried about you, Kim," Liv said. "Alexander told me you asked him to recommend a good custody lawyer. And yesterday Diego came to see me."

"He did what?" Kim's fork clattered to the table. "He was in New York?" And he hadn't even called her.

Liv nodded, worry creasing her brow. "He…he wanted me to give you something. He said he didn't want you to open it alone. I think he's worried about you. When I asked him why he didn't do it himself, he said he was done running after you."

Liv opened her handbag and pulled out an envelope from it.

Fear curled up in her stomach and Kim braced herself.

He hadn't called her. He hadn't responded to her email. Every second of every day for the past week she had been on tenterhooks, waiting to hear something, *anything* from him. And she had a terrifying feeling about the contents of that envelope.

He was going to sue her for custody. He was going to take the babies away from her.

Just the passing thought was enough to plunge her into an abyss of panic. Her hands moved to her stomach and she shuddered. Her lungs felt as if they were seizing up on her.

She sagged to the floor and tucked her head between her legs.

Her palm on Kim's back, Liv whispered something, but Kim could hear nothing past the terror clawing through her. She couldn't even bear the thought of being forced to part with her children, the thought of not seeing them every day for the rest of her life.

How cold-hearted had her mother been to walk away so easily from them? Kim couldn't imagine making that choice if her life depended on it.

Maybe she would have a little girl with a golden gaze and a distinct nose like Diego's, and a boy with jet-black hair and a penchant for fighting. She would love her kids no matter what life threw at her. She would spend every minute…

A choked sound fell from her mouth.

There it was. The connection. The joy she had wanted to feel for so long. She closed her eyes and gripped the feeling closer to her heart. She curled up on the floor and gave in to the tears scratching her throat.

She couldn't share it with Diego. Couldn't tell him of the joy overflowing within her at the thought of the children they had created together. Couldn't tell him she finally understood what he had experienced from the minute she had told him about the pregnancy.

And now he was going to take them away from her.

Liv joined her on the floor and hugged her. "God, Kim. What are you doing to yourself?"

Kim wiped her tears and steadied herself. At least now she had the strength to fight for her kids—she couldn't expect Diego to give up his rights, but she was damned if she would either.

"If you don't want to open this now—"

She shook her head. "No. Better to get this over with…"

Casting her a worried look, Liv tore the envelope. Her mouth tight, she scanned the documents rapidly.

"This is a motion to start divorce proceedings. You're to have full custody and there's a note requesting minimum visitation rights to the...*children?*"

Kim gasped, every inch of her trembling with relief and shock.

"Wait... What does he mean *children?* Oh my God, you're having twins?"

Clutching Liv's hand, Kim nodded. Her vision was blurred. Her head felt dizzy. Delayed shock was setting in.

He was divorcing her. He was giving her full custody...

Liv skimmed through the papers in her hand again. "He will never contest your custody rights in any way. He..."

Saliva pooled in Kim's mouth, followed by a wave of nausea pushing its way up her throat. She kept her hand on her stomach.

Liv threw the papers on the table and knelt in front of her. She squeezed Kim's fingers, her gaze filled with shock. "It's so strange, isn't it? After everything he did to get you into his life, he's agreeing to all this."

An empty chill pervaded Kim's limbs, sucking out every ounce of emotion from her. *This was it.* "He's finally given up on me."

"What?"

"He's finally realized I'm not worthy of him after all."

Liv shook her head violently. "That's BS, and you know it."

Kim wiped her tears with the back of her hand. The sooner she accepted the truth, the better now. She missed Diego as if she had a hole in her heart, but she would tailor her life better for her kids. Starting with telling Liv the truth.

"I lied to you, Liv. All those years ago when Mom left."

Liv stared at her, her gaze searching Kim's. Fear clouded her eyes. "What?"

"I found her note the previous night. She was going to take you with her."

"She didn't say a word to me."

"Because I stopped her. I threatened to tell Dad if she even touched you. I was selfish. I couldn't bear the fact that she would take you from me. I couldn't—"

"You didn't ask her why she wasn't taking *you?*"

"Everything that Dad did to you—it was my fault. If you had left with her… She *did* love you, Liv. You should know that."

Her twin laughed, the sound full of bitterness. "Isn't it weird how you're blind to what she was?" She clasped Kim's cheeks, her own eyes full of tears now. "You can't blame yourself. You did everything in your power to shield me from Dad. And Mom didn't love you *or* me— not enough. The moment you threatened her escape she decided I wasn't worth it either. Don't you see? She wasn't strong enough for that. She was never strong enough for us."

Kim's heart felt as if it was bursting with emotion. The love shining in Liv's eyes was enough to pull the last bit of wool from her eyes.

God, she had been such a fool. She had let guilt and pain rob so much from her. Her mother hadn't robbed it from her. She had done that to herself. And now she was letting her fear rob her of Diego, wasn't she? Failing herself even before she took the leap?

"And even if she had been, do you think I'd have gone with her? Left you behind?" Now her sister's words vibrated with pain. "You are my sister. You're all I had—all I *have*. What I don't get is why you have let it hurt you so much. All these years you just accepted her decision, you let it weigh everything you've done."

"What was I supposed to do?"

"You are supposed to fight for yourself. You shouldn't have let her cowardly decision have so much power over you. You always fought for me. You stood up to Dad every time he came at me. Why do you think you deserve any less?"

Kim's tears ran over her cheeks as she stared at Liv. She had no answer. It was what she was doing again with Diego. Instead of fighting for herself—fighting for her love—instead of fighting for her *babies* she was walking away to protect herself.

So what if he didn't love her? So what if he only wanted their marriage to work for the sake of the children? He took care of her, he pampered her, he understood her stubbornness and he had stood by her when she had been crumbling. It was more affection than she had ever received from anyone.

She scrubbed her cheeks and grabbed the papers from the table. "You're right. I am going to fight for myself." Her stomach churned with fear, but she couldn't let it stop her now. Her fingers shaking, she tore the documents Liv had brought into so many pieces. "Can you please call Alex? I need transportation."

Her eyes wide, Liv laughed as she followed her into her bedroom. Kim plucked at her suitcase, which she still hadn't emptied, opened it, threw the clothes into a pile and started throwing others in. Mostly shorts and tank tops, nightwear.

She slipped her laptop into its case, tucked in the power cord, followed by her cell phone charger and her wallet. She quickly called her assistant, informed her of her travel plans and hung up while the woman was still struggling to grapple with what she'd just been told.

After three years of non-stop work, Kim knew her team was obviously surprised that she was now taking vacations so frequently. But they were an expertly trained team, and she could do her job from wherever Diego was just as easily as she could in New York.

She made another call to her VP of Operations and informed her she should start a headhunt for another CEO. Effective immediately, she was going to cut down her hours. And when the time came she would need maternity leave, too.

Excitement mixed with fear thrummed through her veins, making her a little light-headed.

Liv stopped her with a hand on her shoulder. "Whoa... Kim.... Slow down." Her mobile mouth was frozen in shock. "Wow, you're really doing this."

"Yep, and I can't stop, Liv," she said, walking back into the kitchen and throwing her multivitamins into her handbag. "I have to keep moving, I have to get on a plane before I start thinking. Diego was right. I should get a device that stops my brain from overthinking."

"He said that?"

Kim nodded, the memory of his smile lending her courage.

"Alex's pilot should be ready in half an hour. Do you want me to come with you? Bring Alexander to take on Diego?"

A laugh barreled out of her and Kim kissed Liv's cheek. Hugged her again.

"No. I'm going to be fine. Whether in the name of revenge or my pregnancy, Diego always fought for us." She had to believe that and she had to do the same. "If he hadn't cared he could have sued for custody. After all the things I told him he still trusted me enough, believed in me enough, that I would love our children. He's fought for our relationship with everything he has in him. Now it's time I do the same." She clasped Liv's hands in hers, her throat closing up again. "We're good, aren't we?"

Liv nodded and kissed her cheek again. "Of course. Whatever happens, you always have me."

CHAPTER FOURTEEN

DIEGO HAD NO idea how long he had been pushing himself in the huge state-of-the-art gym that he'd had specially built on the island. His muscles groaned under the rigor he was putting himself through. It felt as if his flesh had morphed into points of torture and then turned inward.

But he couldn't stop. He hadn't been able to stop for the past week, since Kim had left. He had flown back and forth to New York within a day, worked from morning to evening and then punished himself with a brutal workout each evening, so that when he went to bed he hoped to be so exhausted that sleep came.

It hadn't worked. Even with his body turning into a bruising pulp he couldn't fall asleep. He was beginning to feel like a ticking bomb.

The days stretched torturously ahead of him, with memories of Kim pricking into him wherever he turned.

He was beginning to hate the island, after everything he had done to own it.

He'd seen Miguel and Anna poke their heads in a couple of times at the entrance to the gym.

They were worried about him. He got that. But nothing could puncture his need for physical pain right now. Nothing else could numb the emptiness he felt inside.

* * *

It was midnight by the time he walked toward his bedroom. He had showered at the gym, yelled his head off at Anna and Miguel when they'd tried to talk to him and then wandered on the beach for more than a couple of hours.

And he still wasn't tired. Every nerve in him was strung tight. Olivia would have gone to see Kim yesterday. She would have handed her his documents. He couldn't breathe for the ball of pain that was hanging around his neck.

He froze at the entrance to his bedroom.

A breeze flew in from the ocean. The French doors were wide open. The lamp was turned on, the feeble light from it illuminating the woman snoring softly in the center of his king bed.

He felt as if a tornado had hit him in the gut and then tossed him around.

How long had she been waiting for him? When had she arrived?

She was lying on her side, her knees tucked into her chest. Her arms were wrapped around herself. He didn't question why she had returned. He didn't question why she was in his bedroom, of all the rooms in the villa. They hadn't shared a bed even when she had been here.

Kim was back. The woman he loved with every breath in him was back.

He walked toward the bed, his gaze unblinking. His chest tightened and he realized the tight sensation was fear. Every inch of him was shaking with spine-chilling fear. He loved this woman so much and he was afraid to blink. He was afraid she would disappear if he did.

He climbed on to the bed slowly and pulled the cotton covers over her sleeping form.

She wore a silk sleeveless gown in dark blue that clung to the small bump at her stomach and just about covered her knees. The lace neckline fluttered over her breasts with every breeze that flew in through the door. He greedily looked over her, from her hair, which was a mess, to her painted toes.

Her long eyelashes cast shadows on her cheeks. Dark blue circles hung under her eyes. He muttered a soft curse.

Droga, that gaunt look was back in her face again. He rubbed the pad of his thumb over her cheek, his breath hovering in his throat. And then, and only then, did he breathe air into his lungs again.

He ran his fingers over her toned arms. The skin was so soft and silky that he was afraid he would mark her with his rough fingers. His hand shaking, he pulled back.

He was never going to let her go. He had ripped out his own heart to let her go once. He couldn't do it again.

Even if he had to handcuff her to this very bed. Even if he had to spend the rest of his life tearing away her defenses piece by piece.

He didn't care anymore if she loved him or not, if she was as crazy about him as he was about her. All he wanted was to spend his life with her, looking after her, loving her, telling her every single day how much he wanted her, how much he needed her.

He stretched out next to her, feeling the weight on his shoulders dissolve into nothingness. Calm floated over him. His sore body felt lighter. He would just sit here, stay with her, watch over her.

He turned onto his side and pressed his mouth to her temple, breathed in her scent. And closed his eyes.

Sleep hit his eyelids with the force of a hurricane dragging him under, as though it hadn't eluded him at all for that whole torturous week.

Kim drifted awake suddenly, instantly registering the warm, comforting weight around her waist. It was the same feeling all over, actually. From her hair to her toes she felt as if she was encased in the most delicious embrace ever.

She opened sleep-heavy eyes. The lamp she had turned on was still lit, and Diego's sleeping face filled her vision. A soft gasp escaped her mouth. It was his arm that hung around her middle.

Her heart went from a quiet drone to a thundering pace in a mere second.

For a few minutes she just looked at him to her heart's content. He wore shorts and nothing else. She swallowed as her gaze drifted over his long, hair-roughened legs. His abdomen was a ridge of hard muscles, with a line of hair that disappeared into his shorts.

His powerfully built chest rose and fell with his even breathing. The groove where his neck met his shoulders invited her touch. She fisted her hands, her gaze on his face now.

His mouth was a lush line in repose, his features etched with the passion and kindness that made this man. How stupid had she been to walk away from him?

Taking a deep breath, she lifted the arm around her middle and twined her fingers with his long ones. She heard him breathe in on a soft hiss and froze. With a frown, she pulled his hand up and saw the raw knuckles. The skin was broken in several places and crusted with blood.

Tears hit her eyes with a brutal force. She lifted his hand to her mouth and kissed the center of his palm. She dragged her mouth over the rough calluses, learning and loving every inch of him anew.

His breathing altered from its soft rhythm to a sharp intake of breath. She froze with the tips of his fingers on her mouth.

Their gazes collided. Her fingers tightened around his. "You have to stop fighting Miguel and whoever else you are."

Warmth filtered into his gaze. "I wasn't fighting."

She fought to keep the tears at bay. "Then what is this?"

He shrugged.

"It hurts when I see you hurt, Diego. I don't ever want to see *this*," she said loudly, pointing his own fingers in his face, "again."

She couldn't keep the demand out of her tone.

She expected him to mock her, question her, tease her at least.

He said nothing, his gaze raking her face hungrily. His silent nod was too much to bear.

He scooted closer, his body an inviting fortress of pulsing heat and so much more. He still didn't say anything, didn't ask her anything. Just held her, his leg thrown over hers, his open palm on her back.

She pulled his hand to her face.

He obliged her without a word, his long fingers fanning out from her temples to her mouth. She kissed every finger, every ridge and mound of his palm.

She shivered as a sob built in her chest.

She drew a painful breath and tucked her face into his chest. She kissed him, the thundering boom of his heart the only sound filling her ears. "I've torn up the divorce papers. I never want to see them again in this lifetime. I'm never leaving you again, Diego. *Ever*."

She felt his silent nod as he pulled her against him, his arms tight bands around her. *Why didn't he say anything?* His agonizing silence, compared to his usually mocking, challenging, probing self, was beginning to breathe crippling fear into her limbs.

Her throat was choked up with all the words she wanted to say, her strength once again leaving her in her moment of need. But she had to do this. She had to tell him, had to show him her heart.

She struggled against him and he loosened his hold.

Using his strength, she pulled herself up. She laughed, the sound tinged with her fear. She breathed hard, her hands going to her small belly. "I'm already a little clumsy."

He stayed on his side, propped by his elbow, his gaze on her belly. "You've begun to show."

She laughed, her tears finally spilling from her eyes. *He was still speaking to her. It was more than she deserved.* "Every day is making a difference."

"Can I touch you?"

"You don't have to ask," she whispered, wondering if she had already lost him. Because Diego never asked. He manipulated her, he tricked her, he bargained with her. It was the only way she had ever given him anything, the only way she had let him see anything. And his solemn request now pierced her.

He placed his hand on her belly, his huge palm almost spanning the small bump.

She placed her hand atop his and he glanced up toward her. "Aren't you going to ask me why I came back?"

The warmth disappeared from his gaze. He pulled himself up with a smooth movement and joined her against the headboard. "No."

She held his hand tightly, drawing strength from it. One question swirled on the tip of her tongue, gouging into her. Every instinct inside her told her to embrace the silence again, to let it go. If she didn't ask, she couldn't be hurt by his answer. If she didn't ask, she could…

She was short-changing herself again.

"I…I would like to ask *you* something. And I want you to give me an honest answer, okay?"

He nodded, his gaze never leaving hers.

Her throat almost seized up. There was a hot prickle of tears at the backs of her eyes. "You… Why did you take Marissa with you? I… It was the cruelest thing you could have done to me. I knew Eduardo. I would have come with you…"

He touched his mouth to her temple. "Shh…I never meant to hurt you."

His fingers tightened around hers. He didn't smile, but she saw the softening in his eyes. Because he understood how big it was for her just to ask.

"I wanted to take you with me. All I wanted was to hear you say again and again that you weren't disgusted by what I had done, that I was a better man than I already was." His words were soft, yet loaded with emotion. "But, Eduardo, he was always a good reminder to me of what I could become if I let something matter to me too much. Leaving without you was a matter of denying myself, proving to myself that I didn't need you. Marissa…when she requested if she could come I couldn't say no."

"I want to share both good and bad with you, Diego. I want to be the one you lean on when…" She took a deep breath. "I meant what I said before. I'm never leaving again."

A fire licked into life in his gaze. "That's good to know."

"Why are you being like this?"

"What is it you want from me? I will do it."

"You have given up on me."

Fresh tears spilled from her eyes, but she wiped them with determination. This was only one day—the beginning. She would spend this entire lifetime and more waiting for his love. Because this man—he meant everything to her. And she wasn't going to hide how she felt for him either.

"I'm in love with you, Diego." She rushed over words that should be said slowly, softly, without waiting for his reaction. She could do this only one way. "I've always been in love with you. I was an idiot before. I'm going to spend the rest of my life fighting for us, proving to you that I'm worth it. All I ask is—"

In a second he was kneeling over her, his legs on either side of hers. And then he kissed her. She moaned and wrapped her hands around his nape. Gave his kiss everything she had in her. He wasn't gentle with her. His hand in her hair kept her where he wanted her as his tongue plunged into her mouth.

Heat blasted all over her as he pushed up her nightgown with rough hands. His hands cupped her breasts and she whimpered at the pleasure sparking all over.

"Diego, wait…" she managed to say, even as arousal stole through her, lighting an insatiable fire in her body.

He halted, his breathing rough, his palms spread out over her thighs. His face was tight with guilt. "Did I hurt you?"

She laughed and cupped his jaw, her breathing still nowhere near normal. "I won't break, Diego. I want nothing more than to feel you inside me." Stealing her fingers into his hair, she pressed an open-mouthed kiss to his lips. Warmth stole through her. Diego's groan added to it. "But I… You haven't said anything. I understand if you're angry, if you're—"

"Angry?" he said, and the very emotion he was denying crept into his tone. "Try gut-twisting emptiness. I've never been more alone, felt more alone in my life than the past week. Everything I have achieved, everything I have—it means nothing without you."

Her heart leaped into her throat. She felt dizzy—as though someone had sucked out the oxygen from around them.

He touched his forehead to hers. "I love you so much, *minha esposinha.*" His words reverberated with pain. His features were stark and menacing. "And if you leave me again it will destroy the little good there is in me. It almost did this time."

Her heart felt as if it would burst out of her chest. Kim wrapped her arms around him and hugged him so tight that her breathing stuttered. It was more than she had ever hoped for. "You love me?"

His gaze was filled with pain. "I can survive if I lose all this wealth, I have survived rejection from pretty much everyone in my life, but I can't survive losing you. When you left, for a few moments all I could think was that you had gone because everything I had done wasn't enough. *I* wasn't enough."

"No, Diego. Don't say that. You're the most wonderful man I've ever met. I just couldn't bear to be by your side thinking that you would never love me. It hurt so much that you turned away from me. I wanted to ask you. I wanted to…" She shivered and he kissed her temple. "It was nothing to do with you, Diego. I was weak. I…"

"You're stubborn, arrogant, you drive me to the worst of myself and you're so damn hard to get through to sometimes. But you're the toughest woman I know and I love you for everything you are."

He settled his palm on her belly and she wondered if she would combust from the pride, from the acceptance, from the love in his words.

"I can't think of a better, stronger mother for my children."

This fierce, passionate man loved her. She would count herself lucky for the rest of her days. "You really think that, don't you? I couldn't believe you trusted me enough to…"

"Of course I do. You might not feel that connection, but I have no doubt that you'll love our children."

Kim smiled and hid her face in the crook of his elbow, his words washing over her with a warmth she wanted to keep close. She would tell him in a minute. She would tell him how much joy now flew through her just at the thought of their little family.

"Will you promise me you will never stop fighting for

me and you will never give up on me? Even when I don't believe I'm worthy of you?" she said, fear stealing through her.

He met her gaze and smiled, his hands tight against her
waist. And the tenderness in it stole through her. "We will
always fight for each other. We will never let ourselves
settle for anything less than we deserve. It's a promise,
gatinha."

Olivia laughed as strong arms engulfed her from behind
and pulled her hard into a body she would know in her
sleep. She clamped Alexander's arms with her fingers,
tucking herself even tighter into his embrace.

She should have known he would follow her to Diego's
island.

"You left without telling me," he whispered near her ear,
his hands holding her hard at her ribcage.

Liv closed her eyes and breathed the essence of him,
every inch of her trembling with that same happiness that
had marked her life the past couple of months.

"I was worried about her," she said, nodding toward
Kim.

Kim and Diego were walking hand in hand at the edge
of the water on the beach, lost in each other. Liv couldn't
stop smiling at how Diego's hand never left her twin, how
Kim hadn't stopped smiling ever since Liv had gotten here.

Alexander kissed her jaw, his hands inching under her
T-shirt until they found bare skin. She sucked in a breath
at the weight of his palm.

"There's no need, is there?" he asked.

"No need," Liv repeated, knowing that he understood.
"He loves her, Alexander. Like she deserves to be loved."
She swallowed the tears in her throat. This was a time to
rejoice. "I've never seen her so happy and glowing. And
did you know she's having—?"

He turned her around, his blue gaze eating her up with

a hungry intensity that started an ache in her own body. It was always like that.

But he looked haunted, with deep grooves pinching his mouth. "You got on a plane without telling me after we had a God-awful fight, Liv. You weren't answering your phone. I asked Emily. She thought it was really funny that I didn't know where my wife was before she told me. I think my heart stopped for a few moments."

The edge in his words, the way he was holding her so tight… Liv frowned. Damn her and her impulsive head. "I left my phone by accident. And I should have realized Emily would play with you first. I *was* really worried about Kim. And I'm sorry about Emily. I know I shouldn't interfere, but—"

He pressed a soft kiss to her mouth, his hands capturing her face. The love that shone in his gaze took her breath away. "I think I know why you did that. It's a strange feeling to be protected by my ferocious wife. I love you, Liv," he whispered.

God, she would never tire of hearing him say it.

"And I'm glad Kim has found happiness."

Liv nodded and returned his kiss, her own joy making her light-headed. She twined her fingers with his and tugged him forward. "It's time you met Diego properly, don't you think?"

She laughed when he raised his brows in an exaggerated way. Her husband and her twin's husband were just as different as she and Kim were.

Life was going to be really interesting for them, but full of laughter and love.

* * * * *

LET'S TALK
Romance

For exclusive extracts, competitions
and special offers, find us online:

 facebook.com/millsandboon

@MillsandBoon

@MillsandBoonUK

Get in touch on 01413 063232

For all the latest titles coming soon, visit
millsandboon.co.uk/nextmonth